The Adventures of John Harris

Surviving

And

Hell in the Homeland

Post-Apocalyptic America

AJ Newman

*

This book is a work of fiction. All events, names, characters and places are the product of the author's imagination or are used as a fictitious event. The above means that the author made the whole thing up by himself and it is pure imagination.

NOTE: My good friend Cliff Deane has four great Post-Apocalyptic novels on Amazon. If you like Post-Apocalyptic novels, you'll love these books.

Vigilante: Into the Darkness   Vigilante: Into the Fray

Vigilante: The Pale Horse   Vigilante: No Quarter

**These books are available at Amazon:
https://www.amazon.com/dp/B06XG1XPQM**

**Please visit Cliff's FaceBook page:
https://www.facebook.com/mustangpublishingllc**

*

Books by A J Newman

Alien Apocalypse:

The Virus   Surviving (Oct 2017)

A Family's Apocalypse Series:

Cities on Fire – Family Survival

After the Solar Flare - a Post-Apocalyptic series:

Alone in the Apocalypse   Adventures in the Apocalypse*

After the EMP series:

The Day America Died New Beginnings The Day America Died
Old Enemies The Day America Died Frozen Apocalypse

"The Adventures of John Harris" - a Post-Apocalyptic America series:

Surviving   Hell in the Homeland   Tyranny in the Homeland
Revenge in the Homeland...Apocalypse in the Homeland   John Returns

"A Samantha Jones Murder Mystery Thriller series:

Where the Girls Are Buried   Who Killed the Girls?

Books by A J Newman and Cliff Deane

Terror in the USA: Virus: Strain of Islam

These books are available at Amazon:

http://www.amazon.com/-/e/B00HT84V6U

To contact the Author, please leave comments @:
www.facebook.com/newmananthonyj   Facebook page.

*

This book is dedicated to my beautiful wife of over thirty years.

Special thanks to Wes Newman Patsy Newman and Kate Dennis for proof reading my work. Thanks to LTC Clifford T. Deane, US Army, Cavalry, (ret), (ret) for proofing, editing, military accuracy and color commentary.

This is my first attempt at writing a novel and perhaps it won't be a historically significant read, but my aim was to entertain and get a few points across to the reader. If you like this book you will love the next five in the series, please recommend them to your friends.

*

Prologue

America is a losing the war with drug gangs, a flood of illegal immigrants swarm into our country every day and Islamic Terrorists such as ISIS across the world. The terrorists must have numerous sleeper cells established in many of our cities.

Two nuclear EMP blasts would send us back to a post-apocalyptic dark age.

Our civilization is also in steep decline resulting from the poor stewardship of our elected officials for the past 65 years.

This work simply takes into account, through extrapolation, that which our enemies, along with our government are currently doing to destroy the United States of America.

The bottom line is that we end up with a disaster that is called by many different names. Some of them are TEOTWAWKI (The End of the World as We Knew It), TSHTF (The Shit Hits the Fan), SHTF (Shit Hits the Fan), The Collapse, End of Days, and Armageddon.

This novel proposes that Rogue US Government officials and a coalition of Third World Leaders have launched a selective nuclear assault and high altitude Electro Magnetic Pulse attacks on all of the major powers. Exposure to an EMP results in the destruction of all unshielded electronic devices.

This ravaging of our planet has killed nearly 200 million Americans and an unknown number of the planet's overall population.

Three EMP detonations, at an altitude of 125 miles, and centered over Northern California, Kansas, and Virginia, have shut down the power grid, and the lights are out. The devastation reaches across the United States, southern Canada, and northern Mexico.

There is no electricity. Vehicles manufactured over the past 40 years will not run due to the effects of these Electro Magnetic Pulse detonations.

The USA is in chaos with criminals and gangs attacking citizens, and unprepared communities, as well.

This tale begins with the premise that unless you are a prepper, your world ends.

<u>Surviving</u> is the first of a series of six novels that follow John Harris as he leads an intrepid band of survivors through a nation in chaos. Food and water are in short supply. Individual survival is in doubt.

John and his Team are the nation's best bet for surviving.

They fight the gangs, drug lords and the corrupt Department of Homeland Security to return America to a united country, governed by *the rule of law*.

I hope you have as much fun reading this series, as I did writing it.

Surviving

The Adventures of John Harris

AJ Newman

*

Chapter 1

John Harris

Mobile, Alabama

May 20, 2020

Radio studio

Mobile, AL

"Good Morning L.A. I love the U...S...A", the host told his morning audience. "How are all of my Prepper Buddies doing this fine day in Lower Alabama?"

He then added, "The President can kiss my redneck ass. Those bastards got their asses kicked in the midterm elections, and they are trying to make your lives miserable.

Yeah, I'm John Harris, and I hope to have some fun today discussing how to start a fire without matches, lighters or other modern methods.

Then we'll move on to how to cook a rabbit on an open fire. We will begin with a bow and stick and end with flint and steel."

He then introduced his son, Scott, and said, "Scott, tell our listeners how you how to make and use a bow and drill to make a fire."

"How to Survive," was a one hour program on a local A.M. Mobile station that had been in production for three years.

Prepping Buddies was now growing in syndication and was heard on 34 other radio stations, mainly in rural western and southern Alabama, Mississippi, and Louisiana.

This lively morning show had become very popular with the outdoors group, and 'TEOTWAWKI Preppers.' He just spoke from the heart about survival that he had learned from living in the woods and swamps around the Mobile Delta and the Army. John had a great sense of humor and connected with his loyal audience.

He built a small studio in the back of his business so he could start his mornings close to his work. Nothing real fancy, but he would start every morning at 7:00 am with his live show and fill the hour with a combination of survival information and redneck wisdom with a major dash of good old Southern humor.

John got his start as the author of several "Prepper Books" dealing with everything from how to survive in the woods to what food to stockpile for TEOTWAWKI. His works to date were:

Surviving in the Woods

Surviving in the Big City

Surviving - Food

Surviving - Prepping

Surviving Big Government

Surviving After Using Your Concealed Carry Weapon

Surviving our Socialist Government.

These books gave him the idea that he could actually write a series of novels about terrorists plotting the destruction of America to create a worldwide Caliphate.

John wrote under the name "Mac Norman" because he doubted his ability to entertain, thru writing, and worried about the response to his thoughts on society.

Mac Norman's books sold very well on Amazon, but not quite as well in print. However, they were providing him with a steady stream of income that came in very handy.

9

While John was very proud of his work, he was concerned that some of his audiences were wacky cults. What bothered him most was that some of his readers actually might think that he was encouraging a remaking of America thru revolution.

That was the best reason for Mac Norman to exist. Only his close friends knew who Mac was. He always reminded himself that this shit was just fiction and a way to make some money.

His day job earned him a comfortable living, even though his "ex" got half of that for eight more years. His writing and radio show were paying for his toys and paid off most of his bills. Hell, he might even be able to retire before he turned 90

"Harris Body Shops" was the name of John's auto body and custom paint business. His father, John senior, had started it back in the '70's with just the one shop in Mobile. His Dad, however, had little ambition to expand beyond one shop.

John took over the business when his Dad, retired at 65 years of age. John, Sr. went by "Buddy."

His parents, Buddy and Becky, moved to Florida and were staying busy at The Villages.

John was an only child, so there was no fight to see who took charge or any of that nonsense. He quickly fired the shop foreman when he tried to boss John around. Now that was something that did not sit well with Mr. John Harris.

John's best friend, Gus McCoy, managed the Mobile shop and JoAnne Henderson was the Office Manager.

Gus and John met years before, in the service and had instantly bonded. John trusted him with his life. He would gladly give his life to protect Gus.

JoAnne had worked for John's Dad and had become quite close over the years. He'd heard rumors that JoAnne and his Dad had been involved in a long-running affair, but had never seen any indication of it. However, the week after his Dad retired, JoAnne slipped up behind him after the close of business and started massaging his neck and rubbing her rather large breasts on his back. He gracefully got out of that situation and let her know that he was all business.

John was 46 years old, 5'11" and 210 lbs. He had graying hair and wasn't too ugly. He was in great shape and had been a member of a local health club for the last two years lifting weights and

10

running five miles a day. This kept his mind off his personal life when not at work.

John played golf, hunted and fished a lot more since Ann filed to dissolve the marriage.

Ann divorced him for no other reason than she felt it was time to move on. They had been high school sweethearts and were madly in love until John became successful, and she could afford the damn country clubs and other high priced shit.

She spent her day taking golf and tennis lessons. John spent too much time at work and with his "guy friends" to suit her. He had grease under his nails while she was eating snails and drinking champagne.

She'd been gone for over two years now, and John was just beginning to get over her. There had been no woman in his life since the divorce. They remained in contact, and she did help him with the "love scenes" and romantic crap in his books. He had just never had been too good at expressing himself with that stuff.

Their union had produced one child, Scott, who was close to both of his parents but felt a very tight bond with John. They shared the same passion for the outdoors, guns and prepping. Scott lived with John and worked at the shop.

Scott and Gus tried to fix him up with friends, but he just wasn't ready. A couple of blind dates to keep them off his back had ended in disaster.

John was simply not a lady's man like Steve. He just didn't have the confidence or the line of bullshit. Those ladies either left thinking he was gay or simply did not like women.

He had been in the Army Special Forces for two tours in Afghanistan and rising to the rank of Staff Sergeant. The CIA recruited him as a gun for hire.

John provided bodyguard services for foreign nationals in dangerous places. This lasted for a couple of years until he had been able to save enough money to help expand his Father's business, and left the CIA.

He now owned four auto body shops and was slowly adding one every year or so. Harris Body Shops were now in Jackson, MS, Montgomery and Muscle Shoals, AL and the home shop in Mobile. He was hoping to expand the business to Tennessee in the near future.

*

Chapter 2

The Team

Mobile, Alabama

May 15, 2020

Steve royally screwed up several trips with numerous calls from his business and his women.

He said that he just could not live without his cell phone. He got calls from seven different women in one day during his last business trip. The calls were a real nuisance, like fingernails on a damned chalkboard. If AIDS didn't get him, one of his friends would kill him because of a damn phone call just as you sighted in a 12 pointed buck.

These women cared a lot about Steve, but his little head always did the thinking for him when it came to women.

He was a loveable character who could charm the pants off a nun. This always got him into trouble because he did not know when to stop. His newest lady and the current one were always either pulling each other's hair or trying to kill Steve.

He had been married three times and enjoyed the attention of many ladies before, during and after all of his failed marriages.

Steve Jones was an attractive 46-year-old "black" guy that stood 5' 9" and weighed 175. He had jet-black hair, a broken nose that gave him character and a snake tattoo on his right forearm. The ladies loved that rascal's southern charm. Many of his friends attributed his charm to his smooth southern accent. They clung to him in droves. He had told many stories about threesomes around the campfire.

Steve was a Black Man but never was he an African American. When hearing the term, "African-American," he replied that he was 100% American.

He knew that anyone who stayed off drugs and worked hard you could do anything you wanted in the USA. While he was not a Republican, he was by no means a Liberal

Steve managed a speed shop that specialized in building hot rods for rich doctors and lawyers. He had built several '32 high boys and hopped up numerous Mustangs and Corvettes for Mobile's elite. "Toys for Bad Boys," was the name of his shop. John used him to rebuild engines. He drove a V10 Dodge Ram that had a Viper motor and enough chrome under the hood to use as a mirror. Of course, he picked up the ladies in his red Viper.

His business made a great profit, but the cars, ex-wives and girl chasing took all his money. He was pretty much broke even on a good day.

Gus looked like a monkey making love to a football on the last trip, trying to watch the tiny assed screen of an iPhone, strapped to his damn wrist while trying to fish. Try to imagine a grown man standing in the middle of a stream casting a fly rod while attempting to watch a baseball game on a wrist-mounted iPhone.

He fell twice that day, broke his rod and lost the damn phone. Everyone told him not to make bets on games during the yearly outing. He never listened. Gus never lost a lot of money, but bet almost every day on some sporting event. It was an addiction. He would be on his cell phone at night betting on the next day's games. What a shame he wasn't better at choosing his teams.

His friends said that Gus McCoy was born old. While he was only 49, he had always been the one to keep a cool head when trouble was near. This helped keep them out of trouble over the years.

Gus McCoy was Army Special Forces, and he was one tough man who could break anyone in half if pushed but would not hurt a flea if it could be avoided.

He had served in Iraq (the second one) and had won the Medal of Honor for holding off over a hundred enemy insurgents single-handed while his wounded friends were picked up by a chopper.

He took three rounds in his arm and legs but fought on until all could be extracted. He must have looked like John Wayne holding that SAW and mowing down jihadists as fast as they charged his position.

Gus was 6' 1" and 225 lbs. of pure muscle and short-cropped gray hair. Around the shop, he was called the "Grouch."

He liked to debate on almost any topic, but loved politics and hated Liberals and Democrats. Scott would wind him up tighter than a tick by talking about the "Socialist" grand liberal ideas, or government policy turned sour.

It was good-natured, but you could always see Gus' ears turn red when Scott got to him, and Scott *always* got to him.

He and Robin had been married for 24 years; they had three daughters and five grandkids. Robin was the love of his life, and she could never understand Steve's womanizing or John's divorce. Gus was a devoted father and grandfather. His girls were not outdoors types, and the grandkids ranged from three to ten years old. He would take the three boys on camping trips. He tried to raise them "right" as he put it; they would be true outdoors people. John hoped that Gus was right, but their dads were real wussies and roughing it was beer instead of cocktails.

John had known Gus for over ten years and was John's best friend, and he loves him like a brother.

He managed John's Mobile body shop and was the best in the business. John and Gus met in a bar in Italy while on R&R. They both were working on a black ops mission in the Middle East. A friend had said the wrong thing to the wrong guy, and the fight just broke out. Gus stepped in and ended it. He quickly kicked, punched and tossed all five of the bad guys out on their asses. John bought him a drink, and they were friends forever.

Scott's talking drove the rest of them to distraction. It wasn't talking; it was his damn singing along with the music coming from an IPOD. No country, no western, no Carrie or Miranda, not even good old rock and roll, just heavy metal, yelling and screaming. What a pile of crap. They finally got him to use headphones on the last trip so that they would not hear that god-awful noise, but then he just started singing louder along with the music.

This was Scott's good side; he goes downhill from there. He's going to school to become a politician. Yes, a degree in political science and then a Masters.

Everyone kept telling him, "Damn boy, get a real job fixing things with your hands, building engines, repairing cars as a real man. Get your hands dirty kind of stuff." John had said many times, "What a waste of time, a damn politician." He took after his mom, not John; John always made his living with sweat and hard work.

Scott got a late start on college because he joined the Army when he turned 18. He said he did it to find himself and that it had not hurt him any. He was right; the Army made a man out of him. He grew up and started taking life much more seriously, except for his taste in music.

He was in Bravo Troop, 4th Squadron, 10th Cavalry Regiment, stationed at Fort Carson in Colorado Springs. He had a ball operating the Bradley Fighting Vehicles and playing war games. His unit returned from Iraq and redeployed just after his discharge. He did, however, learn a great deal about small arms and reconnaissance during his short stay in the military.

When he got back to Mobile, after his hitch, his best friend Jim introduced him to Joan, who was a friend of Jim's girlfriend, Imelda. Joan was a cute little black haired beauty who was quiet and very low key. At 5'4", she only weighed 110 lbs. soaking wet. They looked like Mutt and Jeff together but made a great pair. What they say about opposites being attracted to each other must be true. They were getting serious and intended to get married after he graduated.

Scott Harris was a good-looking boy of 26 years who stood 6' tall. He weighed 190 pounds with brown hair and blue eyes.

He had real promise too. He had built his own car from many boxes of parts, and a totally rusted out body and frame. It was a '65 Mustang. He still had it and drove it every day. Damn, a 15-year-old who could build his own car now that was damned impressive.

Too bad, he wanted to be a danged politician.

Yeah, Gus and John taught him and kept him focused whenever he got tired or disgusted. They were very proud of him and had plans for him to manage one of John's shops, but no, he wanted to be a damned politician.

Though, Gus and John were always proud of him and now; after The Trip, they respected him as a man.

Jim was a real pain in the ass and was Scott's best friend. He worked at John's original Mobile shop prepping cars for painting; he's quite good at it.

Jim Payne was the worst pain in the ass of all the guys; he snored like a foghorn. No one could sleep. The asshole could be heard for miles. They damn near broke his ribs on the last trip trying to wake him up.

Fish jumped out of the water when he snored, and loose paint flew off the walls. He was awfully loud. Gus shoved a sock in his mouth and nearly was killed on the last trip. Jim jumped up and nearly beat the crap out of Gus and John before they were able to wake him up. No one would have thought the kid was that strong.

Gus was one mean assed bastard when aroused, and John was no slouch. It turned out Jim was a Black belt and could be one mean mother when he got riled up.

Hell, they knew that he played around with all that Jap slapping stuff, but he got a hell of a lot better at it than they had ever thought.

Jim Payne is 25 years old and only 5' 6" tall. He barely weighs 155 lbs. soaking wet. He has blond hair, is good-natured and a dependable worker. He hasn't met the right girl, yet, but has one cute girlfriend, Imelda. They all drool when she visits him at the shop.

Jim grew up at Scott's house; he was usually at their home. John and Ann thought of him as their son.

John knew his parents and did not think much of them. They were into their lives and did not have much time for Jim. Jim was a good boy and was a good friend for Scott since he had no other siblings. Scott started out alone until Jim came along.

John had bitched, moaned and groaned about the others ruining their trips over the years, perhaps John over did it. They rebelled.

That was how the idea for the back to basics trip came about and how they found out what they were made of. You see, they met last winter to plan the next outing and John mentioned a couple of their

16

faults that ruined the past trips and they came out in attack mode. John never saw it coming. He worked hard putting these outings together year after year getting the gear and food ready. This went on for years without knowing how he annoyed anyone. When he started bitchin', they jumped on him like a duck on a June bug.

Never in over 10 years of camping with this crew did John ever hear one critical word about his behavior. He knew that he was no saint, but was nothing like the others. He would never bother anyone. Bullshit. They set him straight. They said that he cussed too much.

John thought, "Me, fucking cussing too much, what a crock of shit."

*

Chapter 3

25th ISA Independence Day

Nashville, TN ISA

Dec 20, 2048

Nashville, TN, ISA

Fireworks had been going off for several days in the country's capital and for that matter throughout the whole country. The people of the Independent States of America took their freedom very seriously and celebrated vigorously with each state conducting ceremonies tailored to their contribution to the overall victory over the USA and Mexican Drug Cartels.

Hwy 24, near Smyrna, TN, ISA

Josh Logan drove from Nashville on Hwy 24 East about 20 miles to Smyrna, Tennessee to interview the daughter of one of ISA's founding fathers. He wanted to interview John, her father, but John had not spoken with any news reporter since '43 when a "Northern" Reporter printed an article that twisted the truth and made him come across like a mad man.

Josh was a rather good-looking 30-year-old, 6'1" tall with black hair. He had the looks and personality to be a star in the news business.

Josh worked for the closely monitored Conservative News Group based out of Indianapolis. He and his company had promised on live TV that they would only broadcast Jenn Harris' words without any analysis. CNG was the only News Organization based in both countries, and they had broadcast just the facts throughout the entire war and ongoing Cold War between the two countries. They said that they would let the viewer form their own opinions.

He had taken a train from the border crossing at Fort Louisville yesterday. He spent the day in the ISA's capital doing a little sightseeing and trying to interview the nation's leaders. He caught a few congressmen, but no one noteworthy.

Josh traveled on a News Reporter's seven-day visa and knew that he was being followed.

The Big War had been over for six years between the USA and the ISA. There were still major differences, and a Small War had been fought just two years ago.

The ISA was prosperous while the USA wallowed in debt and had large ghettoes. The ISA was based on "You work, You Eat," while the USA had extremely high taxes and over 60% of the population either worked for the Government or was on welfare. In the ISA, military service was mandatory, and anyone who did not fight for their country was not allowed to vote. The USA was a socialist country with a strong central government while the ISA had a president and congress, but the true power was based in the states.

The USA was made up of the Northeastern and upper Midwestern states. Wisconsin and Illinois were the westernmost states while Indiana, Ohio, Pennsylvania and Maryland were the southernmost.

The border between the two was heavily fortified and the ISA had a mile wide strip on their side that had fences, landmines and machine guns wired to sensors and would fire automatically. Just the hundreds of thousands of claymore mines and land mines discouraged any uninvited incursions. There were 15 floating forts spaced out along the Ohio River and land based ones from Pittsburgh to the Atlantic.

The ISA was made up in the south of 16 southern states stretching from Virginia thru Arizona. Idaho, Montana and North Dakota made up the northwestern boundary.

The Pacific States of America was made up of all of the West Coast states plus Alaska and Nevada. Since LA, San Francisco and Seattle had been nuked; the survivors had become very conservative but did not want to join the ISA.

They enjoyed the protection of the ISA's Pacific fleet, which was based in Hawaii. The ISA kept control of the San Diego Naval Base and 10 miles around it in payment for the protection. The ISA also took the top 10 miles of Mexico below San Diego to help protect the base. The PSA was not as prosperous as the ISA but was doing well. While they did not totally embrace the strict conservative philosophy the ISA, they were far more conservative than the old USA and made sure that everyone worked that could, and everyone paid taxes. The PSA was continuously fighting small border wars with the Drug Cartels that had taken over Mexico after the TSHTF (the shit hit the fan). The ISA had been a big help with Intel and air cover for the major battles. The ISA also funded the ongoing battle along the entire length of the old USA border that was the main line of defense between the ISA and PSA with the lawless, ever probing Mexican Cartels.

The USA was particularly upset about four major issues. The first was that the ISA had deported its entire poor and disadvantaged people to the USA and Mexico. The ISA always countered that they were offered work and refused.

The story goes that John Harris gave them a choice of where to go, but they could not stay in the ISA unless they worked and contributed.

Several thousand were shot when they rioted and burned a town to the ground. The USA took their case to the UN, but the ISA sent a note to the UN saying, "We do not recognize the UN and any attempt to meddle in the affairs of the ISA's will be considered an act of war."

The second issue was that most of the old USA's military had defected and joined the ISA making it the major power in the world.

They defected when the President refused to retaliate against the perpetrators of the nuclear attack. He wanted to negotiate with our enemies, but had no problem bombing and killing thousands in the breakaway states led by Harris.

Most of the remaining Navy battle groups were now stationed in Hawaii, San Diego and the Gulf, or at Charleston protecting the ISA and making it the only remaining major nuclear power.

The third issue was that the ISA had helped the far western states to secede from the USA to become the Pacific States of America.

The fourth and most heinous crime, according to the USA, was that the ISA was directly involved in the deaths of the United States President and over 3,000 Liberal leaders in 2024.

The truth was that that President and 3,000 of the ringleaders and traitors were tried in a court of law, found guilty of high crimes and treason and legally executed. Both the President and one Vice President were directly responsible for the deaths of over 200 million Americans. Worldwide deaths were estimated to be in the billions.

The UN tried to take advantage of the now weakened USA. They believed the United Nations could become the world government of their dreams, along with the accompanying power. The UN was then made up of mainly Middle Eastern and African countries that hated the West and wanted to dominate the world.

These "Tin Pot Dictators" believed they had the opportunity to use the UN to push their radical Islamic agenda.

The UN finally backed down when the Aircraft Carrier Group, John F. Kennedy, accompanied by USS Texas took out Cairo, Riyadh, Tehran, Tripoli, Jakarta, Mogadishu and 150 other Muslim cities with nuclear weapons.

Those were the homes of the largest concentrations of radical Islamists, and the countries that funneled money into the cause.

That was the beginning of what the ISA named, "The 2nd Purge." Most of the people outside of the ISA, jihadists called it the 2nd Crusades and publicly denounced the ISA. Non-Islamic nations, in private, were thankful that the radicals were being dealt with.

The ISA's military was constantly bombing radical Muslim strong holds as fast as they were identified. The European allies were assisting as much as they could. It was a constant battle until Radical Islam became only an unpleasant memory.

Josh pulled up in front of the Harris house and quickly noted the massive fence and guards. He parked and walked up to the guardhouse and was quickly searched and told to wait. After a few minutes, a beautiful young lady came down to meet him. He immediately recognized her as Captain Jennifer Elizabeth Harris, John Harris' daughter and a Captain in the ISA Army. She greeted him with a big smile and a handshake, and then took him to the front porch. There he found two chairs, a table and a pitcher of lemonade with glasses.

Jenn said, "Josh would you like something to drink? We have sweet tea, beer or lemonade." Josh indicated that the lemonade would be nice.

Jenn Harris was 27, worked with the National Defense Agency as a Field Agent and still lived with John and Beth Harris in their home in Smyrna. She had been born during the time between the SHTF and the start of the breakup with the USA.

Jenn smiled at Josh and said, "I guess we need to get started, don't we?"

Josh replied, "Let's get started by telling me about yourself, then we will go back to the time before the war."

Jenn had started from just before she was born. Her Mom, Beth, and John had been together for a year and had met while camping in Montana. She was the youngest of four children and the only one from Beth and John.

Her older brothers, along with her father, were considered heroes in the ISA and terrorists in the USA. Beth fought in the last war; she had been wounded several times during the battle for Northern KY. Both sides disagreed on who started it, but the ISA finished it and kicked the USA out of KY and south of the Ohio River all the way to Pittsburgh.

She told about the treason by the ex-CIA Agents and Foreign Governments and jumped into the first war.

Josh interrupted her and said, "You're skipping over the "Trip." Is that intentional?"

Beth replied, "Dad wrote a whole book about it, and there is a movie, what could I possibly add that you don't already know?"

Josh smiled and said, "You can add some of the colorful quotes from your Dad and leave out the less than accurate parts. What about the love story between your Mom and Dad? The book and movie downplayed those. You demanded that we only tell the story you tell us, and we only demand the truth and the whole story."

She started the story by telling Josh about John and The Trip.

•••

Jenn had been talking about the early years for about an hour when an older man walked into the room with a gun in his hand, pointed it at Josh and said, "If you publish any of my sex life I will personally hunt you down and shoot you myself."

Just as Josh recognized the man, the man pulled the trigger. A stream of water hit Josh in the face.

Jenn yelled, "Daddy stop, he'll piss his pants."

Josh looked up and was staring John Harris in the face.

Jenn said, "Daddy, this is Josh, and I think that you will like him. John sat down and joined the meeting.

*

Chapter 4

The Trip

Mobile, Alabama

May 15, 2020

The Trip was meant to be fun for five friends getting away from it all. It was understood that it would be mentally and physically challenging.

No one dreamed that The Trip would change all of their lives and set them up for some of the greatest challenges a man could endure.

The Trip was meant to be fun. The Trip was meant to help old friends patch up some differences. It was meant to be many things, but damn; it *was* just a trip.

Who would have thought their lives would be in danger and that they would suffer so much and pay such a dear price?

They had all agreed that there would be no radios, TVs, cell phones, CD players, gadgets or the other extraneous bullshit tapestries of modern convenience. These things always ruined their other outings and strained their relationship.

This was to be the trip to end all trips. This was not to be a run up to the lake or a walk in the park. Other trips had been fouled up by each of them trying to get away, but always taking their work or commitments with them on their yearly outings.

They were the best of friends, but they annoyed the hell out of each other at times.

This trip was set up from the get-go to stress hunting, a little fishing, and fun. No work, no women, no distractions.

Books, magazines and the Internet; they researched the topic very well and came up with an unusual and challenging two-week visit to the great outdoors that would give them a taste for the real outdoors. The plan was to relive Jim Bridgers or any of the 19th-century trapper experiences.

Other than First Aid supplies, the only modern equipment would be their fishing gear. Guns would be black powder just as Daniel Boone had. Everything else had to have existed in the early 1850's or be left behind.

Of course, since they were all Preppers, they would take their Bug out Bags and personal survival weapons, but there was no expectation of needing them.

They all had concealed carry permits, and each one had a personal weapon on them at all times. John carried a KEL-TEC .380, but the rest had Ruger LCP .380s as concealed carries.

The KEL-TEC was the lightest and barely made a bulge in his pocket. Some of their other friends and coworkers made fun of them at times, but they paid no attention. Being prepared was a way of life for them. They often proclaimed, "I don't carry a pistol because I fear being attacked. I don't fear a fire either, but I have an extinguisher."

Gus wanted to take them down to Florida, to a Lake just about 80 miles from Lake Okeechobee. No research, just from the gut. They had been to Florida five or six times, and no one was interested.

Scott wanted to go to Colorado, out east of Colorado Springs for some trout fishing. He had been stationed at Fort Carson for two years and loved the area, but had never been able to go back due to family commitments and school. Jim always agreed with Scott, does the boy *have* a brain?

John didn't care where they went, but quite a few of his radio call-in fans had recommended the Great Adventures Outdoors Co. to help them plan their trip.

The past two years had been rather difficult for him, the divorce from Scott's mother, Ann, had been a terrible experience and John just wanted to get away from the shop and everything else.

Steve looked up the "Great Adventures Outdoors" on the Internet. Based out of Salt Lake City, they flew clients into selected wild areas all over the upper Southwest, Four Corners area and Mid-northwest.

He corresponded back and forth with them for over a month and obtained brochures for various outdoors experiences and a list of references.

They flew groups into the great outdoors, landed on a lake, left them for a week or two and then returned to pick up the group. They had over a dozen planes ranging from a couple of DC3's to modern 12 passenger twin-engine floatplanes.

Maria, the GAO representative, and Steve became internet friends because of the prolonged dialog. Hell, you know Steve; he wanted to get in her pants simply as a matter of course. Being unable to see or talk to her in person just made it more intriguing.

She sold Steve on hunting and fishing trips to Idaho, and he sold the rest of the group.

Steve told Maria of their need to experience the great outdoors without all the distractions, a real roughing trip. Take very little food or water and living off the land. Catch some fish to eat and hunt the rest of the time. Maria had just the place in mind, guaranteed fish, game and drinkable water. It was in Idaho, just south of the Montana border.

A lot of work goes into any trip; normally it took a week to get their gear together. This time it was much easier. Each man had a black powder rifle, fishing gear, a pup tent, a knife, two changes of clothes, a few cooking utensils, and a first aid kit.

Their Bug out Bag was a standard backpack, and all had three days' food, water purification tablets, thermal blankets, weapons, and ammo.

Most also contained numerous other survival gear such as a magnesium fire starter, folding saw, buck knife and other assorted gear.

John's also had a KEL-TEC P11 9mm and a Mark I Ruger .22 pistols with 100 rounds for each. The others all had 9mm autos accept Gus who carried his Colt 1911 caliber .45 automatic.

The group just had to drive from Mobile to Salt Lake City and leave the rest to GAO. They could have flown to Utah, but Jim and Steve could not afford the airfare, and while John's book royalties paid for the trip, he didn't want to be seen as "The Patron," so would not cover any extra costs.

While John's business was quite profitable, the divorce had financially hurt him. Ann got half of the current business profit. He kept any money from expanding his body shop and custom car work business.

The guys met at the shop the night before and loaded up their gear with road trip food and beverages. The rented RV was 35 feet long and slept six, but it seemed that everyone brought everything they owned. Gus quickly took charge and had them pare down the extra bullshit.

"Steve, this ain't no fashion contest. All you need is a pair of jeans, some shorts, a couple of shirts, socks, and underwear."

Gus chortled and added, "You don't need two big ass suitcases to go hunting."

He made all of them unpack their crap and repack to his specifications.

Jim got after him, "Gus, I don't remember you being my Momma or being put in charge of my ass."

Gus came over, wrestled Jim to the floor and then tickled him until he almost pissed his pants.

Scott went over to John and exclaimed, "Gus must have got laid last night, I've known him most of my life, and that's the most fun I can ever remember seeing out of him."

John slept at the shop that night but was up by 5:00 a.m. He checked things out and made a pot of coffee. He again went over his bullet points for his show that morning and quickly moved on to eat some sausage and biscuits he had nuked in the microwave. Scott had arrived just five minutes before the show started.

"Good Morning LA, I love the U...S...A,"

John asked his morning audience. "How are all of my Prepper Buddies doing this fine day in Lower Alabama?"

He then added, "The President can kiss my redneck ass. I'm John Harris, and I hope to have some fun today with my son, Scott, discussing how to put a Bug out Bag together and what to put in that rascal that might save your neck one day. Scott, tell 'em what to put in their bag."

Scott proceeded to describe every item, and why it was important. This took about 45 minutes with John inserting jokes and his personal experiences. He took two callers, answered their questions and moved on.

John then added, "I know a few of you don't appreciate guns like the rest of us, but one of these days you will say to yourself, I wish I had listened to old John and put a gun and ammo in my darned old Bug Out Bag. Now I have a Ruger MK I with 100 rounds of hollow point LR and a "P11, 9mm also with 100 rounds of hollow point ammo.

"I know, I know, John, why hollow points, they are more expensive, and ball ammo is just as deadly?

OK, good question, and one I'm glad *I* asked, so listen up. I carry hollow points for three simple reasons.

One: Hollow points are what the FBI use.

Two: Ball ammo is likely to go right through your target and injure an innocent standing nearby.

Third: If I am must use deadly force I want to be able to say that I use hollow points because of reasons One and Two.

After all, if the FBI thinks it's the best, and safest ammo then so should I.

That is a point you may have to make in a Liberal court facing homicide charges against some gangbanger who was about to kill you then rape your wife and daughters. All right, nuffsaid 'bout that.

I chose these two weapons because they give me the ability to put the game on the table and protect myself from bad guys.

As I always say, "a pistol is just a tool until you can get a real big long gun.

I'm also looking at adding one of the breakdown .22 survival rifles made by Henry. You might just kill a rabbit or two with that one.

Now it's time for cool trivia stuff. Did you know that the primary long guns carried by Lewis and Clark were actually air rifles? Yeah, that's right, the Girandoni model 1790 caliber .46 air rifles. The only downside was pumping those things 1,500 times to get 800 fps... Modern versions are just a smidge better, howsoever."

John ended the show by reminding his audience that he was on vacation for the next two weeks and that they would hear the best of "How to Survive" during his absence.

• • •

John went to the restroom to take a shower and freshen up before the rest of the guys arrived. He took a long hot shower thinking about Ann and wondering if he could get back with her. She was good in bed, even if she was above his raisin'.

He walked out of the shower buck naked right into JoAnne who smiled and asked him if he was happy to see her. He looked at her and saw that she had a halter-top that just barely covered her breasts and the shortest white shorts that he had ever seen. He then remembered to grab a towel for cover.

"What are you doing in so early on a Saturday morning, JoAnne?" John asked.

"Well, I was just worried about you, with no wife to take care of you. I want to make sure that you are taken care of," replied JoAnne, with a come-hither grin.

She then walked up to him and wrapped him in her arms while rubbing her body against him. John forgot himself for a few seconds before coming to his senses and pushing her away.

John calmly told her, "JoAnne, you are the best person for your job, and you never have to do anything like that again. Your job just depends on your work. Sex is not a part of your job description."

He also told her that he had wondered why so many women quit their jobs here before he started working at the shop.

She told him that his Dad got much better at hiding his womanizing after John and Gus started working.

John then told her," I'm not interested in any woman at this time. The only thing you have to do is your job."

John did not believe in dipping his wick in the company inkwell.

JoAnne gave John a peck on the cheek and thanked him for being a gentleman, then excused herself and walked away. As she walked away, John had to admit she had one fine ass. Just as he started to smile, she turned and looked back, smiled and walked away.

John took a few minutes to call Ann, his ex-wife, to fill her in on this issue. He knew that JoAnne and Ann had been close at one time and he wanted her to look in on JoAnne while he was gone.

"Good morning, Ann, how are you today?" John said in his friendliest voice.

She replied, "What time is it, is the sun even up this early?"

John filled her in on what had happened and what JoAnne had told him about his Dad and JoAnne.

She sarcastically said, "John, you dummy, everybody in town knew what a womanizer Buddy was, even your mom knew.

John, I'm worried about you. JoAnne rubs her body on you, and you didn't give in and make love to her. I'll bet you haven't been laid since I left you."

John stammered and could not come up with a thing to say.

Ann piled on with, "John, you were boring but great in bed, so to help you I am going to set you up with one of my friends from the club. She's 40, great looking and horny as hell. Even you will get laid if you spend a minute with her."

John quickly replied, "I'll find my own girl in my own time. I certainly don't need you to find a woman for me."

"So you think that you will just stumble over a perfect woman fishing and hunting out in those nasty woods that you so love. It won't happen, Dumb ass. John, even though you don't believe it, I still care for you and want you to be happy. Now find a woman and treat her right. Take her on trips and buy her beautiful things," Ann chided.

"Ok, Ann, I have listened to you lecture me for ten fucking minutes. Yes, I was a good boy; now will you check on JoAnne?" John asked.

Ann replied, "John, you cuss too much. I promise that I will check on JoAnne, but if you had just bent her over her desk and ravaged her, she would be happy, I would be happy, and even you might be happy." Ann laughed and hung up.

John thought, "Well that went rather well."

30

*

Chapter 5

Great American Outdoors

Mobile, Alabama

May 16, 2020

They finished loading up the RV and hauled ass across the Gulf to Salt Lake City. The drive was only a little over 1,900 miles, and with five drivers, it took just 29 hours.

While they all took turns, John drove most of the way. He was not a big drinker and was a lousy poker player.

He would think about the plot for his next book and used a voice note-taking program on his phone so he wouldn't forget anything.

Everyone made sure that the driver was sober; roughing it meant no beer, so they enjoyed themselves while they could. There was an ongoing poker game, and Steve took all everyone's money. Drive, drink and play poker, at least they didn't have to stop for a bathroom, just a dump station.

Salt Lake City

The intrepid group arrived in Salt Lake just before 8:00 a.m. and stopped for breakfast before driving on to the GAO office at the airport.

As usual, there was an argument on where to eat, and no one could agree, so John pulled into the parking lot of a local family run restaurant.

They all started complaining, and John said, "Shut the hell up and either stay in the RV or come in and eat with me. I'm buying; I don't care which choice you make."

Of course, they all piled out and went in with John. He was paying, and they were cheap bastards.

They were seatedquickly, and the waitress was very friendly. While waiting for their food, they overheard three older gentlemen having a rather lively discussion about, "How those damn Mexicans and Muslims were moving into the area and ruining the place." Naturally, Gus had to nose into the conversation. He went over and joined in just as if he had known them all of his life.

Gus asked, "What is all the fuss about the foreigners?"

The one in the red shirt told Gus, "That damn hunting trip company keeps bringing in these foreigners instead of hiring decent local folks."

Gus asked, "Do you mean the Great American Outdoors?"

All three started complaining about GAO and kept talking over each other.

The red shirt guy told them to pipe down and said, "Yeah, those guys are bringing in them damn Mexes and Mooslims. I think they's moving out into the country to form one of danged sleeper cells we hear about."

Gus asked, "How many have you seen? A small company like that couldn't use a whole bunch of workers."

The guy replied that he had seen at least 50 different Mexican workers in the last six months and that there were never more than 6-7 working at the airport at any one time. They also said that Muslim looking men flew in and out about once a month.

One of the guys said that the Muslims never came into town and kept a low profile while at the GAO operation. The old boys then gradually changed the subject and started talking local politics, which also interested Gus. He returned to the group just in time for breakfast to be served.

Gus told them about the conversation while they were eating. Between bites, he added his two cents and thought that something smelled about GAO. The rest of them were not as concerned and were just too excited about their trip.

They arrived at the GAO office at 10:30 a.m. The GAO office was south of the airport at Utah Lake since they had several floatplanes. As they drove up, Gus saw some of the float planes at the dock, two DC 3s and what looked like an old Huey helicopter were parked close to the office.

Gus and John were both fixed wing and Chopper qualified. They co-owned an old biplane that had been a crop duster. John's shop had converted it to a four-passenger toy to fly to NASCAR events and just have some fun. It was very slow, but lots of fun and would haul a lot of luggage. Thank the Lord for small favors, the plane had been in Gus' name, or half of his half would have been snatched by Ann.

Steve went into the office to find Maria while the guys stretched their legs. They walked around the compound and found that it was much larger than they would have guessed, especially for such a small operation.

There were the expected office and hanger, but also a warehouse building that had a couple of armed guards. When they approached, one of the guards came out to stop them from getting any closer.

The Mexican guard told them that they needed to go back to the office or they might miss their plane. Jim noticed that the guard had an unusual tattoo on his forearm. It appeared to be a small monster with a big head and large teeth.

When Jim asked about the tattoo, the guard smiled and said, "It's just a Tasmanian Devil."

Jim said, "You know it looks like one of those mythical Mexican monsters. I can't think of the name, but it'll come to me."

The guard looked mad and told them to get back to the office.

"What the heck is the delay?" Gus asked the pilot.

Gus was impatient and was growing grouchier by the minute.

Roger, the pilot, replied, "Just performing my preflight checks."

Maria came out of the hanger with Steve; both were laughing and carrying on like old friends. She wore a tank top, short shorts and a figure that women die for and men kill to possess.

John thought aloud, "Damn, she is one good looking gal."

Everyone could see that Steve was using all of his charms on Maria. They heard him invite her down to Mobile.

She laughed and said, "I'd love to, but we are so busy. I can't get away now, but maybe later in the year."

Maria tried to flirt with Gus just to cheer him up and get his mind off the delay. It didn't work.

Gus had flown many planes over the years and was sure that the pilot was just in a delay mode. This pissed him off.

Gus came over to John and said," I think he's pulling our chain, let's get this flight in the air."

John gruffly replied," Gus, don't get your panties in a wad this early in our trip."

John was also wondering what the delay was himself when a pickup pulled up, Roger and a ground crewman started loading up several boxes into the cargo bay. One fell and broke open. Scott and Jim tried to help Roger pick up the contents, but the crewman ran them off.

Scott whispered to Jim, "Drugs?"

Jim said, "That's what I thought I saw."

They weren't sure and said nothing to the rest of their friends. The crewman saw them whispering and did not appear to be pleased. He caught another Mexican off to the side, and they talked for a few minutes. It was obvious the Mexican was angry at the crewman, he gave him hell.

Roger walked over to the group and said, "Let's get this plane loaded and in the air."

They loaded up and took off. Maria stood beside the lake, smiled and waved to them as the plane lifted off.

*

Chapter 6

Back at the Home Front

Mobile, Alabama

May 17, 2020

JoAnne had called Ann and set up a lunch date at the club. John would have a fit if he knew that the business was paying for a membership for JoAnne, as well as Buddy and Ann. They met at 1:00 p.m. with a hug and a kiss. The girls were old friends.

Ann started the conversation laughing as she said, "So you finally made a pass at John this morning. Why didn't you get him in bed like we planned?"

JoAnne replied, "Oh My God Ann, you make me blush. I can't wait to get him in bed."

"He apparently has more self-control than you thought, or that hunk is gay. I've never failed to get a guy in bed before. I even loosened my halter top and shoved my boobs in his face."

Ann laughed and said, "John is still in love with me and wants me, and only me. That's why I want you to seduce him and give him a taste of another woman, so he will stop coming after me."

JoAnne smiled and replied, "I may have to tie him down and rape him."

Ann said, "He likes margaritas, get him drunk and then lay that boy down."

Ann asked, "What is going on with this new secret lover of yours? So, come on and tell everything about the new man of yours, down to the last detail. Inquiring minds want to know."

JoAnne grinned and said, "I am dying to tell you all about him, but he swore me to secrecy. I can tell you that he works for the government and is good in bed."

Ann laughingly replied, "This conversation is heading towards the gutter quickly."

"Buddy was the best, but my new guy has raised the bar. Of course, Buddy still gives it all he has."

"Joanne, you are still banging Buddy?" Ann asked.

"Yes, as long as he pays the bills, he expects me to deliver," said JoAnne.

Ann asked, "But isn't John paying the bills now? Even though he doesn't know it."

"Yes, but Buddy hints at telling John if I don't deliver. Thank God he's in Florida most of the time," replied JoAnne.

They carried on the banter for over an hour, before JoAnne excused herself and went to the hotel to meet Robert.

*

Chapter 7

Back in Mobile

Mobile, Alabama

May 17, 2020

Robert was a nice looking man about 40 with slightly graying black hair and stood 6' 1" with a muscular physique.

He was sitting on the bed in a Holiday Inn in Mobile wondering how he got this assignment and what it had to do with DHS. The phone rang, and he knew his contact was on the other end.

The voice on the phone said, "Are you making any headway with the secretary? I mean besides screwing her brains out?"

Robert replied, "You think I like screwing her? Well, I do, I do. She is beginning to trust me. I have most of the names and info on all of the shop's employees and a lot of info on Gus and John."

The voice said, "Good, now gain her confidence and get the entire story. We need more Intel about guns, ammo, and anything that will help our cause. You've been working with her for a couple of months now. It's time to tell her how you love her more than life itself. Continue buying her expensive gifts. Hell, take her on a trip while the guys are out of town."

Robert laughed and said, "Yeah, more than life itself, right. But, to tell you the truth, she is gorgeous. Oh well, the things we must do for our country. It's a dirty job, but someone has to do it."

About an hour later, there was a knock on the door. Robert opened the door, grabbed JoAnne and kissed her passionately while telling her how much he missed her. He kicked the door closed while continuing the kiss.

He said, "I missed you so much, I want you to be mine forever. I think I love you, baby."

JoAnne was confused at first because she thought this was just a booty call while she tried to land John.

She replied, "Robert, I had no idea that you cared so much."

He said, "Close your eyes and hold your right arm out." She did, and he placed a very expensive diamond tennis bracelet on it.

He said, "Open your eyes baby." She looked at her wrist and got very excited because there was a $10,000 bracelet on her wrist.

"Robert, I am so surprised, I know you like me, but this is so personal and so over the top," she said.

Robert replied, "I hope that I am not going too fast for you, but I love being with you and our sex is so wonderful that I can't bear to be away from you.

JoAnne replied, "I care for you, too, but we need to get to know each other before we push this too far."

Robert looked annoyed for a minute then recovered. He said, "JoAnne, you are a very special woman, and I don't want to miss out on the love of my life."

She put her arms around him and started taking his clothes off. She did not trust love at first sight, but she knew expensive jewelry when she saw it. He was a very happy man that night.

*

Chapter 8

The Crash

Idaho

May 17, 2020

North of Great Salt Lake

As the plane cleared the end of the lake, the guard went into the hanger and called his boss Manny. He told him about Roger dropping one of the boxes. He told him that one of the boxes of drugs had broken open and that at least one of the men had to have noticed. He then mentioned the tattoo.

Manny cut him short and told him, "Not to worry, Karl will know how to handle this little hiccup."

The plane was a twin-engine six passenger with Roger and Steve up front, Gus and John in the middle. Scott and Jim sat in the rear.

They flew directly over the Great Salt Lake and then headed out to some very desolate country. Steve chatted with Roger who had calmed down a bit since the takeoff. Gus and John slept while Jim and Scott were in awe of the terrain below them.

After a while, Scott whispered to Jim, "I'm sure that box was full of drugs, it looked like how they wrap cocaine in the movies."

Jim replied, "Are you sure? What the hell was a brick of drugs doing on a bush plane going to Idaho?"

Scott said, "As soon as Dad wakes up, we'd better tell him; he'll know what to do."

The plane droned on; the sky was clear and the sun was bright. The weather forecast was excellent for the next two weeks with no rain for at least a week.

Steve and Roger kept each other company while Gus and John slept. Jim and Scott sat uncharacteristically quiet in the back. They were still heading towards Sun Valley as planned when Roger got a transmission over the radio that appeared to be giving him instructions.

He replied, "Yes, I know where it is, we're only about 20 minutes from there. Okay, okay, damn it, I'll land there."

He then spoke some words that Steve could not understand and then started to make small deliberate changes in direction. Steve questioned him about it.   Roger replied, "Oh, Karl, my boss, just told me to make my cargo delivery on the way out instead of on the way back. I now have to go north and pick up some tools from a mining operation before I drop you off."

Jim and Scott were busy trying to guess what the boxes of drugs meant and where they came from. Their minds ran wild.

The plane banked, and Roger began the approach to a large lake east of a large city. Roger told them they were landing on a reservoir just west of Pocatello.

Gus woke up and wanted to know what was going on. Steve told him, and Gus complained then rolled over and went back to sleep. They made a smooth as silk landing and taxied up to a dock in front of a group of small cabins. Several rather tough looking Hispanic men greeted Roger and helped him unload the boxes. Jim and Scott watched closely.

Jim pointed and asked," Do you see the guy behind the tree by the far cabin on the left?"

"Yeah," Scott replied.

"Well, he's got an M-16."

"Let's tell Dad," Scott whispered.

Jim replied, "No wait, we'll look foolish if we're wrong. Let's watch this play out a while."

Just at that time, Roger got back into the plane and quickly started the engine. They taxied out onto the lake and took off. Roger saw Scott and Jim whispering in the back and knew trouble was on the way. He'd also caught a glimpse of the M-16. Scott and Jim knew that something was wrong, but had no clue how right they were.

Roger flew the plane up to cruising speed and soon received another transmission. Roger did not like what he had heard. He argued and then complied as if he had been threatened. Steve overheard Roger's part of the conversation.

Roger's answers were, "We made the drop...Why there? Yeah, I know you are the boss. Okay...Okay...We're 40 minutes from there." Again, "Are you sure? Yes, sir, I've got it, Roger out."

Steve questioned Roger," What's going on this time?"

Roger answered with," My son of a bitch boss wants me to work straight on through the weekend to get those tools back to the mine. I had a hot date."

Steve asked him what was waiting for them 40 minutes away.

Roger said, "That's how far we are from our landing and your camp."

Gus, butted in and stated, "Just a while ago you said that we were only twenty minutes away, which one is correct?"

Roger apologized and said that the 40 minutes was correct and that he didn't remember saying 20 minutes if he said it, he had been wrong.

Gus was becoming concerned. If he knew, what Scott and Jim had known, he would have been much more than just concerned.

The time crawled by. Roger said, "Your destination is right there, over the right wing." Roger began a slow circle over the largest lake in a chain of lakes.

The largest one was about a mile long and perhaps a quarter of a mile wide. It looked shallow and murky, not what they had expected at all.

This area was known for its deep clear bodies of water. There were several islands on the north side and dense forest all around.

It was one of the most beautiful sights Scott had ever seen. He thought that this would be home for the next two weeks. Just as he

41

was picking out likely fishing spots, he saw something shiny in the woods to the south. He watched the area closely and saw a bright flash and smoke.

He yelled, "Someone is shooting at us."

Gus took a quick look and hollered, "Roger, dive, incoming."

He had spotted the missile. Roger brought the plane into a steep dive at a right angle to the incoming rocket but was too late. There was a thunderous explosion, and the plane rocked and felt as if it had been blown sideways. Shrapnel blew through the floor and out the top; they were hit, blood splattered, and everyone screamed just like in the movies.

Scott thought, "*I know it sounds corny, but it seemed like it was in slow motion.*" Shrapnel began bouncing around the inside of the plane. No one would fail to shed blood.

John's first thought was that they were all dead. He prayed all he could in about two seconds. Whatever he had done, that was wrong; he promised never to do it again if God would save them.

Roger had blood all over him from a wound in his shoulder and Steve was yelling, "My ass, my ass, oh shit my freaking balls are gone."

A jagged piece of metal had gone into his seat and hit his butt.

Gus shouted over the rush of the wind blowing through what was left of the plane, "Is everyone okay, or at least alive?"

All were hit with bits of shrapnel, but only received cuts and scrapes, it could have been much worse.

Scott was pulling a small shard of aluminum from his cheek, and Jim said that he had a slice in his thigh. Steve had checked his ass and had a bad cut, but was keeping the pressure on it. Roger still had his balls, for the moment. All would live, at least for now.

The plane was barely in the air. Gus saw large holes in the wings. The left engine was severely damaged, and the right engine was barely running. The plane was bucking and jumping as it careened toward the lake.

Roger was mumbling, "That dirty fucking Karl."

Gus quickly assessed the situation and yelled, "Roger, get us out of here." Gus reached over and gave the remaining engine full throttle.

Gus said, "John, we only have one engine, a pontoon has been blown away, and only God knows what is holding this damn plane together."

The missile had hit one of the pontoons and expended most of the explosive force on the destruction of the pontoon. The pontoon had performed as standoff armor.

Gus then told Roger to aim for the farthest lake to the north.

Roger yelled back, "The plane won't make it that far; I'm landing on this one."

Without warning, Gus cold cocked Roger and took the controls.

John screamed, "What are you doing? Did you kill him?"

Gus shouted over the roar, "John, someone just tried to shoot us down with a Stinger and only Roger and his company knew where we were landing."

He then added, "I think we crapped in someone else's sandbox. Now that shit is flying, and it stinks."

Steve and John pulled Roger into the middle seats. John moved up front with Gus.

"Can you land this damn thing?" John asked. "John, this piece of crap is going down whether I land it or not. With only one pontoon we will crash. Does that answer your question?"

Gus then said, "See the lake over to the right with the small island on the north side?"

They all saw it and replied with a rather shaky "Yeah."

Gus told them, "I'm going crash this thing between the island and the shore.

"He then added, "Get your seat cushions from under your asses, then wrap them around your ears and buckle up. We are coming in hot, and we are going to make a big splash.

John told them, "If your right about the missile, those guys will be on us like stink on shit, be ready to un-ass this junk pile on impact, 'cause this fucker is gonna' sink like a freakin' stone."

John began searching the cabin and found a loaded 9mm and a bag of candy under the seat. He told the others to find anything that could be useful. Grab Gus' and his Bug out Bags, which were in the cabin behind Scott. He thought for a brief moment that this trip was at least starting out with a bit more bang than the others had been.

Gus ordered them to get all the gear that was in the plane when the missile hit and told Scott and Jim to try for the guns in the cargo hold if they could.

Gus told them that he was going in and for them to get ready. The plane was all over the place as Gus tried to bring it down onto the water. Gus touched the one remaining pontoon onto the water, it immediately broke off and ripped part of the flooring out with it. The plane bounced back up into the air.

Gus yelled, "Damn it, we can't make another pass. We are goin' down, now!"

He then brought the nose up and almost stalled, but did manage to keep it alive. The plane slammed down hard and started skipping on the water. Without pontoons, the plane became a sled. As it abruptly came to a stop, the fuselage dug nose first into the water and flipped over leaving everyone hanging upside down in strapped to their seats.

Fuel began pouring all over them. Smoke from the engine rolled into the tangled mass. They quickly kicked the doors open and jumped out, leaving Roger hanging from his seat belt.

John said, "What about Roger?"

Gus said, "Screw him; he's the one that did this to us."

John said, "You don't know that, and anyway this is still not what we were raised to do. He must know something about why we were shot down. He goes with us, at least for now."

Screaming, Steve said, "Ya think the drugs might have something to do with getting a Stinger up our ass?"

Steve and John pulled Roger from the plane while Jim and Scott tried, in vain, to open the cargo hold. The plane was floating in about 12 feet of water and was sinking fast. There was no way to get the guns or other equipment.

Gus asked them to grab what they could and swim to shore. John towed Roger, who was now sputtering as he began to awaken.

They swam only about 50' before reaching a muddy bottom allowing them to wade to shore. This was the shallow end of the lake, and there were trees growing right up to the water. John saw a rabbit and some birds at the edge of the forest and thought that they would not starve.

Steve and John pulled Roger out of the water and dropped him on the shore like a sack of potatoes, he groaned, then passed out.

Gus looked at Roger and told John, "That's one lucky sumbitch'. If you weren't here, I'd of let his ass drown."

John turned towards Gus and stared him down, "Gus, shame on you. You are the one who has been after me for years to be more religious and caring of my fellow man."

At that point, Scott observed, "Whatever happened, they don't like him any more than us. They obviously didn't care if he was collateral damage."

Scott gently kicked Roger in the ribs until he woke up. Then he asked him, "What was in those boxes? Don't lie; we saw some drugs."

Gus said, "What drugs?"

Scott answered, "Gus, Roger dropped a box and bundles of drugs fell out. We were going to tell you after Roger let us out."

John pointed the gun at Roger's head and said, "You have one chance, to tell the truth and live."

Roger told them that he thought that it was a drug smuggling operation, but was distinctly light on detail. He told them that the GAO paid him well and he didn't ask questions.

Turning their attention to their wounds, Roger had the worst of it with a deep gouge in his right shoulder and a nasty slash in his ass. Scott spread something from the First Aid kit on his injuries. He then secured it with gauze and a medical tape from the First Aid kit.

John made Steve pull his pants down, and they saw a puncture wound on his right butt cheek. John poked at it with the end of a pair of scissors to see if anything was still stuck in there causing Steve to jump and scream like a 12-year-old little girl.

"Quit acting like a baby, you big wussy, ignore the pain," growled John.

Scott also spread some of the same gook on the wound and applied a large Band-Aid.

Scott said, "Steve I think you'll live, but it only missed your balls by an inch or two. The ladies would have been very sad back home."

The rest of them just needed a few Band-Aids and were okay.

John told Jim and Scott to go back to the plane and try to dive down and get some of the gear. They swam out and dove down to the plane.

Scott brought some gear to the shore while Jim continued to dive. They had only gotten John's Bug out Bag, a black powder rifle and some assorted gear. The plane had rolled over and was blocking the hatch to the hold.

Gus spread out all the gear that they were able to salvage. They found:

- a 9mm Berretta,
- a 9mm KEL-TEC,
- a .22 Ruger with ammo,
- a .22 Ruger MK1 and 500 hollow point rounds,
- a black powder 50 cal. Hawken rifle,
- a compass,
- field glasses,
- a bag of candy,
- one pint of black powder,
- a seven-inch hunting knife
- four pocket knives,
- about 30 feet of nylon rope,
- a first aid kit,
- several cans of tuna,
- two jars of peanut butter.
- magnesium fire starter
- thermal blankets
- one flare gun with three flares
- five chocolate bars
- their Concealed Carry weapons, five .380s with ten 6 round magazines.

Gus laughed and said, "It ain't much, but we can shoot some game, cook it and keep warm. It could be a lot worse."

John replied, "It would be nice if we had some bullets for the Hawking."

Jim said, "Sorry, I just could not find any."

Roger very gingerly stood up behind them and blurted out, "We had better get off the shore and into the woods before they spot us.

Gus heard him and quickly turned the 9mm on him. "You had better not move again without permission or I will put a big assed hole in you, you worthless piece of shit."

Roger yelled back at him, "They had a plane stashed in a cove back there on the other lake. They should have already been here by now. We have got to get into the woods now!"

Gus took over the conversation and said, "Let's get out of here."

They quickly gathered their equipment and headed into the wood line. Gus had tied Roger's hands behind his back and was pushing him ahead as they walked under the canopy of trees.

 John was in the lead with Steve bringing up the rear. Steve told them to keep going, and he would go back so he could listen to see if the plane was approaching yet.

While Steve was gone, Scott took the Hawken and loaded it with a double load of powder and three small pebbles in a piece of cloth for a patch.

Scott said, "It won't go far, but it will do up close."

Steve had walked back towards the lake and was out of sight for a minute. He came back at a full run, yelling for them to move out quickly. He told them he had seen a plane circling over the lake as if it were looking for them. They took off at a quick pace into the woods heading northeast towards higher ground.

Steve was joking that the plane was probably coming to rescue them or was full of women.

John stopped and told them to go on about half a mile then wait for him. He then told them that he would catch up after he found out who was on the plane.

John looked at Steve and said, "I know there ain't any women, but it would be a shame to starve in the woods hiding from our rescuers.

If I don't show up in one hour, just keep heading north for about a mile then head due east. This will take you away from the lake, and I will know where to find you.

We crossed a highway about 30-40 miles back, and that is our best bet to find help. I'll be up in an hour or so if everything goes well. If not, then goodbye."

Scott protested and tried to come along with him, but John told him to take care of the others and keep his head low. Gus tried to make John take the 9mm, but he refused and took the Hawken instead.

John told the team, "There are five of you and if those bastards catch up, ya'll gonna' need as much firepower as you can get. If they see me, I'll take one shot and run like hell. Remember I still have my .380 and this hunting knife for close up fighting."

John added, "This has already started out much more exciting than any of our other trips."

He only got a couple of half-hearted laughs in reply.

• • •

Manny and the four GAO men watched as the missile struck the floatplane. They saw the explosion blow off the pontoon and shred the bottom of the plane.

Smoke rolled from the right engine and Manny yelled, "That bitch is coming down."

The others cheered. Then the plane rocked side to side and bucked like a horse as Roger poured the coal to her. The plane stabilized and started to gain altitude.

Manny told the others, "Karl won't like it if those bastards get away, let's get in the air."

They piled into the plane and took off in hot pursuit.

The pilot, Red, was a sinister looking man who was 6'2", bright red hair, very muscular and had scars all over his arms. He also had ugly face from a scar that ran from his nose to his left ear.

Red had been with Manny for over ten years. He seldom spoke and was loyal to a fault. No one doubted for a second that Red would die for Manny.

He had been in the Russian Air Force before settling down in South America where he and Manny met and became friends. He probably had some weird Russian name but went by Red Smith. Only Manny knew that he was wanted by half of the governments of the free world and the entire breakaway Russian states for God knows what.

Manny Cortez was afraid of Karl but was not afraid of anyone or anything else. He was a trained killer and combat veteran of many South American bush wars. Manny was 36 years old, 5'6", 160 pounds, black wavy hair and brown eyes that cut through people at a glance.

Manny was a midlevel operator in a major crime family based in South America who specialized in drugs and smuggling people into the USA. His wife, Carla, and six children lived in Paraguay in an old mansion on a large compound.

Manny was dedicated to The Cartel first and his family second. He was a trusted right arm man in Karl Mendoza's North American operations and would soon be moving his family to the states. This would enable him to spend more time on his business and less time traveling.

As the plane climbed, Manny got on the radio and called Karl.

Manny said, "The plane was hit and going down, but it appears that there may be survivors."

Karl replied, "Check the crash site and call me if there are survivors. I have plans for them."

Another GAO soldier in the back seat was Jesus Sanchez. He was a cold-blooded killer who had been with Manny since their childhood.

Manny had a crush on Maria, but she never showed any interest and called him her brother. She had joined the group about a year ago and had become like family. The two remaining thugs were Jose and Pepe who had just flown up with Karl on Monday. They were now assigned to Manny to help him get ready for the big push.

Karl was only visiting the outpost in Idaho when the security breach occurred. When Manny told him that the plane had been hit, but got away, Karl thought that he would mix business with a little fun. He thought that he would show these lazy Americans the other side of the hunt.

He replied to Manny, "Allow the Americans to escape. Stay close, but don't let them know you are following them until I arrive. I am also going to take care of *our* pilot; he will never foul up anything else for us."

He then ordered his personal pilot, Maria, and his three bodyguards to load up his plane for a two-day hunting trip. He told one to bring along a good hunting rifle and plenty of ammo.

He then went to his luggage and gathered clothes and his shaving kit just in case. Even though he would come back to the outpost at night, he always thought it was best to be prepared.

He searched his suitcase, found the little black leather case holding his special toys. Smiling to himself, he thought of Roger.

Manny's plane landed and taxied to the end of the lake where the crash had occurred. The water was still muddy, and there was an oil slick. He had one of his men dive down to the plane and search for survivors. The man surfaced and told Manny that no one was left on the plane. Manny quickly got on the radio and told Karl that the Americans had survived and that he was unable to determine the extent of their injuries.

Karl received the message and ordered his crew to prepare to leave. They taxied to the far end of the lake and then took off.

Karl enjoyed the beautiful landscape and thought how these Americans took this wonderful country for granted. He would remember to teach his children never to spoil the land, God would not like it, and Karl was a very religious fellow.

Karl read a book to pass the time until landing. The plane landed and taxied beside the sunken wreck, which had nosed in toward the shore.

Manny greeted them, shook Karl's hand and began telling him that from what he could tell everyone aboard had somehow survived the crash.

Karl asked, "Are they armed?"

Manny replied, "We cannot tell for sure, but they only brought black powder muzzle loaders with them. The guns were loaded in the planes' cargo hold, and the door is jammed in the mud. "

Karl thought that perhaps a few old weapons in the hands of a couple of businessmen "wannabe hunters" could add some excitement to an otherwise dull hunt.

Karl turned to Red and said, "Red, are you still able to track man or beast without them leaving bread crumbs to mark their trail?"

Red laughed and said, "Karl, you know that I can track anything that leaves tracks. I can track a fish if you want me to."

Karl joined in the laughter and said to all, "Let's start this hunt so we can finish before dark."

It was about 1:00 p.m. and there were nearly six more good hours of daylight. Manny reminded Karl that the Americans had at least an hour and a half lead on them. He also said that Roger might have a pistol. Karl was not concerned, if it takes a couple of days, so be it. This was to be the highlight of his visit to the states.

• • •

John backtracked and came out of the woods about one hundred yards from the crash site. He kept low and spied through the field glasses on the people as they were apparently searching the crash site.

One dove down to the wrecked plane several times and then swam to the shore. Another came out of the woods and looked familiar; he was Manny from GAO.

Manny appeared to be directing the others. He had a tall red haired guy searching up and down the shore. A small Latino man was checking out the spot where the vacationers had regrouped before slipping into the woods.

He thought Scott and Jim were correct; the bastards from GAO were the ones that tried to kill us.

John decided that he had better get his ass back to join the others when he heard a noise a few yards away. He crawled under a brush pile and tried to disappear. While John could not see much, he could catch a glimpse of the one with the red hair standing behind the brush. The Latino was walking up towards the pile from the direction of the plane.

That saved his ass because he walked over John's tracks and Red did not notice his trail. Red and the Latino were discussing what they thought someone called Karl would do to the Gringos when they were caught.

The red-haired thug said, "Jesus, what has made Manny so mad at Roger, he seemed to be a fair pilot?"

Jesus answered, "I don't know, but the fool dropped a box of cash and drugs in front of the Gringos. It made no difference if the Yanquis did not notice. Any potential error must be fixed. You know how Manny and the GAO are about keeping this operation secret. Karl will cut his tongue out and then gut him."

Red laughed and said, "I guess it is just lucky for us, we get to have some fun hunting the great white hunters."

John thought that without a doubt Roger was a dead man and would die a very slow death. The rest of them would be hunted down for sport.

They sat down on a log and shot the shit about the good old times down in South America. Apparently, they had been mercenaries for several banana republics. They talked a good story about warfare, rape, and murder during several of their campaigns.

Both then also talked about their leader Karl who apparently was the number two guy in a very large South American drug operation based in Paraguay.

Jesus mentioned that they were a year ahead of plan in taking over the West Coast operations in the US. Apparently, the Colombian Cartel was not, yet, well established in the northwestern half of the US and some battles had been fought for control of the drug trade. They both agreed that they would earn their money as they pushed into the eastern half of the US.

"It will be a bloody battle all the way," exclaimed Jesus.

Red answered with, "The bloodier, the better, I hate Colombians more than I hate Americans."

He pulled a 9mm auto out of his holster and aimed it right at John. John held his breath, but nothing happened. Red re-holstered the gun. John noted that Jesus appeared to have a similar weapon.

Jesus told Red that their most daunting task was to hire competent Gringos to help run their operations on the east coast. Cubans were available for Florida, but the North was still in the planning stage.

Red thought that he could recruit some of the Russian mob, but Jesus warned him that Karl and his boss would not take kindly to involving the Russian mafia.

Red groaned and said, "I am not into politics, I like the adventure, wine, women and a good fight. This drug running is not a good thing for a soldier."

He added, "I will kill anyone needing killing, but the drugs make me feel dirty."

Jesus smiled and replied. "It's all about money my friend; we have to have lots of American dollars to fund our cause. I, also, have worries about smuggling in those Arabs, even though Karl wants bombs going off to keep the Feds busy, I just don't like it."

"The Americans like the white powder, and we need their money. It's a marriage made in heaven. We must be taking tens of millions of dollars out of the western half of the US, right now. Wait until we get the east coast operation up to speed," Jesus told Red.

John had been thinking their cause was selling drugs. However, that comment made him start wondering what they were up to and what was the Arab connection, and what bombs?

This was much worse than John thought. These weren't just some local bad guys. They had stumbled into a hornet's nest. Even if they escaped, The GAO had their home addresses along with John's credit card info.

John knew he needed a well thought out plan. Now, just saving their sorry asses was no longer the prime concern. Their family's lives were at stake. John had to get back to the others to warn them. This group had to find a way to return to Alabama to save their loved ones.

They talked for over 10 minutes when John heard another plane landing. John thought that this must have Karl and crew aboard. Red and Manny left him in the brush pile and rejoined their friends in welcoming the newly arrived Karl and his merry band of hunters.

John silently watched as the new group unloaded weapons and supplies. One of them was the girl, Maria, from the GAO office back in Utah. Damn, Steve will be surprised to see this sweet young thing with the big gun strapped to her hip. They all wore side arms, and three had AK 47s.

A big blonde man had a hunting rifle with a high-powered scope. The others acted as if he was the big cheese. While they gathered around the tall blond haired man, John moved in closer in an attempt to discover their plan.

The blond guy was Karl, and there was no doubt that he was in charge. He spoke very softly, but they hung on every word. His plan was simple. Red was to track them down, and Karl got to shoot them like the wild pigs they were.

John's thoughts kept turning to his son and the others; they must survive to warn the authorities. These people must be stopped. He then slipped into the relative safety of the dense forest. He

53

headed back to his friends as quickly as possible so that they could get prepared for the eventual conflict.

As he slinked away, John couldn't help wondering if Mac Norman would write a book about this or should John Harris write it as a true story. He finally decided it would make a good yarn regardless of who wrote it.

＊

Chapter 9

Beth

The Iowa/Montana Woods

May 17, 2020

John saw something ahead in the bushes. Someone was squatting down trying to hide. Damn. Oh shit, he was only about twenty feet away when he spotted her. He could only see her backside but did notice that she was blond, had great legs, a slim waist, and a great tan. He realized that he was misbehaving and was silently embarrassed; however, he kept watching. He could not take his eyes off this gorgeous vision.

He had been in a hurry and just ahead of the GAO hunters when he came upon this wondrous vision. She was about 35 and about 5'5", and built like a brick shit house with revolving doors and a toll booth.

He was deep in thought about this gorgeous woman, when a twig snapped and brought him back to the real world. He surveyed his surroundings and heard one of the GAO coming up to him from the other side of his newly found beauty. She would be spotted in a second, he knew. She had turned, now facing to his right. He sprang to his feet and lunged towards her.

She was in a world of her own and did not react until he grabbed her around the waist and closed his hand over her mouth. She struggled, but he quickly overpowered her and dragged her to the ground. She was laying half in his lap with her head beside his, cheek to cheek. He thought that she must think that she was about to be raped.

She was horrified and struggled quite a bit. She even managed to elbow him in the ribs as he overpowered her. The more she struggled, the tighter he held her. He held her firmly and prayed for her to be quiet until they passed.

He finally whispered for her to listen.

He said, "I'm not going to hurt you, look, see those guys?"

The main body of the group was about twenty yards behind the point man.

"They are killers. See the guns. We can't let them find us."

She stopped struggling.

He told her, "I'm John Harris, and these guys are trying to kill my friends and me.

I am not going to hurt you. If I take my hand off your mouth, will you be quiet?"

He could tell she was watching the group and could easily see their assault rifles. She nodded, and he took his hand from her mouth. He was still holding her with one hand on her bare stomach and the other on her shoulder. They watched as the last guy, who was trailing the main group by another twenty yards, faded from sight. She slowly moved his hand off her stomach and moved away from him.

He asked, "What's your name?"

"Beth," she whispered.

He asked, "Are you okay? I am sorry that I had to pull you down so hard."

Red faced, she asked, "how long were you watching me?"

He replied, "Oh, only a second before I knocked you down."

His grin probably gave him away because his face was also bright red.

She looked at him and gave him the once over, she frowned and said, "I think that you are a pervert and were watching all along."

He told her, "You name a man that would not have watched such a beautiful woman standing in the woods."

He added, "If I had not been there, the killers would have found you and done horrible things to you."

She blushed and said, "A true gentleman would have never stared at me."

He then told her about the events so far. She said that they had heard some noise in the distance and had heard the plane, but did not think much of it.

She thanked him for saving her from those men. She then slapped the shit out of him while saying, "I'll bet you think twice about stalking a strange woman in the future."

He backed away, rubbed his jaw and said, "I will most assuredly behave myself in the future."

He reintroduced himself and asked for her full name. She said that her name was Elizabeth Fox and that she was a teacher from Smyrna, TN. She was 38, divorced and had two kids, Kristie who is 16 and Randy who is 14. She had a small home in Smyrna and taught at the local high school. She liked country music, hiking, kayaking and anything to do with the outdoors. While she talked, he took in the beauty that she radiated as effortlessly as a diamond or a sunset over Mobile Bay.

Smiling now, she said, "Oh, I like pina colada's and getting lost in the rain."

She had shoulder length honey blond hair, weighed about 135 pounds and was about 5'6" tall. Her smile warmed him down to his toes. John was lost in her gaze. Just as Ann had predicted, here was the perfect woman alone in the forest. He'd have to thank her if he lived long enough.

Then he heard her say, "I can see that you aren't listening to me, you were probably fantasizing about me."

He quickly said, "No ma'am, I was just amazed at how utterly beautiful you are."

She smiled and said she did not believe him. "You are a dirty old man, and you will probably never change my mind," she exclaimed.

John realized that probably was the optimum word. "Oh, crap, I think I may have just met my next ex-wife."

He asked her how many were in her party and how did they get here.

She said that there were four others in their party, Bill James and his wife Janet, Fred Allen and his girlfriend Alice Myers. They were all from the Nashville area, and Alice Myers taught History at the high school with Beth. All but Fred taught at the same high school. Fred was the assistant football coach at the middle school in Murfreesboro. They were all outdoors buffs and had planned this trip for over a year.

They had driven from Nashville to Dillon, Montana in Bill's rented RV. Their plan was to hike from the south end of the Beaverhead National Forrest in Southeast Montana to Yellowstone Park in the Northeast corner of Wyoming. The trip covered about 70 miles over some rough country. The plan was to hike an average of 10 miles per day through the forest, camping, and fishing along the way. They would finish their trek and camp in Yellowstone for an additional week before catching their ride back to Dillon.

John asked, "Where the fuck, are we? I thought we were in Idaho?"

Beth gave him an icy stare and then told him that they were in Montana, about 45 miles from the tristate corner of Montana, Idaho, and Wyoming.

He then asked where her camp was.

She pointed in the direction that the GAO group had gone, turned white and nearly yelled, "They are headed right to our camp."

He told her to keep her voice down and to follow him. The GAO creeps left a trail that a blind man could have followed. It was apparent that these people were not concerned about covering their tracks or being attacked.

The forest was dense, and traveling was slow at best. John told Beth that he did not want to go too fast or they could run right into them. Twenty minutes later, they heard a scream and much loud talking.

John said, "Beth when we get to the camp it may be a bad scene. We may not be able to help your friends, and they may be dead."

She was visibly upset, but said, "Let's go and try to help them if we can."

He told her that he only had the Hawken and a .380, while the thugs each had side arms and automatic rifles. The two of them would not stand a chance in a head-to-head fight.

She replied, "Then let's be careful when we kick their asses."

He liked the girl's attitude.

They quietly moved closer to the camp and observed from 25 yards out. One man, John later found out to be Fred, was lying on the ground in a pool of blood. His girlfriend, Alice, was at his side crying and sobbing.

The tall red haired man was wiping his hunting knife on Fred's shirt, laughing.

He then grabbed the grieving woman and began to grope her. Maria came out of one of the tents and kicked Red in the ass. He turned and fronted Maria, his hand raised as if to strike her; Manny stepped between them and pushed Red away. The woman, Alice, fell to the ground.

While they could not hear everything that was said, it was apparent that Karl was not pleased that Maria had stepped between Red and Alice.

Karl called for Manny, "Get your bitch under control or I will take care of her myself."

Maria yelled back to Karl, "I don't need anyone to watch over me. Red is a pig and what he was about to do will not move our cause forward."

Karl only laughed and replied, "Jesus, take her to one of the tents and tell her to stay inside; Red needs to have a little fun with this Gringa."

Jesus grabbed Maria's arm and pushed her into the furthest tent from Red. Karl then told Red to have fun with the girl. Red knew what he wanted to do, after all, it had been over a month since he had a woman and this one's last name was Myers so that Karl would watch with pleasure.

Red ripped Alice's clothes off and then stripped her of her underwear. She fought, but Red was twice her size. He slapped her around until she complied. He grabbed her, and she kicked him. He then shot into the ground yelling, "Bitch, do as I say, or the next one is in your head."

She stopped struggling and submitted to the bastard. He savagely raped her.

Beth heard the shot and watched Karl's violent behavior. John had to grab her and hold a hand over her mouth again. Alice kicked and tried to scream.

John covered Beth's eyes with his chest. He reminded her there was nothing they could do since these guys outnumbered them, and each was heavily armed. John then swore to her that he would make them pay for this atrocity.

John continued to hold Beth while Red, Manny, and Jesus took turns raping Alice. This was the worst thing that he had ever had to witness. The feeling of being helpless while someone was being tortured was nearly more than John could endure. He steeled himself and tried to console Beth to keep her calm.

Beth's friend, Bill, apparently had snapped while watching Red abuse his friend. He tried to knock Red off Alice, but Jesus and Manny stopped him. They kicked Bill and beat him until he could no longer resist. When they finished with Alice, Red moved towards Janet, but Karl waved him off.

"Red, you had your fun, now get back to work. Let's deal with these campers and return to the hunt."

Karl had Jesus bring Bill to him.

"I do not want to dirty my hands on this inferior piece of shit, who wants to kill him?"

Red replied, "Let Maria kill this bastard as proof of her allegiance."

Karl liked the idea and had Jesus bring Maria from the tent to face Karl.

Maria had heard the conversation and blurted out, "So, I have to prove myself after being a loyal supporter for over a year?"

Karl glared and said, "Yes. Kill the son of a bitch."

Maria took Karl's Glock, hit Bill across the back and marched him to the edge of the camp, directly in front of them. She put the gun to his head and pulled the trigger. Bill fell to the ground.

"Does this make me any more loyal to you? Karl, what do I have to do, kill ten more to impress you? I am loyal, but I do not like unnecessary killing. I will do whatever it takes to further our goals, but random killing is barbaric and beneath us."

Beth again had to be restrained as her friend died. John quietly pulled her back another hundred feet from the camp so they would not hear her cry.

"I have lost two good friends today, and there is no telling what they will do to Alice and Janet," she sobbed.

60

John told her that they would quickly bury Bill and Fred to keep the animals from eating them until someone could come back for the bodies.

Alice was lying on the ground sobbing and pounding her fists into the ground. They finally heard Karl command the others to dress Alice and to bring the two captives along.

Beth and John quickly went into the campsite and buried Fred with rocks and what dirt they could scrape up with a frying pan. While John finished covering Fred, Beth went to start on Bill's grave. Suddenly John heard her gasp and saw her back away from the body.

Then she said, "He's alive."

John checked his pulse, and she was right. John then checked his wound and found it to be a deep graze to his right forehead. This would hurt like hell for several days, but would not kill him.

Beth got a canteen and splashed water on his face. He awoke, but was very groggy and was speaking nonsense. She cleaned the wound, applied a bandage from an FA kit and gave him some painkillers. John took a smelling salts vial from the kit, broke it and placed it under his nose. He sat straight up and began thanking God he was alive.

Bill asked about Janet and the others and Beth filled him in on what had happened to his friends. He was distraught about Janet and kept blubbering that he prayed she had not been raped like Alice.

Meanwhile, John grabbed some food, a butcher knife, three sleeping bags and a few supplies from their gear. They stuffed all they could get in three small bags. They also grabbed jackets, and Beth pulled a pair of pants on over her shorts.

John told them that their best chance was to catch up to his party and to try then to get the ladies away from these killers.

They agreed and set off at a fast pace toward the location he assumed his friends would be waiting.

They both supported Bill and moved as quickly as they could push him. The brush and small trees were thick, but they still made a good time. Bill soon recovered enough to walk by himself. They finished filling him in as they walked.

They had traveled for about an hour when John heard his name called out by Scott. "Dad, are you okay? Who are these people?"

At the same time, John saw the rest of his group spring out from cover in the brush.

John said, "Let's move on out of here. Some really bad guys are only a few minutes behind us. We'll fill you in as we go."

"This is Beth Fox and Bill James. They were camping about five miles back when the GAO overran their camp," John explained.

Beth noticed that Roger had his hands tied and started to ask about it, but John poked her in the ribs and waved off the questions for later. John then proceeded to fill them in on his surveillance of the GAO group and the killing at the camp.

John conveniently left out how he met Beth. She later thanked him and said that he might become a gentleman after all. He got her off to the side and told her about Roger being part of this gang of dope smugglers.

*

Chapter 10

One Step Ahead

The Idaho/Montana Woods

May 17, 2020

They marched through the woods without stopping to rest with Gus constantly ordering, "Keep moving, they are on our tail."

"My best guess puts us about a half-hour ahead of them." John estimated as they started across an open area of about two hundred yards.

Gus told them to move as fast as they could while crossing. He also had them split into three groups with the fastest two of the three taking a looping course that would meet back up about a quarter mile into the next wooded area.

"That trick may not slow them down much, but this ground is harder, and we won't leave as much of a trail," Gus explained.

Beth, Bill, and John were taking the shortest line across the open area. Beth and John began filling each other in on their groups. She was surprised that Scott was John's son even though there was an obvious resemblance after taking a more thorough look.

"That Steve thinks he's a lady killer, doesn't he?" she asked.

"Well not like our friends chasing us, but he does have a way with the ladies back in LA," John replied.

Beth had a puzzled look on her face. "LA, I thought that all y'all were from Mobile," she stated.

"Yes, we are from Mobile, and LA, Lower Alabama, to you Northern types."

She fussed and reminded him that she was from Tennessee.

As they were just about to enter the woods, John took a last look over his shoulder and caught a glint of light from the far side. He barely got the word "duck" out of his mouth when Bill was grazed on the left arm and blood flew. They ran the last few feet into the woods and ducked behind a large log. Several rounds hit the log, and then the firing stopped. While Beth tended to Bill's wound, John peeked around the end of the log and saw the GAO group.

Karl had the rifle leveled and aimed at them, John dropped and a round hit beside where his head had been. John leveled the KEL-TEC, took careful aim and squeezed off a shot. The shot was high and about a foot wide of the tall blonde guy. It struck a tree and showered him in bark. All of the GAO thugs scattered and ducked. John thought that would slow those bastards down.

John told Beth and Bill that they all had to start thinking smarter or they'd all be dead. They had been very lucky so far, but luck always changes. They had to be more careful to make sure that they were not caught in the open again.

They scrambled to catch up to the others and found them in only a few minutes. Bill was okay; only a flesh wound as they say in the movies.

"That was an honest miss; however, I don't see how Maria could have missed killing him back at the camp," John told the others.

They continued to march south for about an hour. Gus and John trotted side by side trying to come up with a plan to get them out of this mess. The sun was going down soon, and it would be getting dark quickly because the dense forest blocked out much of the sun. They debated waiting until midnight and raiding their camp versus an ambush when Scott came up with a brilliant idea.

"Dad, you told us that these guys are traveling with a point guy and a tail end Charlie protecting their rear end didn't you?" Scott asked.

As John said yes, it struck him, "Oh hell, yes, we could pick one or two off at a time without confronting the others."

Scott said, "Yes, we can split into three groups, one shoots the point man, takes his weapons and makes a hell of a racket to draw the main body forward and away from the prisoners. When our tail end Charlie team hears three shots, they slip up on the rear guard, slit his throat and take his guns."

"I'll make a crude bomb out of the powder can and some rocks. We'll lob it in front of their main group when we hear the ruckus up front," Gus added.

John said, "If it weren't for their prisoners I would just lob it right in the middle of those assholes. Let's give it 30 seconds, and then throw the bomb. I want to make sure that the bad guys have rushed to help the point man and gotten as far away as possible from the girls."

Everyone except Beth liked the plan, but even she knew they had to kill or be killed at this point. Her main concern was for the safety of Janet and Alice, who as far as they knew, were still with the others.

Beth grabbed John's hand and pleaded with him to save her best friends. John promised her that they would do their best.

Roger, who had been quiet until now, spoke up, "Even though these guys have killed and injured you and your friends, you can't take the law into your hands."

"So says their accomplice in this nightmare," Steve replied.

John then added, "You are damn lucky that we don't string you upside down by your balls and start a fire under you, you bastard."

Gus stuck the 9mm under Roger's chin, "As Dirty Harry said, make my day, asshole."

Gus then clubbed Roger on the side of the head with the 9mm, not hard, but enough to smart like hell.

Roger then said, "Stop walking for a minute and take my left shoe off and look inside under the inner sole. Oh, there is a .38 strapped to my leg."

Gus shoved him down and pulled Roger's left pant leg up and took the pistol, then asked, "If you had this gun, why didn't you use it to kill us or escape?"

"Look in the shoe," he exclaimed.

Gus took Roger's shoe and dug into it, then brought out what appeared to be a driver's license.

"What the hell is this? It looks like an ID for the FBI with Roger's face and a different name," growled Gus. Roger was clearly getting impatient with Gus.

"You idiot, do you think that I would go undercover using my name? I could have killed all of you if I was one of them."

John examined the ID and told Steve to cut the rope tying Roger's hands.

"He had plenty of opportunities to escape or kill all of us; I think he's telling the truth. Cut him loose," John ordered.

All agreed except Gus. He finally cut Roger's bindings. John took Roger's gun from Gus and said that he would keep it until he trusted Roger a bit more than he did now.

"Roger, you've got some explaining to do. Give us the 15-second drill now."

Roger told them that he had spent over a year working into the GAO's organization as a bush pilot delivering campers and drugs. He had been given a contact in the organization that had been working for the FBI for years. He only communicated through notes, so Roger said that he did not know who it was. He must have been at the GAO office this morning because he passed him a note. It said that the money was being used to buy a rather impressive arsenal and that there was some connection to a right-wing skinhead group in Idaho. He thought that the skinheads handled the Cartel's dirty work and was charged with eliminating competitors who would fall in line with the GAO.

Roger also told them that the GAO was just the US branch.

They were known as the Chupacabras south of the border. The Cabras were ruthless and seemed to love removing tongues and heads just to make a point. They would not only kill you; they would kill your whole family and your dog.

Quite a bit to digest in 15 seconds, John thought. John thanked Roger and told the group, "We've got an ambush to execute."

Roger angrily replied, "That's what I'm trying to stop. As I said earlier, what you are about to do is against the law, it would be cold-blooded murder. We can outrun them and go get help."

Gus jumped between them and punched Roger in the stomach, hard enough to knock the breath out of him.

John pulled Gus off Roger and said, "Look, you ignorant bastard, these guys have killed one of us, and they won't stop until we are all dead. We are going through with the plan, with you or without you. You can leave now, but if you warn them, I will kill you myself, and I will use Cabras methods."

Roger gave in and said that he would not stop them, but he would not take part in killing any of the GAO. He also wanted to try to get the two girls away from the bad guys when they attacked them. He said that he thought they had a good plan and when the bomb exploded, he and another volunteer could get the girls and run with them in the confusion. Bill and Beth volunteered to help Roger free the girls.

John tried to talk some sense into Beth and Bill, but they wanted to help their friends.

"Okay," he told them, "but, I will go with Beth and Roger to free the girls. I don't want Roger out of my sight. Scott, you and Jim take the rear guard. Are you able to kill him? You know that you will have to slip up on him and slit his throat, or the rest will come running if they hear any commotion."

Both Scott and Jim swore that they could, and would do it, but John was worried. They were big fearless guys, but killing does not come easy.

"Steve, you and Gus are with Bill. You'll hit the point man, Gus will shoot him, and Steve and Bill will grab his weapons. Then you must quickly put up a short stand to attract the others. You will continue to fire on them long enough to give us a chance to get the girls," John added.

They all agreed. John thought *'Avengers R Us', no task too big or small for the boys from Mobile.* John accepted the inescapable facts that it was them, or us, and that made ordering his son to kill a man a little easier.

It was now about 7:00 p.m. and the sun was going down behind the trees. It would be dark in about an hour.

Gus and Scott chose the ambush site. It was not the perfect place as you would see in the old time western movies with the Indians up high in rocks shooting arrows down on the Calvary, but it would have to do.

The ambush site was in the dry creek bed they had been following. This helped make it less obvious that the hunters were walking into an ambush. The creek bed was about three feet below the adjacent ground level and was about twenty feet wide at the starting point where the rear guard would be taken out. The creek bed eased a bit more downhill. It gently fell toward a crèche of boulders cut through them before making a narrow right turn. This left only a hundred feet from the chosen spot to take out the rear guard. At this point, it was only about five feet wide, stayed narrow for another fifty feet. There were dense trees and undergrowth at the ambush side.

John wanted to hit them just as the main group started into the narrow section, but before the captives entered.

The trail now took a steep grade over rocks and small boulders. This terrain would significantly slow the main body. This was the spot where the larger group would be attacked. This bottleneck would hobble any attempt to go forward quickly to help the point man.

The point man would be about twenty yards ahead of the group. This would place him out of the narrow channel, and out into a much wider section with a smooth surface. The point would die here.

At about seven thirty, it began to rain. John smiled; this was in their favor since the rain would muffle their steps.

Even though it was still quite warm, the rain sent a chill down his spine. His clothes were quickly soaked and clinging to his body. He was happy that Beth had a jacket with a hoodie.

The rain reminded him of the summer showers along Mobile's coast. He and Gus had to take cover on many occasions while fishing on the Spanish River. "C'mon, John, focus on the now, dumbass."

The others were in place waiting on their pursuers to arrive at the ambush point. They must have been further behind them than John had thought. They should have been here by now.

At that instant, they heard the thugs talking as they slowly came thru the creek bed. John was about one hundred feet from them and could not quite hear what they were saying, but they were only a few feet from Scott and Jim.

They stopped about halfway between Scott and John and appeared to be ready to camp for the night. John could now hear them talking, but could not tell who was saying what.

They continued discussing the women as if they weren't there. On several occasions, John heard the women struggle and moan from being grabbed and pinched.

John hoped that none of their people overreacted. They mustn't attack before the GAO people were in the right spot.

If the others had half as many butterflies in their stomach as he did, they could be up the creek without the proverbial paddle.

Knowing that you were about to slit a guy's throat was not like waiting in the locker room for the big game to start.

Taking a slow, even breath, John relaxed a bit and knew that Gus would make the kill when he had to.

Beth leaned against John, buried her head into his chest and quietly sobbed as she heard the abuse that her friends were taking.

She whispered that she was thankful that Janet's husband, Bill, was too far away to hear the discussion. "Damn," John had forgotten the connection. Bill must be going through hell knowing that his wife was in the hands of these bastards.

Beth pressed her body tightly against John to help them both stay warm. He placed his arms around Beth, hugged her, whispering to her that he would get them free and make the bastards pay for what they had done to the girls.

He kissed her on the head and continued to console her, the best that he could. She continued softly crying as the rain kept pouring down. She was dry from her waist up thanks to the jacket taken from the camp.

• • •

"We can't camp for the night at this location," Red exclaimed.

Karl replied, "Red, what is your hurry? The men need a little rest and some loving."

"Karl, you *are* the boss, but we need to catch these tourists and kill them today before they escape. Besides, haven't any of you noticed that this is a dry riverbed and it is raining?

Look, you can already see small streams of water under our feet. In an hour, this could be a river washing us into those rocks ahead. I am not worried about the tourists; however, I do not want to drown tonight in my sleeping bag. Let's move on downstream to the high ground on the other side of the ravine ahead," Red implored.

The voice that John had figured out was Karl's, told them to get up and move out. He could see them as they passed by, only fifteen feet away.

*

Chapter 11

Ann

Mobile, Alabama

May 17, 2020

Ann kissed Dan on the forehead as she got out of bed and went to the bathroom. She got into the shower and watched him for a moment.

She thought about him, wondering if this romance would go anywhere special. Dan was a midlevel manager in the city government. He had family money and did not have to work, but wanted to get into politics, and his goal was to become the mayor of Mobile.

Dan was adequate in bed; however, was he marriage material? She was looking for Mr. Right but wanted to make sure that she didn't end up with Mr. Right Now.

Ann looked at herself in the mirror and was pleased with the reflection. It was the best body that Mobile's plastic surgeons and personal trainers could deliver. She spent a lot of her alimony on making herself beautiful, and the rest was invested very wisely.

She dressed and made sure that she had everything before checking on Dan as she left. He was sleeping peacefully, but snoring very loudly. He looked like a little boy, curled up in the fetal position, hugging his pillow.

She checked her bag to make sure she had everything. She saw her wallet, keys, and the .380 KEL-TEC. Ann was thankful to John for the many hours on the firing range. She was secure in her life and did not worry a lot about bad guys.

Ann locked the door as she left, got into her Jag, started it and left quickly. She noticed a black Explorer following about 100 feet as she pulled out on the highway.

The SUV turned off at the next exit, and Ann wondered if she was becoming paranoid. She drove down Highway 65 to Azalea Blvd. and stopped at her favorite café for coffee and a blueberry muffin. As she got out of her car, she looked over her shoulder and saw another black Explorer parking at the end of the block.

She remembered seeing a black SUV outside of Dan's house, and recalled one of John's sayings, "Being paranoid, doesn't mean they're not out to get you."

She went into the shop and placed her order. While waiting, she turned on her Kindle Fire to check out her Facebook account.

Peering over the top of the Kindle, she saw two men get out of the Explorer and sit on a bench across the street. They were trying to appear to be reading newspapers, but she could tell that they were looking over the papers and not at them.

*

Chapter 12

The Ambush

Deep Woods Somewhere in Idaho

May 17, 2020

Bill and Steve were in place and remained very still as the point man came up to their position. Gus could hear the point man's feet disturbing the gravel as he walked. As he came into view, the man appeared to be talking to himself.

Gus thought for a brief moment that the guy might be praying, or maybe just singing to himself.

Gus kept the 9mm aimed at the bastard's heart, as he got closer. Somehow it made Gus feel better about what was about to happen if he thought of the guy as a very evil person. He made sure that Bill and Steve were not in the line of fire.

The guy was a Latino in his late 30's. He had jet-black hair and such an evil-appearing pockmarked face that could have been in the movies. He was the classic bad guy. Gus wondered if he was married, did he have any kids and where did he live?

The gun bucked in Gus' hand. The flash was bright, the noise deafening. He had pulled the trigger without giving it a second thought doing what he knew must be done. Damn, he thought that might be his epitaph.

The man fell but was not yet dead. He grasped his chest and raised an AK-47 just as Steve landed on him. A spasm caused the trigger to fire off a few rounds as Steve slit his throat. Bill grabbed the AK-47 and Steve got the dead man's ammo belt with his 9 mm and all of the magazines for both weapons.

• • •

The going was rough and the footing rougher for the GAO group as they entered the streambed that had been chosen for the ambush. While it was still twilight, the trees blocked most of the remaining light. It was damn near pitch black.

The men continued to argue over the women when Maria scolded them, "You guys act like you have never seen a woman before. Karl, I thought that I had joined a class act, but all I have seen today are rapists and punks. Surely, you are not going to continue to be a party to this continued debauchery. Who is in charge here?"

Karl glared at her and shouted, "Bitch, shut the fuck up." He was mad, but not at Maria, because, he knew she was right.

The leader of the North American GAO operation could not act as a common punk. He caught Maria off to the side and apologized to her and told her that she was correct, however, he would not stop the boys from having fun.

Looking into her eyes, he knew that he wanted this feisty bitch. He would try to keep her happy, at least long enough to find out if she was as feisty in bed as she was about her ideas.

"Everyone must be on alert; this looks like a good place for an ambush," Manny whispered.

Jesus replied, "These gringos are running for all they are worth. They do not have the guts to stand and fight." The words were still coming out of Jesus' mouth when the first shots rang out.

"Let's go, Move." Karl ordered.

They all rushed toward the noise, leaving the women behind.

• • •

The first of the bad guys rounded the corner and dove behind the rocks, upon hearing the gunfire.

Gus shot at them with the 9mm as they scattered and hit the dirt. Gus kept them pinned down but didn't think he had hit any of them.

Jim and Scott had plenty of time to size up their prey since the group had practically stopped right in front of them. They had discussed for several minutes about who had the nerve to kill the guy. Both agreed that shooting him was much less personal than using a knife. Jim finally convinced Scott to flip a coin. Jim won or lost depending on how you looked at it. The job had fallen to Jim.

Their target was an American. He stood about 6'1" tall and built like a prizefighter. He was armed with an AK-47 and a 9mm automatic strapped to his right thigh. He lit up a cigarette as soon as the others traveled around the bend of the small canyon. Not a professional, Scott thought.

Jim and Scott heard the gunfire and jumped the rear guard. Jim grabbed his head, covering his mouth and reached to drag a knife across his neck, to sever the jugular.

The damn guy was quick, he grabbed the blade with his bare hand, and even though that blade sliced to the bone, he kept it from his neck. He yelled, for Rodrigo to help him, but the rain made it impossible for his friend to hear.

Thankfully, the AK was dangling from its strap, and the asshole could not get his hand to the trigger. Jim wrestled with him for a few seconds but was unable to finish the job.

Scott came from around the backside, unsheathed his knife, plunged it into the rear guard's kidney and ripped upwards. His body twitched in spasmodic waves as he died.

They began to strip the body of all weapons, and anything that might be useful. Jim grabbed the guy's coat while Scott took his hat and ammo belt. Scott took the AK, and Jim liberated the 9mm and its magazines.

The entire portion of their piece of the operation had only taken a minute. They had expected to hear the bomb go off seconds ago. It did not.

They rain had so dampened sound that their mission had remained silent to the rest of the trackers. No one ahead had heard even a peep; their part of the mission was a success. Scott was worried about Gus and his Dad, had they been injured? Did Gus and Steve's part of the plan go as well as theirs had? He thought, *"No purpose in worrying about the others now."* They ran quickly to help free the hostages.

Beth, Roger, and John heard the shots. Beth looked at John's watch as he started the countdown. Roger got the cigarette lighter ready, and John held the can of gunpowder with the homemade fuse. John had kept it under his coat in a plastic bag to keep the fuse dry and hoped that he had been successful.

Beth punched John's arm and said, "Light it."

Roger flicked the wheel of the lighter and nothing happened. Roger kept trying to get fire from the lighter to no avail. John reached deep into his pocket and brought out one of his handy dandy contraptions that should not have been on this trip and prayed. The battery powered electric lighter came to life, and the fuse sputtered and caught.

Beth pointed, "Throw it over there. The girls are out of the way."

John heaved the bomb as hard as he could and was right on target. The can rattled and then exploded.

John strained to see the bad guys through the darkness, and he could tell that they had done more damage than had been anticipated.

Beth hoped her friends were okay. John heard several pain-filled moans and groans as they ran to help free the captives.

• • •

Alice and Janet heard the gunfire and dropped to the ground. The two guards that had been following behind them rushed to the front of the column.

"Keep low to the ground and follow me; this is our chance to escape," Janet whispered.

Janet helped Alice towards the right creek bank, and they were just about there when there were a loud explosion and a big fireball on up the creek bed in the direction that the guards had gone.

They then heard the sounds of mass confusion and cursing. They hoped that their captors had all been killed by this mystery explosion.

"Come to me, and we will get you away from them," Beth called.

"Oh my god, it's you, Beth. Where have you been?" the girls cried out.

"Later," Beth told them. "Let's go now." she urged.

Roger grabbed Alice and scared her until Beth said it was okay. John took Janet by the arm and led her away from the creek bed. She was soaked to the skin. John helped steady her as they scrambled away from the creek.

Beth was leading the way towards Gus' team she saw Jim and Scott running toward them. They heard yelling, and shots were coming from behind.

Several rounds hit the rocks to their rear, and Roger fell. Jim and Scott returned the fire while Beth tended to Roger. John emptied a ten round magazine from the Ruger .22 pistol at the thugs. I hope that that would pin the bastards down, John prayed. The situation was not looking good at all. Roger had been hit in the back, his spine was severed, and the bullet had exposed his large intestine.

"John, come here," pled Roger in horrible pain.

John bent over him, and Roger groaned out, "Take this to the FBI." He held out a small pouch.

"I know I'm dead, take this note to my wife, tell her I loved her and was thinking of her when I died."

With that, Roger screamed one last time, then slumped over and was gone.

"Come on, we have to get back to the others before they find out the women have escaped," John said.

The others wanted to bury Roger, but John made them leave him where he lay.

"We will send someone back to get him after this ordeal is over," John ordered.

"Move out."

• • •

Just ahead of them, something flew through the air, sputtered, sparked and hit the ground.

"Grenade! Hit the ground," several GAO thugs yelled all at once.

They had run right up on the bomb as it hit the ground. It blew up before they could react. Lucky for them it was just a can full of gunpowder instead of a pipe. The tin was shredded and flew out like shrapnel, but was in small pieces except for the top. The top embedded in Pepe's head and killed him outright. The rest all received wounds from head to toe. They had been hit by bits of tin or gravel that the bomb blew from the streambed. Several had wounds similar to small caliber bullets, and the rest had buckshot type wounds. No others would die, but it hurt like hell.

Karl and Manny faded back as the others rushed to help their point man. Both had been hit by rocks, but only had bruises and a few small nicks. Karl was in no rush to die; that's why he paid these men so well, to do his fighting for him.

Maria had been hit by several small pieces of tin but was okay. One piece had hit her right breast just about an inch above her nipple. It had bled just enough to soak through her blouse. She knew that she would catch hell from the guys at daylight.

As they regrouped, several shots came from their front and right side, bullets ricocheted, and one hit Jesus in the right forearm. The bullet was just about spent after glancing off the rock wall but still punctured his arm. They scrambled and wildly shot in all directions. Karl ordered them to stop and not shoot until they had a target. Karl had one guy stay to tend to Jesus, and the rest surged forward to hunt down their attackers. They found the point man lying on the ground with water backing up in the creek bed; his body had become a dam of sorts.

"Damn, Jorge finally found something that he is good at. Don't worry Jorge; we will find your killers and torture them before we kill the bastards."

There was no one to be seen, and the GAO crew was taking as much cover as they could, they did not have a clue what had happened and were only guessing the tourists did it.

"Manny, take Maria with you and go back and get the women; the rest of us will stay here until you get back. We will find a place to camp tonight, and then tomorrow we will chase these assholes down like the dogs they are."

Manny and Maria kept very low as they went to where the women were expected to be and heard someone moving in the bushes. Manny began shooting at the sound, and Maria shot into the air. Suddenly they saw flashes and bullets were hitting all around them. They fell to the ground. Maria landed on the rear guard's body.

• • •

They ran as quietly as possible towards the rest of their friends, while Bill and Steve were helping Alice and Janet. Beth led the way. After what seemed to be an eternity, they broke into a clearing and almost ran over the rest of their group. It was pitch black by this time, but Gus checked everyone over and asked about Roger.

"He gave his life saving us," cried Janet.

Bill was holding Alice and not paying much attention to his wife. Bill took his jacket off and wrapped it around her. Steve was helping Janet, and Janet was glaring at Bill.

Gus looked at John and whispered, "I don't know if I want to know why Bill isn't holding his wife."

John replied that Steve did not appear to mind that he was comforting another man's wife right in front of him.

They quickly filled each other in on the results of the ambush, which by all accounts had been very successful.

Gus started with his brief account of their accomplishments. "One enemy dead and we grabbed one M-16, a 9mm and 100 rounds for the AK-47 and 3 – 16 round magazines for the 9mm."

Scott followed with one enemy dead, one AK and a 9mm captured. He thought they had about 120 rounds for the AK and three plus mags for the 9mm.

John followed up by pointing at the ladies who they had freed and told them that he thought they might have killed one or two with the bomb, but could not be for sure.

They then reissued the weapons.

"Gus, you take an AK, you are the only one here that won't shoot all the rounds up in one burst. Scott, you take the other AK, and move the selector off fully automatic."

"I'll take the .38 if it is ok with you, I used to shoot my Dad's old .38 when I was a kid," requested Bill.

Gus said, "Yeah, that's okay with me. Steve, Jim and I will take the three 9mm handguns. Hey, Jim, you take your Hawken, we just about forgot about it. You have one shot...er...rock. That'll at least scare the hell out of somebody."

"Janet, how many were in their group before the ambush?" Steve asked.

"There were nine men and a woman," she replied.

"Well we have cut them down by two known kills, and several must have been wounded by our little bomb," Gus added.

"I think the bomb did a lot more damage to those bastards than we had hoped. I'm sure that most of them were hit by shrapnel and gravel. It may have taken some of the fight out of those assholes," John said.

"I'll lead the way, and I will do a hell of a lot better job than their point man did," Gus exclaimed.

Gus was already pushing them to move on and get away from the GAO while they had the chance. They gathered their possessions and headed south; still with the idea of finding the road that, they had seen on their inbound flight.

It was very difficult to make any time in the dark as they kept tripping over vines and logs. The brush was very dense, and everyone was scratched to hell and back by sticker bushes. After about an hour, John halted the group and asked Jim and Scott to backtrack a few hundred yards and see if anyone was following. By now, it was 10:15 p.m. and inky black with no moon or stars.

"Gus, while the lads are checking our backside, why don't you find us a place to spend the night."

"Okay, John," Gus grunted and trudged off into the night.

Beth caught John and said, "You sure do boss people around a lot, don't you John?"

John looked at Beth and said," I'm sorry, I had not realized that I was bossy."

"John, I was only joking with you, it's obvious the others look up to you, and you are a good leader. You have saved my ass and helped save all of the others from harm several times today," replied Beth.

"Don't give me too much credit and remember only this afternoon you were calling me a pervert for looking at a beautiful woman."

Beth moved closer and gave him a kiss on his cheek.

She said, "Thanks for saving my life this morning and you can watch my ass anytime you want to."

John threw his arms around her and pressed her against his chest. John kissed her quickly, and she rubbed her cheek against his.

A half hour later, Steve said, "Someone's coming toward us; I think it's Jim and Scott."

Steve had been on lookout since the boys left on their scouting trip.

"Hello, don't shoot, it's us."

They stood in the middle of the group and filled them in on their scouting trip.

Scott said, "Dad, you were right, the bomb killed one and wounded all of the others. None has life-threatening wounds, but several are in great pain, and the others were peppered with tin and gravel. Only Karl and Manny appear to have escaped with no more than scratches. Even the girl was hit in the chest by shrapnel from the can. Her right boob got hit by a piece of tin, and they were making fun of her."

John asked, "How could you know all of this, son?"

"Dad, we snuck right up on their camp. They are only about a mile or so behind us and have a roaring fire in a cave on the bank of the creek.

I suggest we plan another attack tonight and do away with the whole bunch. They are sitting in the open at the front of the cave. You can see all of them huddled around the fire, several had already bedded down for the night and the rest are drinking heavily."

John replied, "Son, wait until Gus gets back and then we'll discuss this further.

Remember our main goal is to escape from them, not necessarily to kill all of them. Besides this cozy camp, that you're telling us about sounds somewhat suspicious to me. Sounds like a trap or else they are just plain stupid."

81

Steve again warned them that someone was approaching. Everyone ducked behind trees and logs, for they were not going to be ambushed as easily as the thugs had been.

This time the person stayed in the shadows for several minutes before Steve hollered, "Gus, we see you, get your sorry ass in here now."

"Damn, I'm getting too old and slow to sneak up on a bunch of tenderfoots like you."

Gus approached the group with a smile and quietly whistled a tune.

"I didn't find a five-star hotel, but I found a place about a half a mile on down the creek where we can get out of the rain, but sorry, no fire tonight. We'll be cold camping."

*

Chapter 13

The First Night

Deep Woods Somewhere in Idaho

May 17, 2020

They walked alongside the creek bed to stay out of the now rushing water as much as possible but had to cross the creek or walk in the middle of it several times.

The rain continued to pour down, soaking most of them to the bone. At least all the women had the jackets from their camp to keep their upper bodies dry.

While Alice was not in shock, she was traumatized by the abuse that she had suffered earlier in the day. Bill, Janet's husband, was helping Alice.

Steve continued to help Janet as they made their way towards the campsite and Janet appeared to be handling her trauma well, almost as if nothing had happened. She stayed very close to Steve.

Beth and John were walking and talking.

"What the f...err heck is going on," John whispered to Beth.

"I don't know, but I had noticed Bill and Alice sneaking away from camp several times over the last week. They were going out into the woods and making love right under Janet's nose. Janet does not need an unfaithful husband right now," Beth added.

John said, "But hell, Beth, look at Janet and Steve, she hugs up to him and looks deeply into his eyes every time she gets a chance."

"She may be reacting to the rape, or Bill being all over Alice. Hell, I just do not know. I thought I knew those two, but whatever is going on, they kept it from me," she told him. Then she said, "Hon, why don't you just ask Steve what he knows?"

"Beth, you just called me Hon. Please don't do that unless this can go somewhere. I am 10 years older than you are and live 400 miles from your home. Don't tease me because..."

Beth interrupted, pulling him close to her and said, "Hon, I don't know you well, but I like what I've seen so far."

Smiling, she walked ahead to join Janet and Steve for the rest of the walk to their camping spot.

The group rounded a bend and Gus pointed to an outcropping of rock that jutted out over the creek from a wall of rock on its right. John pulled a tiny single cell flashlight out of one of his many pockets and shone it all around the area that Gus had pointed out, looking for critters and snakes.

Steve saw the light and exclaimed, "I knew that you just could not abide by the rules of this camping trip, but this time your gadgets are welcome. Ya' got any more?"

John replied to Steve," I always have a few tricks up my sleeve, now let's make camp."

There was a hollowed-out place in the rock wall, just below the outcropping, that was large enough to provide shelter from the rain. The floor was sand that had washed in from the creek during high water. They began walking up to their home for the night. It was about five feet up above the bottom of the creek bed and was like walking up a steep sandy beach. The ground consisted of dry sand and would make as nice a place to sleep as they could have found. John saw no snakes or other creatures, and they sat down in the sand and started going through what gear they had.

After setting their gear down, Beth poked John in the shoulder, "I am so hungry, I could eat the southern end of a northbound skunk."

They had been so busy surviving that none of them had thought about food. None of the group had eaten since breakfast, but at least Beth's bunch did have sandwiches for lunch.

"John, didn't you get some of our food when we grabbed the gear back at our camp?"

"Damn, you're right Beth, I forgot all about it."

He had been packing the small duffel bag since they left Beth's camp. He also had the candy and candy bars from the plane. He dumped the bag's contents on the ground and searched through the pile on the ground.

"Damn it, John; I can't see a darn thing."

"Hold on Beth," with that he pulled the tiny single cell flashlight out and illuminated the contents of the bag. "You can have the flashlight."

"Thanks, Hon," Beth replied as she squeezed his hand.

They then sorted through the food to see what to eat tonight and what to save for later.

Gus took charge of the food and told them up front that he had no idea how long they would be in the woods.

"With these people on our tail, we can't stop to fish or hunt so what we have here is all there is for two to three days," Gus warned.

Each person received a can of beans and franks and a piece of bread for their supper. The beans reminded Gus of all the jokes about farting from the movie Blazing Saddles, but the humor was lost on all but Jim. Gus did give a mint to each for desert after they finished their fine, gourmet meal. The creek supplied the water. They all agreed to save the remaining food and candy for tomorrow.

"Jim, grab that rope you've been packing and those empty cans. Let's set up some early warning systems," Gus said with a wicked smile.

"John, I'll take the first watch, and then you finish up the night. The rest of these guys need their beauty sleep."

"Okay with me, let's git 'er dun," John replied as he reminded Jim to fill Gus in on what they had seen on their scouting trip on the GAO crew.

He then caught Steve and asked him, what the heck, was going on between Janet and him.

"Now John, don't make too much of it, I am not trying to take advantage of a poor girl in a weak moment. She and Bill were already breaking up. She and Alice are still good friends even though Bill's been seeing Alice for about three months."

"Why the hell didn't they just get a divorce like normal people, and then screw their brains out?" John asked.

"Remember, they all work at the same school; they were trying to work out a job change for Bill so that none of them would get fired if it leaked before they were ready."

"Well anyway, are you and Janet a couple?"

"Damn John, I've only known her for a few hours, but I like her and want to protect her from any more harm," Steve responded.

Steve thought for a minute and said, "John, what about you and Beth, we can all see you two holding on to each other."

"Steve, your imagination is just running wild because you are feeling guilty yourself," John replied.

"Bullshit," was his answer.

While Gus and Jim were out setting traps, they gave each of the women a sleeping bag that they had brought from Beth's camp.

Everyone spread out under the outcropping and prepared for a well-deserved rest. Janet had placed her sleeping bag, under shelter, but as far from everyone as she could. The rest, including Beth, kept close together as close to the rock wall as possible.

Everyone stripped down to their underwear and hung their clothes on bushes and rocks to try to dry them overnight. The men had fresh dry underwear and socks from their duffel bags, salvaged from the plane, but Beth and John did not think to grab clothing from their camp for the women. They gave each of the women a T-shirt to sleep in, while their undies dried. With the rain continuing to pour down, there probably would not be much drying accomplished tonight, but it was great to have some dry clothes next to their wrinkled skin.

John looked over the camp and saw Gus on guard and the others sleeping. Like a shepherd watching his flock, John knew he could not sleep until they were safe. John walked over Beth and sat down next to her. He told her that he was too keyed up to sleep, maybe later.

86

She told him that she couldn't sleep either. Beth and John talked about their families and friends back home. He enjoyed her company and felt that he had met someone special.

"John, why did you and your wife get divorced, did you run around on her?"

"No, it wasn't anything like that. I think that we just grew apart over the years. We were high school sweethearts who finally got married and grew up, and then apart."

"Well how did you change and why did you want the divorce?" Beth asked.

"Again, it was not like that at all. I was still in love with her and was happy when she sprung the news on me.

I didn't beat her or run around on her; we had a nice house and enough money. I run a successful chain of body shops in the Mobile area, and we were set for life," John answered.

"Well, why did she leave you then?" she pried.

"Beth, you are getting kind of personal here, aren't you?"

She smiled, "Yes I am, now answer please, I want to know all about you."

John said, "I guess that your ex cheated on you and might have been abusive."

She gave him a peck on the cheek and said, "It was rough, and I could never go through that shit again."

John lay down on the sleeping bag with her and then he told her about how Ann had walked in one day and said that she needed her space. She packed her bags and told him good-bye. The court delivered the divorce papers to the shop a week later. Crushed, he felt for a long time that somehow it was his fault.

He told her that Scott had his own theory. It was because his mom came from the old money in Mobile and that their life was just too plain for her.

John said, "Hell, the kid could be right. She's always in the paper on the arm of one rich guy or the other."

They lay there with him spooned against her back. She squeezed his leg and fell asleep. She had a slight snore, after falling into a sound sleep.

Gus woke John up at 4:00 a.m. from a light sleep that was chock full of nightmares and boogiemen. The last thing he remembered saying to Beth was about his ex. Not exactly what you want to be discussing with a sweet young thing that you want to get in good with at the time.

He remembered the dream was about making love to Beth; it seemed so real. He took a minute to watch Beth sleep and knew that he was falling for her. Maybe he was falling in lust...or maybe something more. Time would tell if there was time.

They moved away from the group so that they could talk for a minute before Gus woke the others up. The rain had stopped, and the air was already beginning to warm.

The clouds had passed, and the stars were bright. It was a beautiful night with a half-moon shining down on the forest. A very heavy fog lay close to the ground and looked like a scene from a Sherlock Holmes movie in England with wisps of fog dancing around in the gentle breeze.

Gus said, "Jim filled me in on what they learned from watching our pursuers. Based on that, I just think we just need to bug out of here early and leave these animals behind. The law can deal with them."

John said, "I agree, while part of me wants to sneak back there and finish them off; we chance getting more people hurt or killed. We should be on the move by 4:30 a.m. We should only be about 10 – 15 miles from it, and if the women can move a little more quickly, we can get there tomorrow or the next day in the worst case."

Gus left to take care of business, and John felt happy for the first time in years. It was very quiet with only the sound of the water rushing in the creek and an occasional owl hooting in the night. This was the most peaceful time that he could remember having in quite a while. It gave him a moment to reflect on this beautiful woman.

John heard a noise behind him and saw Beth walking towards him. "Hon, are you okay? Would you like some company?" She smiled.

"I'm okay. Are you amped for the long march? We leave in 30 minutes," John responded.

"I'll be fine. Remember I'm a hiker from way back, I will walk you into the dirt," she laughed.

"You are probably right; I'm getting too old for this shit."

She popped him on the shoulder as she sat down, "Don't say that, I like you just the way you are."

She then kissed John before he could say a word.

John tried for another, and she waved her finger at him and said, "Don't be a pig."

John replied, "Beth when this is over I'd like to see you again."

She said, "Didn't you see enough of me yesterday?"

John laughed and replied, "Maybe I'd like to see more."

She gently slapped him and told him to be a good boy.

John looked at his watch, "We have to get the others up in fifteen minutes. Gus wants us to be on the trail by oh dark thirty."

She put her arm around him and lay her head on his shoulder for the next few minutes. Neither of them said a word and just enjoyed each other's company.

• • •

Beth and John went around shaking each one until they opened their eyes. Jim jumped up and exclaimed, "Good morning LA." Gus kicked him in the ass and told him that there were ladies present. All were laughing at Jim and Gus. They all quickly put their rather damp clothes on and packed up what little gear they had in their possession and made ready to leave. Just as they started down the creek bed, they heard tin cans banging and someone cursing. Apparently, the bad guys had the same idea about getting an early start.

"Let's haul ass folks. That was one of my trip wires, and it is only a hundred yards out. Move it. We need to get to civilization." Gus exclaimed.

John knew that today they had to keep on the move and rest less than their pursuers or be caught. They had just been lucky back there when Gus' trap had warned them.

Just then, they heard a scream and a burst of gunfire.

Gus laughed, "I'll bet they just found my punji sticks. That will slow one of those bastards down for a while. They will be looking for traps everywhere now." I hope that it will give us what we need, time.

• • •

Maria woke up with Manny softly stroking her hair with one hand while the other was resting under her blouse. She shoved his hand away from her hair and slapped the other one.

"Manny, you are just making me hate you more and more, yet you say you love me."

"I do love you, and I also want you in the worst way," replied Manny.

She replied, "Well, I will never want to be with you if you keep trying to rape me like those other women."

All of the others were awake and had already gotten their gear ready to travel.

"Hey, Maria, ju ready to go? We got to catch those Janquis before they get moving this morning," said Jesus.

Maria said, "I'm not going anywhere until I take a trip behind those rocks over there and Jesus make damn sure that Manny doesn't try to peek."

They bickered for a minute, and Karl said, "The Lady has to go."

Maria went behind the rocks to do her business in private but had to watch over her shoulder the entire time to make sure that Manny or one of the other perverts were not watching her using the outdoor facilities.

She also knew that she had to get away from this bunch one of these days, but she also wanted to slow them down so that the tourists could escape.

She took her time until she knew that Karl would be upset. She finished, returned to camp and picked up her part of the gear, then followed Red along the creek bed.

Red said, "Be very quiet, I think that they camped rather close to us and with a bit of well-deserved luck, we may be able to surprise them this morning."

The sun was just peaking over the horizon, and they had traveled only about a mile when one of them tripped one of Gus's warning devices. The tin cans clattered and scared the crap out of the guy and those around him.

Pepe, one of Karl's guards, then laughed and started forward again when he screamed in pain and fired off several rounds. They all ran over to him and found that he had stepped off into a shallow pit and had impaled his leg on a sharpened stick. Ten short sticks sharpened to a point were stuck into the bottom of the pit. Pepe was screaming in agony and bleeding profusely from the wound. The stick had entered above the ankle and come out at mid-calf, tearing a large hole in his leg.

"Hold Pepe still while I get a tourniquet on his leg above the wound."

Red and two others grabbed him and held him down while Jesus used his belt to make a tourniquet above the knee.

"Maria, do we have anything for pain?"

"We've got aspirin."

"Well give him what you have, and then we move on," said Karl.

Karl went over to his trusted guard.

"My old friend, there is little that we can do for you now and moving him will just cause the bleeding to get worse."

Karl said, "Maria, bind the wound and leave the aspirin with him to dull the pain. As soon as we kill the Yanquis, we will come back for you."

Karl said, "Perhaps these Yanquis are more skilled than we had thought. We must be more careful and watch for other traps. Anyone can make punji sticks, but to hide them well enough that one of my best men falls on them requires a lot of skill."

Karl then motioned Red to lead them in pursuit of the Yanquis.

They had gone only another hundred yards when Red waved for them to come to him. He pointed out a black fishing line stretched across the path. He took a long stick and tripped it. A rope with a large noose came up out of the leaves and sprang upward into the branches above.

It was a snare trap large enough to catch a man, but unless it caught his neck it probably would not kill, but again the trap put them on notice that perhaps they were picking a fight with the wrong people.

That one slowed them considerably, even with Red scouting their path. They were all spooked and just waited on the next trap to be sprung.

Maria taunted them with, "What happened to all the big talk about these touristas and how you big bad guys were going to hunt them down for sport?"

Karl replied, "Manny, shut the Bitch up or I'll forget that she works for you and gut her."

• • •

"Have any of y'all figured out yet that they have no problem tracking us since we continue to follow this damn creek bed?" asked Scott.

Gus replied, "Speak to me boy, what you got in that tiny brain of yours?"

Scott replied, "Well I was just thinking that we are just barely staying ahead of the bad guys and just a bit of bad luck and our asses are six feet under.

Have any of you thought that we might want to try to throw them off of our trail and perhaps take a parallel course about a mile or so east or west of this creek?"

"Damn, John, the boy is right, we ain't thinking. We need to quickly think up some kind of way to throw them off our trail by leaving some diversionary tracks and then head off quickly in another direction for that half mile or so," Gus asserted.

"What about how the Indians always doubled back on the Cowboys by turning around while walking in water and then slipping out of the water without leaving footprints in the bank?" Beth exclaimed.

"Damn good idea," came from Gus.

"Until we get to some water deep enough, let's take turns splitting off to the left and right to perhaps slow them down or at least confuse them," John added.

Steve and Scott peeled off out of the soggy creek bed and doubled back for several hundred yards then turned away from the creek and came back towards the others several times. John saw them moving at a trot but staying far enough away so that their tracks would not be seen. They then quickly rejoined the main group.

Gus and Jim took off and were not in sight for a long time. They were offsetting several snares and misleading trails. Then John spotted Gus leading Jim back towards him, he was grinning from ear to ear.

Steve asked, "Gus, what kind of foul trickery did you leave for them?" Just then, John noticed that Jim was no longer packing the Hawken. Gus laughed while he told them about setting several traps for the bastards, with the first one being the Hawken set to blow up like a pipe bomb.

Gus had made the trap so that no one could spot it. The fishing line was tied to a stick that when stepped on would trigger the Hawken at knee-high level. He had filled the barrel with gravel, which would either result in a shotgun blast or blow the whole gun up. The stick and line were covered with bits of leaves and other sticks so that it blended in with the surroundings. The other traps were a mixture of punji traps and tin cans that would rattle and scare the hell out of the bastards.

They kept walking for about half hour when they heard a loud boom that made every bird in the woods fly off. They must be at least a mile back and will go slow now with more dead or wounded.

• • •

The Hawken did not explode, but the gravel peppered Karl and Maria on the legs just enough to sting and make them think they were hurt badly until they pulled their pants down and checked their legs. Karl was pissed. He got on the satellite phone and raised hell with someone.

*

Chapter 14

The Cabin

Idaho Woods

May 18, 2020

They had hiked at a fast pace most of the morning when Gus caught Scott off to the side.

"Scott, I hate to say it, but these women are slowing us down, and we *are* going to get caught if we don't do something," Gus said quietly.

"I was thinking the same thing, and I think Jim and I should go back and ambush them again," said Scott.

"Whoa boy, I meant that I would go back and kill some of those bastards," exclaimed Gus.

Scott gave Gus the time out signal and gave him his plan.

He told him, "Jim and I can pull off the ambush then run like hell back to the main group or hide out if necessary. Gus, I know you can kick any man's ass, but Jim and I can run circles around you."

Gus begrudgingly agreed and gave them some extra magazines for the AK and the 9mm. Scott filled Jim in, and they fell back and disappeared.

About two hours later, they stumbled into a clearing. The house was in the middle of a very dense stand of trees. They would have missed it had they not come out of the woods right at the front door. It was a fancy log cabin with rather large bay windows on either side of the front door.

John had dreamed of having a log cabin like this one, but Scott's mom was a city girl and would have none of it. The more John thought about the house; he began wondering if he had spent most of his adult life trying to please a spoiled girl who just needed a spanking. Well, too late. John pleased her and never got the cabin in the woods. His last thought before Gus got after them was that he would never make that mistake again. Love is wonderful, but sometimes you have to please yourself and take care of number one.

The cabin's roof was covered in solar panels. There were two large propane tanks behind the house. There was a large fenced garden, which held a large variety of vegetables. Spread throughout the large clearing was numerous fruit trees.

Gus and John agreed that these people must be Preppers like themselves. They wondered aloud about what kind of stores and food they would find.

Gus made them move back into the woods until he and Steve checked out the cabin.

John took Bill and went to the closest side of the cabin, where there was a log garage big enough to hold two cars. Looking inside the garage, they found a Ford pickup and two four wheelers. They searched for the keys, to no avail. Damn, these people thought there might be thieves out in these beautiful woods. In front of the garage was a stone path to the house, it was just pieces of flagstone laid into the dirt. They then crept around the back of the cabin and looked into the windows and back glass doors. There were no signs of the owners, so they continued to look all around the front end of the cabin.

They went to join the rest of the crew and saw Gus wave them in from the cabin's front door.

"There's no one home, but they must have just left," Gus told them.

They looked around and saw that someone had eaten and left the dishes on the table. The beds were unmade, and clothes were on the floor.

The cabin was a three-bedroom, two bath modern house with all the conveniences. It even had satellite TV, but there was no phone.

Beth made several comments about how cute the log home was and that she was jealous of the people who owned the cabin. She went from room to room exclaiming how much she loved the way the cabin was laid out and decorated.

Gus said, "We only have a short time to waste here; we don't know that we have lost those creeps for sure. Bill, let's see if we can get the truck started."

Steve then jumped in with, "Search the cabin for anything we need to help us move on."

They then spread out and quickly searched each room for food, clothes, and weapons.

Beth and John walked into the master bedroom and frantically opened all closets and drawers. John was looking at the family pictures on the dresser when he heard Beth giggling. He turned and there she was bare ass naked, slipping a pair of panties over her well rounded behind.

John stood there and took in the view then finally said, "Damn, I think that you are the sexiest woman that I have ever laid my eyes on."

Never wanting for words, Beth looked him in the eyes and said, "I knew that you were a pervert, your eyes are bulging right out of your head."

John pulled her to him, kissed her passionately and then replied, "I like what I see, but I want to get you safely out of this mess before we finish this discussion."

Before John could stop her, Beth had pushed him down on the bed and jumped on top of him. She covered his lips with kisses as she lay on top of him.

"That's all you get for now. Gus will be after us any minute." Just as she finished, Gus poked his head in and saw them on the bed.

He turned red and said, "O Lord," and quickly slammed the door.

Beth quickly dressed in dry, but poor fitting shorts and a rather tight top and then grabbed an assortment of underwear and clothes for the other ladies.

She told John that he stank and ordered him to change his dirty clothes.

John thought that it was just too bad that he didn't have time for a shower or to finish what Beth started.

They met the others in the great room to share what all had found. There was an assortment of food, clothing, knives and one Ruger LCP .380 auto with two mags that Alice had found hidden in an end table. Steve offered it to the women. Neither Alice nor Janet was interested, but Beth grabbed it and stuck it in her pocket. John was beginning to think this was one gal that could take care of herself.

Gus then caught John off to the side and said, "The pantry is well stocked, but I expected to see whole rooms of food and water from what we saw outside. I also expected to find a cache of guns; this guy *is* a Prepper."

John agreed but thought they did not have the time to keep looking.

Gus told John, "Scott and Jim went back along our trail to give us warning if the thugs get near."

John was surprised that he had been so busy with Beth that he hadn't noticed his son was missing. John did not like that one bit. He knew his son could handle himself normally, but these were hardened killers.

"I couldn't get the truck started, Steve went out to the truck to see if he could hotwire it so we can get the heck out of here," Gus added.

John said, "We can load the truck up with some supplies in case we run into trouble."

Janet walked up to John and Beth, looked John straight in the eye and said, "Good Morning LA, I love the U...S...A..."

John started laughing and said, "Are you a fan or are you making fun of my show?"

"Both," she replied, "My husband Bill is a big fan. I thought your show stank."

Beth had a puzzled look on her face and added, "You are the John Harris, the Survival Show host, and author?"

"Yep, that's me alright, although I never thought I'd use this training to fight drug lords in Idaho," Janet called Bill over and told him about John.

Bill ran to John and began shaking his hand and thanking him for saving their lives.

Beth said, "No wonder you sound so familiar, I listen to your show every chance I get."

Gus chimed in, "He's got a big enough head already so please don't add to the fire. Now I'm gonna' need a hatpin to deflate his head so he can get through the danged door."

John snickered and quickly changed the subject. He showed the others the family pictures that Beth had found in the bedroom. A tall, dark haired man about 45 who looked like a ballplayer and an attractive blond woman were in several pictures. The other pictures had an older teenage girl, a young boy and small girl in them.

Gus told them, "The guy is an accountant, and his wife is a nurse." Steve asked him where he found his crystal ball.

Gus replied, "Don't need one when you see all kinds of accounting manuals and the American Journal of Nursing magazines laying all around the house. Oh, well, yeah, I knew that."

"C'mon, let's eat. This place is well stocked, and we can leave them some money," Beth was hungry again.

John wondered how she kept that slim and trim body. He thought that perhaps he should see what her mom looked like before he got too serious. Then John thought, already too late dang it.

Gus threw them a candy bar and said to grab additional clothes and more food. "Don't eat it here; we'll eat as we march, the hell, out of here.

"Those bad guys are hot after us, and we need to get a move on," he urged.

John got his wallet out and pulled some rather soggy bills out to pay for what they had taken. He counted out five one hundred dollar bills, left them on the island counter and had Beth write them a nice note thanking them for what they took and told them that they were sorry, but it was necessary.

. . .

Dave and Julie Kantor were returning to the cabin from dropping the kids off at the neighbors and going hiking.

The kids were going into town with the Martins who would bring them back home later that evening. They were discussing how the kids were finally getting used to living in the woods after being born, and raised, in Los Angeles.

Dave had been with the FBI as a forensic accountant working on major crimes. Julie had worked at a local doctor's office, and both became burned out by all the crime and violence in L.A.

Then after the incident, they just could not live in L.A. anymore. The perps got off without even a slap on the wrist, after committing one of the most heinous crimes in local history.

"You know, we haven't been alone for a long time, looks like we can run around naked and have a ball until about dark," Dave said with a big smirk.

Julie answered with, "I'll bet I can get my clothes off faster than you can buddy."

Dave was looking forward to a few hours alone with his wife because the kids had been a pain in the ass since the move. Julie had been smothering the kids since the move from L.A. Other than school; this was the first time since the move that they could get away from their kids.

As they cleared the last turn and saw the cabin, Dave slammed the brakes on then backed up out of sight of the cabin. He said, "Julie, grab your shotgun and get into the woods with me."

Dave had seen several armed strangers come out of their cabin. Dave jacked a round in the chamber of his KEL-TEC KSG Shotgun and followed Julie into the woods. His shotgun looked like a short assault rifle but was a 12 gauge that held 14 rounds in the twin tubes. His was loaded with double ought Buck that would tear a man in half.

Julie's Mossberg 500 was loaded with No. 4 buckshot that was just as deadly but had a wider pattern that made it harder to miss your target.

They had practiced many times for this, were excited and scared shitless to be executing what they had played out so many times in the past. Dave wondered if Julie thought he was responsible for their lack of preparation four years ago when they lost so much.

They watched from the woods as these strangers were trying to get the truck started.

Dave laughed and said to Julie, "I'll bet they never find the hidden anti-theft switch," he chuckled to himself. "They all have their hands, so they did not find our armory," he added.

The strangers were eating but weren't carrying any electronics or jewelry. This was odd, but perhaps the robbers had already loaded up the good stuff before they arrived.

One guy appeared to be in charge of the group, and he was rushing the others to little avail. Dave whispered to Julie that they needed to work their way closer to the thieves so they could learn more about what was going on before capturing them.

Dave desperately wanted to catch these bastards and turn them over to the Sheriff and put their asses in jail where they belong. Years of built up frustration led him to feel that he wouldn't mind killing a couple of them. The weak California laws that coddled criminals placed his family in such danger that they decided to move into these woods to get away from gangbangers and common thieves.

While they had to keep hidden in the woods, Dave and his wife were able to sneak up to the garage and get within 30 feet of those trying to get the truck started.

He took a good look at all of the intruders and only one had a gun on his hip, but knew he had to assume all were armed.

Dave told Julie his plan and motioned for her to stay put and be ready to take on these assholes. Dave circled back around the house to come up around the corner of the cabin just beyond the front door. He peered around the corner and could see his wife hiding behind a tree while his targets were finishing loading the truck.

He watched while one of the men cussed and another opened the driver's side door and stuck his head down under the steering wheel.

Then he heard, "The dirty bastard has a damn kill switch on this blankety blank Ford." Dave knew that they had to take action or watch these thieves drive away in his truck.

He caught Julie's eye and signaled, then sprang into action. He shot a round of buckshot into the air and yelled, "Get your hands up or die." At the same time, Julie shot into the air and ran in from the opposite side of the truck.

Gus and John knew that they had been caught with their pants down. They all complied quickly and were rounded up and lined against the cabin.

John remembered that Scott was not with the group. He just hoped that Scott would not do anything stupid. These people just wanted to get the police.

Dave came over to John, hit him in the stomach with the butt of the shotgun and yelled, "What the fuck are you doing here and did you think that you would get away with ripping me off? I have eaten up and spat out much tougher trash than you."

While John was doubled over in pain, he couldn't help but think this asshole sounded like a script from Dirty Harry. Didn't matter, John wasn't holding the gun.

John looked Dave in the eye and said, "Look, you have got us all wrong, and the really bad guys are going to come out of the woods at any time."

John started to tell Dave about the upcoming peril, but Dave just stuck the shotgun in John's face and slapped him hard, blood flew.

Dave ordered them into the cabin, made them sit down on the floor and sent Julie for something to tie their hands.

"Look, man, what's your name? We are running from..." John exclaimed just before Dave tried to butt stroke him in the head. John grabbed the shotgun, and all hell broke loose.

Beth jumped on Dave and scratched the hell out of his face as she also grabbed for his gun. Gus made a move to help, but Julie fired a shot over his head as Dave threw Beth to the floor and kicked her in the side. John saw red.

John and Bill jumped on Dave while Gus and Jim grabbed Julie and fought for her gun. Julie lost control of her shotgun but quickly began kicking the shit out of both Gus and Bill. She was moving like Chuck Norris, kicking and blocking counter punches with her arms. She had put Bill out of action and started on Gus when Gus got tired of fighting a woman and just hit her upside the head and knocked her out.

Steve had pushed Alice and Janet out of the way and came charging at Dave who was fighting with Bill and John for control of the shotgun. He hit Dave in the jaw with his elbow and dropped him like a sack of potatoes.

Bill and Gus tied Dave and Julie with a clothesline and then threw a pan of water in their faces. Steve took Dave's shotgun and put it in Dave's face and said, "Shut up and listen, you dumbass cracker."

They quickly checked each other out, made sure there were no serious wounds, and only needed a few bandages. Beth walked over to Dave and kicked him hard in the side.

"Next time you will shut up and listen when someone is trying to save your pathetic life, you sorry piece of crap. John, how do we know that they aren't part of that bunch of killers?" Beth screamed.

Julie was laying on the floor crying and sobbing, "Don't kill my babies, God, please don't kill my babies."

"Julie, shut up," exclaimed Dave.

"We didn't plan on hurting you two until you attacked us, you miserable assholes," yelled Bill.

"We just wanted to escape from the killers and borrow your truck to get into town to get the law after them," said Beth.

"Why did you attack us?" chimed in Steve.

Julie kept blubbering about them not killing her babies, nothing she said made sense. John came over, picked Julie up, kicking and screaming and put her on the couch. He then told Dave to get his ass off the floor and calm his wife down. It took a few minutes, and Julie was gently sobbing, but would not open her eyes.

John said, "I guess you *will* listen now."

He proceeded to tell them as much as he could in five minutes. John stressed that the killers had to be close and that they were all in danger.

He then told them that he was John Harris and that he had noticed that they appeared to be Preppers. Dave said that they were, but why did that matter. John then shouted out his corny opening for his radio show.

"Holy crap," Dave exclaimed. "Was that crap supposed to mean something to me?" he added.

John told him about his radio show, and Dave didn't have a clue, but when John mentioned the survival book series, Dave stood up. John shoved him back onto the couch *hard*.

"I bought those books, look on that shelf," Dave said. John went to the shelf, opened the book to the last page and put the author's picture next to his face.

"Look Dumbass, that's what I looked like before you slugged me," said John.

Julie started laughing and cried, "You are not here to kill my babies?"

"Not you or your babies," said John. He then asked Dave what the fuss was all about killing her babies. John freed Dave while Beth untied Julie and told all to keep an eye on them.

John took Dave out on the front porch and asked, "What was the talk about killing her babies?"

Dave told him their story about life in Los Angeles and their previous jobs in law enforcement and nursing. He told John that his team had broken some lower level pushers and got the goods on the local head of the "Cabra's" drug gang.

Before they could close in, the gang tried to kill every single team member and their family. Dave and Julie were away with their two younger kids when they attacked their home. Their 15-year old daughter, Kim, was alone with her best friend. Both were savagely raped, and their heads were cut off. John looked back to the house and saw Beth just a few feet away, crying.

Beth went into the house, sat down next to Julie, gave her a hug and told her how sorry they were for bringing in this grief on them. They both cried for a while, before composing themselves.

Beth then looked at Dave and said, "Do y'all have cell phones, we need to call the police?"

• • •

Scott and Jim doubled back about two miles staying 50 -100 feet to the West of their original trail and peered through the dense foliage for the GAO group. They had decided to sneak back to meet them and cut them down to size a bit. Another ambush could get two maybe three of them.

"I'll shoot the tall blonde guy, and then the redheaded one with the AK while you get as many as possible with the 9mm. Take no more than five shots and fall back. Then do it again after half a mile or so. Then we run full speed back to the cabin," said Scott.

Jim added, "All of that track we ran in high school might pay off."

Scott knew that he could outrun the thugs, but knew Jim was not in the best of shape, too much Imelda and beer.

Jim said, "I'm not a soldier like you and your Dad, but what if they don't follow us?"

Scott didn't get a chance to answer because they saw the thugs coming towards them through the trees. They were following the big red headed guy as he followed the signs in the disrupted leaves and bushes. They were about 75 yards away.

Scott and Jim got into position and made sure they had cover for their retreat. Jim pointed out Maria and the blonde man. Blondie was laughing and hanging on to Maria while bossing the others around. When he put his hand on Maria's ass, she slapped him and ran to the front of the group.

Scott thought that except for the big red head, this bunch looked like they were on a Sunday stroll. We should achieve total surprise.

• • •

As they got closer, they heard Red shout out to Karl, "When will the others get here?"

Karl replied, "In a couple of hours or so. What's wrong? Don't you think we can kill these putas?"

Red replied, "I think we may have something more than putas ahead of us. Sometimes you get to eat the bear and sometimes the bear eats you. I'm not sure *what* we have here. They have set some effective traps, taken our hostages and killed several of us. We have only killed Roger."

Red thought that Karl was too full of himself and that they might have bitten off more than they could chew. He was going to slow the chase and wait on the re-enforcements that Karl had coming to join them.

Karl shouted at Red and ordered him to come back to him. Scott and Jim could only hear every other word, but Karl was furious. He was telling Red that he was the boss and that Red had better do what he was told and shut up or Karl would gut him like a pig.

Red quieted down, said something very quietly and went back to scouting the trail. What Red did not see was that Manny and the white guy backed Karl while Maria and Jesus had their guns pointed at Karl.

．．．

After the confrontation, none of the GAO soldiers were watching too closely or talking at all. Scott counted six of them and decided to change the plan and wait for the line to draw even with them.

They would target the blonde-haired man and Manny. Scott hoped the rest would stop the chase without their leader. The team would then kill as many as possible and run west for a while to throw them off the cabin, and then ambush them one more time if they followed

Just as Scott was about to fire, a snake crawled in front of him. He could tell it was not poisonous, but still, he knew a bite would be painful. The snake crawled straight towards his face. When it got about four feet away, he started blowing at it to run it away. The snake kept coming at him until it was just a foot from his arm. Scott quickly reached out, grabbed the snake just below the head and threw it as far as he could. The snake landed in a bush. There was just enough noise to alert Red.

Scott fired first and dropped Blondie, then shot Jose in the head. His head exploded into red chunks of brain flying out the back. No doubt, he was dead.

At the same time, Jim took aim at Red and pulled the trigger, Red fell. Jim then shot at Manny, but only grazed him. The girl, Maria, must have thought there were snipers in the trees for her shots were high and wide. Jesus returned their fire, put a slug into a tree beside Jim, threw bark in his face and then put another one in Jim's shoulder before Scott's shots got him. Jesus fell screaming to the Lord to save him.

By this time, they were receiving return fire, and bullets were whizzing all around. They fired several rounds each to pin the GAO down and then crawled back about a hundred yards where Scott checked Jim's shoulder. It was a flesh wound high on Jim's left arm. Scott applied a piece of his shirt as a bandage and then drew it tight with another piece of his shirt.

"You won't die of this you lucky bastard, "he told his friend. But keep your head down before they shoot it off," he added.

They started running while shooting back at the GAO to make sure they knew where to follow.

• • •

Karl only had a deep scrape on his right side and wondered if he had a broken rib. He was cursing these demons and was threatening them, their families and everyone they knew.

Manny took a bullet to the fleshy portion of his left bicep, and could still use his arm. Jose had his head blown away, and Jesus had an ugly wound in his stomach. Red walked up to see how they were.

Jose took a flesh wound in the side but vowed he could soldier on. That left only four relatively unscathed and Jesus with the severe stomach wound. Maria did not get a scratch.

"Jesus, do you have any fight left in you?" asked Karl.

Jesus held his stomach and replied, "I'll do whatever it takes to please you, Karl, just tell me what you need."

Karl looked him in the eyes and said, "Die." He then shot Jesus in the forehead.

Maria exclaimed, "Why did you do that; he did *not* have to die?"

"Look, you dumb bitch he was dying, I just put him out of his misery. He would have slowed us down, and we could not leave him behind and take a chance on him getting caught by the local police."

Maria said, "Karl, killing your men is not the way to endear them to you."

Karl struck her across the face and knocked her down. Karl nudged Maria with his foot and made her get up, then pointed his pistol at her and said, "Perhaps you should give me your gun, just in case you hold a grudge against me."

He laughed and shoved her until she started following Red. Karl was worried, but furious at the same time. He'd lost three of his best men and three of Manny's to these amateurs. Madre de Dios, he would even the score regardless of the price.

Karl gathered the others and said, "I will not allow you to give up, we only need to keep after them and wait for help. Then we will attack with many more men and heavy weapons."

106

Red agreed and said, "Let's track the bastards down and make them wish they weren't alive." He then said, "Karl, you pay me to handle security, and something's wrong here."

Karl turned to Red and glared, "What is wrong, my friend?"

Red said, "That ambush was halfhearted, and I am sure that there were a couple of them just trying to keep us away from the main group. We need to keep following the main trail and attack them. Watch closely for another ambush, but concentrate on the main group."

Karl thought for a minute and replied, "You are the warrior, I defer, but in the end, I want them all dead."

• • •

Later, Jim said, "Scott, do you hear a helicopter?" Scott replied, "I hear something and hope it's a SWAT team."

Scott said, "I don't have a good feeling about this, they did not follow us, and a helicopter shows up." Scott then added, "Let's get back to the cabin ASAP."

They quickly noticed that the helicopter was also heading towards the cabin.

• • •

The pilot had directed Karl to a clearing about a half mile from the cabin. The pilot brought five well-armed men plus enough ammo and weapons to start a small war. They landed and quickly off-loaded the supplies. Karl took stock of the weapons and told the new men his plan.

He said, "I want you to mount the M 60 in the door and be ready to kill any that try to escape. Did you bring the RPG and the night vision equipment?" Karl was not going to underestimate this bunch again. He was now prepared to kill all of them. Each man was armed with AK47s, 9mm side arms. The copter also brought one RPG with four rounds, and a couple of tear gas grenades. There were five pairs of night vision goggles. Karl's plan was to surround the cabin, talk the "Campers" into surrendering and then rape the women and kill the men. Then, when done with the women, he would kill them also. If they did not surrender, he would blow them off the face of the earth.

Red led the group to the cabin and then gave each instruction on what he wanted them to do. He sent two men back into the woods to ambush the two bastards that had attacked them a few hours ago. He had the rest surround the cabin and get ready to fire one shot through each window just before Karl told them to surrender. He went over to Karl and said, "We are ready and waiting for your orders." He had barely gotten the words out when there was gunfire in the woods.

He said, "We got the SOBs that ambushed us earlier today," and slapped Karl on the back.

Karl shook his hand and said, "Things are finally going our way, and the end is near."

Karl thought it was going to be dark soon and he knew they had surprise on their side. Finally, he would destroy these pests.

• • •

Scott saw the gang first and started firing as Jim joined in with deadly aim. The firefight was intense, but one sided. The Mexican gangsters had only gotten off a couple of random shots before they died. Scott and Jim quickly stripped the bodies of two AKs, two 9mm and several mags for each.

Jim rolled the bodies over face up and exclaimed, "These are new bad guys. The helicopter must have brought in re-enforcements."

Scott added, "We have to get our asses to the cabin before they attack."

Scott looked at Jim and said, "Remind me to start going to church. God has been with us on this trip."

Jim agreed. They shouldered the extra firepower and took off at a full run.

• • •

Dave made the 911 call and had trouble convincing the dispatcher that there were numerous men trying to kill them. Dave then told her that he was retired FBI and that she had better get the FBI and State Police out here quick.

He gave her the names of the State Police Commander and Section Chief for the local State Police post and emphasized that he was friends with both of them. He demanded to talk with one of them. It took a minute, but she patched the FBI into him.

Dave told the Special Agent the description of the group, their arms, and that a missile shot down their plane down. That was all it took to get an intense response.

In a few minutes, the FBI section chief was on the phone and told Dave a major team was on the way. The response included FBI, State Police and a Terrorist SWAT Team. Dave begged them to hurry since they were not sure that they could hold out and that his kids were due back home in an hour. The dispatcher told him that the SWAT team would be there in about three hours and the rest would be another hour behind them, he added that he would have local police block the roads out of town to block the kids or other innocents from entering the area.

Dave told Julia that help was on the way and she was relieved a bit. She could not rest until her children were safe in her arms.

Dave told the others, "Help is about three hours away."

Everyone started talking at one time.

*

Chapter 15

The Stand

At the Cabin

May 18, 2020

Gus said, "Shut up and deal with it. We have to survive about three hours before the Cavalry gets here. Let's get prepared."

Beth quickly asked, "What can we do?"

Gus replied, "Well, first make sure that you have your weapons loaded and spare ammo close by. This could be a two-hour battle so hit the bathroom and get some food and water down."

Steve added, "We might want to place some buckets of water around in case they try to burn us out. Also, I will go outside and spray the roof and bushes close to the house."

John also took Beth outside to move the SUV while he put the lawn furniture in the garage so they would have clear fields of fire.

John went to Dave to get the keys, and Dave said, "Please follow me to the bedroom."

They went into the master bedroom, and Dave reached under the left corner at the foot of the bed and the end of the bed tilted up to show a doorway with a ladder going down under the house. On both sides of the doorway were various pistols, assault rifles and numerous magazines already loaded and ready to go. There were also several smoke grenades and flash bangs.

John exclaimed, "We were right, you are a major Prepper. What's down in the cellar?"

Dave replied, "More guns, food, medical supplies and Bug Out gear for our family."

They came back in the room with two-12 gauge pumps, four AR 15s, six Glock 9mm and the grenades.

Gus said, "Christmas came early. I almost feel sorry for those dumb sumbitches." Dave and John gave out the weapons and ammo while Gus showed the ladies how to use them.

An explosion suddenly shook the cabin and rattled the windows; they all ran outside. There was a cloud of smoke rising about a half mile away in the direction of the town.

Julie cried out, "That's towards town. You don't think..." Her voice tailed off.

John said, "Don't assume the worst, but it can't be a good thing." John said a prayer to himself that it wasn't Julie's kids.

• • •

The sun had been down for an hour, and a mist was forming in the air. It wasn't quite fog, but soon would be. John had Dave turn on the light at the end of the walkway by the end of the driveway. They also turned the light on at the front of the garage and one at the back of the yard. John turned off the lights in the house and told everyone to stay low and not present a bigger target than necessary.

John then went to Beth and gave her a quick hug and said, "How about a date when we get back home?"

She laughed and said, "Your timing sucks, but let's get out of here alive big boy, and I'll think about it."

As he left, she pinched his ass.

John turned around, smiled and said. "Payback is rough around my neck of the woods."

Gus took charge and said, "Quit playing grab ass. Get your weapons and be ready, we have to keep them out of the house.

Steve and Bill, take the kitchen. John, Beth, and Julie take the front door and living room. Dave and Alice, take the master bedroom. Janet and I'll float and be ready to handle any surprises."

They all started moving furniture in front of the doors and windows from which they were not planning to shoot.

He barely got the sentence out of his mouth when the windows exploded and rained shattered glass on all of them. The cabin rocked from the explosion, and part of the porch roof fell. Luckily, the glass and shrapnel hit no one. They all hit the floor and jumped under, or behind whatever they could find. John shielded Beth while shooting through the window to slow the attackers down.

Steve yelled, "Is everyone okay?"

All answered that there were no serious injuries, just some cuts from flying glass and bruises from hitting the hardwood floor. While no one was seriously hurt, the women were scared, and Julia was sobbing again. Beth was also visibly shaken and trembled in John's arms.

John told her, "Don't worry, we'll get out of this, and I promise you that these bad guys will be dealt with."

Dave yelled, "I'm turning on the outside flood lights, be ready to shoot. They are bright, cover your eyes." Dave flipped the switches, lit up the lights and flooded the outside of the cabin with bright white light.

The attackers were caught flat-footed. Shots rang from the cabin and the GAO scattered like cockroaches in a cheap hotel. Gus had a bead on two that were caught in the open trying to sneak in the back door. He fired a burst from the M 16, and two bad guys fell.

John missed as he tried to shoot the red headed bastard and another attacker as they came around the end of the garage. He did have them pinned down behind a couple of trees and was covering them with bark and dirt when he fired.

John saw someone aiming an RPG at the cabin. He fired a burst into the man, shredding him. John saw the RPG lying on the ground and told the others not to let anyone get close to it. He knew the RPG could blow them to hell and back. One guy tried, and Julie got him in the stomach; he was screaming in agony before he hit the ground. His pitiful agonizing cries for help caused the attackers to be even more careful. Fear works both ways.

Beth missed her target but forced him to run back to the road and hide in a ditch. Bill and the women were laying down a withering fire that kept the bad guys pinned down.

Red and several others opened up with heavy fire while two others tried to get to the RPG. They shot out most of the floodlights and just as the two got to the RPG, John and Julie braved the fusillade and took both of them out with accurate return fire.

A ricochet burned a crease on John's side. Julie was hit in the chest. In shock, she was smiling at Dave as he walked towards her. She told him that she loved him and then her head slumped over. Dave shook her then started crying.

Janet came over to console Dave, but he pushed her away. He ranted and raved about killing all of those Mexican sons of bitches. Dave lost it and was out of control. Gus and Steve grabbed him and kept him from running out the front door in a suicide attack.

Beth looked at John's side and picked out a piece of the bullet that had shattered before ricocheting. She taped a bandage to his side, slapped him on the butt and said, "Get back in the game and save us, Big John. Please kill the bastard that killed Julie."

John replied, "Painkillers please?"

Beth smiled and said, "You are such a wussy."

Janet and Gus kept the remaining GAO pinned down while the wounded were patched up.

John looked over to Gus and said, "These aren't your run of the mill crooks: RPGs and choppers, we have pissed off some very bad people."

Gus replied, "You thinking what I'm thinking? When we finish these bastards, a hundred more will be coming for our families and us."

John replied, "Yes, that's what has me really worried. We need to clean this mess up and wipe out our trail. We do have experience at that crap, you know?"

Gus replied, "That we do, but I'm afraid that we can't get all info contained or enough of them killed before they do some serious damage."

• • •

Scott and Jim heard the explosion and stopped to see where it had come from but there were no visible signs of an explosion.

Jim said, "I think it came from over that way. Shouldn't we head that way?"

Scott countered with, "No, Dad and Gus will try to hold the cabin. I don't know what that was, but I would bet the GAO just got some help. Be ready for anything." Again, they started running full speed towards the cabin.

They were panting heavily, but managing to make good time when Jim saw a clearing up ahead. He heard the pilot even before they saw the chopper in the clearing. He was chattering away in Spanish to someone. Jim spoke Spanish well, so they stopped to eavesdrop. He listened for a minute, then quickly took aim and shot the pilot. He slumped to the side, never knowing that death was about to take him to Hell.

Scott shook Jim and said, "What was that about? We could have gotten info from him."

Before Jim could answer, they heard a volley of gunfire coming from the direction of the cabin.

Jim said, "He was telling someone that their leader, Karl, had given orders for all of us and our families to be killed to set an example. I don't think I stopped him in time."

Scott replied, "We have to get to the cabin, kill these bastards, get back to the GAO office and clean house. They have our home addresses, next of kin and Dad's credit card info."

They ran up to the copter and Scott calmly walked up to the pilot. He pulled out his pistol and shot him between the eyes, just for spite.

He then said, "I guess you won't threaten my family again."

Scott then went to the copter, opened a fuse box and took a couple of fuses to disable it. Then they continued to the cabin.

• • •

The remaining GAO troops regrouped back into the trees. There were only Karl, Red, Manny and Maria left alive. Karl, Red, and Manny had flesh wounds, and Maria had taken some minor pieces of buckshot, but all could continue the fight.

Karl ordered, "We have to get the RPG. *I am* tired of screwing around with these hombres; send them to hell. I must kill them all and make examples so that no one fucks with GAO ever again," Karl swore as he glared at Red.

Red stepped towards Karl and said, "Karl, we are beaten, we should retreat while we can. Trying to get the RPG will be suicide, they will mow anyone down that gets out in the open."

Manny added, "Karl, I know you are right, but we cannot do what you ask. If we are not victorious, we will all die when we get home."

Karl pulled out the Sat phone and called the GAO office. He started with, "What did you find about these pieces of shit?"

Jorge, the head guard, told him, "I talked with a lady that works for their leader and found out about the whole group, where they live and who they love. She thinks I am a news reporter doing a story about their leader."

Karl asked, "What's so special about him?"

Jorge replied, "He is a local redneck who was in the army and is now a survivalist who has a radio program."

Karl said, "Be ready for my return, you know what to do, make them pray to die. We will capture some of these assholes and put them on the phone to hear their women and children die. Get more info from the puta."

Karl then added, "Have you reported any of this back to the Wolf?"

Jorge said, "Yes, I thought that you would want the news to go back home that you are victorious."

"Thanks for having a head on your shoulders, be ready for more responsibility and pay my friend." Karl hung up. Jorge thought that the mission must have turned to shit for Karl to call him his friend.

While Karl was on the phone, Maria got Red off to the side and tried to get him to help her get Karl to retreat.

Maria said, "Red, you know that I am dedicated to our cause and making all that money is great, but dead people don't enjoy the fruits of their labor. What can I do to convince you to help me stop him from getting us all killed because Karl is pissed at a bunch of redneck Gringos."

"The Wolf will kill you if you screw with his fair-haired boy. We can only try to talk him out of this madness. Also, watch out for Manny, he will back Karl to the end."

Maria placed her hand on Red's arm and said, "Red, if you help me stop this I will be yours forever. You could take Karl's place in our organization. We just shoot both of them now."

Red slapped Maria hard enough to knock her down. He bent down and shook her; she was groggy.

Karl turned just in time to see Red checking on Maria. "What the hell is going on behind my back?"

Red replied, "She got smart, and I guess I hit her a bit too hard. Anyway, the bitch will watch her mouth in the future."

Karl motioned for Manny to come to them and said, "Manny, go get the RPG. Red and I will throw the tear gas grenades and lay down suppressing fire to pin them down.

Manny was visibly upset, but replied, "Karl, anything you want I'll do." With that, he left to get in position to fetch the RPG. Both Red and Karl threw the tear gas grenades as far as they could, but only got them about 50 feet from the cabin. They began shooting at the cabin's windows. The return fire from the cabin was heavy and hit all around the three of them. Manny got his courage up, charged out into the open, grabbed the RPG and ran for cover.

• • •

Gus had warned them that there would be a last ditch effort to get to the RPG and that their lives depended on stopping them.

Dave saw Manny's shadow as he skulked around the edge of the forest to get closer to the RPG. Dave told them to get ready because the shit was about to come down. He was about to shoot when the covering fire began. A bullet hit him in the throat and knocked him back across the room. Janet ran over to him and applied pressure to the wound. The rest concentrated on shooting at the guy trying to get the RPG.

• • •

Scott and Jim heard the gunfire and agreed that it was only about 100 yards in front of them. They were dog-tired but sprinted towards the gunfire. Jim saw the cabin and signaled Scott to stop. They could see a man crawling towards the cabin. He was heading toward a pile of bodies and shooting at the cabin. They stopped, dropped and got cover before shooting.

Scott saw flashes from the woods in front of the cabin and told Jim he was going to circle around behind them. He said, "Try to hold fire until I am in position and take the first shot."

Jim patiently waited for Scott to get in place. He alternated taking a bead on the guy in the open and then the guy crawling towards the pile of bodies.

The people in the cabin were putting out an enormous rate of fire. Jim knew Gus and John had all of them armed to the teeth and ready to kill. He told himself that John would start writing about this episode before they got the RV back on the road.

Scott got in place directly behind the two that were firing on the cabin. Just as he started to shoot, he noticed someone to his left. The person was sneaking up behind the shooters with a pistol in their hand. He got up and followed just behind. He got close enough to see that it was Maria. She raised the gun and shot the tallest man in the back. As the other one turned, Maria and Scott shot him at the same time.

Scott rushed Maria and overpowered her. She fought like a wildcat, but Scott finally hit her with the butt of his AK and knocked her ass out.

Jim started firing when he saw the flashes and heard gunfire behind the two GAO guys. He put a whole magazine into them and watched as each round hit. He thought it looked as though the men were receiving electrical shocks. He did not realize that he had stopped the RPG attack.

Once the shooting stopped, Gus called a cease-fire. The silence was almost deafening. It was only seconds before one could hear tree frogs and cicadas.

John peered out over the window seal in time to hear his son's voice saying, "Dad, we got them, you can come out."

They came out of the cabin slowly and looked in every direction for potential snipers.

Jim ran up and started hugging everyone. Scott was slowly walking towards them carrying a limp body. They rushed towards him.

John saw that it was Maria and said, "Son, that's the GAO Bitch."

"Dad, I think she's on our side. She killed their leader. I only had to knock her out because it was dark and she thought I was going to shoot her."

Janet came out of the cabin crying and told them that Dave had died.

*

Chapter 16

Vengeance and Heroes

The Cabin

May 19, 2020

Everyone was hugging their fellow survivors and thanking God for being alive.

Jim yelled, "*QUIET!*"

They all turned and looked at him.

"John, it's not over. I don't want to be a wet blanket on the celebration, but these assholes know where we live and have information about us. They will soon come after us. We have to kill the rest of them."

Jim then told them what the pilot had said.

Gus said, "Jim you are right, let's quickly think this through. Let's go in the cabin and quickly come up with a game plan; the SWAT team will be here in 60 minutes."

John took charge and said, "Beth, Alice, Janet and Bill, they do not know you or have anything on you. Take the truck and get back to your RV, and head home *now*. Do not stop, do not waste time, get out of here."

Bill stopped John and said, "What about Fred?"

John said, "Oh shit. We forgot him. Gus, come here."

Gus hurried across the room and asked what was wrong. John filled him in.

Gus grabbed all four and said, "Do you want to live?"

They all said yes. Gus added, "Do what I say and exactly what I say, and you will live."

They hung on his words. Gus thought a minute and said, "Y'all go back to your camp. Fred has a GAO bullet lodged in his head. Cut Fred's head off and take the body and head with you. Clean up your camp take everything with blood or evidence. Get rid of it on the way.

Dump the head, with the bullet, in a river on the way home. Take the body with you and when you get about 100 miles from Nashville create a crime scene that will pass inspection. Above all, get your stories straight and match up. No one goes off script; no one folds. Blame it on some crazy guy that needed a ride.

Shoot the RV up and make it look real. Now, above all, you were never here. Your camp was 500 miles from here."

The three listened in stunned silence but knew they had to protect themselves and more importantly their families.

John grabbed Beth and took her off to the side. "Get a pay-by-the-minute cell phone and don't use your real name. John scribbled something on a piece of paper and gave it to Beth. Call me at this number in three days, and I *will* find you. I love you, but you are in danger *GO*."

Beth grabbed John, kissed him passionately and said, "John, I love you too."

Beth's group picked up their weapons and left.

Jim, Scott, Gus and John laid out a plan to pile most of the bodies in the cabin, burn it and take the chopper to the GAO office and clean house. They were taking Red and Karl's bodies with them. This would help their alibi if captured.

"You can't do this; it's vigilante justice. You will go to jail," Maria yelled.

John turned and faced her; he said, "That's big talk for a GAO tramp running drugs and plotting to overthrow the government."

Maria replied, "John, I am a Homeland Security agent, I was working undercover with Roger to nail these bastards, and you just can't kill people because they are bad."

"You wanna bet? If we can kill 'em, they are already dead. I guess you have an ID in your shoe and a .38 strapped to your leg like Roger?"

She took her shoe off, showed him the ID and pulled a KEL-TEC .380 from just above her ankle.

John said, "Guys, start cleaning this place up. Gus, bring the chopper here. Chop Chop, amigo."

Steve came over and gave Maria a hug, then told her, "Maria, do you have a family? They are in danger; these guys will kill our families without a thought."

Maria said, "I have a five-year-old daughter and parents, but the government will protect them."

"You believe that the government can keep a drug cartel from finding your daughter and raping and killing her? They will rape and cut that little girls head off just to make a point."

Maria thought for about two seconds then replied, "Okay, I'm in. What's the plan?"

• • •

They didn't say a word for half an hour, then all spoke at once, everyone babbled on and on for about five minutes.

Finally, Beth said, "All right, we have to man up and get this done. Are you two up to this task?"

They said that they were, but weren't sure they could cut Fred's head off.

Beth jumped in with, "I can do it if I have to."

They didn't say another word until they got to the camp. They drove straight to the camp and loaded up everything into the RV, every leaf, twig or rock with blood on it. They put them in trash bags.

Fred was where they had left him days ago. You could tell that animals had found him, his eyes had been pecked out and one of his arms had big chunks of flesh missing. They placed the body on a tarp and said prayers that Fred would be rewarded in heaven. After a while, Beth went to the RV and came back with a butcher knife.

She placed the knife against his neck and started slicing. It took a while, but she finally got the head severed from the body, then went into the woods and vomited until she was left with only dry heaves.

• • •

It was about two in the morning, and John knew that they had to haul ass to get the plan executed and get down to Mobile. John said, "Leave a few of the pistols and an AK, but grab all other weapons and ammo, we might need it if these pendejos retaliate."

John scoured the area around the cabin and even cut a bushy limb from a tree and dragged it around the cabin to hide evidence. Gus, Jim, and Scott had already put all of the evidence and bodies in the cabin and poured gas throughout the cabin.

As Gus landed the copter on the lawn, John threw a burning torch into the cabin door and yelled, "Let's haul ass out of here."

• • •

The SWAT Team arrived about 20 minutes after they lifted off and found the cabin totally engulfed in flames. Since they were not aware of the GAO, they began standard operating procedure and started investigating the crime scene. They found hundreds of spent casings on the ground and blood everywhere, but no bodies were found.

The SWAT team leader said, "Something very bad happened here. Why did someone try to half ass clean the crime scene up? There are scads of evidence everywhere. Where are the people who called this in?"

His assistant looked at the burning cabin and said, "Maybe the bad guys cooked them."

The FBI arrived a couple of hours later. They immediately sent for a CSI team. They began searching the woods for survivors and placed markers by every spent round, or blood spatter. A guy in a blue suit arrived with the CSI team. While not in charge, he appeared to have the run of the crime scene.

• • •

The blue suit went to the back of the house and pulled a satellite phone from his coat pocket.

He dialed a number, waited and said, "Yes, it was Karl. That dumbass has caused problems for our plans. Our GAO operation is finished. However, I have a plan B. Let's meet at location 7."

• • •

While the SWAT Team was looking for evidence, standing around scratching their ass, John and his team were landing about half a mile from the GAO office. They had the AK 47s, the RPG with four rounds and a will to use them. They quickly found the guards, neutralized them and moved on to surround the office.

"Let's stick to the plan, kill as many as possible without firing a shot. Then get our data and burn the bodies and buildings to the ground."

Maria said, "Your records will be in the black four drawer filing cabinet by the safe. I'll find them."

It was 4:00 a.m. and very dark. Gus could not see his hand wave in front of his face. They all had nylons over their heads and latex gloves on their hands. The fire would hide the fact they had been there. They were slowly hunting down every GAO slime ball and slitting their throats. Jim snuck up on the last guard, and just as he put his hand over the guard's mouth and shoved the knife into his kidney, the hat fell off. It was a woman.

As she fell, she turned and looked at Jim and mouthed, "Fuck you!"

Jim dropped her and started shaking, and tears came to his eyes. John rushed over, hugged Jim, and told him, "Jim, she was a hired killer. That puta would have killed us without a second thought."

Jim replied, "I know, but it is still a woman, and she looks just like Imelda."

John looked at the girl and replied, "No, Jim, your mind is playing tricks on you. She looks nothing like Imelda."

John knew this was a lie, but a well meant one. He did not want Jim thinking about killing this bitch every time he looked in his girlfriend's eyes.

The sun was barely up when they saw several cars drive up. Four Hispanic men got out of the cars and went into the office. They were about to go into the office when a minivan with two adults and three children arrived.

Gus said, "I'll take care of them. I'll have them gone in a minute." Gus walked over to the driver's side of the van and talked with the driver for a minute. The van then backed out, and sped out of the parking lot, squealing tires as it left. Gus stood there waving at them as they disappeared.

"Jim and I'll blow up their planes. We'll save a DC 3 for our trip. John, you, Scott and Maria take the office and destroy all records," Gus said.

They walked into the office with AKs aimed at the GAO thugs.

"Hands up or die," said Gus.

There were four of them in the office, two raised their hands, but two grabbed for their weapons. John was a blur; he killed the two that had tried to draw their weapons and shot the other two in the shoulder.

Scott went to John and said, "Dad, the other two did not draw their guns."

John said, "You need to grow up, son, and today is the day."

John then proceeded to make one of them open the company safe and ordered them to pile the contents on the floor.

There were piles of records and several large bags. He also made them empty the filing cabinets and stack the records on the floor. Scott searched the bags and took the largest one.

Maria rifled the records cabinet but did not find their file.

John looked at the gangsters and said, "Where is our info, you know, records of our trip and credit card data?"

Neither looked up, and both tried to ignore John. One said that they needed to go to the hospital.

John placed his 9mm against one of the thug's head and said, "The first one of you that gives me our records lives, the other dies."

The other goon said, "Bullchit, ju are de goo guys, ju call the cops. We go to jail, get out and then we come to jour casa, rape and slowly keel jour wife and kids in front of ju, den we keel jour sorry asses."

John quickly aimed at the thug's foot and shot him.

John said, "You obviously made the mistake of messing with the wrong, good guys. Maria, pull the employment records on these turds. Scott, search them for ID."

They piled the documents on the counter.

John took a minute to review their info and said, "You two idiots have this all wrong. Both of you are already dead. You just haven't fallen over, yet. After reading your files, it goes like this. We leave, you die, and we burn down this building with you inside. Scott will douse you in gas in a minute and burn you alive unless you tell me where the records are."

He pulled a driver's license and said, "Martin, your wife, and two daughters live here on Mesa Ave, your mother and all six brothers and sisters live in Yuma, AZ.

If you don't give us the info in sixty seconds, or fail to give all of the info I want, I will hunt them down, cut their throats and kill your dog. I'll burn down the house with them inside. You are right about one thing. We are just the good guys. We are the *NEW* good guys, and ju, amigo, ju don't mean chit to me."

John then shot the other goon in the foot. "The next round goes to your nads. I understand it takes about 25 minutes to bleed out. Oh, don't worry; the fire will kill you before you bleed out.

"Speak up. You are already dead, save your families now."

He pulled the trigger, castrating the mouthy bum. The other one started crying and yelling where the records were.

The records were all there, but Maria also noticed that someone had made notes on each of them. She did not mention this to John.

He turned and shot both men in the head. Maria started screaming at John and tried to hit him.

He grabbed her and told her to put her big girl panties on and get a grip.

"Maria, you do what you have to, but don't trust the Government to protect you. There are no witnesses, and perhaps with some luck, all of us can go home and live safely. Scott, you'd better clean out the valuables in the safe and cash drawer, then, burn it down."

John pushed Maria out the door while Scott poured gas in every room, lit a torch and threw it into the office. The office exploded as if a bomb had gone off, and knocked Scott to the ground.

Maria said, "John, you just killed two unarmed men. Can you live with yourself?"

John replied, "Yes, I can. If we keep these monsters from killing my loved ones, I'll sleep sound all night, every night, and when I stand before God to be judged, I will stand by every shot I have taken and will take in the future.

Remember, these animals cut innocent men, women and children's heads off. They rip tongues out to make Colombian neckties, just to scare people. They raped and killed that young girl, then laughed."

The plan was to knock Maria out. This would give her an alibi. Red had already given her a cut and lump on the head.

Jim and Scott jumped in the RV and headed for Mobile while Gus and John headed for an airport close to Mobile so they could get home and prepare for retaliation if it came their way.

John would rent a car and take the extra weapons to his home in the middle of the night. They would wait a day then fly to an airport closer to Mobile.

John started the fire and ran over to the Gooney Bird, which Gus had warmed up, and was ready to fly. They took off and flew straight to an airport just north of Montgomery so they could quickly get home from there. They would then fly to Satsuma to meet up with the RV.

• • •

The four of them argued for the first 100 miles when Bill remembered, "Damn, we are not expected back for three days. We have time to camp at a different place to help our story.

We all watch CSI and all those other TV crime scene shows; we have to come up with an unbreakable story."

126

Beth added, "Well we can sit around the campfire telling TV plots."

They all laughed for a minute and then reality set in, the story had to ring true. Alice talked them into driving over to the "Craters of the Moon" in Idaho to spend their time.

They drove on, making sure they only paid cash for the fuel and supplies. Alice was the only one to get out of the RV while Bill filled it up. She had a ball cap and sunglasses hiding her face.

They skipped several high-end campgrounds and stopped at a nice, but older RV Park where their rented RV wouldn't stand out. They had solved their major problem by making a large makeshift ice chest for Fred. None wanted a quickly decaying body as a roommate.

They got their stories down pat. They all were fans of police TV shows and knew that their stories had to be good, but not appear scripted.

The prepared central theme of being forced off the road, robbed, Fred was taken a hostage and the attackers leaving in a hail of bullets. It was dark; they had masks, "yaddayadda."

They knew their families' lives depended on them sticking to the story and the authorities not finding Fred's body for at least a week.

• • •

"You know this is just great, what the fuck is John Harris doing hooked up with drug lords and terrorists in a battle in the Northwest? You just can't make this stuff up," said the blue suit to Agent Black.

There were five men and one woman spread around the table. There was nothing in the room, but a table and six chairs. They had never met in the same room or the same city for their once a month strategy session. They did not know who was above them or who supplied the money to cover their very expensive projects.

They got an update on the GAO Chupacabras and John's exploits then a heated discussion took place.

The woman said, "We needed someone to take the fall for the upcoming changes in our country. Our average Joe Blow wants to make the changes but does not have the guts to do the dirty work. Moreover, where are all of these damn skinheads when you needed a

127

Socialist President killed? This has to happen before our President, and his cohorts execute their plot against the USA.

We had John set up to take the fall and now the dumb asshole screws up our plans. He was perfect. He rants and raves about our out of control government and has a Special Forces background."

Blue Suit added, "Hold on, the Cabra's are tailor made to be our fall guys, the shame is we have to keep John Harris from killing all of them before they take that fall.

We'll make John and his dipshit countrified redneck friends National Heroes. The people will rally around John, and us, when we show them that these despicable narco-terrorists killed their wonderful president and attacked them."

The woman said, "Can we tie the Iranians into the plot?

Blue Suit replied, "Sure, we just have to add a few bits of evidence."

They all agreed and decided to adapt their plan to blame the "Cabra's."

Blue Suit said, "Miss Brown, you handle the media and Agent Black will handle the Law Enforcement groups. Let's make a HERO!"

Their underground compound was to be completed in a few weeks, and they could stop all of this clandestine meeting bullshit and begin to make things happen. It was time for planning to end, and execution to begin.

• • •

The DC3 was 75 miles from Satsuma when John's cell phone started playing, "You're So Mean" by Taylor Swift. While not a Swift fan, the song fits his ex-wife to a tee.

John answered, "What do you want now; you got all my money?"

Ann replied, "Okay smart ass, get someone else to proof your trashy books next time."

John quickly changed the tone of his voice and said, "Darlin', what can I do for y'all today?"

"I just wanted to make sure that you are okay, I heard on the news about the horrible things that happened on your trip. I know the media exaggerates a lot, but did someone get killed?" she asked.

John said, "What did you just say, you heard what from the news?"

Gus started cussing in the background and John gave him the sign to pipe down.

John gave her a brief update and said, "Well, we tried to keep this secret so that there would be no retaliation from this bunch of drug dealers. Ann, this is a very well organized group with vast resources. They will be coming for us."

Ann said, "Well, it's too late to keep it quiet; the mayor is getting the city geared up to give y'all the key to the city. ABC, NBC, FOX, CNN and everyone else is descending on Mobile to camp out at your house."

Ann added, "Well, first you can call off your PI who has been watching me for the last two days. You know I got my half of our money fair and square, catching me sleeping with Paul won't do you any good."

"Ann, I promise you that I do not have anyone watching you, I have no idea what you are talking about, and maybe you pissed some guy's wife off. Look, seriously, it could be one of the guys that attacked us. By the way, did you check on JoAnne, how is she doing?" John asked.

She said, "I checked on her twice, and all appeared to be going well. I saw her with David Meeks, the city parks commissioner on Friday. She does not seem to miss you one bit. I *told* you to bend her over the desk."

Ann then thought about the mystery man in JoAnne's life.

John suddenly said, "Ann, I am over you and won't need JoAnne's services. You won't believe it, but I met the perfect woman for me deep in the woods of the Northwest."

Ann laughed and said, "Yeah, right, you are just trying to get me to stop working to get you laid. Maybe then, you can get over me."

John replied, "Ann who?" and hung up before she could answer.

John started thinking about who could be following Ann. He finally thought that he would call one of his cop friends to look into it.

• • •

Scott and Jim were yakking away about their adventures and then about how much they missed their girlfriends when they heard some big news breaking on the radio. Jim yelled for Steve to join them in the front of the RV.

They heard, "While the details are still unfolding, it appears that a terrorist group has suffered a major setback in an attempt to implement a large-scale attack on the U.S.

While sketchy in detail, it appears that the Chupacabra Drug Cartel was plotting to shoot down several airplanes including Air Force One. The attacks, aimed at planes carrying DEA, Federal Marshalls, and the President.

Fortunately, for the USA, a group of hunters from Mobile, AL stopped them in their tracks. There was a furious gun battle, and the good old boys from Mobile wiped the bad guys out."

The newscaster went on to say that, the FBI was on top of the case and had teams searching for other conspirators.

Just then, Scott's phone rang and John was on the line. "Scott, meet us at the Satsuma airfield. We need to get our stories straight; now we are *heroes*. Don't get a big head. The Chupacabras will still be after our asses, and now we're sure they know all about us."

• • •

John called the tower for landing instructions and received a surprise; the attendant asked if he was the famous John Harris.

John said, "I don't know anything about famous, but I am John Harris.

The attendant said, "I have someone here who wants to talk with you."

Blue Suit said, "John, my friend, I am with the government, and I am here to help you."

John replied, "Okay joker, who are you and what do you want?"

"I am with the government, one of the groups that you and Gus used to work for. I need you to land and taxi to the hangar at the far south end of the airpark. The reporters are at the Main Office, and you need to avoid them until we talk."

John asked, "Do I have a choice?"

Blue Suit said, "Well that's a good question, and no, John, you don't. However, we intend to make you and your guy's heroes since you screwed up our investigation into the Chupacabras, but somehow did it so spectacularly that our boss wants a hero out of this mess."

John asked, "What if I just fly on by and skip your sorry asses?"

Blue Suit replied, "Another very good question. John, look to your east along the horizon and see the attack helicopters. There are three of them that will either force you down or shoot you down, your choice. I get paid the same. I can be your friend or your undertaker, again your choice."

John quickly said, "I think we want to be heroes, we're coming down."

They landed and taxied over to the hanger that they as instructed and parked.

The hanger had five Black SUVs surrounding it and had about ten men dressed in black suits serving as guards. Gus and John got out of the plane, chocked the wheels and went towards the hanger.

Blue Suit walked up, shook their hands and said, "My heroes are finally here, come on in and join your friends."

As John entered the hanger, he saw his RV parked in the back. Suddenly, Scott, Jim, and Steve ran up to welcome them. They all shook hands and hugged one another.

Blue Suit said, "Well enough homecoming, let's get down to business. He told them to sit down around a table that was placed in the middle of the hanger. Blue Suit started explaining how John and the team had to be heroes to keep egg off the faces of some high-level men in Washington or face the death penalty for killing all of the innocent GAO personnel. Yep, Heroes or Zeroes.

John asked, "What about the Chupacabras retaliating against our families?"

Blue Suit replied, "First, we have them on the run; second, y'all are some big bad mamma jammas who can take care of yourselves, and third, we don't give a shit if they kill you because you screwed up our operation.

However, it is your lucky day because our boss cares about you sorry pieces of shit. We will keep a guard on all of your families for the foreseeable future."

John replied, "So we are the bait to draw the bastards out of the woodwork."

"Bingo, "replied Blue Suit. He added, "You assholes can keep all of the guns and ammo except for the fully automatic weapons. You are all military types and can handle yourselves."

He then spent half an hour giving them their story.

Blue Suit finally said, "Now you have your story, go meet your adoring public."

"Oh, wait, just one more thing," John said, as he grabbed Blue Suit by the Adam's apple and squeezed just hard enough to maintain the lock. "Now, you listen to me you hotshot dickweed. Don't you ever speak to me or mine like that again, or I will enjoy ripping out your miserable fucking throat." With that, he added just a tiny bit of additional pressure. Blue Suit's eyes bulged. John added, Capiche?"

Blue Suit gurgled, "Ok, Ok."

John smiled, and said, "Good, now we can all be friends again."

John then released his hold on Blue Suit, slapped him on the back and said, "Great, c'mon, old buddy, let's go and meet our adoring public."

The entire incident happened so quickly that none of Blue Suit's entourage had time to react.

As they walked away, Blue Suit glared at John. He attempted to appear threatening, but John returned his stare with piercing eyes of gray steel. Blue Suit's composure collapsed, and he looked at the ground for the rest of the walk.

His mind, however, looked forward to his ultimate revenge.

• • •

It was dark when they left the hanger. John's phone rang. It was his literary agent. His agent told him to blow off the press because he had sold their story to a book publisher and that he had FOX news paying to have the first interview.

Gus said, "John, can we share in your heroic story?"

John placed his hand on his best friend's shoulder and said that they would all share any profit equally. The agent also told them to go home, kiss their loved ones and get ready for their adoring fans, accompanied by many news interviews and parades.

· · ·

Gus went home to his wife, Robin, who was thrilled to see him and welcomed him as the conquering hero.

After a short stop at the hospital to get his wound treated, Jim went to his girlfriend's apartment, spent the night making love to her and asked her to marry him.

Scott hugged his Dad and went to his girlfriend's house only to find his mom already there. They spent the rest of the evening catching up on the event. Following Ann's departure, Scott and Joan went to the bedroom, and Scott fell asleep with her in his arms.

She looked at him and wondered when he would ask her to marry him. She loved him and wanted to spend the rest of her life with him.

Steve went to his favorite bar, entertained all of his friends and played the big kahuna to all of the women. He started to take one home and bang her all night, but thought of Janet and went home, alone.

John went home after checking on things at the shop. All was well, but he found that JoAnne had taken two weeks' vacation. She had not been seen since the boys had left for the trip.

John got to his house after dark, went in and checked all of the rooms, then tried to fall asleep on the couch. He could only think of Beth and had to hold her. He smiled as he thought just how many teachers named Beth Fox could live in a small town like Smyrna, TN. He knew he could *not* wait for her phone call. He fell asleep with a big grin on his face.

· · ·

Robert dropped JoAnne off at her front door, kissed her and left. JoAnne was walking on cloud nine; she had finally found Mr. Right and just needed him not to find out about her past. The only thing that nagged her was that Robert had continuously asked questions about Gus and John. He explained that he was a bit jealous and they to be a big part of her life.

JoAnne opened the door and sat her bags down in the hallway. Just as she reached for the light switch, she felt a hand cover her mouth and another drag her down to the floor.

She heard a voice say, "Bitch, keep your mouth closed, or you die." The hand left her mouth, and the lights came on.

A Latino looking guy stood there with a big gun aimed at her chest. He reached up and cupped a hand on her right breast, and she slapped him. He hit her on the side of her head with the gun, and she fell like a stone.

He pulled out his iPhone, started filming and said, "beg for jour life and maybe I will spare ju." JoAnne started crying and begged for her life

She asked him why this was happening, and he replied, "Senorita, Jour amigo, John, well, he joss fock with the wrong hombres."

*

Chapter 17

May Fred Rest in Pieces?

Tennessee

May 20, 2020

They dropped the rest of Fred's body off in Buck Snort about 100 yards off Highway 40 around 2:00 a.m. They then drove about ten more miles toward Nashville and ran the van through the fence on the side of the road.

They made sure no one was on the road and then begun to shoot up the van and a couple of trees. Bill took the pistol about a quarter mile down the road and threw it in the trees. Beth, Alice, and Janet took turns tearing their clothes, slapping each other and rolling around on the ground.

When Bill got back, they assaulted him to make his story look good. He already had the bullet wound so their story should be credible.

Bill tried to flag down a car, but after many attempts, no one pulled over. Finally, a police car drove up with lights flashing. Soon, there were ambulances and a dozen cop cars all around.

The cops took down their stories and took them to the Jackson Hospital. They all played their roles to a tee. Bill was in shock, and the women were alternating between crying and screaming about poor Fred.

Once they calmed down in the hospital, a Homicide Investigator took their stories one more time. He thanked them and asked if he could get them a ride home. Beth told him they had a ride and were thankful that he was going to get Fred away from those assholes. Since they only had bruises and scrapes, they were released to go home.

Beth had the police call her uncle when they arrived. He got there about an hour after they were released.

Her Uncle Tom arrived with her cousin, Sam, in tow. Tom was 6'3" and looked like a boxer, complete with the mangled ear and scars on his chin. He turned the corner, saw Beth, ran up and picked her up in the air. He bellowed out that he would personally kill the sumbitch that hurt his little girl.

The rest of the group introduced themselves and settled in for the two-hour ride back to Smyrna. Beth acted as if she was asleep so she wouldn't have to answer Uncle Tom's questions.

Her aunt and uncle had practically raised her and were the closest things to grandparents that her kids had. Her parents had died in a car crash when she was in the 6th grade, and they always had there for her. Her cousin, Sam, was four years older and was the best big brother a girl could have.

They got to the Smyrna area, dropped the others off and took Beth to her uncle's house. Her kids had stayed there while she was away and her Aunt Sally just had to take care of her baby girl.

They agreed to tell the kids that mom had been in a car wreck, but was just fine. Beth looked in on the kids and found them still asleep since they had been up for several hours after Tom got the call. Kristie was 11, Randy was nine, and were very good kids. While their father was too busy with his new wife, Beth, Aunt Sally and Uncle Tom gave them a lot of love and education. They were very lucky kids.

Beth was exhausted. She lay down and passed out.

***

Aunt Sally woke the kids up at 10:00 a.m., fed them and asked them to play quietly while their mom slept. They begged her to let them see her, and she let them peek in on her. This helped, and they were soon on their iPads and Game Boys.

Tom got his wife and Sam off to the side and said, "Something is rotten here, I would normally believe anything our girl says, but this sound like a TV show."

Sally said, "Now Tom wait until you have all the facts and give her the benefit of the doubt. We both know that if she is keeping something to herself, it's for a good reason. Remember she was raised right and is a great woman. I trust her with my life."

Tom and Sam agreed.

Sam added, "Dad, we will kill whoever hurt her."

Tom said, "You got that shit right. Maybe we need to clean our guns."

***

"Good morning L A. I love the U...S...A.... How are all of my Prepper Buddies doing this fine day in Lower Alabama?"

"Oh, yeah, the President can kiss my redneck ass.

You won't believe the story that I'm about to tell you," John exclaimed. "Also we are simultaneously broadcasting live on FOX news. Jim O'Reilly is here in the studio and will interview us heroes.

You won't hear our story on any of those Socialist Lapdog stations. This story may even be better than my last book, and that's why it is going to be my next book, and possibly a movie." John exclaimed.

O'Reilly started the interview with Gus telling the audience about the background concerning their annual trip. Then he proceeded to have each one give a thumbnail sketch about themselves, and their backgrounds with an emphasis on what gave them the ability to survive and then prevail over these very dangerous terrorists.

John couldn't wait for the show to be over, even though it meant that being well known, as a hero would increase his book sales. He just wanted to hightail it to Smyrna to see Beth.

John had awakened that morning on a mission from the minute his eyes opened. He called the rest of the team and checked on them. All were fine, and he told them that he was okay, would do his morning show, and then be out of town for a couple of days on a trip to Nashville concerning a new shop he planned to open in that area.

He left the studio, got his Bug Out Bag and some artillery, loaded them into his old Jeep and took off towards Nashville. His Jeep was a '68 that had been modified and made better than new. Steve's shop performed all of the running gear work and the engine swap. Since John was a Prepper, he kept the motor free of all modern electronics. The Jeep didn't have any microprocessors because every Prepper knew that a solar flare or EMP would fry all of that crap.

Along the way, he burned up his iPhone asking Siri to look up addresses for Beth Fox and Elizabeth Fox in Smyrna. He got four addresses.

He also called the Commercial Realtor that had been working the Nashville area for him. John said, "Miss Woods, what have you got to show me today? I will be in the Nashville area by noon and want to look at businesses or properties. I will be there for two to three days. By the way, do you have anything in the Smyrna area?"

Miss Woods replied, "I have several in Nashville, but I'll have to check on the Smyrna area."

***

John got off Highway 65 at the 840 exit and headed over towards Smyrna. It was only 15 minutes, and he got on Highway 24 and headed west towards Smyrna. He got to exit 70, exited and headed east into Smyrna on Nissan Blvd. Frankly; there wasn't much on it for the first several miles.

Then he saw Smyrna High School on the left. This is where she taught. Too bad, it was summer break, or she could be found quickly.

He drove several more miles and saw the large Nissan plant on the right and a Wal-Mart on the left. He continued and noticed the road had changed names to Sam Ridley. Another mile or so John saw a golf course on the right, then a large airfield just behind it. He kept driving around the area for a while then drove to the first house on his list of Foxes.

He sat outside of the house and saw a family of six with a multi-racial mix. Check, not the right one.

He drove to another neighborhood in an older section of town and was sure that the house might have had some drug dealers so another no check.

He was hungry and checked the time; it was 1:30. He drove back to Sam Ridley, went to Cheddars and had a good meal and a couple of beers. Now full and feeling good he continued hunting for his honey. If he got lucky, he might even find a location for his new shop. He thought, *I hope her kids aren't a bunch of brats.* He had just finished raising Scott and Jim and didn't know if he was up to it again.

John then went to the realtor's office and spent the rest of the day looking at property. He spent the night at a hotel at the intersection of I-24 and Sam Ridley.

John got up at 6:00 a.m. determined to find Beth; he missed her. He didn't know how he fell so quickly for her, but she had also fallen for him, and that was the most important thing.

John stopped for breakfast at the Cracker Barrel, then drove down Sam Ridley and stopped to get gas. The old Jeep had a 351 Cleveland and mostly Ford running gear. Gas mileage was not a strong suit, but it could go anywhere.

He got back on I-24, headed back to exit 70, going west until he got to One Mile Lane, and turned left. He drove around until he saw the street he wanted and parked a couple of houses down from the address.

He waited for a while, a Ford 4x4 pulled into the drive, and two guys got out and went into the house. One was a real big guy, and the other was just a bit smaller. You did not want to tangle withthem. They were in the house for about 15 minutes and came out carrying a bag and several women's garments on hangers. They drove off and then John thought BINGO. Maybe Beth needed clothes because she stayed at a relative's house. He thought it was worth a try. He eased out and followed the Ford.

They only went a couple of blocks before pulling into the driveway of a nice house with a detached garage on a large lot. It was a real nice house. Two kids ran out to meet the guys and helped them carry the clothes into the house. Beth has two kids about that age, and a boy and girl match what Beth had told him. Again, he parked across the street and tried to look like he was checking a map.

Beth woke up and couldn't go back to sleep. She heard Uncle Tom and Sam come into the house and was eager to see them. She put on a housecoat, combed her hair and went out into the kitchen. Sally hugged her and gave her a cup of coffee. The guys came into the kitchen, hugged her and started asking her how she was.

Tom looked through the kitchen window and said, "Sam, come help me out at the truck for a minute.

Sam, do you see that black Jeep across the street from the Patterson's?"

Sam replied, "Yeah, and it looks just like the one parked across from Beth's house. Do you think it's one the guys who beat her up?"

Tom replied, "I don't know, but let's find out."

They went out the back door and circled back towards the Jeep. They caught John totally by surprise, and when he looked up, he had a Colt 1911a1 under his chin.

He heard, "Partner, I don't know who you are, but you are about to meet your maker if you make one wrong move."

John slowly raised his hands and told them that he was just a man lost in Smyrna trying to find Main Street.

Sam asked, "Then asshole, why is there a .45 in the seat beside you?"

John replied, "Son, there are some bad guys out there, and I know a young lady that needs some protection. I am trying to find her."

Just then, John's phone rang. John asked if he could answer it. They both said, "Sure, go ahead.

He answered and said, "Hello Darling, I hope all is well with you, and I miss you so much. Beth, do you know two big guys that are a bit over protective of you? Yes, well talk to this guy."

He handed the phone to Tom. Tom said hello and instantly recognized the voice on the phone. Tom said, "Beth do you know this guy?"

He then hung up and told John to get his ass out of the Jeep and follow them.

Before they could cross the street, Beth came running out of the house and jumped into John's arms. They kissed for a minute, and Beth said, "I guess we have some explaining to do."

Uncle Tom said, "Girl, you got that right."

When they got in the house, Aunt Sally took one look at John and said, "I saw you two kissing. Isn't he a bit old for you Beth? He is handsome in a rugged sort of way. Well, I guess love is blind."

Aunt Sally stopped and thought a minute before saying, "Where the hell did you two meet him and how did this in love thing happen so fast?"

Beth replied, "I'll fill you in on my trip and my new love."

She squeezed John's hand as she talked with Aunt Sally.

John interrupted and said, "Beth, have y'allnoticed that the police have about zero interest in solving Fred's murder?"

Uncle Tom said, "You know I expected them to be bothering Beth, what gives?"

John waved off Tom and took Beth into the kitchen and asked, "Beth do you trust your Uncle with the whole story, and before you answer the CIA, FBI and probably Home Land Security are involved.

They are making my Team out to be heroes, and your group just stays out of it. Y'all are home free no worries."

Beth said, "Yes I trust my Uncle Tom, and he could come in handy. He's a lot like you and Gus. Can I tell my friends not to worry, they are scared shitless?"

John replied, "Tell them not to worry about the police, but to keep an eye out for any strangers, or anyone following them. Tell them this is just me being overprotective."

They went back in the living room, and John told Tom and Sam to get comfortable.

Thirty minutes later Tom said, "Holy Crap, normally I would call that one tall tale. If Beth weren't part of it, I would not believe a word of it. How much danger are we in?"

John laughed and said, "You jump right in, don't you?"

They discussed their backgrounds and compared notes from their stints in the Marines and Army. Tom and Gus could have been twins. Scary thought.

Sally and Beth had made breakfast while John and Beth alternated on telling their story. Everyone enjoyed breakfast and got to know each other for about an hour.

Tom was retired from a job with a corporate security group. His team had provided training and bodyguards for corporate executives traveling to foreign countries. Sam had just gotten out of the Army and had served two tours in Afghanistan. Sam worked at Nissan, but was going to MTSU and was majoring in Law Enforcement.

Beth got off the phone with Alice, looked out the bedroom window and saw a van parked across the street. She then stepped out the back door and saw a guy on a bicycle between the houses behind her Uncle's house. She went into the living room and motioned for John to come to her.

She grabbed a pen and paper and wrote, "Someone is watching us from a van in front and guy in the hiding in back of the house."

John showed the note to Tom. John motioned that he would check out the front and Tom and Sam handle the back.

John took the pen and paper and wrote, "Capture if possible."

He showed Tom his .45, 1911a1 and the Glock. Tom and Sam both pulled out 1911's. John gave thumbs up and got Beth's attention.

He whispered, "Beth I need you to walk out the front door and go to my Jeep to distract them. I'll slide out a side window and sneak up on them. When you see us get close to their van, hide behind the Jeep. I love you."

***

Brown Suit and another guy were watching when Beth came out the front door and walked towards them. Just as they were getting nervous, she stopped at John's Jeep and opened the passenger side door. She appeared to be getting something when an arm reached in and hit the guy in the head with a gun.

Brown Suit heard, "Put your hands in the air or die."

A .45 was aimed at his chest. He started to move, and he was hit in the back of the head and passed out. John looked across the top of the van and waved the .45 at Beth.

142

He said, "This is one heavy assed gun, I hope I didn't kill the bastard."

They moved Brown Suit over and drove the van into the garage, unloaded both guys and took the van out to the street. Tom and Sam came in the back door dragging the other guy. They tied all three up in the garage.

John called Gus and told him that he needed his help and quickly explained. He told Gus that his gut told him that the shit was going to hit the fan and they needed to make sure everyone was safe until they could get information from these goons.

He then said, "Gus, you might bring some interrogation tools."

Gus said that he would get all of their families to the Bug Out location and to get his ass back to Smyrna ASAP. He would bring Scott, and the others would guard the families.

"Drive safe," John added.

Gus laughed and replied, "Drive hell! We'll be there in a couple of hours. Pick us up at the Smyrna airfield. I'll call when we're 30 minutes out."

Gus called about 3 hours later and told John he was landing the DC3 in 20 minutes. He told John that he had brought some artillery so be prepared to stuff the Jeep full. John took Tom's truck and drove to the airfield. Scott, Gus, and John loaded the truck with several M4s, ammo and his tool bag. John gave him more detail as they drove back to Tom's house.

Gus said, "There has to be something that *we are* missing, there just has to be more to this. John, I think that we stepped right in someone else's litter box just as the game was about to begin and fouled things up."

John agreed and said, "Gus I think that you are right. How the hell do we keep our loved ones from being harmed while we get to the bottom of this mess?"

Gus said, "Well the ones back home are safe. No one knows about the Bug Out Bunker except the ones in it and us. We just need to get Beth and her family safe."

They arrived at Tom's house and unloaded everything while John introduced Beth's family. Gus asked where the captives were and Tom took him to the garage. All three of the captives were gagged and tied to chairs. Sam was guarding them and had a

Bushmaster .223 aimed at Brown Suit's belly. Gus removed the gag from Brown Suit's mouth and told him not to yell.

Brown suit said, "You are way over your heads and fucking with the wrong people."

Gus slapped the crap out of him and then said, "No you are fucking with the wrong Gus."

John laughed and said, "Look Brown Suit, we'll get what we want out of you, and if you are lucky, we might let you live after you tell us what we need to know."

Gus began with Brown Suit's companion and began with waterboarding, then took a pipe and hit the soles of his feet while the others watched. Gus took some gas from a can in the garage and poured some on the guy's crotch. He began screaming and begged Gus to stop. Gus took a cigarette lighter out of his tool bag and started flicking it at the guy.

The guy said, "I'll tell you all I know, just stop."

Brown Suit yelled, "We will kill your wife and your kids if you talk."

Gus took the guy into a bedroom and the guy told him that he could not talk or his family would die. Gus took the lighter and lit the gas on the guy's crotch. The guy started talking. Gus put the fire out. The guy said that he was just a security gun for hire and did not know the overall plan of this group.

He went on to say that, they were up to something very big, it involved people from several countries, and he had overheard that the world would change in 30 days. Gus asked when he heard that. The guy said *28 days ago.*

Gus filled John in on what he had learned, and they put the next guy through the same routine and got more of the same.

John said, "Gus, Brown Suit will be tough to crack."

Gus said, "No, not at all, now here is my plan."

Gus went into the garage, got a syringe out of the bag and filled it with some blue liquid. He then proceeded to slap and beat Brown Suit up pretty severely. He then asked several questions which Brown Suit ignored.

Gus then gave him the shot of blue liquid and said, "This will make you talk."

Brown Suit woke up and pulled against the restraints. He had wet his pants and had to relieve himself very urgently. The garage was very dark, and he couldn't see anything. He heard someone talking through the door to the house. He tried to scream, but the gag just cut into his mouth. Finally, after an eternity, the door opened, and Gus came in with a candle. He was able to look through the open door and saw a Coleman lantern in the kitchen. Then, he saw John come into the room carrying a lantern.

Gus said, "Well, now are you ready to tell us what you sons of bitches did to our country?"

Brown Suit replied, "I have to go to the bathroom. What do you mean? How long was I unconscious?"

Brown Suit looked down and saw he was wearing sweat pants and a tee shirt.

Gus said, "Here is the bucket, take a dump, and then we talk."

Brown Suit said, "Why can't I use the restroom?"

John replied, "Because whatever y'alldid has taken out all power and utilities."

Brown Suit relieved himself in the bucket with guns pointed at him the whole time. He looked at the clock over the workbench and saw that the date was four days from when he was captured. He had lost four days. What the fuck was the blue stuff that had been shot into his veins and what did he tell them?

John tied him back to the chair and said, "We don't need you now. If you have a God, start praying, because when you are done, you're dead. We won't spare any food for the likes of you."

Brown Suit asked, "What happened to my men?" Gus went to the other side of the garage and pulled a tarp back. There were his guys, dead.

Gus said, "Sorry, but we got all the info from all y'all, and we just *will not* feed you."

Brown Suit began to panic and said, "You just can't kill me, I know a lot more. I know which cities were bombed in the second wave. I also know who the contacts in the USA are and some of the Iranians."

John looked at Gus and said, "That stuff won't help us so just go ahead and kill him now."

Gus said, "John, maybe he can tell us which cities got bombed, so we'll know if we have to move to avoid radiation."

John said, "Okay, talk and live." Brown Suit told them all he knew. He just thought that it had happened already. He told them there were 16 cities that were to be bombed. This wouldbe blamed on right wing Christian groups.

With the USA out of the picture, Iran could take over the Middle East. Mexico, Venezuela, and Cuba would invade the western USA and divide the southwest into equal shares.

John said, "That explains the earthquakes and loss of all electronics."

Brown Suit went on to say that DC, New York, Philadelphia, Detroit, St Louis, Miami, Chicago, San Francisco, LA, Boston, and Seattle were to be sacrificed first.

He laughed and said that what was funny is that two of the bombs came through Nashville about midnight on the day they captured him. They were for the second wave and were for Dallas and Memphis. The other bombs had been prepositioned days earlier. The last two had been delayed due to a foul up with the Home Land Security Agent who had been paid to let them get through. Two hundred thousand dollars had convinced several HLS agents that they were letting a load of cocaine slip through.

John asked, "How did you get the bombs through a city like Nashville without being caught?"

Brown Suit laughed nervously, and said, "The bombs were in special trucks that were built to be a traveling museum covering the Atomic Bombing of Hiroshima and Nagasaki. The trucks had pictures of Atomic Bomb blasts going off on both sides. One of the earthquakes was Memphis going up in flames."

Brown Suit went on saying that the two that came through Nashville started out from the port of Baltimore and came down Highway 81 to Highway 40 then the last truck would go on to Arkansas before dropping down to Dallas.

The combination of drugs and thinking that the bombs had already gone off loosened Brown Suit's tongue and he just went on and on.

Gus said, "Enough, we are running out of time."

John replied, "Kill the others and keep this sick bastard."

Gus pulled the tarp off the two and shot each in the head with his Ruger MK I. The .22 made some noise, but not enough to be heard outside the garage.

Brown Suit said, "I thought they were dead."

Gus said, "No and it's still the day we caught you; you dumb ass."

Yes, they had set the clocks ahead and fooled the bastard. No one thought it would work, but it sure as hell did.

*

Chapter 18

TEOTWAWKI
(The End Of The World As We Knew It.)

Smyrna, TN

May 22, 2020

Beth's family home
Smyrna, TN

John yelled for the others to come to the living room. He told them the cliff notes version and said that they only had 16 hours before the bombs were to be detonated.

They discussed calling the police, FBI and the Department of Homeland Security, but quickly decided that no one would believe them and the authorities would swarm on them.

They already knew that the Department of HLS, FBI, and CIA were compromised. Who could they trust? They agreed that Tom would call some contacts in the Marines and Gus would call his Army contacts. They would give them warning about the bombs and get off the cell phones quickly. John and Gus would warn their families and friends in Mobile.

John said, "We have to stop two trucks from leaving the Nashville area at all cost. They both contain nukes; one is going to Dallas and one to Memphis. They would ruin the whole path from Dallas to Columbus, Ohio. We have 16 hours to plan and execute a hijacking and then get rid of these bombs."

They started planning when suddenly Sally spoke up, "I don't think you want to attack them in Nashville, I watched 24 on TV, and I just know the bombs will explode when you attack the trucks."

Tom said, "I don't think that could happen if we quickly kill the driver and guards."

Beth said, "But, John, we can't take the chance."

The men discussed this for a while and finally agreed that it was not worth the chance. They had to plan an attack that would yield the least possible loss of life and keep Nashville free of radiation and fallout.

Tom said, "John, you and Gus plan the attack while we load up the weapons and head out I-40 East to catch the trucks as far from Nashville as possible.

About halfway to Knoxville is our best bet. Sam and I will search the map for the best place to attack the trucks that will yield the best case for survival."

They took John's Jeep, Tom's pickup and Brown Suit's car. Gus and John rode in the Jeep, Scott in Brown Suit's car and Sam and Tom in Tom's pickup which was loaded to the gills with weapons and ammo. They stayed in touch with Tom's cell phones in case the bad guys were monitoring John and Gus's phones.

They were just past Lebanon when Scott had the best idea of his life. He called Sally and said, "Please put the speaker on. Ladies, y'all need to go to as many different stores as possible and buy food water, ammunition, gold, and silver. If this shit is true, we will need to survive for about six months before we can grow our own food.

Use the cash from the GAO. Max out the credit cards. Spend it all. If nothing happens, we can always return everything.

Call close family members and tell them to do the same. Don't argue, just tell them and hang up. Call them while driving to the stores. Get back home and hunker down. Phones won't work. Tom says that there are two walkie-talkies in an old ammo can in the garage. Don't get them out until after the lights won't come on."

He then called his Mom, Gus's wife, Beth and a couple of friends in Mobile. He thought that he should do more, but that was the best he could do on such short notice. He told his Dad and got a verbal pat on the back.

***

East Tennessee

The driver of the lead truck said, "Jimmy, I have never been paid so well just to deliver a rolling museum to Dallas."

Jimmy thought the driver was a dumbass and got tired of the idle chatter. He was being paid more to make sure the driver got the truck to Dallas on time. He was sanctioned to kill the driver if he got in the way of delivering the truck on time.

He replied, "Don't you ever shut up?"

The driver said, "Sorry if I'm bothering you, but it gets lonely on the road. Hey, there's a truck stop up ahead; we need fuel. I gotta take a piss and get something to eat."

The truck stop was halfway between Crossville and Lenoir City. Scott was in the lead about a mile ahead of the rest when he saw the truck stop. He called John and told him that he was going to make a drive through and make sure they weren't behind the building.

In a couple of minutes, Scott called and said, "Bingo, Dad, they both just pulled in and are sitting out on the left side, there is one guy in the cab of each one."

John replied, "We will be there in a minute."

They pulled up beside Scott and Gus said, "We will kill the guards then get the two out of the restaurant and kill them. Then we will take the trucks on Highway 70 and stash them in the first barn we see. Scott in five minutes, go in the restaurant and get the others to come to their trucks. We'll take care of the guards."

Gus and John each took one of the trucks. They crawled under the trucks until they got where they could climb up into the cab and see the guards. They shot one round into the guards' heads, got behind the wheel and got ready to haul ass. Scott and the two drivers came out of the restaurant walking very fast towards the trucks. Sam and Tom jumped out and shot both of them.

Gus and John headed out of the truck stop towards Highway 70; the others took their vehicles and followed. In about 20 minutes, they saw a big old barn off by itself; they drove both trucks in and closed the doors.

They only had about 50 minutes before the first bombs were to go off. They loaded as much artillery that would fit in a Jeep with five guys. John got back on I-40 West and hauled ass. He was passing a string of cars going 90 mph when the car's lights went out, and the cars slowed to a stop. They saw a bright light over the horizon and in a few seconds heard a deep rumble.

Gus said, "John, slow up some, some of these folks may not get off the road. We don' want to crash into them."

The scene ahead of them reminded him of several books that he had read about the after effects of an EMP blast. There were cars pulled over, and a few crashed cars. People were standing beside their cars in the dark. Almost all waved for them to stop.

They saw a bright flash that lit up the sky a couple of miles ahead and then heard an explosion coming from the same direction, and guessed it was a plane falling out of the sky.

It only took a couple of minutes to get to the site of the crash and what they saw was something they would never forget. The plane had tried to land on the interstate, but the road had several cars and a semi in their landing path. The plane had hit several cars and the semi and had disintegrated into many small sections and two large ones.

They saw several people still strapped in their seats which had been burned beyond recognition. The plane was a 737, and there were hundreds of bodies lying everywhere. They had to drive around the wreckage and bodies but saw no one alive.

Gus said, "Guys, say a prayer for all of the poor souls that died tonight."

They all said prayers for those poor souls, but all of them also prayed for the ones who had to rebuild this fractured country.

***

Blue suit was back at home at a fancy restaurant in Virginia when he saw the bright flash coming from DC. He ran to the door just in time

151

to see and feel the shock wave and see it blow windows out all around him.

He told his wife, "The dirty bastard nuked us before we could kill his sorry ass."

***

The U.S. President, President Chaves, President Ahamedad and the new dictator of Chile were in Paraguay for a top-secret meeting to begin discussions on developing a lasting peace for the entire world.

They were staying at the country estate of the richest man in South America, Pablo Cortez, who had been pushing for this meeting for years. Their goal was one world government with peace for all and only one military to keep all countries equal. They had met all day and were now guests of Pablo for a rather extravagant dinner. An aide came to Pablo, and he quickly excused himself. He took the phone and listened.

He said, "Bueno, send the right hand to me. Did you get the required information? Gracias, you will be rewarded when you finish the mission."

Returning to his dinner guests, he said, "I am sorry for leaving my distinguished guests, but one of my children needed advice." They all laughed and got back to running the world.

It was only 15 minutes later when the President's aide came to him, and he excused himself.

He asked, "This is the secure phone?"

The aide said, "Yes."

The President politely asked for privacy.

"Hello, okay, now when will the event be concluded? Yes, L. A. and Miami?" The President hung up and went back into the dining room.

He went over to Ahamedad and whispered, "It's begun, my friend."

Just then, several staff members came into the room yelling for everyone to come to the sitting room to see the TV.

The President's aide said, "Mr. President we have to get you to your plane, the USA is under attack."

152

The President followed them to the limo.

***

John was weaving from side to side of the highway to avoid stalled cars, and several people tried to get them to stop. He ignored them and drove past as carefully as he could.

Gus waved his .45 at several who tried to stop them. They all moved out of the way when confronted. Right before they got to Lebanon, they saw a guy in the middle of the road yelling and waving; he jumped in front of the Jeep and ran them off the road. Gus jumped out of the Jeep, hit him across the face with the .45 and knocked him out. Scott ran up and saw a woman and two kids on the ground.

All were crying; the woman was pregnant and very much ready to deliver. She told Scott that her contractions were getting closer together. Scott went to his Dad and explained the situation. They knew they had to either deliver the baby or get them to a hospital. Civility had not, yet, been completely lost in this new world. Civilization, however, was now absolutely dead and gone.

They loaded the woman into the Jeep and left Gus and Scott to take care the man and his children.

John drove straight to the hospital in Lebanon. They pulled up in front of the hospital, but there was no one to greet them.

Tom got out and went in to get someone to take care of the woman and finally found a nurse.

She told them that most of the staff went home to be with their families. She told him to bring the woman in, and she would do her best. John brought the woman in and left her with the nurse.

They drove back to get the others and hoped that the woman and baby survived. They loaded the man and kids up and drove back to the hospital, dropped them off and drove away.

Scott said, "A lot of people are not going to survive the next 30 days. Diabetics, people with pacemakers, dialysis patients and anyone needing specialized medical care will go first. Starvation will kill millions. Gangs and Outlaws will kill the next wave. We will be left with a solid group of survivors at the end."

He was met with a stony silence, with everyone nodding their heads.

153

Tom got on the walkie-talkie and was amazed, but thrilled that the walkie talkie worked.

Beth had a million questions and did not stop talking. She finally calmed down when Tom said that they were all okay and the mission was successful.

He asked her how the shopping trip had gone. She replied that they received many questions, but all of the stores had loved their business. Beth added that the gun shop in Hendersonville only wanted to sell two boxes of each type of ammo, but she got the manager and gave him $1,000, and he sold them every 12 gauge, .223, 9mm, .45, .22 and .308 in the store. She had purchased over 10,000 rounds of ammo.

Sally had purchased enough food to feed them for a year. Sally grabbed the walkie-talkie and said, "Tom, I bought a bunch of rice and beans."

Beth got back on and said, "I bought several hand pumps that will pump gas from storage tanks."

That put a smile on John's face.

What Sally didn't have time to say was that she and Beth had contacted Alice, Bill, several of their friends and family and told them to do the same, but that they had to go to LaVergne and Antioch so there wouldn't be a bunch of people making a run on the same stores. Sally drove their RV to Sam's Club in Murfreesboro and practically wiped out their beans, rice, salt, sugar, spices and canned meat departments. Sally gave $100 each to a bunch of stock boys to motivate them to load the RV up at a record pace. They all made several trips and had to make up a bunch of stories about why they were stocking up on so much food.

John's were the only lights on the highway and every time they passed a stalled car; the people tried to get them to stop. They got to the Smyrna exit on Highway 840 when they saw a policeman waving for them to stop and help at a wreck at the top of the ramp. They went off the road to go around him while he frantically waved and shot his service pistol in the air. Gus had his .45 aimed at the cop and was glad that he did not have to kill him.

There would be many choices to make in the future, and most would be between good and evil, but many were like this one, family over strangers. Another layer of civilization peeled away like the skin of an onion.

John said, "Gus, in all of the books that I have read in situations like this, the cops or bad guys always try to commandeer any vehicle that will run."

Gus replied, "TRY." He then waved his .45 Colt 1911 and said, "From my cold dead hands." He added, "That applies to my damn truck, also."

John asked, "Hey, what about the DC3, will it fly?" Gus thought for a minute and said, "Damn good question. It probably will, but all of the modern avionics will be fried. No radio and no GPS. I can use one of the portable short wave radios to communicate with you."

***

Mobile, Alabama

The Mexican broke into John's house and placed JoAnne's head on the mantel. He then went to Gus' house and left a hand on the kitchen table. He laughed and thought that this would scare the shit out of John and his friends.

He would come back in a couple of days and start the campaign of terror ending with all of the pendejos dead. The murderer had missed them by hours and did not realize that they would never come back to their houses.

***

North of Mobile, Alabama

The Bug Out Bunker was about 20 miles northwest of Mobile. John had bought an old farm with 200 acres that had an old, but nice house, and a 5-acre lake that was fully stocked. He buried twenty overseas shipping containers for emergency housing and storage.

155

The facility was designed to support 20 people for 18 months as long as they liked rice, beans, fish and any vegetables could be raised.

There was an old house with a well and plenty of garden space. He had planted over a hundred fruit and nut trees to get it ready to survive at least a year without outside help.

John paid a local farmer to grow a large vegetable garden and let him sell most of the crop at the farmers' market. John and Scott took lessons from the farmer on how to raise a garden and became quite proficient.

There were a dirt landing strip and hanger for John's old four-seater Cessna and the antique crop duster just north of the house. John had flown in and out several times.

Gus and John used the Cessna for vacations and trips around the southeast, but it would only carry four people plus a lot of gear. The plane was from the early 60's and had all of the original EMP proof equipment plus modern avionics. John made sure that it would be useable after a nuke or solar flare.

Ann was flitting around the place as if she owned it and that pissed Robin off. Robin didn't hate Ann, but she knew that John was a great guy and Ann should have stayed with him. Hell, Ann had even brought her boy toy, Dan, to the bunker. Robin had been slow to convert to the Prepper lifestyle but was now as much into it as Gus and John.

Scott had called Robin and Steve and had told them to round up the family and close friends. They were to get to the Bug Out Bunker before midnight. Robin brought her family and chased down Jim's girlfriend. Steve called Ann, and Scott's girlfriend, Joan. He told them to get their families to the Bug Out Bunker. The immediate families all arrived, but most of the extended families thought it was crazy. They were told to bring a week's worth of clothes and all the food, water and weapons that they could load into their cars.

Gus also told them to bring all of the antique cars that they could find. Steve loaded up his three old hotrods on a car carrier and brought them to the bunker. Several brought their hot rods and old pickups. Only fifteen total people showed up against the thirty that John had expected.

Ann had tried to find JoAnne, but there was no answer when she called. She even ran by JoAnne's house, but no one was there. Ann was very worried about her friend and knew that John would not have them bug out to the bunker if things weren't going to get very bad, very quick.

While John bored her, she did respect his judgment on prepping for disaster. He had trained her how to shoot, hunt and fish. While she was a city girl, she could handle herself.

Steve gathered everyone and filled them in on what he knew and what was probably going to happen over the next few days. He started giving work assignments when Ann's boyfriend, Dan, balked and said that he did not come here to work and was only here to please Ann.

Steve told him, "You are right you don't have to work, but if you don't work you don't stay. So, decide now if you want to contribute or get the hell back to Mobile."

Dan replied, "I will stay as Ann's guest, and no 'Nigrah' is going to make me leave."

Steve walked over to Ann and said, "Get his sorry ass out of here before I shoot him."

Dan charged Steve and grabbed his left arm. Steve turned and kicked Dan in the nuts and hit him on the chin with his pistol. Dan started to charge Steve again when Robin fired a shot into the ground at Dan's feet.

She yelled, "I will shoot you if you don't get the fuck out of here now. Get in your car and go."

Dan begged Ann to go with him, but she told him that he was a lazy coward and that he was lucky that Steve hadn't killed him on the spot. Dan left and was never seen again.

Ann apologized for Dan's behavior and went to the house ashamed about the whole situation.

Robin came in and said, "Ann, no one is mad at you. Yes, Dan is a racist jerk, but you set him straight and sent him packing. That's what counts."

Ann said, "Robin, I never heard you cuss before."

Robin hugged Ann and said, "That turd bird pissed me off. Steve is a good friend, and the color of his skin makes no difference to me."

Ann thanked her and rejoined the team.

Steve got the entire team together and told them that they only had a few days before outsiders would try to take their food and water. He went on to say that, he was starting round the clock guards and training for everyone on how, and when, to shoot.

Jim replied, "Steve I can help with training in hand to hand combat, and shooting."

***

Smyrna, Tennessee

They arrived at Tom's house and immediately had to explain to the neighbors how they had a vehicle that would run. Tom handled that and had to get a little rough with a couple of guys that wanted to take it from him.

John went to the Jeep, got one of the short wave radios out of their metal box and called for Steve at the Bunker. He gave the designated call sign repeatedly for about 30 minutes when he heard Steve's voice.

"Hey, Buddy how are you and the folks doing up north? We are all fine down here. I rounded them all up, and we circled the wagons at the fort. We could not find JoAnne, but nearly everyone else made it."

John replied, "There is a lot of chaos, but we are all fine and may be visiting you in a week or so."

Steve replied, "Good, watch your ass on the road. There will be bad guys. We are hearing gunfire towards town and can see several large fires on that horizon."

John signed off and felt relieved, and terribly sad.

***

By 7:00 a.m., all of the friends and relatives of the group from the immediate area had arrived. Most had to walk, but a few had older trucks or cars and drove to Tom's house. There were 18 adults and 21 children counting John, Gus, and Scott. These were all good people who should get along and help each other survive.

After everyone had a great breakfast, Gus gathered all of the adults and said, "We have several decisions to make and have to set

158

a plan to survive the next 90 days and then a longer term plan for the next year."

They all listened.

Gus said, "Don't everyone speak at once." He then laughed.

Tom replied, "Gus, John, you and I have the experience to lead this group. Most of our family does not know what has just happened, much less how to survive it."

Gus backed up and spent about 15 minutes explaining what happened and what was likely to happen. He told them how, soon, sane people would try to kill them for a loaf of bread. They all listened and started to ask a thousand questions.

John stood up and said, "There are several questions that have to be answered now. They are:

Where are we going to get food and water?

How are we going to protect ourselves?

What will we do for medical care?

Where can we protect ourselves with the fewest losses?

How will we heat our homes?

How do we handle sewage?

How do we handle looters, general bad guys and

anyone, who will anyone try to take our stuff?"

Again, they all listened then suddenly broke out in numerous discussions.

Alice said, "Won't the government come to help us? We can just stay in our houses and wait on them, can't we?"

Gus replied, "The government has its hands full with the big cities and probably guarding against foreign invaders. They won't be much help to small cities and the open country. I hate to scare people, but the government may cause more harm to us than help."

Beth caught John off to the side and said, "John, these guys are great people, but you and Tom need to take charge and tell us what to do. They will either go with your plans or leave and take their chances."

John agreed. John got Tom off to the side and told him about his discussion with Beth. They both agreed to take charge and let the chips fall where they may.

Tom banged a spoon on a pot to get their attention and said, "John, Gus and I are going to take over the leadership of this group. We are trained to handle bad situations and know what has to be done. If you agree, stay here; if not, please leave."

One of Tom's neighbors, Will, spoke up and said that this was a democracy and everyone had a say in what they were going to do.

John told the group, "No, we have lived in a Constitutional Republic with the principles of democracy. Those days are gone, you all can do whatever you want, but the people who stay in this house when I am done speaking will follow orders, or be removed from the group."

Will said, "That's not fair, we should all have a say in how the group is led and how we do things."

John heard several tell him to go. John said, "Will, you are right, it is not fair, so what, new world, new rules. Those that agree stay, those that do not agree, please leave now."

Will started to argue again, but Tom grabbed him by the arm and shoved him out the door. Gus and Tom watched him and his family walk down the street telling all that would listen about how, "Those assholes have plenty of food, but want everything for themselves."

Tom got the group back together and said, "We will be asking for your input on all plans, but we will make the final decisions. As a team, we need everyone except John, Gus, and I, to go into town and get more supplies. We need more running trucks to haul supplies, and in case, we have to haul ass. Older diesel powered trucks may still run.

Scott and Sam will coordinate the efforts. Bill, we need you to see if you can get some kind of tanker or tank on a trailer so we can stockpile fuel.

We don't have even an inkling of the skills we will need to make this enclave work, but right now, we need a Doctor, Nurses, Veterinarian and all the medical supplies we can find. Don't take "no" for an answer.

Buy anything, and everything you can think of that, we might need. Spend your cash, max the credit cards, today.

Remember, if things sort themselves out, we can always return what we buy. I do, however, promise you that money, as we know it, will not be worth anything 24 hours from now."

160

The government was concentrating its efforts on helping the areas that were supportive of the president and the liberal agenda. Tennessee would never see any help and was to be targeted for help of another kind.

Over the next several weeks, the Department of Home Land Security quickly took control of Baltimore, Boston, Harrisburg, Columbus, Charleston, Jacksonville and Mobile to try to begin taking control of the nation's remaining resources.

DHS tried to take control of Fort Bragg, Fort Knox, and Pope Airbase, but the Military Commanders refused them access to the bases.

The Marines had to return fire on the DHS troops when they tried to ram through a checkpoint. The 50 DHS members were killed, wounded or taken prisoner.

This caused major infighting between DHS, the President, and the Joint Chiefs. The Joint Chiefs stood firm, no civilians would take direct control of the military, and the military would not take up arms against the United States Citizens.

In a private meeting of the Joint Chiefs with the President and the Secretary of Defense, the President was told that the Military would protect the country against any overreaching by the President.

They would help keep the peace, but would not violate their oath to defend the Constitution of the United States of America.

The Military leaders were very thankful to John and Gus for the last minute warning since it allowed them to quickly cut their losses and arm the troops. It also enabled them to prepare for attacks from a dozen enemy countries. The military quickly began bringing our troops home and began preparations to defend this country, at their disposal, to include, in dire circumstances, the potential use of thermo-nuclear weapons.

***

John, Tom, and Gus met for a couple of hours while the others foraged for supplies. They had agreed that their houses in Smyrna were not defensible; however, John's bunker was. This was the major decision that had to be made. It was 450 miles from Smyrna to Mobile, and the roads were packed with stalled cars, desperate people, and many other perils.

They decided that they needed the safety of the country, the seclusion and security that it provided.

They needed dependable transportation, fuel, and intelligence about what lay ahead on Highway 65 to Mobile. Their plan was to obtain vehicles, fuel, and supplies during the next week then head to Mobile to make a stand at The Bunker.

Gus said that he would fly to Mobile and travel as slow as possible along their route so he could scout for potential dangers. He would take the children with him and take as many supplies as possible.

***

The next day Sam was on guard at the front of the house when he noticed a crowd gathering at the end of the street. He called for Tom. They watched the crowd for a while and saw several were drinking and most had guns. Tom went into the house, got the other men and took them into the garage.

Tom told them, "I may be wrong, but I think those people are about to come down here and try to take our supplies and trucks."

Gus said, "I guess we must remember Thermopile. They'll have to come and take them."

John added, "Let's go out in force and set up a perimeter about three houses down, so we shoot on their home ground and not ours. Arm the women and have the kids duck."

One man broke out of the crowd and headed towards Tom's house; the crowd followed. Gus had the men set up behind cars and a stone fence. He stepped out of the shadows and told them to stop.

Gus asked, "What are y'all doing out here late at night making all this noise?"

The lead guy said, "That's none of your business, old man, now get the hell out of my way before l put you permanently out of my way."

162

Gus leveled a 12 gauge at the guy's stomach and said, "Look, big boy, we don't want trouble so tell me what you want."

The guy said, "We want some of those trucks and food that y'all have been stockpiling for the last few days. Give us half, and we will let you keep the other half."

Gus replied, "Get your ass back home before you get killed."

The guy raised his rifle and started to point it at Gus just when Gus shot him in the gut and dived behind a tree. Hell arrived; these neighbors were no match for Gus and his crew.

John shot two before they could take aim; they fell dead in the middle of the street. Tom and his son took out two more, and the fight was over.

The rest dropped their guns, and John made them sit in the street with their fingers locked behind their head. There were five dead, three wounded and six captured. Just when they were putting zip ties on their hands, a small group of women came walking slowly towards them with a white flag.

Several of the women broke down when they saw their husbands and boyfriends dead in the street. One ran over to John and slapped him.

John pushed the woman away and told her, "Your man got just what he deserved, and if any of you try to attack us again you will be shot.

Y'all need to get your asses in gear and figure out how to survive without stealing from us because the government will not help you. They may, in fact, be your greatest nightmare. Send someone down here to get this trash, or we will burn them where they lay."

One of the women walked up to John and said, "I am sorry, we tried to talk them out of this, but the ones that came out to fight were mostly drunk and worthless before this mess started."

John told her, "I'm sorry that we had to shoot them, but we won't allow anyone to steal what we worked hard to get."

The woman went back and got some men to come and get the bodies and, as they left, she promised that there would be no more trouble. John took her and her husband off to the side and gave them a 15-minute course on survival. He also told them that they would leave some food to help them get started. They thanked him and left.

They left several men to make sure that there was no further trouble. Then Gus came out from behind a tree holding a hand on his ass and limping.

John saw him first and asked, "Gus did you get shot in the butt?"

Gus replied, "Yes. That sumbitch got a lucky shot off before I dropped him."

They took Gus into the kitchen and made him lie down on the table with his ass in the air and his pants at his ankles.

Sally and Sam cleaned the wound and probed for the bullet, luckily it had only penetrated just below the skin. They gave him some pain meds and antibiotics and, put a patch on him. John came over, slapped him on the ass and told him to get up and get to work. Gus gave him a good cussing then apologized for 10 minutes to the ladies who were all laughing.

Still laughing, Sally said, "Gus, don't you go get shot in your butt again, that danged thing is just way too hairy to be pickin' pellets out of."

*

Chapter 19

On The Road to Mobile

Highway 65 Mayhem

May 27, 2020

Smyrna, Tennessee

They spent several days scrounging for supplies and trucks to carry them in but knew they had to get on the road before chaos set in across the land.

Gus, Tom, and John met and decided that they had to leave on the 28th. They got everybody together, and John said, "We are leaving tomorrow.

They loaded all day on the 27th, had a hot breakfast and prepared to leave.

Gus, Bill, Sally and several of the women loaded the children into the DC3 and got ready to fly to Mobile. The others left a half hour after Gus took off so that he could radio back about any issues along the road to Highway 65 and the first part of I-65. He was in pain and tried to sit on the cheek that hadn't been probed, but had to shift from time to time and winced in pain at every move. He did not want to take too many pain meds while flying. That was never a perfect plan, but Gus could still report to John any major roadblocks or impassable bridges.

The plane was loaded with supplies and a bunch of kids. Gus had all of the adults armed with binoculars and M 16s. He had instructed them on how to spot trouble on the ground and in the air.

Since the plane's modern electronics had been fried by the EMP blasts, Gus was following the roads as if he were driving a car. This matched the route that the convoy had to travel so Gus flew as slow as the bird would go and stay in the air. He kept the plane high enough that run of the mill average idiot wouldn't take a shot at the plane, but low enough for the spotters to see what was happening on the highway.

Gus loped along until just before the Tennessee/ Alabama border, then shoved it into wide open to get on down to Mobile. They had not seen anything that worried Gus, and he thought that he could get back in the air soon enough to survey the next leg before the team got there.

***

Gus and the spotters were flying above the clouds and did not see the helicopter or Humvees parked below the bridge on I-65 South between Huntsville and Decatur. There were five Humvees and three Black SUVs hiding below the overpass. They had blocked the road and were turning people back. They told them to go home and that the government would take care of them. A few resisted. They were murdered, right where they stood.

The men operating the roadblock heard the plane fly over and alerted their commander.

The Captain asked, "Sir, I thought that only government planes would be airborne after the attack, could this be a foreign power exploring our defenses?"

The Leader replied, "While I can't be certain, I would guess the plane is from one of our military branches."

The Captain replied, "But Sir we called them on every frequency available to no avail."

The leader was not concerned and told everyone to get back to their duties. He had never been in the military and was not thinking about threats; this would be his downfall one day.

The leader of this DHS Team was surprised that his fellow Southerners were so resistant to his authority, but told his team that

166

they only had to execute a few and the rest would fall in line. He was on a tour of his new area of responsibility and had to visit Ft Rucker, Redstone Arsenal, and several major National Guard Commands to make sure that he had their support in keeping the peace and helping his people through this crisis.

The President had personally met with the fifty DHS Commanders chosen to govern each one of the states. He told them that they were his "Field Marshalls" and would represent their respective state until the Federal government could sort out the traitors from those friendly to the Government.

Their only mandate was to bring law and order out of the chaos and root out those who opposed the President's will. He told them that they only had one year to have their operations ready to support his new program.

Deke Jones was 55 years old and had been a lifelong liberal politician with major connections in DC. He was a black man from a poor family who always tried to prove that he was as good as his other schoolmates. He had been a star running back at Auburn and helped New England win several Super Bowls.

He was, for a short time, a darling of Hollywood. He had been in several utterly forgettable movies and was married to super liberal movie star Jane Joplin.

Deke was born and raised in Mobile, Alabama and would soon make that city the new capital of that state.

Each of the "Field Marshalls" was given a minimum of one thousand DHS agents, ten helicopters, one hundred armored vehicles and enough weapons and ammo to start a small war.

They all wore black fatigues and boots topped off with black body armor. Most were a mixture of long-term, big city, law enforcement officers and raw recruits hurried into service 90 days ago. Their main attribute was loyalty to superiors and not asking questions.

Deke had opened his combination DHS and FEMA office in Mobile a year ago. It was off Airport Boulevard about halfway between the airport and Big Creek Lake. The building was located at an older manufacturing complex. His office occupied the original front offices for the aircraft company that had occupied the buildings for 30 years.

There were three buildings with over 1,500,000 sq. ft. of total space and had double fences around the 120-acre compound. At first glance, the compound looked like a prison due to the razor ribbon wire on top of both fences and the guard shacks at all entrances.

The citizens of Mobile were told that this major complex would be used to protect the Homeland, and would focus on efforts to help when disasters struck the southeast.

The Mayor and many distinguished citizens attended the big ribbon cutting ceremony when the DHS office was opened nine months ago. Local citizens asked what would be stored in the large empty warehouses. They were told emergency equipment, food and first aid supplies for disasters were to be stored.

With this cover story, no one cared about the numerous train cars unloaded day after day. The armored cars, Humvees, weapons, ammunitions and food filled the largest building.

All of the buildings had been rebuilt on the inside with no changes apparent from the outside. Each wall was reinforced to withstand hurricanes or earthquakes, and several bomb shelters were constructed over 100 feet below ground level.

All buildings had access to large underground water, gas and diesel storage tanks. The interior walls were lined with steel. All doors and windows had metal coverings.

Several large diesel generators were delivered and stored. The generators were designed to supply sufficient electricity for a medium sized town. Since the generator area was restricted, it was unnoticed that each of these huge generators was stored in a metal cage.

There were living quarters for over 2,000 people when necessary in the hardened buildings. Construction had begun on three five-story apartment buildings at the back of the lot that could house an army.

**

Tom and his son, Sam, led John's group out of Smyrna on Highway 24 East. They stayed about a quarter mile ahead of the main group looking for roadblocks and trouble in general.

They were driving a pickup that had steel plating welded to the front back and doors for some protection against small arms. They stayed in near constant contact with John who had Beth, Alice and Bill in the Jeep.

Everyone in the convoy was armed and stayed vigilant against attacks.

The main column, followed by another pickup was guarding the rear of the group. The supply trucks were positioned in the middle of the convoy because Gus and John felt they would be major targets for any bandits.

They immediately began passing people still walking along the highway trying to get home. The group stopped a couple of times to give water and a bit of food to families with small kids but quickly knew that they would never get home if this continued. They also could not spare food for everyone on the highway.

They drove around these folks, and people cursedthem or had rocks thrown at them. John told everyone to poke a gun out both side windows, and the rock throwing would stop.

They were on HWY 840 about halfway between Interstate 24 and Interstate 65 when they saw a group of rough looking people suddenly come out of the woods and created an obstruction in the middle of the highway.

There were about 40 adults and 60 children ranging in age from toddlers to teens. They were all dirty and looked like they had not eaten in a week. The lead vehicle approached them, and the group quickly blocked the road.

Tom slid to a stop and then backed up about a hundred feet when the group charged at them. Tom fired his pistol over their heads, and the crowd stopped and then slowly walked towards Tom and Sam. Tom backed up again, but the crowd kept coming at them. Tom shot two rounds into the dirt, and they stopped again. This time a single man walked towards them with his hands raised in the air.

He stopped about ten feet from the pickup and yelled, "You are not getting through here without giving us half of your cars and half of your food and water."

Tom replied, "I only see a couple of guns in your group, just how will you take our stuff?"

The man replied, "We have Molotov cocktails and will burn your cars to the ground if you try to get through without sharing."

Tom said, "Okay, let me check with our leader." Tom drove back to the main group and filled them in.

John and Tom were discussing backtracking and going around these bandits when Beth said, "I'm guessing that this will happen several more times. If we backtrack every time, we will never get home. Let's shoot the leader, and the rest of the bastards will scatter."

John and Tom agreed. The plan was to drive up to tell them to get off the roads by 100 yards or die. If they did not move, the leader would be shot. If they still didn't move, keep shooting the adult men until the threat was removed.

Four trucks with ten men drove down to the bandits. They stopped about fifty feet away, and John yelled, "Get off this road and get out of sight or we kill you first and then the rest if you don't get gone."

The man that had walked up and talked the first time shrank back into the crowd and hid.

An old woman came out of the crowd and said, "I am the leader, and I know you gentlemen wouldn't shoot an unarmed lady."

John saw several men light several of the firebombs. He raised his M 16 and shot the woman right between the eyes. He then yelled at the rest of the group, "Your leader is a dead crook who thought she could rob us. Get gone or die."

Several of the people started shooting and tried to hit the trucks with the Molotov cocktails, but they were too far away. John's team quickly shot nine of the men. Sadly, even this did not stop the group. The men and women kept charging the trucks.

John said, "Shoot all of the adults and anyone else that try to harm us."

The gunfire was horrible, and bodies began piling up. Only a few of the kids tried to throw the firebombs. They died quickly.

Another inevitable layer of civilization's onion peeled away. The new reality was now family, or clan was all that mattered. Only the strong survive in this brave new world.

Only five adults and most of the young ran away from the fight and escaped into the woods. They rounded up several of the children and began questioning them about why their parents had tried to rob them.

One of the older girls said, "They wanted your trucks and guns, we don't have any trucks that run and only a few guns."

John asked, "Did they do this becausey'allare hungry?

170

The girl said, "No we live on a big farm back in the woods and have plenty of food and water."

John said, "We are sorry about your parents."

The girl stopped him and said, "Most of us were kidnapped years ago and have been used as farm labor and other bad things."

She was thirteen and a beautiful blond headed girl beneath the grime and dirt. John took her to the side and asked, "I hate to put you on the spot, but are any of these kids, besides you, worth saving. I mean, are any of them as bad as the adults?"

She looked him in the eyes and said, "Most are good, but some of the boys were rewarded with their choice of the younger girls. A couple of the girls are really bad, also."

John knew he was taking a chance, but he questioned several other girls and got the same story.

One older girl had a very different story about how their parents were starving and desperate. John weeded out the bad apples and told them to head back to the farm. They left. There were twelve children left that John felt good about, nine girls and three boys below five years of age.

John waved for the rest of the group to join them and had the shortest town meeting in history. The bottom line was that he wanted them to accept the children and raise them as their own. All but a few agreed, so it is written, so it shall be done. John's ragtag band now had, even more, kids. They ranged from thirteen to two years old. The women took over their care and loaded them up, and the band of wanderers took off again for Mobile.

***

Gus was about an hour out of Mobile when he got on the radio and called the compound to let Steve know that they would arrive soon.

Steve informed him that all was well and that he would check the runway to make sure that it was clear.

Steve took a pickup, drove the length of the runway and found all was okay. He then started checking the perimeter of the compound to make sure that the fences were intact and that the guards were guarding the place. He found all was going as planned until he got to the south side of the compound.

171

One of the guards saw him and said, "I was just about to call you on the Walkie talkie. There are several guys out there about 250 yards with field glasses looking us over."

Steve aimed his rifle at the figures and looked at them with the nine-power scope.

They peered back at him then quickly hid in the brush. Steve had a very bad feeling about this and wished Gus was here. Steve knew he could hold his own in a firefight, but Gus knew tactics. He knew how to fight a war.

Jim was training most of the women and a couple of men on shooting safety, how to reload their weapons and improving accuracy.

He was using pellet rifles and .22 pistols to train the newcomers to firearms to conserve ammo. They were all doing very well. He looked up and saw Steve waving as he drove towards them.

Steve gathered all of the men that were not on guard duty and told them about the situation. He needed five volunteers to go with him to check out this bunch that was watching them.

The ad hoc 6-man team grabbed AR15s, 9mm Glocks and plenty of ammo. They met on the north side of the main house. Steve had them slide into the woods that ran on the west side of the property to remain unseen as they began working their ways south. It only took about 20 minutes to work their way to within 50 yards of where the strangers had ducked into the woods.

Steve and one of the volunteers crawled another 40 yards towards the strangers when they heard voices.

One voice said, "Yes they have a lot of guns, and when they got here they unloaded a bunch of what looked like food and water."

Another replied, "And we will take all of it away from them when our reinforcements arrive."

Steve saw three guys sitting on the edge of the woods and knew what he had to do. He shot four times and dropped all three.

As he rushed up to them, one tried to raise his rifle. Steve shot him then put a head shot into the others.

***

Tom was driving, and they were about 40 miles north of the Alabama border when the windshield exploded in their face. He swerved off the road and got the truck stopped when several bullets slammed into the truck.

He yelled at Sam to duck when he saw Sam slumped in the seat with blood all over his chest. He pushed Sam down below the metal armor and checked the wound. Sam was hit in the shoulder. If Tom could get the bleeding stopped, he should be okay.

Tom was busy with Sam when a shadow went across the side window. He looked up and saw about ten men charging towards him. They all wore black BDUs and were heavily armed with M4s and side arms. They also had body armor and hand grenades on their chests.

He carefully aimed and started dropping them with carefully aimed shots to their legs and groin. Just when he knew that they would be overrun, he saw the enemy begin dropping like flies. He saw bullets hitting them. He could not hear any gunfire.

What he couldn't see was the DC3 circling above him with three men firing their AR15s down on the DHS forces from a thousand feet.

Their fire was not accurate, but they made up for it with volume. Gus spotted three Humvees and a couple of 5-ton trucks parked behind a stand of trees and motioned to the rest to be ready to fire on them. He circled several times and could not find any signs of life. Gus raised John on the walkie-talkie, directed him to the ambush and told him about the Humvees.

Gus said, "John, be careful, we killed a bunch of them, but I'll bet you are heading into an ambush. Watch your ass."

John told him, "Thanks, and we will watch for ambushes."

"I'm glad I circled back before heading on to The Bunker, "Gus said as he banked the plane and headed towards Mobile.

• • •

Gus landed the DC 3 without any problems and taxied up to the closest gate to the compound. As he came to a stop, he saw Steve driving up in a pickup with three bodies in the bed. Gus thought that the fun had started down here and would get worse quickly. He just hoped that John and the rest would get here before this mess got out of control.

Most of the people at the compound heard Gus circle before landing and came out to meet the plane. He unloaded his passengers and introduced them to the home team.

After some handshaking and proper introductions, the kids went to the house for a good meal while the men met with Gus and Steve. Steve filled all of them in on what he had heard and why he killed the three men.

Gus agreed with Steve's action and said, "Well this is about to get as real as it can be. Is there any indication of how many men and weapons they have?"

Steve replied, "No, they just said the others. I'm no military genius, but the guns they had were hunting rifles, as you can see they are dirty and were packin' very little ammo."

"Good observations, Steve, I agree they don't seem to be well armed, and they defiantly aren't professionals," Gus added.

• • •

Ann was working with the cooks, preparing their supper. She hated cooking but knew that the others thought that she was just a spoiled rich bitch. She desperately wanted to win them over. She had changed into a tee shirt and shorts with no jewelry or makeup. Ann knew that she needed to fit in and join the team.

Robin had just walked into the kitchen when several windows were shattered, and Brenda fell to the floor with half her brains splattered on the wall.

Ann screamed and ran down the hall waking the men and yelling for the women to turn off the lights and duck. She hid in the bathroom and then noticed blood and gore all over the front of her blouse. She vomited until she dry heaved, then slapped her face and went back to the kitchen.

Steve looked out a window and saw roughly 30 men that were shooting at the house as they climbed the fence. He asked himself, "Damn, is this what Custer saw at the Little Big Horn?"

Ann and Joan grabbed their rifles and started returning fire along with Robin, Nancy and Brenda's twelve-year-old daughter.

174

The three were making every shot count. Ann wondered how Nora could fight with her mom dead on the floor.

Gus ordered Steve and several men to go out the front door and circle back to flank the intruders. In a few minutes, Gus saw intruders start dropping one after another, and the survivors had dropped to the ground looking for cover. Unfortunately, for them, there was very little cover, and all of those returning fire were behind cover and well protected.

The intruders had mainly handguns and hunting rifles, while the home team had AR15s, Bushmaster .223s and a couple of M14s. The attackers were cut to ribbons in a very short time.

Steve and the men scouted the area and saw what looked like four soldiers dressed in black BDUs and automatic weapons. They ran to a Humvee, and high tailed it out of the area. Steve could not imagine the connection.

He posted guards, and then directed the other men to take the bodies out beyond the fence and use the backhoe to bury them. They stripped the attackers of any weapons, ammo, and any documents that might help explain the attack. They found many pre-1965 silver coins on most every one of the attackers.

When they found the attacker's cars and trucks, they found them loaded with MREs and whiskey bottles.

Gus posted extra guards, then had a roll call to see how banged up the team was. He was surprised to find that there were only one dead and two with minor wounds from windows being shattered. Their training had paid off.

Gus got on the short wave and called for John. He took only a few minutes to fill John in.

John then told him about the ambush. Gus told him about the men dressed in black with the Humvee.

John informed him that the Humvees and ambushers that attacked Tom and Sam were also dressed in black.

• • •

John had hoped that the government would be a force for good, but these were signs that the government was perhaps the enemy of "We, the People..."

*

Chapter 20

History Lesson

Present day Smyrna, TN ISA

Dec 20, 2048

Josh had become so wrapped up in the story that he hadn't noticed that it was now dark. When the fireworks started exploding overhead, he just about fell out of his chair.

Jenn burst out laughing and said, "You have never been in a firefight, have you?"

Josh's face turned red as he replied, "I was in college and grad school during the last Disagreement, my family is well connected and pulled some strings."

Jenn replied, "I got a bullet in my thigh and lost three close friends during the last Disagreement. Don't y'all know that the last war was fought because your government tried to kill our entire Senate with a suicide bomber?"

Josh countered by reminding her that their President and over a hundred of his advisors had been hunted down, and killed before the alleged bomb incident.

Jenn fired back, "Your crappy President had become an enemy and traitor long before his death, but suspending the constitution and declaring himself to be President for life was the straw that broke the camel's back.

Let us not forget that he killed himself before his capture. Congress should have impeached him for treason, but the liberal media, threats, and bribes kept him in office. The Pacific States of America tried all of the others, found them guilty of treason and legally executed each one."

Josh laughed and said, "You may be right about some of that, but you will never convince the people in the USA, he is still godlike to most of them."

While John stayed quiet, the look on his face could kill a grizzly bear.

Josh thought for a minute and said, "You are right, I am here to hear and report the other side of the story about how the USA became three countries."

He quickly smiled and added, "But, no stories about John's sex life will be reported."

John and Jenn laughed.

"Seriously, no one in the North knows about the terror that was perpetrated against the early leaders of the ISA movement; this is great stuff, but is this story stretched a bit?"

Jenn replied, "Josh, we are downplaying the real atrocities because no one will believe the actual events. Murder, terror, and mutilation were their tools. Who would have believed that our President would be right in the middle of this plot?"

Josh continued the interview with, "The people of the USA think you made up the part where the President and Ex-President conspired with the Iranians to bomb our own country and another 12 countries around the world.

Unhardened electronics failed, not in a day, but in a single second. U.S. citizens still think that a group of ultra-conservatives committed the atrocities. Do you have any proof?"

John interrupted and said, "Yes, we have proof, and you will see all of it. It took five years to track down all of the traitors.

We found the former President hiding under a house, and President Wilton still has a bounty on her head. The trials, conducted by the PSA presented the evidence to take away the perception of bias. All were proved guilty, as charged.

The PSA reopened Alcatraz in 2026 just to store the large volume of traitors and crooks found guilty of treason and high crimes. The executions of several billionaire liberal supporters, the Speaker of the House, the Senate Majority Whip, and 13 other ringleaders immediately followed the trial.

The executions of three thousand others followed within six months. That piece of shit, Ex-President escaped the gallows by taking his own life. I was there. I saw him hanging from an overhead sewer pipe."

Josh said, "But why were over fifty media executives and reporters executed?"

Jenn said, "Because they were on the President's payroll and manipulated the news to support the President's, and future President Wilton's reign of terror."

Jenn added, "We also gave proof to DHS, CIA and the FBI, but by that time your next Socialist President had purged all who had not drunk the Kool-Aid.

At least the CIA took it seriously, but after Benghazi and the massacre in Montana, they were gunning for the bastards. We have the proof, and want to get it out to everyone in the USA."

Josh said, "Oh yeah, this is where I come in."

Jenn said, "Only if you can be trusted."

Josh said, "A small part of the USA believes that John personally nuked the cities and caused the downfall of the USA. I will follow the evidence, and write this story as it truthfully unfolds, whether the government editors will let it stand is another issue. I have no control over that."

Josh laughed and said, "Even if it is printed as written, I'm not sure how many will believe it. We have our kooks too. It may be difficult to get anyone to believe your proof."

Jenn replied, "We only want to get it in front of the people and let them make up their own minds."

John left the room, brought back a bottle of Jack Daniels Black Label and poured three fingers for each of them, over ice. Josh said, "Jack Black, my favorite."

THE END of THE BEGINNING

The Adventures of John Harris

Hell in the Home Land

Post- Apocalyptic America

AJ Newman

Prologue:

America is currently in a losing war with drug gangs, and illegal immigrants inside our country and Islamic Terrorists across the world. They probably have numerous sleeper cells already established in the States. Two nuclear EMP blasts would send us back to post-apocalyptic dark ages. We are also in decline thanks to the poor stewardship of our elected officials for the past 25 years. This story just takes what our enemies and our Government are currently doing to destroy the USA and expands on these misdeeds.

"Hell in the Homeland," is a novel that tells how John Harris leads a group of survivors through the chaos of a country that has been attacked with nuclear bombs and EMP blasts. A coalition of rogue US Government criminals, Radical Islamic terrorists, and a Drug Cartel has attacked the major nations of the world. There is very little food, and water and many people have starved or been forced into relocation camps. The grid is down; people are dying due to lack of medicine and criminals are looting and ravaging the cities. John and his followers fight back to survive and protect their loved ones.

I hope you have as much fun reading them as I did writing them.

*

Chapter 1

The Confederates

15 Miles Northeast of the Bunker

May 28, 2020

It was midnight, and there were four old trucks in the ragtag convoy bouncing at every rut and bump in the dirt road. The convoy consisted of an old Chevy farm truck and three pre-60's pickups. The lead pickup was flying a Confederate battle flag.

George Washington was driving the lead pickup with his wife, Shirley, and his dog in the cab. George was worried about his family's safety since TSHTF.

Several Skinhead groups had begun killing people of color on sight, taking all they owned, raping the women and killing all when they were finished. George thought the rebel flag might keep those assholes from chasing them if they were seen. To avoid attention, the convoy traveled mainly at night.

George knew that there were many decent people out there, but you could not tell what a man was thinking until it's too late, so the plan was to continue traveling at night until law and order were established.

George and Shirley were singing tunes from the '70s to pass the time and to keep George awake. George had a deep baritone voice that was always off key, but Shirley had a lovely voice.

They truly enjoyed each other's company, so the time passed quickly each night. As Shirley did not like to drive at night, she managed to talk George into doing all of the driving. He was okay with this since he felt better about his driving skills to get them out of trouble if something bad happened on the road.

George was 53, six foot three inches tall and built like a boxer. He had kept the Marine look; short cropped hair with a mustache. He had served for six years as a Marine Corps Infantryman. George returned home to help his dad on the family farm.

He was a registered Democrat that found his party had left him as they became more and more liberal. George was a Conservative that thought Republicans needed a little heart but were on target about foreign politics, taxes and big government.

Their sons, Marvin, Sammy and Sonny were following with their families spread out in the pickups and farm truck. His two daughters, Ginny and Mary, were riding in the back of the farm truck with Ginny's two kids and Marvin and Sammy's four children. Ginny's husband did not come home from work the day of the attack. The family searched for him to no avail.

George's five kids ranged from Marvin at 26 to Mary at 18. They were all good people, who raised their children in a Christian home and for the most part, they stayed out of trouble. The farm had plenty of work to be done, and all had to work in George's family. When staying at home they went to God's, and George's rules.

Marvin is married to Tonya, his childhood sweetheart. They have a boy and a girl, five and four. Sammy is married to Karen, and they have three-year-old twin sons and an eight-year-old boy from her previous marriage.

Karen is white and was the wife of Sammy's best friend. Karen's husband died while fighting insurgents in Iraq. Just before he died, Sammy promised to take good care of her. George's family accepted her, and her son, except for George's mom who did not approve. She thought they were both going to Hell.

Sonny was still in the Marines and had never married. He was home on leave when the lights went out. With no way to get back to the east coast, he decided to stay home and help his family.

George and all of his boys served in the Marines. George's father and grandfather's service had been in the Army.

The small convoy had been driving for several hours after midnight when George spotted what he thought were headlights over the hill in front of them. Signally with three short taps on the brake, he waved everyone off the road and into cover.

He gathered the boys and said, "Marvin, stay with the family while Sammy, Sonny and I go over the hill and see what those lights are about. Be ready to haul ass."

Marvin replied, "Maybe you should take the deer rifle and leave the shotgun with me."

George thought that was a good idea and making the weapons exchange led his sons to just below the crest of the hill. They had gone into the woods on the west side of the road and made as little noise as possible while moving towards the light.

Sonny said, "I hear music."

George and Sammy agreed. They started to get a whiff of smoke from a campfire and began to hear voices. They crawled to the top of the hill and saw a black Humvee and several people jumping around a large bonfire.

"Dad they aren't jumping, they're dancing."

DHS roadblock, Alabama

There were four men and two naked women dancing around the fire. The men were obviously drunk. The three of them crawled to within ten yards of the dancers and now realized that the men were DHS agents from the markings on the Humvee. One person still had his uniform on. They also saw that the girls were very young, maybe fourteen or fifteen. There was a tall blonde and a short brunette. Suddenly one of the guys took the rest of his clothes off and started rubbing his body on the blonde girl.

She resisted, and he punched her in the face. Then he forced her to the ground. He was quickly on top of her, but she was a fighter and kicked him in the crotch. Upon recovering from the kick, he started punching her.

A shot rang out as Sonny charged the group. He was a blur, charging the enemy. George tried to get up to join in the attack, but Sonny shot all four men before George and Sammy could get a round off. The men didn't even have a chance to resist. Sonny shot three in the torso and one in the shoulder.

The brunette rushed to the aid of the girl lying by the fire while George and the boys secured the DHS Agent's weapons. The girls then noticed the three black men standing around them with guns and started screaming. George grabbed two shirts from the DHS crew and gave them to the girls.

George told them, "We won't hurt you. Where do you live? Can we help you get back home?"

One of the DHS yelled, "Those girls are ours, and you are going to die you black ass son of a bitch."

George looked the man in the eye, took his .44 Bulldog and shot the man right between his eyes.

He then walked up to the next one and said, "Ya'll are supposed to be helping these people not raping them, you bastard."

George kept the gun on the Agent's nose and asked him several questions. The piece of trash had pissed his pants and was shaking uncontrollably after answering all of George's questions. He asked the other one the same questions and got similar answers.

"May God help your souls," George said. He then put them out of their misery with shots to the head. George then told Sonny to get the rest of the group to join them.

In about ten minutes, the convoy drove over the hill. The women were shocked to see the carnage. Shirley walked up to George and told him to give them a Christian burial even if they were bad men. The women took charge of the two captives while the men turned the headlights off on the Humvee.

Tony organized the other men to dig a grave.

The blonde-haired girl was in shock, and the brunette started telling Shirley their story. The blonde's name was Linda, and the brunette was Sandra. They were neighbors and had just barely enough water and food to keep their families alive after the power died.

The DHS guys arrived that morning and promptly shot Linda's dad when he couldn't give the agents any alcohol. Sandra's dad ran out of his house to see what the shooting was all about and they shot him as well. They then rounded up all the rest of their families and tied them up. They took turns raping the girl's moms and then killed everyone, but the two girls.

Shirley wondered, "How could they shoot just shoot people, especially children?"

They salvaged everything useable and hid the Humvee deep into the woods. George thought a Humvee would draw too much attention by the government, and other trash would try to take it from them.

They found four bulletproof vests, six M4s, four Beretta 9mm, several boxes of ammo, and MREs. They also found several walkie-talkies and a large box with jewelry, gold, and real silver coins.

They dragged the four DHS men into the woods and placed them in the grave. Shirley opened the Bible and said a couple of verses and the Lord's Prayer over the graves. George had everyone grab some brush to get rid of all of the tracks and had the kids pick up the brass. They then drove about ten miles and pulled off into a clearing in the woods at daybreak.

George gathered everyone in a circle and thanked God that none of their clan had been killed rescuing the girls. He then told them what he had learned from the DHS men.

Recruited by the local DHS headquarters in Mobile, the men were to confiscate any guns and encourage everyone to go to Mobile to stay at the relocation camp.

They were to trade the people for free meals and security from gangbangers and motorcycle gangs that were looting the countryside.

If the people did not agree to go, they were to scare them into going by raiding their houses in the middle of the night.

The government wanted everyone to move to these relocation camps for their own safety.

The Agents were told to use any fear tactics that would get the people to the camps. Rape, murder and molesting children became common practice according to these scumbags. The government did not approve of this but didn't stop this deviant behavior, either.

George and Shirley sought a private spot and tried to fathom how this chaos could happen so quickly after the power went out. George theorized that the government had planned and executed the entire disaster to get tighter control of the US citizens.

Shirley said, "George, we have a Black President who loves his people, he couldn't do this, could he?"

187

***

Oval Office of POTUS

The President called his advisors to a meeting at his retreat in upstate New York. He was trying to understand why the civilian death rate was so much higher than his staff had anticipated. There simply wouldn't be enough people left to do the necessary work if they continued dying at this rate.

Whole cities were devastated by the rioting and gang violence. He expected approximately eighty million casualties from the nuclear bombs, but those mainly killed the welfare bums and other people who did not contribute to society and were a drain on the national resources.

Only the President and his two closest confidants knew the entire plan. A vision that was to reshape the United States of America into a much stronger nation based on sharing the wealth and everyone contributing equally, "Each to his needs." Of course, he would be the Benevolent Leader of this new country. He would give it the firm, loving hand and guidance needed to reshape society and the business world into his vision.

Everyone, of course, would flock to this new America, as all would benefit and there would be no freeloaders. The lower class Democratic votes would no longer be needed since he was a leader for life and their drain on the economy was solved with a few nukes to strategic cities.

The President looked across the room and spoke, "I called you together to adapt Phase II of Operation Brave New World to our current situation. Phase I achieved all of our objectives, except for gaining the support of the majority of the military, but it killed many more of our future workers than planned. We need more laborers."

The Secretary of Labor said, "You are correct Mr. President. We have lost almost one hundred seventy million people so far. The bad news is that the deaths are still occurring at an alarming rate."

General Walls spoke up, "Mr. President, we got played by the Iranians.

General Walls knew that this would piss the President off, but someone had to reach the arrogant bastard and shake some sense into him.

"There never was a plan to use EMPs on our own country. The nukes were more than enough to accomplish our objective of cleansing the riffraff, but the EMPs destroyed the grid and took away our ability to maintain our cities. That is why our people are starving, rioting and killing each other. We need to nuke the

Iranians and the rest of our enemies in this debacle before they nuke us, again."

The President replied, "General Walls, the President of Iran has sworn that his country did not launch any EMP devices at the United States of America and, in fact, claims that our own bombs caused the EMP destruction."

"Respectfully, the Iranian President is a liar and a traitor to our cause. Mr. President, we tracked the missiles from their points of origin, to the blasts. They came from ships off our coasts. That bastard and some of his friends intend to take our country from you and us were played a fool. Iranian submarines and surface craft are staged in the Gulf of Mexico waiting to join in an attack on our country.

Friends in South America tell us that there are major troop movements taking place and they are all heading towards the border with Mexico. The Mexican President is on TV telling his fellow countrymen that it is time to help the United States by giving support to what was once the northern part of Mexico."

The President pushed a hidden button, and suddenly the room was full of Secret Service.

The President told them, "Please remove General Walls from this meeting, turn him over to the DHS and have him placed under house arrest. Have Field Marshal Williams join us to finish the meeting."

***

Port Arthur, TX

Port Arthur, Texas was much better off than most cities in the United States of America after the bombs fell. The Mayor, Police Chief, and several other high-ranking officials, were ex-military, and most were dedicated preppers.

Since they were on the Gulf Coast, the town was well prepared for hurricanes and flooding. Under the guise of getting better prepared for hurricanes like Katrina, the Mayor and city council spent a fortune for backup generators and survival supplies. The generators were EMP proof, as was the main power plant for the city. They had seen what happened to New Orleans and more importantly the small towns around it when the starving people and gangs moved to higher ground.

Chief Charlie Adams had been in Army Special Forces and carefully selected his police officers from honest ex-Military Police and Special Forces when he could find them. He was always first in line to get surplus military arms, ammo, and equipment. He had five armored cars and three armored personnel carriers plus hundreds of M4s and side arms.

Besides protecting the civilians, his team's major job was to seal off the town when TSHTF. There were only three major roads and a handful of small two lane roads coming from Houston and Beaumont to block off from the outside. In a pinch, he was prepared to blow a dozen bridges and make Port Arthur a safe island with virtually no way to get in or out of the city via land.

Port Arthur's most significant asset was that the majority of its citizens were ready to fight to protect their town if push came to shove. A large number were also preppers and had at least a year's worth of food, arms with ammo survival supplies.

Chief Charlie taught a course in survival and self-protection at the local college. The police in New Orleans taking guns from its people sickened them, and Obama's attempt to take away their weapons only stiffened their resolve. They had become believers in the Second Amendment, and most were armed and ready. Chief Charlie knew that he could have a small army in a matter of hours.

Crime was not an issue in Port Arthur since Charlie, and the Mayor decided that criminals had to leave Port Arthur one way or the other. The legal system got rid of most. Others were secretly taken out to the Gulf and dropped overboard with chains wrapped around them. Only a very select few knew about the more harsh methods used to purge the town of criminals, but everyone in town loved the results. They still had the usual small town problems with wife beaters, DUIs and car wrecks, but there hadn't been a violent crime in over four years until the end came.

The night that lights went out found the Mayor sound asleep during a major rainstorm. There was some fool pounding on his door. He woke up and remembered one large lightning bolt that rattled the windows and shook the house. He tried to turn the lights on, but there was no power. He looked at the alarm clock, and it was blank. Grabbing his Glock, the Mayor threw on a robe. He then told his wife to wake up and get dressed. He peeked through the spy hole, saw Chief Charlie at the door and told him to come into the house.

"Mayor, we've been attacked. It appears, from what I can learn, the whole country is under attack from nuclear weapons."

The Mayor responded, "Now Charlie, calm down. Are you sure about this and by the way how do you know that we were attacked?"

"First, my officers saw several jet planes fall out of the sky at the same time. Second, there is no power, and most cars won't start. Several of my guys were driving down the road when their patrol cars just died. They got out of the cars and saw the planes falling to the ground. One hit in the middle of Groves and wiped out most of downtown. I think we were nuked with EMP devices and God knows what else. We need to put our plan into action now."

"Okay, Charlie, round up the city council and our town leaders and let's get moving. We should have about two to three days to get fully up to speed with our plan."

*

Chapter 2

John's Home

Nashville, TN ISA

Dec 16, 2048

The sun was coming up, and a rooster was crowing in the distance. Josh rubbed his eyes and tried to open them. His head was throbbing, his mouth was as dry as a cotton field, and he was hungry. He also had to piss like a racehorse. He jumped out of bed, tangled in the sheet and fell flat on his face. He lifted his head and looked into the most beautiful eyes he had ever seen.

Jenn said, "Good morning, Mister Graceful, did you have a good night?"

Josh looked at her, stammered and asked, "Did we?"

She kicked him in the side and said, "I should kick your ass, but you're probably still drunk, thanks to Dad."

He looked at her and took the vision in. She was wearing a pair of short cutoffs and a halter top showing her midsection. She had a skull and bones tattoo on her right shoulder and several scars. She was gorgeous and sexy in a rugged sort of way. When she turned to leave, he saw another tattoo peeking below her shorts on the inside of her left leg. It looked like the feet of a cartoon character. The feet were orange, and there were a couple of yellow feathers lying by the feet. He wanted to see the whole bird.

He ran to the bathroom and took a cold shower, but could not take his mind off this beautiful lady warrior. He really wanted to get to know her better but knew that his job was to get the story, not chase women. He found his clothes and got dressed.

Jenn and John were at the breakfast table, and an older version of Jenn was in the kitchen cooking. Josh noticed that there were eight plates on the table, but didn't see anyone else.

Jenn saw Josh and said, "Mom, this is Josh; Josh, Mom. Josh is a reporter for CNG, the Conservative News Group."

Beth replied, "So, you are one of the good guys. Can you actually report the news without changing the facts to suit your boss' political needs?"

Josh said, "Ma'am, I will always tell the truth about a story and make sure the facts speak for themselves. I'm also honored to meet you and your family. I know that you have been maligned by the press and I assure you that only the truth will be reported."

Beth asked, "Josh, do you go to church?"

Josh replied, "Yes Ma'am. My family is Baptist, and we attend the Cedar Crest Baptist Church in Columbus, Ohio. We're not that religious, but we believe in God, hard work and hate abortions. My mom and sister stay in trouble with the local and state authorities picketing abortion clinics.

Mom is a high school teacher, and Dad is the sales manager for a used car lot. They both would be a great fit for the ISA, but they will not leave home. Our family settled in the OH-KY area over 250 years ago. Does your family go to church?"

John replied, "Every Sunday since I married Beth. We are also Baptists, and Beth is the spiritual leader who keeps our family active in the church. Beth, Lindsey, and Kristie are Sunday school teachers and Randy is a deacon."

"Good morning Mom and Dad," said a beautiful young amber-skinned young lady as she strolled into the room.

John looked up and yelled, "Lindsey, get your ass back upstairs and put some clothes on the young lady."

She walked up to John, sat down in his lap and said, "Now daddy, I am wearing more than I wear to the beach."

Lindsey wore a white halter-top and tiny white shorts that barely covered a rather voluptuous body.

John gave her a kiss on the cheek and said, "We have company," and pointed at Josh.

She jumped up out of his lap and ran up the stairs just as the front door opened and a bunch of kids came into the house yelling and running all around. John got up and met them as they entered the kitchen. They swarmed him. Their parents Randy and his wife shook Josh's hand and sat down at the breakfast table.

John rolled on the floor with the kids for about thirty minutes while everyone ate and then yelled, "Church in one hour, everybody get dressed. You, too, Josh."

Josh said, "I think there is another story that has been overlooked because of all of the warfare and serious events."

Jenn said, "What story?"

Josh replied, "An epic love story." He smiled and walked away.

John walked up behind Jenn and said, "Are you getting sweet on that boy? I like him, but I can't trust him yet."

"Dad, yes, I like him and would like to get to know him better. You know being your daughter makes it hard to meet any man who's not afraid of my father. Josh has great respect for you, but is not afraid of you."

"He'd better learn to be afraid of me."

*

Chapter 3

The DHS

North of the Alabama border
May 28, 2048

North of the Alabama Border

The team had cautiously pulled up to Tom's shot up pickup. Tom was on his knees giving first aid to Sam. Tom looked up and saw the team getting out of their trucks and running towards him.

He yelled, "Do you have anything to stop the bleeding?" Several yelled back at him to keep the pressure on the wound.

He replied, "No shit Sherlock! Now get me something to stop the bleeding."

Beth came running and pushed through the group and dropped to her knees beside Tom. She ripped open a package of WoundSeal and told Tom to move his hand off the wound. She poured half the contents on the bullet hole. She then placed a wad of gauze on the wound and told Tom to put pressure on it. She then lifted Sam's shoulder and performed the same process on the exit wound. Beth took a pill from a bottle and made Sam swallow it with a drink from her canteen.

Beth told Sam, "That was a pretty strong pain killer, and you will sleep for several hours."

She told the group that Sam would live, but may have a lot of shoulder pain the rest of his life. She told Tom that the bullet had a clean entrance and small exit wound.

John added, "Looks like a .223 wound, but couldn't be a military round, not from the small exit wound."

Tom looked at his son and said, "I love you son, but I will kick your ass if you die on me."

Sam squeezed his dad's hand and passed out. Beth had Sam loaded into the back of one of the five-ton trucks where she and one of the women could tend to him. Tom joined them and said several prayers for God to spare his son's life.

Beth made Tom calm down and let her examine him against his protests. He only had a few cuts on his face and neck from the shattered window during the ambush. Beth prayed that she would not have to nurse many more wounded friends and relatives.

John asked several of the men to gather the weapons and bury the DHS goons. He went to the Humvees and quickly decided to take them back to the bunker. All four had twin M-60s mounted.

These could make the difference in the next fight. John felt in his gut that they had not seen the last of the DHS. He was sure there was either an ambush or a large group of these DHS goons between them and the bunker. He did not know this, but that is what he would do.

He sent Scott, Bill and a couple of the other men out to scout the area. He told them to split up, and each group was to go two miles down the road in opposite directions and report ASAP.

John got in his truck, got a shortwave radio out and tried to see if anyone was broadcasting while waiting on Beth to finish nursing Sam and the scouts to get back. John turned the dial for a few minutes and heard a couple of men talking about the disaster.

He heard, "Most of the world is in the same shape. The Israelis, Brits and our military took out most of the Islamic Country's militaries that participated in the attack on the western countries and Japan. Russia and China nuked each other when China tried to invade Russia. Only a few countries in Africa and South America still had power and no destruction from nuclear weapons."

Beth heard the radio and joined him. She asked, "Why don't you ask them where they are?"

John replied, "Darling, we don't need the government tracking us down. It's easy to pinpoint the location of anyone who broadcasts over shortwave radios. We just don't know what they are up to yet. They ambushed our friends who were driving along minding their own business. I just don't trust them."

Beth gave him a kiss and said, "John thanks for knowing what to do to keep all of us out of trouble. You know we have not had a minute alone since we met and I need some time alone with you John."

She ran her hand under his shirt and rubbed his belly. John pulled her close to him and kissed her while rubbing her backside.

He said, "Darling, I think we need to go for a long walk after we set up camp for the night."

She smiled and continued kissing him. Scott interrupted them.

"Get a room," was all he said.

Beth threw an empty soda can at Scott. She continued to listen to the shortwave while John debriefed the scouts who had returned.

She learned that even though as many as 15 major cities had been nuked, there was very little damage to the rest of the country except for the power being off. The US government had moved to Harrisburg, PA since DC was now a pile of cinders. She also learned that most of the Tea Party Congressmen were in Dallas at a conference and were safe; however, the rest of Congress had been decimated.

Beth said to John, "Am I correct, but over fifty million people have been vaporized, and most of them were on welfare or government assistance? They were also mainly Democrats. The United States of America is now a predominately Conservative country."

John told Beth that he despised the liberals that had been running the country, but he never thought that they would be burned alive in a nuke attack. He didn't say it aloud but hoped their worthless President and his minions had been vaporized.

John remembered that they had captured the two nukes that had been heading to Memphis and Dallas. Not only did they save millions of people from being incinerated, but they had also saved the future leaders of their country. He thought that God must have been watching over them and guiding their actions that night. He also wondered if he could activate the bombs if needed due to some dire unforeseen circumstance.

Beth searched for other people broadcasting and found over twenty; several were close by. She made a list of the channels and what they were discussing. She learned that no one really knew what had happened and how bad the damage was. By piecing the discussions together, she found that there was a mixture of people banding together to survive and a great deal of lawlessness and looting. About half of the people didn't give their exact locations, but most of the country was represented, with the majority being in the South.

John ordered them to get back on the road and asked Scott to ride with him since Beth was back in the truck tending to Sam. As usual, he had scout vehicles about a quarter mile ahead and behind the main body to make sure there were no surprises or ambushes.

John asked Scott how he was doing and what he thought about the recent events.

Scott said, "You will be very lucky if Beth doesn't adopt about a half dozen of those kids we freed back there. She is already beginning to mother them."

John laughed and replied, "You know, I think that woman is pretty strong willed so I may just be along for the ride. Besides, I did pretty well with you and Jim. Didn't I?"

Scott said, "Well Dad, Mom did most of the raising until I was about 12 years old so I don't know how you'll do with little kids."

John just laughed.

Scott asked, "How do you think Mom and Beth will get along?"

John replied, "I don't know, I hadn't given it any thought."

Scott broke out laughing and said, "Dad, the fit will hit the shan. My God, both of your women in the same bunker will be funny."

John sternly replied, "Your mom is not my woman."

Scott replied, "You're taking a sexy younger woman back to meet your ex-wife. This will be like introducing a match to a can of gasoline."

John got his walkie-talkie and checked in with Gus. They spent a few minutes filling each other in on the day's events, and then John steered the conversation to Beth and Ann.

Gus stammered for a minute then said, "Man that is something I had not thought about. Fireworks are what come to mind. Don't you think we should keep them about a hundred miles apart?"

198

They had driven for about 20 miles when the lead scout vehicle called to tell them to stop. John saw Bill and Tom dismount and look at the left side of the road for about five minutes then get back in the truck and head back to the convoy.

Tom got out, walked up to John and said, "We saw signs where a large group of guys stopped for a break. There were MRE wrappers and empty water bottles all over the place. I think they were there about three or four hours ago. Judging from the tracks and footprints, there are 5-6 vehicles and 30-40 men."

Scott said, "Dad, pull out the map of this area. We need to see if we can spot a likely ambush position."

John fetched the map and spread it out on the tailgate. They followed Highway 65 from their current position down to the Alabama border until Scott said, "I'll bet they are at the overpass where Hwy 64 crosses 65. They can ambush us and have cover from the air by ducking under the overpass. Gus killed ten of them, and they never saw it coming. They have to be scared of being attacked from the air again."

John and Tom agreed and started planning how to ambush those bushwhackers.

***

DHS Ambush Site

The scout saw the vehicles approaching and radioed back to the Sergeant. "Sir, there are six trucks heading my way, they are going slow, and they are armed. They are scanning the road ahead and appear to be expecting trouble."

The Sergeant replied, "Call back when they get in the kill zone."

The Sergeant was sure that these people were connected in some way to the plane that had strafed and killed over ten of his men earlier in the day. He ordered his men to take cover and to kill all but five of these criminals. He also warned them to keep an eye out for that damn airplane. He wanted to take prisoners back to Deke for interrogation. Deke wanted to find out what was happening in the other states around Alabama. Even the government had only sketchy info on most of the country since the nuclear attack had destroyed almost all communication.

The President had sent an appointed leader over a year ago to govern each state in the event of a national emergency until the Federal Government could get the power and communications back in operation. Each "field marshal" had several thousand the United

States of American men, weapons, armored vehicles and ammo to use to restore law and order in his state.

Most field marshals were from one minority group or another. They were a mixture of misfits that could not make it in the real world and political appointees that had blindly supported the President who was responsible for the downfall of the United States of America.

The Sergeant did not communicate back to his home base in Mobile about the disaster that morning or the upcoming ambush. His ego overcame his training, and he thought that capturing these people would make him look good to Deke.

The Sergeant wanted to kill or torture everyone of these assholes for killing his men earlier in the day. The scout radioed back that the target just had to come another 100 yards and they would soon be within range but had stopped. Just as it was dawning on him that something was wrong with this picture, the Agent next to him slumped down to the ground. Then he heard the shots and ducked.

"Take cover; we're under attack. They're coming from the woods."

He and his men were pinned down by withering fire from the woods on either side of the road. Twelve men were down, and more were falling.

The Sergeant tried to rally his men to counterattack, but they could only return enough fire to keep from being overrun. He just hoped that he could hold the attackers off until help arrived. Then it dawned on him that central command did not know about the attack. He remembered that he had left his satellite phone in the Humvee. He desperately crawled for a few yards hiding in a low spot, but now had to get up and run to the Humvee. He got up and took two steps before a bullet knocked him to the ground.

***

The remaining DHS couldn't use the firepower of their two Humvees because Scott and Tom had them pinned down by using the twin M60 machine guns mounted on two of the Humvees that they had captured. The twin M60, 7.62 mm machine guns were destroying the enemy troops and vehicles. The massacre had only lasted about twenty minutes.

John ordered a cease-fire when there was no return fire for five minutes. He sent the Humvees in to check for survivors and found all but three dead, and they were all wounded. Scott took a

200

team to make sure the dead were actually dead. A shot rang out a couple of times.

Scott yelled, "Them Sons Uh Bitches was playing possum."

Beth and Alice came over to the wounded men and tried to start first aid, but John asked them to leave.

Beth protested, and John took her to the side and said, "These guys won't need first aid. We will interrogate them, try them and execute them."

Beth said, "A hard man for hard times. Baby, can you live with your actions?"

John replied, "Yes when these men were going to ambush us and kill everyone. Darling, I *am not* a cold-blooded killer, but I can do what is needed for us to be safe and survive."

Scott forced the DHS sergeant, to stand up and walk to the front of one of the Humvees and tied him to the front and facing away from the grill. Bill and a couple of the men made the other two sit down to watch the interrogation. John came up to the Sergeant and saw that he had been shot in the right arm and right side. He asked when he would get a doctor to fix his wounds.

John said, "I am going to shoot you in the other arm with this .22 if you don't answer my questions."

He pulled the Ruger out of his belt and put it against the guy's left arm.

The Sergeant replied, "You know I only have to give you my name, rank, and serial number."

John smiled at him before pulling the trigger. The report of the gun surprised the rest of the team and caused one of the other prisoners to soil his pants. John had the other two moved out of range and asked again, and this time he spilled his guts.

The other two had much the same story but did not know as much about the headquarters in Mobile.

John learned that there was a major complex in Mobile that was the state headquarters and manned by over 2,000 men. The Sergeant told him that the complex had bomb shelters, food, and water to cover the army for six months. He added that there were numerous armored vehicles and helicopters readied for battle. There also was an internment camp with tents and a ten-foot high fence around the perimeter. The camp would hold ten thousand United States citizens until they could be resettled. All three told John about how the DHS was forcing people to relocate to the camp even if they were doing okay. They told him that the mandate was to relocate everyone to the numerous camps around the country and to use the people as labor to get factories and state-run farms back up into operation.

John quickly dispatched the three DHS scumbags.

Before John could speak, Bill said, "Come on people, you know the drill, bury the dead and grab anything useful to the team."

John patted Bill on the back and helped salvage weapons, ammo, and food. They were getting efficient at burying the dead and picking over the remains. It only took an hour to accomplish the task and get on the road. They were only able to salvage 20 M4s, 26 9mm, a lot of ammo, assorted backpacks and 40 cases of MREs. Several of the M4s had grenade launchers mounted below the barrel, and they found two cases of grenades holding 24 grenades each. The vehicles and .50 cal. MGs were shot to hell. They only saved a couple of spare barrels for the .50 cal. along with a cleaning kit.

They drove south on Hwy 65 south for about 15 miles and decided to camp just north of Athens. It was about an hour before sunset and John did not want to go through Athens and Decatur. He wanted to avoid all cities if possible, and they would get up early and try to get past Athens and Decatur before most people were up for the day. They pulled off the highway and set up camp by a creek in a stand of trees. They dined on MREs for supper, and except for the guards, everyone went to bed early since they knew they had to get up before daylight in the morning.

John and Beth snuck out of the camp and went about a hundred yards into the woods. John pulled a plastic sheet out of his back pocket and spread it out on the ground. They talked and cuddled for a while before Beth asked John if he had protection.

He drew his .45 Colt, and she laughed and said, "I guess we just take our chances one time and I'll be checking out the next gas station or pharmacy."

Their chances ended up conceiving a beautiful daughter.

Beth lay in John's arms for several hours while they talked about the future.

Beth asked, "Isn't Ann staying at the bunker, John?"

John thought, "Oh shit," and replied, "Yes, she is, but I don't think that will be an issue. She doesn't care for me or me for her. We have been friends, but that's all since the divorce."

Beth said, "That sounds good, but if she even looks at you, I'll scratch the bitch's eyes out."

John had arranged for Beth and him to have the last watch of the night, but Scott still caught that they came to guard duty from the bushes and not from camp.

He said, "Ya'll find that room?"

Beth walked up to him and smiled while she grabbed him by the cheek and twisted.

She said, "Next time, I'll spank you son."

Scott replied, "So you found a room and a preacher, Mom?"

She kicked him and left with John doubled over laughing.

Scott, Bill, and Alice were taking bets on which of John's women would win the first showdown.

Scott ended the discussion by saying, "I think Beth is one hell of a woman, but I know my Mom and she can be a real bitch and can get real nasty."

Just as he finished, Bill and Alice broke out laughing.

Scott felt a hand on his shoulder, and Beth gave him a ten-dollar bill and said, "That's ten dollars on me, Sonny Boy."

She kissed him on the cheek and walked away, like a woman on a mission.

They were all up and ready to travel by 4:00 a.m. John and Beth were yawning during the morning meeting with Scott making fun of them behind their backs. John told the team that they would drive slowly with no lights until they got past Decatur, which was a total of 20 miles driving in the dark. He asked Scott and Bill to take two pickups with six heavily armed men and stay about 100 yards ahead of the main body. He also had another pickup trail the main body by 100 yards.

John told them, "I don't know what is waiting for us around Athens, but we cross Lake Wheeler just outside of Decatur, and I would have a roadblock there if I wanted to block entry into the area. We need to remember that there are a lot of good people out there that don't want just anybody traveling through their towns and property."

They got just about five miles below Athens when Scott radioed back for the group to stop. He said he thought there were friendly people on the road. He had seen a van on the side of the road with a man, three women and four kids just getting up for the morning. Scott and several of the men walked up to within 30 yards of the van and Scott went ahead to not scare the people. He stood behind a stalled car and hailed the camp.

The people ducked behind the van and told him to leave them alone. Scott told them that he and his people were just trying to head south on Highway 65 and meant them no harm. He even asked if they needed any supplies.

Scott talked with the group long enough to know that these were just people caught on the road and meant no harm to anyone, but he also knew that a cornered man was a dangerous man.

He radioed back to his dad and told him the situation. John told him that he would come up and talk with the people.

John arrived in about five minutes with Beth by his side. They walked up to Scott and hid behind the car while Scott gave them an update and pointed out where the people were.

John told him that he and Beth were going to talk with these people and then walk up to them and see if they could stop this impasse so there would be enough time to get past Decatur before dawn. Beth called out to the group and told them that they needed to hurry up and get on past Decatur before daylight.

A woman spoke up and said, "Why should we trust you? You might just kill or rape us."

Beth replied, "If we wanted you dead, you would be. We have over 30-armed people in our team, machine guns, and Humvees. We also have food and supplies. We don't want to hurt you."

Two of the Humvees with the dual M-60 MGs pulled up and turned their lights on. This scared the crap out of these folks and shook them to the bone.

Beth said again, "As you can see if we wanted to hurt you it would have already happened. Come on over and let's talk."

The others huddled for a minute, walked out from behind their van and laid their guns on the ground.

The man said, "Please don't hurt the children. Do what you want with us, but don't hurt our kids."

John, Scott, and Beth went up to meet with them and shook their hands and introduced themselves.

John said, "We really do have to get on across the river before daylight, but we can give you food if you need it."

The man replied, "We certainly could use some food, but I wouldn't get in a hurry to try and cross the river. There are about a hundred bikers and escapees from the prison just on the other side.

They are making people pay tolls to cross the bridge into Decatur, and when they do get across, they kill the men and kids and take the women. Also, the I-65 bridges are totally blocked by several burned out tractor and trailers, and you have to go through Decatur."

John said, "How do you know this?"

204

The man's wife, Pat, replied, "We originally had 15 adults and 13 kids in our group. We paid the toll in old silver coins and half our guns and ammunition.

When we crossed the bridge, they ran a bus across the road in front of our column and tried to block the backend, but that bus stalled and would not start. Two cars and our van turned around and ran back up Hwy 65.

They chased us and ran the two cars off the road. We were in the lead and got away. As we pulled away, we saw them shooting everyone in the cars. While we are ashamed that we left them, we would have also been killed."

John told them, "In those circumstances, I would have done the same. You saved your kids."

The rest of the main body joined them, and since they weren't going on to Decatur, they stopped and fixed a big breakfast. John and Beth introduced the new people to the team and then filled the others in on their story, but kept the bunker out of the conversation.

Pat's husband, Mark Taylor, her 2 sisters and their kids had left Columbia, TN a week ago heading for the gulf coast. Looting and a riot had just about burned the whole town down, and they had all lost their homes. Pat's brother-in-law was murdered trying to find food for his kids. Two days into the trip, their leader snuck out before dawn with most of their supplies and their best truck.

*

Chapter 4

The Road Home

North of Decatur

June 2, 2020

I-65 North of Decatur

John did not want to walk into a trap, so he sent scouts out in several directions to make sure there were no surprises other than the one across the bridge at Decatur. He sent one group to make sure that Mark was accurate about the bridge at I-65 being impassable. Mark was correct; it would take a week with a dozer to clear the wrecks off the bridge.

The other scouts were gone for two days and brought back a wealth of information. The area north of Decatur was safe and had law and order.

The people were mainly farmers and were well armed and kept the trash from Decatur on their side of the lake. They had plenty of food and a lake for water. They had seen DHS vehicles and choppers but had not been bothered by them so far.

The Prison on the Decatur side of Lake Wheeler was a different story. When the power went out most of the guards left to go home to their families. The warden tried to get help, but with no electricity, little water, and food running out he let the nonviolent prisoners go to be able to keep the most violent behind bars.

The plan was working until one day a biker gang showed up and overwhelmed the guards. These were Aryan Nation criminals, and they killed all of the guards and most of the minority prisoners.

They put five of the prisoners, a live guard and a knife in a cell and left them to starve to death or eat the guard for supper.

The scum then rode into Decatur, killed all of the police that they could find and started killing or raping all Black and Mexican women in the town. Most escaped during the first day, but some tried to fight back and were killed.

They captured over a hundred women and young girls and had them locked up in a hotel to be used and abused. All girls younger than ten were killed or run out of town.

Local farmers had picked up a few, but they also found piles of dead men, women, and children. They buried more than a thousand citizens during the first two days of the gang's siege of the city.

Scott had found a game warden that had some topographical maps of the area that had excellent detail. They spread the maps out and started making a plan of attack, but John quickly knew he had to get eyes on the gang to determine their strengths and weaknesses.

He sent a team out to find a boat, so they could go across the lake and infiltrate the city. The team found a canoe with oars. John and Bill rowed across the lake above Decatur, to get a close-up view of the enemy. They went across at night to make sure that they were not spotted.

The streets of Decatur were empty at 5:00 a.m. There were a couple of rough looking men standing outside of a Value Inn and six more on the Decatur side of the bridge. They were armed with M16s and 12 gauge shotguns. All had biker jackets, no hair and multiple tattoos on their arms and faces. These were the night shift, and the six at the bridge were passing a pipe and a bottle of whiskey around. They were obviously drunk and overconfident.

John and Bill were under the back end of a truck in a parking lot on the northwest side of the road from the bridge leading into town. To the west was the Value Inn with the two guards and due east were the six guards standing behind some cars that were making up a barricade in the middle of the divided highway.

John and Bill had been up all night learning as much about the town as possible. They had been watching these animals for several days and found out quite a bit about where they slept and what they were doing. They observed their schedules and made notes on routines and activities.

There were around three hundred of the vilest quasi-human scum occupying the town that John had ever seen. Most stayed at the Executive Hotel at the corner of Highways 67 and 41.

They stored their captive women at the Holiday Inn by the bridge and had about thirty guards at all times spread about the town. It was a very large brothel for these degenerates. The leader charged the men for every "date."

The gang was systematically looting the town one-bank or jewelry store at a time. There was an explosion about every two hours as the men broke into another bank, jewelry store, police station, liquor store or gun shop. They were amassing a fortune.

Bill said, "You know, John, we could blow up the hotel with them in it and take all of the stuff that they have been stealing."

John laughed and replied, "What about the good citizens who this stuff belongs to?"

Bill said, "Oops, sorry. I got greedy."

***

"I want everyone ready to roll in two days. We'll hit Cullman, Birmingham, and Montgomery on the way down to Mobile."

The men were afraid of Jerry for a good reason. He killed just for the fun of it. He didn't need a reason, and no one wanted to give him one. He had a Bowie knife and machete hanging from his belt.

He liked to torture men and women who pissed him off and made a sport of trying to cut their heads off with one blow from the machete.

"We'll check out the cities for women and drugs, but I want to join up with the DHS by next Friday. Deke Jones will let us do our thing as long as we bring prisoners to him. We can keep the loot and best looking women, young girls and a few young boys for you pervert."

The men cheered and patted Jerry on the back while praising him for their success.

"Snake, go fetch my women. I need some loving before we start packing up."

***

John and Bill walked back into the camp and gathered the senior team together. Scott, Tom, Beth, Alice, and Sam joined John and Bill in planning the assault on Decatur.

Bill kept to his plan to blow up the hotel while the bikers were sleeping and to his surprise, no one disagreed with this brutal, uncivilized planned massacre.

Beth said to Bill, "Hard times make for hard decisions. Those bastards have raped or killed just about everyone in that pitiful city. Let's help them meet with God and let him sort them out."

Everyone laughed. They worked on the plan for over six hours, and at the end had a plan they felt would succeed with minimal losses on their side.

The key to their plan was a before dawn attack while the guards were both tired and drunk, blowing up the hotel the gang stayed in and snipers picking off the guards. They all agreed that the entire gang was to be executed down to the last man.

The advanced team, led by Bill, brought five cases of dynamite taken from a mining company, 50 one-gallon milk jugs filled with gas, and chains to lock the doors on the Executive Hotel. Team Two, led by Scott, was to infiltrate the Value Inn and liberate the poor women who had been sex slaves for the bikers. Team Three, led by John, was to kill all of the guards and mop up any gang members who escaped.

Bill and his team slowly crawled between cars to get close to the hotel. Bill walked right up to the two men guarding the front of the Hotel and asked where the head biker was. Both laughed, but Bill's team grabbed them from behind. Bill's accomplices quickly slit the thug's throats and let them drop to the ground.

The same tactics were being used successfully at the side and back doors. The bikers were drunk or stoned as expected. No one had challenged them since the massacre at the prison, and they were complacent.

Next, they threw the gas jugs into the hallways from the rooms to the outside entrances. Bill placed dynamite with short fuses in the lobby and threw dynamite into the hotel while another poured gas from one end of the hotel to the opposite end.

209

They then chained the doors shut and pushed cars against the doorways. They finally placed dynamite all around the hotel with two-minute fuses and lit them.

John radioed the other teams and said, "Go!" They backed off and waited for the thugs to try to break windows to escape.

The explosion rocked the entire town and rained pieces of the hotel down on a large section of Decatur. Team 2 reacted immediately, stormed the Value Inn and quickly eliminated the guards who were either half asleep or in a drug-induced stupor. The women and children were told that they were free.

Scott was caught by surprise and was blindsided by a gang banger who stabbed him from behind. The knife sliced through his backpack and only stopped when it struck the .223 magazines. The thug had Scott by the throat and tried to get the knife loose and finish him off. Scott did not know the asshole had a knife and thought the bastard was trying to choke him to death. He stomped the man's foot, then kicked his knee as he twisted around and got free. He was now facing the thug with a big assed knife coming at him. Scott had a Glock in his hand, shot the bastard in the chest twice and once in the head.

Scott told the body, "That's what happens when you bring a knife to a gun fight."

Scott was shaking as he scanned for other targets. He knew that the pouch holding the magazines had saved his life.

Alice and Janet lay in concealed positions outside of the Inn to kill any of the scum that got out of the Inn alive and to watch for any surprise attacks.

Alice only had two gang targets present themselves as they tried to escape. She was sad that she felt very little remorse for killing the scumbags but knew it had to happen.

Janet, on the other hand, found that she got a rush every time she shot one of those scumbags. After being savagely raped a few weeks ago, she found herself enjoying killing these men.

She shot five and watched them squirm around on the ground before shooting them again in an arm or leg. She took four shots to kill the last bastard. "Hell hath no fury...," she whispered to the dead and dying bodies.

***

"What the fuck is going on out there? Snake, send some men out to shut those drunken bastards up."

Snake and four men rushed out of the door, and they met a wall of bullets. Jerry panicked, ran out the door and tried to get to his truck to escape. He heard a shot, felt a searing pain in his left calf and fell to the ground.

He turned in time to see a woman with a big rifle pointed at him. He tried to shoot her, but she was faster and shot him in the shoulder. He pulled his machete with his other hand and swung it at her legs. She blocked it with the butt of her rifle and knocked it from his hands.

"Go ahead and grab your knife. I'll put a bullet in your brain."

Jerry said, "I've raped, tortured and killed much better looking bitches than you will ever be, you sorry piece of ass."

Alice aimed the rifle at his hand that was near the knife and shot his wrist. He screamed in pain and continued cursing her. She placed the muzzle on his balls and pulled the trigger. He screamed again and passed out. She put two bullets in his head and smiled, "Maybe so, you miserable bastard, but you won't hurt another woman."

***

John waited until the Executive Hotel blew up in a ball of smoke and flames. He then started picking off the guards stationed around the town. The explosion at the hotel leveled it and all of the structures within a hundred feet all around it. No bikers jumped out of windows. Over two hundred hardened criminals died in that explosion, and none was prepared to meet God at the pearly gates.

John hoped that there were no innocent people in those buildings around the hotel. There were, but John would never know that detail.

Beth hid in the shadows and shot each one of the gang members that crossed her path. She dispatched eight in about four minutes. Her only thought was that she really needed a suppressor to reduce the noise. Taking out the trash was becoming easier by the shot.

Scott posted several guards while the rest of the team drove to the Value Inn parking lot. John held a brief meeting with his team and gave everyone heartfelt thanks for a job well done.

He ended with, "Bill do you think you had enough dynamite?"

Everyone laughed. They had killed approximately three hundred gang members and only had ten wounded, six from flying glass during the attack. They had achieved total surprise on a bunch of drunk and stoned bikers.

Beth, Janet, and Alice then went into the Value Inn and had to persuade the captive women to come out of the building. They were afraid the bikers would shoot them. The group was traumatized and barely able to function.

Beth asked if any of the women had any police or military experience. Five women stumbled forward. They appeared badly beaten, both on the in and outside, but with each step grew both stronger and determined.

Over the next three hours, several hundred of the town's citizens gathered to find out what had happened. They were like sheep and appeared to be in a daze. John gathered the women who had been captives and the citizens who continued to filter back into town and addressed the crowd.

He said, "Citizens of Decatur, you are now free of the gang that killed, raped and looted this city. A few may have escaped, but there are about three hundred dead scumbags, and about fifty are lying around your town starting to rot. You need to clean up the mess before rats get to them and disease spreads."

A woman tried to interrupt John, but Bill told her to shut up.

She yelled, "I am the Mayor of this town, and you killed them, you clean up the mess."

One of the women who had been a captive said, "Why weren't you with us in the hotel? Were you hiding or helping the bikers? Our Mayor is an anti-gun liberal."

John started again with, "If the Mayor interrupts again, tie and gag her.

People, you have to take charge of your town, or this happens again. Elect a real Mayor who will fight for a strong defense of this town, start your own army and protect yourselves or die.

Don't rely on others or the government to protect your town. We are leaving you enough weapons and ammo to fend off an army of scum. You just need the backbone to fight those that try to take your liberty."

One of the crowd asked, "No, you have to stay and protect us? You have a duty to protect us."

John replied, "You are what is wrong with this town; you want someone else to do your dirty work. We're leaving, and we genuinely hope that you want to survive, but assholes like this jerk should be run out of town.

Now, look to your women and children who had been held captive. If that doesn't give you the intestinal fortitude to man up, then........well, then you deserve your fate."

John waited for his words to sink in and added, "Do any of you have military or police training?"

Only five former women captives and three men came forward. However, they had a wealth of experience, and several had fought in Vietnam and The Middle East. John told them to report for duty at 7:00 a.m. sharp by the waterfront.

John then asked volunteers to become the town's police and The Decatur Defense Force. He told them that he would get them some initial training to protect their families and the town. About a hundred women and forty men came to John to "Man up."

The next morning John found that one of the men had been a Marine drill Sergeant and two of the ladies had been MPs, so he left all of the biker's guns and ammo, but did accept half of the silver that had been collected to cover his teams time and trouble taking the town back.

As John, Beth, and Gus walked away, three women came up to him and told him that they would like to join John's group.

The one that appeared to be the leader of the three spoke up and said, "John, we can earn our keep and fight when necessary. Karen was an MP, Jill was a supply Sergeant; both were Army. My name is Meg. I was a Warrant Officer and helicopter pilot. All of us saw action in Iraq and have had to kill a few times.

Honestly, I just don't think we can live with these sheep that let this happen to us. We hope you understand."

John listened and replied in his most sincere Alabama drawl, "'Course, ya'll are welcome to join, but this ain't gonna' be no cake walk."

Meg replied, "John, ya'll saved our sorry asses. We want to make sure that we repay you, and are able to help others." They all shook hands and headed out.

The convoy was back on the road early the next morning.

*

Chapter 5

On the Road Again!

North of Decatur

June 8, 2020

I-65 North of Decatur
     Highway 65 South was a sea of stalled cars, trucks and many people walking to only they knew where. Perhaps in many cases, Only God knew.
     Most of the people kept to themselves, but several groups tried to get the convoy to stop to no avail. It was hard driving past so many women and children who just wanted food, or a ride to anywhere besides where they were.
     They were shot at a couple of times. No one was hurt, and only one window shot out.

Beth pointed at the numerous tractor-trailers parked among the stalled vehicles and said, "I wonder where they were going and what they are carrying?"

Almost screaming, "What an idiot!" John hit the brakes and came to a full stop behind the nearest trailer. Beth looked nervous as he waved to the team to gather around him.

John addressed the team, "As ya'll obviously know, the power grid is down; food and water are getting scarce and, whether we like it or not, *we* are the law.

Beth just pointed out that most of these trailers that we've been passing must have supplies that we need. We're going to start checking them for food, weapons, and supplies. We'll take as much as we can to The Bunker. Aw man, I feel like an idiot for not thinking of this. Well done, Beth."

Scott replied, "We need to commandeer a couple of trailers to pull behind the trucks so we can carry more supplies. Let's get Steve of the horn and tell him to do the same."

Everyone agreed. Scott led a team to go find four trailers while John led the team to start checking the semi-trailer's contents."

Bill took a crowbar and removed the lock from the first trailer they found. The lock came off easily, and the door was opened to deliver the smell of rotted meat. Lesson 1 was, don't open refrigerated trailers.

John opened the next one and found that it was loaded with canned goods and grocery items. He had hit the mother lode. Several of the convoy members helped him go through the contents.

Scott brought a trailer over, and they loaded it full of canned meat and vegetables. John found six different flavors of Spam and was sure that God was smiling down on him. Jalapeno Spam was his favorite. As John watched the last case loaded on the trailer, he wondered why no one else was raiding the stalled trailers.

They found one tractor-trailer with vegetables that were still barely edible, but in others, only car parts, plumbing supplies, and several other trailers with rotted meat, but nothing else usable was found. The sun was setting, so they decided to make camp and go at it again in the morning.

They had only covered about five miles due to their trailer inspections.

John surprised the cooks and started frying Spam by the pan full. Fried Spam, corn on the cob and fried potatoes were enjoyed by all that night.

Scott took several of the men and two trucks to drive back to a town that they had just passed about three miles back. He hoped to find four abandoned trailers or at least trade for some trailers with food, ammo and some of the guns they had captured. They knew that they had to be very careful approaching the town because even good people could shoot first and ask questions later.

They got about a quarter of a mile from the town. Scott took one of his crew to scout the town to determine if they were friendly and if there were any trailers that could be used.

The closer they came to the town the more they noticed that there was no one in sight. The town was the typical Alabama farm town that had many gas stations, churches, fast food restaurants, and a Wal-Mart.

Scott used binoculars to scan the town for a few minutes and saw several burned out cars and buildings. There was also evidence of a large battle that left pockmarks on buildings and thousands of shell casings scattered around the streets.

In front of the courthouse was a black Humvee that was shot up and partially burned. There were no bodies or for that matter, any signs of people anywhere.

They entered the town and slowly crept down a side street while being careful to keep cover nearby. They finally spotted about twenty trailers in a Tractor Supply parking lot. Most were small, but several were sixteen feet long and a couple of goosenecks with enclosed thirty-foot horse trailers. Scott used a walkie-talkie to get the others to join them at the trailers.

They arrived in about ten minutes and were hooking up the trailers when one of the guys went to Scott and said, "Scott, I saw something move between those buildings on the right."

Scott replied, "I'll slide away and sneak up behind the building and flush them out. You go over towards the front. Be ready if they come that way."

Scott backed out of the group, circled around the building, and went into the back lot, which had a hedge that gave him cover. He stayed behind the hedge and covered about two hundred yards when he heard people talking.

He listened to the conversation for several minutes and heard them trying to decide if they should make contact with these intruders. The argument revolved around trying to hook up with a larger group or keep hiding from the DHS.

Scott shouted, "We're friendly." When no bullets came his way, he stood up and raised his hands to get their attention. They raised their weapons towards him as he walked towards them.

He said, "I'm Scott Harris, and we only came here to get four trailers. If they belong to you, then we would like to trade for them."

There were three young women and two older men standing in front of him with guns aimed at his chest.

Scott said, "If you lower the guns we can talk about ya'll joining us and what happened in this town."

One of the men spoke up and said, "Lower your guns, he's not here to hurt us."

He looked at Scott and said, "Where did you get the fancy military guns?"

Scott replied, "We took them from some bad guys who were trying to hurt us. It looks like ya'll have had a run in with the same folks. The DHS was supposed to be helpful to citizens, but it appears they have become an occupying power with an agenda that is not in our favor."

By this time, Scott's backup had walked up to the group with his rifle aimed at the group. Scott waved for him to lower the gun. They all walked over to a picnic table and sat down to share stories.

The leader was Pastor Falls. He led the First Baptist Church and was in the Army right out of high school.

He told them that the DHS had come into town several times trying to talk them into moving into the relocation camp. The mayor and city council met with them and adamantly told the DHS leader that the citizens of Pineville are doing well and did not need help.

They suggested that the DHS go find someone who needed help as they had plenty of food, water, and all other necessary supplies. The folks here about are mainly farmers.

They even had several mechanics that were getting many of the trucks and cars running by retrofitting them with engine parts from the 60s and 70s.

The DHS leader told them that there were many bands of criminals out there raiding towns like this and taking women and children as sex slaves.

The mayor told him that he had over five hundred armed fighters that could handle themselves.

All went well that week, but several families came into town reporting that raiders had hit them during the night, shot up their cattle and drove trucks all through their crops. Every day afterward the violence escalated until there were farmers and town folk being killed, or burned out.

The raiders killed a family of five and hung their naked bodies from a tree at the edge of town. The woman and three girls had been raped and sodomized and had words carved into their chests.

This scared the hell out of the women. Whole families started to travel to the camp in Mobile. It didn't take long until only a couple of hundred people were left around the town and nearby farms. That was when the DHS came back and tried to force the remaining people to go to the camp in Mobile.

The Pastor said, "They came with four armored Humvees, five trucks, and ten buses. They were ready for the people to drop their arms and load up like cattle. Well, the bastards were wrong."

He continued to say that many of the locals had gone home to get a few personal items. They were ready to load up when the DHS told them no pets or guns could be taken to the camp.

When the people balked, one of the DHS men butt stroked a man with his rifle. All hell broke loose. Two men tackled the Agent, and the DHS shot them.

Suddenly, everyone with a gun began shooting at the other side. The town folk had the upper end in just a few minutes. They killed almost all of the DHS men and burned all of the buses and trucks before the DHS could get the Humvees into the action.

Sadly, the townspeople failed to keep all of the DHS bastards away from Humvees. The twin machine guns on each vehicle quickly put the fight to an end, and the remaining town folk went into hiding.

There were only ten DHS men left alive at the end of the battle, and they only got out alive because they were in the armored Humvees. The Pastor then said something that scared the crap out of Scott.

He said, "You know those bastards are overdue, they usually come back through every two to three days about this time, and we haven't seen them in five days. We usually pick off one or two and go hide until they leave."

Scott replied, "We need to get the hell out of here. What can we do to help you?"

They told him that they needed some more powerful weapons.

Scott gave them their M4 rifles and ammo. He told them, "Look, ya'll have to stop ambushing them in your town. They will eventually carpet bomb your asses. Hit them on roads ten to twenty miles from here. Hit different locations.

Our home base is only a short distance away, and we need allies. We also need a pastor to marry my dad and soon-to-be mom. We will bring you better weapons, ammo, and teach better tactics."

The Pastor replied, "Thanks so much for the help and I would love to conduct the ceremony."

They shook hands and parted.

***

Scott's team arrived with two horse trailers in tow, and their friends warmly greeted them. Scott quickly told the others that they had to go back and get the other flatbed trailers. He then told them about the town's experience with the DHS.

John told Scott to take a couple of extra men along with a load of rifles and ammo for the town. He also took Scott's advice on watching for the DHS on their way to the town.

They were only gone about two hours and came back with two flatbed trailers in tow, and another piled on top of each trailer.

Scott reported that the town was excited to get the guns and ammo and would be happy to work with them to defeat these DHS assholes.

John and Beth had the last guard duty slot for the night and reported in for duty at 4:00 a.m. Bill informed them that he and Alice had heard something or someone messing around the last trailer that they had opened.

John told Bill that he would check it out once the sun came up. They grabbed a cup of coffee and toured the camp while talking about the world falling apart.

After making a couple of laps around the camp and finding nothing unusual, they sat at their post and quietly told each other their life stories.

They had been on duty about thirty minutes when they heard sounds like someone rattling pots and pans. John told Beth to go wake up Scott and Tom and get back quickly.

John got down on the ground and crawled towards the sounds, which appeared to be coming from behind a car about fifty yards away. John got to a pickup about 10 yards from the noise and took cover. John was displeased when he heard his backup crew before he saw them. He waved them to join him behind the pickup and told Scott and Tom to go around to the back of the car while he went to the front.

Scott lunged around the tail of the car and found himself staring at a big gun aimed at his chest. The gun was in the hands of a very scared little boy of about eight years. He was standing in front of two toddlers about two to three years old.

Scott said, "I'm not going to hurt you or the others."

219

The boy looked Scott in the eye and said, "I know you won't."

Just then, Scott saw someone tackle the boy as there was an explosion knocking Scott to the ground. He felt a searing pain in his right side and wondered if this kid had just killed him.

John had knocked the boy to the ground just as he pulled the trigger on the Colt 1911. The blowback nearly knocked the kid to the ground. The bullet hit Scott's pistol and drove it into his ribs, reeling him backward. Bill ran up and took care of the boy while Alice led the two little kids to the camp.

Beth had Scott take his shirt off to determine the extent of his injuries. There was no blood, but he would have a hell of a pistol-shaped bruise on his side.

John helped Scott back to the camp where they saw the kids being fed.

Scott had the kid's Colt in his belt, and the kid said, "Give me my gun back."

Scott both grimaced and grinned as he replied, "So, 'Little Gus' wants another chance to shoot me."

The group broke out laughing. Beth placed the boy in her lap and asked him where his parents were.

The boy's name was Billy, and he talked a mile a minute. He told them that about two weeks ago some men drove up to their farm and ordered everyone to come out of the house.

His mom hid his sister, brother and him in the basement. Then she and his dad went out to meet the men.

There were gunshots and screams, but the kids kept quiet and hid until there were no sounds coming from the front yard. Billy left the younger kids in the basement, went upstairs to his parent's bedroom and got the Colt out of a closet. He loaded it, and then went out the back door. He stayed out of sight until he could make sure that the bad guys were gone.

As he peered around the corner of the house, he saw two men dragging his parent's bodies back into the house. Then the men doused the porch and front room with gas and set the house on fire. Billy wanted to shoot the men, but he knew he had to get his brother and sister out of the burning house.

He dashed through the back door and down the stairs. The kids were asleep. He woke them up and carried his brother while urging his sister up the stairs. The whole front of the house was ablaze when they cleared the door.

Billy had them stop so he could make sure they were not seen and then ran to the barn and hid until the bad men drove away.

The house burned to the ground, and only Billy knew that their mom and dad had been burned along with the house.

While Billy was only eight years old, he worked on the farm with his dad and was more mature than his age would indicate. He quickly started looking for food, water and anything that would help them survive. He found a couple of hams in the smokehouse, a case of bottled water in the barn and several knives. He placed the supplies and his brother in his toy wagon and left home for good.

***

They continued their trip to the bunker the next day, and the kids rode with Beth and Alice. Beth told Billy about their situation and where they were headed. The two bonded quickly, and Billy opened up to her about being scared that they would starve without help. Beth assured him that she would make sure that they were taken care of.

The group continued to open up trailers on the way to Mobile and quickly determined that they needed to get a large truck and trailer running to haul all of the canned goods and supplies. They filled every nook and cranny with supplies until every vehicle was nearly overflowing. They were also able to fill their tanks with gas and diesel from the stalled vehicles without much trouble.

During the break for lunch, John asked Beth how the kids were doing.

Beth replied, "John, they are so cute and special. Billy has fed and protected them for several weeks, and he is only eight years old.

Bill and Alice want to adopt Rich, and I'm sure that many other families will want to adopt them.

John said, "It's good that they are black. It reminds me that we have got to make sure no one comes into our community that finds that a problem."

John took Beth by the hand and asked, "Beth, where are we going in our relationship? I hate to suggest that we adopt them when we aren't "we" yet. I love you and want to live with you forever. We could adopt them."

Beth gave him a kiss and said, "Oh Hell Yes."

John asked, "Ok then, yes, we will adopt?"

Beth said, "Yes we will adopt Billy and Lindsey, but what I also meant was, yes, I will marry you."

They kissed and then got the group together and announced their engagement.

Scott was the first to congratulate them.

He said, "It's about time. The whole camp was wondering when you'd make an honest woman out of my new mom."

The rest of the group hugged Beth and John and wanted to know when they were getting married.

John asked, "Does anyone know a preacher?"

They all laughed and looked at each other.

Bill said, "Well we need to add a preacher to the list of skills we need. A real doctor would come in handy also."

John, Beth, Bill, and Alice got all three of the kids and discussed their future with them. The two little ones were too young to understand and sat in Alice and Bill's lap. The kids felt love again and lapped it up. Beth asked Billy and Lindsey to live with John and her.

Billy said he was worried about his brother, but John explained that they all lived at the same place so he would always be around his brother.

*

Chapter 6

Confederates at the Bunker

North of Mobile, Alabama

June 9, 2020

The Bunker

Gus had expected his friends to take three to four days to get to Mobile, but they were long overdue. He was resisting sending a search party out to find them. Steve was even worse than Gus was. He missed Janet and wanted her with him. He had only known her for a couple of days and already could not imagine life without her. He guessed Armageddon had that effect on people.

Their imagination was running wild with all of the bad things that could have happened to their friends. Finally, they came to their senses and decided that John and Scott were well trained and were both born leaders. They could handle themselves. Whatever had slowed them down had been dealt with, and nothing could stop them from getting to the bunker.

Then Gus said, "If the bastards don't get here within three days, I'm taking the DC3 and heading north to find them."

They agreed and got back to work.

Steve left to go on patrol while Gus went to check on Jim and his latest crop of trainees. Gus walked over to the barn and watched Jim training a bunch of ladies how to shoot BB guns.

Jim's girlfriend was keeping guard on him and making sure that no flirting was going on. Gus thought to himself that she had reason to be worried, not because Jim was a ladies' man, but because there were two women for every man due to the attack. He knew that women would be either cherished, or turned into slaves. No sane man would kill women in this new screwed up world.

Imelda was by far the best shot as she had attended three of Jim's training sessions and was ready to graduate to a real gun. Each of the men or women that took the full three days of training was moved up to the .22 rifles, then to a combat weapon. Gus then watched Robin for a while and prayed that she would never have to fire a shot in anger.

***

The women were of various ages from fourteen to late fifties and were all chained to the wall without any clothes, but their panties. Several guards had dragged them from their cells, stripped them and chained them to the wall by their wrists. The guards took turns watching the door and molesting the women for about an hour before the door opened.

A large black man walked into the room and told all but one of the guards to leave. Deke walked over to one of the young women and ran his hands all over her while she struggled. He told the guard that she was a keeper. Next, he went to one of the older and very attractive women. He tried to place his hand on her breast when she kicked him in the leg. He slapped her twice and told the guard to leave her chained for later use.

He felt up all of the women until one tried to kick him in the balls. He pulled his pistol and shot her in the head. The blood and brains splattered several of the women. Two started to cry, and Deke shot them.

He then turned to the guard and said, "Tell the men to come back and take these two to my quarters and all of the rest to the brothel except for the old bitch. Tell the men to take turns with her until they get their fill and then shoot her."

***

Steve was on a four-wheeler riding along the perimeter of the compound just after noon when several men with guns stepped out of the bushes and confronted him.

Steve had his M4, a 9mm strapped to his side, but saw five big black guys surrounding him and they looked like they knew what they were doing. He decided to play along with them and see what they wanted.

The oldest of the group stepped forward and said, "Drop your guns and let's talk."

Steve replied, "Let's talk and I keep my guns."

The reply was, "Drop your guns or we drop your sorry ass."

Steve dropped his M4 and used two fingers to pull his pistol and drop it to the ground.

The leader said, "Now we can talk. What are you doing out here and why should we trust you?"

Steve replied, "You should trust me because I say so and none of your business."

George started laughing and had to force himself to stop.

George said, "The bottom line is, is it safe for black folk around here?"

Steve replied, "So because I'm black I know everything about blacks being safe? No, blacks aren't safe around here; however, whites and Chinese aren't safe either. What you need to ask is "Can you join our team as equals?"

George replied, "I guess you cut to the bottom line there buddy. We'd like to get to know you and your team. We were just passing through, but this looks like a good area to check out."

The men took Steve back to their camp and introduced him to the rest of the family. They compared notes on their recent experiences and when George told him about the fight with the DHS Steve knew why the DHS had not come back to the bunker. Steve asked for more detail, and George gave him a blow-by-blow description from finding the girls being attacked to hiding the Humvee.

Steve asked, "Do ya'll want the Humvee? If not, we may be able to use it to fight those dirty bastards."

George said, "We don't need it, and you should be careful it stands out and would draw more of those DHS assholes."

Steve laughed and replied, "That is exactly why I want it, cheese to bait the trap."

George asked, "So ya'll are strong enough to take on the US Government?"

Steve replied, "Not in a face-to-face all-out battle, but we have a few veterans that know how to handle themselves, and I'll bet you and your crew have some military experience. Together we can start with harassing them while we grow strong enough to defeat them."

The camp was just waking up. Shirley and the girls were preparing a big ham and eggs breakfast when they saw the men walking towards them.

Several kids ran up to George and asked him what he had brought back for them.

He pointed at Steve and told them he had brought them an Alabama redneck. They all laughed. George introduced Steve to his family and the girls. Steve told them his story during breakfast. Steve was careful not to tell them too much detail about the bunker or their supplies and weapons. He really liked this family and felt that they would fit in well with his people. He asked if they wanted to come with him to the farm to meet the rest of his people, and perhaps settle down for a while at the farm.

George asked Steve to take a walk for about fifteen minutes while the family had a meeting to discuss joining Steve's team.

Sandra and Linda started walking with Steve when Shirley walked up to them and said, "Where are you two going? We are having a family meeting."

Both stared at Shirley and then Sandra said, "We know that you are being nice, but we really aren't part of your family."

Shirley replied, "You two are good people, and we would love for you to join our family."

They walked off to the meeting.

George's Camp

Steve walked the perimeter of the camp and saw a man about 200 yards out at each end of the camp on Lookout. He was pleased that these people were vigilant. They could contribute to the safety of the group and would not be a hindrance.

He heard something and looked all around when it dawned on him to look up. He saw a helicopter about a mile north of their position heading east. While he knew, they could not be seen, he knew that the helicopter was searching for something and he did not want them to find the bunker. He ran back to the camp to warn the others and saw that they were already hiding in the brush in case the helicopter came back their way.

When the helicopter disappeared over the horizon, George rounded everyone up and said, "I want to travel to Steve's group and talk about joining them. Get ready to travel."

George said to Steve, "We will be ready to travel in thirty minutes and may want to join your group."

Steve nodded, shook George's hand and told him that he felt sure that adding his family could only strengthen The Bunker community.

"I hope this is not a problem, but my group has mostly white people."

Shirley responded, "Do they believe in God? Are they good people? That's all that's important."

"We all believe in God, and yes, they are great people. We have a few hard heads, but they are good and would give you the shirt off their back."

Steve told them that they were only a couple of miles from the farm and that he should go in first by himself to make sure that there were no accidental shootings.

He led them to the farm, had them stop about five hundred yards from the perimeter fence and went on in to be met at the gate. He checked in with the guards and then drove up to the house.

Steve filled the team in on the newcomers, and the team was glad to have more good people join them. There was, however, some concern about food and supplies.

Gus told them about the semis, and that they had just found several truckloads of can goods. He told them there were many more out on the roads and to get them before someone else did. The gardens would be expanded to become a true farm, so there really was no food concern. The group decided to welcome the newcomers warmly and make them feel at home.

Steve led George's family into the compound and introduced them to their new family. They were welcomed, and the women took over figuring out living accommodations.

Alice, Ann, and Shirley hit it off from the start and quickly got Shirley and her daughters and daughter-in-laws into the cooking and guard schedules. Shirley was an excellent cook and took over the kitchen, which hurt no one's feelings.

Ginny tapped Imelda on the shoulder and pointed to the horizon. It was just before sunset, and she had seen a glint of light just below the tree line about a mile out. Imelda raised her rifle and used the scope to check out the tree line.

She said, "Darn, I hope they are friendly because there are a bunch of vehicles heading our way."

They called for Gus. He drove up to their position with Steve and Jim in the pickup.

Gus said, "That's John and Scott bringing the rest of our crew home."

Ginny replied, "You could have told us. What if we had shot at them?"

Gus said, "John told me that he wanted to test our defenses. Ya'll passed the test."

Imelda ran back to the house to tell everyone that the crew from Tennessee had finally arrived. They all came out to greet the rest of their ever-growing family.

There were fifteen trucks in the convoy, and all were towing trailers full of food, water, guns, and supplies. The string of trucks drove through the gate and on up to the house with John and Beth in the lead vehicle.

John jumped out, shook Gus's hand and said, "Well we made it, and everyone is alive, and except for Sam, all are well and sound."

Gus gave Beth a big hug and asked her, "Has John been good to you?"

She replied, "Yes, he is wonderful. Gus, where is your wife, Robin? I want to meet her."

Gus turned to see Robin and the rest of the group approaching them. Ann was leading the group and walking fast. Gus introduced Robin and Beth and then left with Jim to help get the trailers unloaded.

Ann walked up to John and gave him and Scott big hugs.

She said, "Now, John, where is this new girlfriend of yours? I want to meet her."

Beth walked up to John and held his hand.

She said, "I'm John's new girlfriend, and you must be Scott's mom. He's told me so much about you."

Scott said, "I got to go help Jim and Gus, bye."

He took off running.

Ann said, "John, did you and Scott think that I would make a scene? Ya'll probably have this girl afraid of me."

John said, "Ann, I don't believe Beth is afraid of anything. However, I did not bad mouth you."

He took off to help the others.

228

Ann took Beth by the hand and said, "Beth, you don't have to be worried about me. I just got rid of John two years ago and am not interested in him."

Beth replied, "Thanks for clearing the air, but I really wasn't worried."

Ann looked at Beth who was wearing short-shorts and a tight fitting tee shirt and was very beautiful, and said, "I'm sure you weren't darling."

They both smiled at each other, but before anything could happen, Steve interrupted them and yelled for everyone to gather around him so he could introduce the newcomers. He introduced the people from Mobile first.

John asked, "Where is what's his face, Ann's boyfriend?"

Steve said, "A long story, but Ann kicked his racist ass out of here."

Steve then introduced George's family and the people that George's team had brought in to join the team. John finally introduced the group from Tennessee to everyone and was ready to get back to work when Steve motioned him over to the center of the crowd.

Steve said, "We have one last introduction and then y'all can go about your business. For those of you who have joined this band of misfits, John Harris is our leader. Say something John."

John looked over the crowd and said, "Welcome to The Bunker. I can't think of much to say now, but you all know that the country has gone to hell in a hand basket. It appears that elements of our government have actually turned against us and are forcing people into concentration camps. We have food, water, shelter, and weapons, but need to keep gathering as much of those as possible until we can expand the garden and find out how dangerous Mobile is. We all need to work together and share the load. That's it for now. Have a good night."

As the crowd broke up, Ann said, "Beth, come on into the kitchen, and we'll get some sweet tea and get to know each other."

Beth agreed, and they went into the house. The rest of the women stayed away and waited for the inevitable fight. They came out of the house about an hour later laughing and acting as if they were best friends.

Steve walked up to Beth, gave her a hug and said, "Ya'll cost me two extra hours of guard duty. Several of us bet that there would be a fight."

Ann hit him on one arm while Beth hit him on the other.

John and Gus helped get the vehicles unloaded and made sure everyone had a new home, then went into the barn and compared notes on the past several weeks.

*

Chapter 7

Day after Independence Day

Smyrna, TN

Dec 21, 2048

They all had a good breakfast, then went to their rooms and got ready for church. They had started a tradition of attending church on the day after the Independence Day celebration. Josh came out of his room and bumped into two men who were obviously security guards. They moved out of the way and stood by the front door.

Josh walked into the living room and saw another pair of guards by the front door. He expected to see security for the ex-President on the ISA, but this appeared to be overkill.

Most of the family was in the living room with John keeping things lively and stirred up. He was dressed in a suit and tie so he was not rolling on the floor but was still playing with his grandkids.

He heard steps and turned to see Lindsey and Jenn walk down the stairs. They were two of the most beautiful women that he had ever seen. They both had M4s and bulletproof vests in their hands.

Jenn smiled at him and said, "Just like the Swiss, every adult in the ISA is armed and ready to protect our country. We are on high alert today because of the 25th anniversary of the Republic."

They all began walking out to the waiting cars when Josh noticed that there were three limousines and a dozen up-armored Humvees making up a rather impressive convoy. John motioned for Josh to join Beth and him in the middle car. Josh got in and saw that the windows were about an inch thick. These were bulletproof cars built for the leaders of this country.

Josh slapped his head as he remembered that several of the founding "Fathers" of this country surrounded him. They would be a prime target for any enemies foreign or domestic.

John and Beth filled Josh in on the events planned for the day, and Jenn gave him advice on what to do if there was an attack.

Josh asked, "Are you really worried about a real attack or is this just a way to remind me that you still have enemies after all of these years. After all, there have been no hostilities between the two countries in years."

John replied, "That's what your country tells you. We have averaged six attacks a year since the last war. Just five months ago, those bastards tried to bomb the kindergarten that my grandkids attend. We will eventually unleash holy hell on the USA, and you should not go back over the border. You appear to be a great guy, and I can't hold Scott back much longer."

They drove for about fifteen minutes through a very scenic route and arrived in front of a majestic old church with massive oak trees lining the street. The preacher was at the front door greeting everyone and shaking hands. The preacher was a very distinguished young black man that could have passed for a politician running for office.

Billy "Gus" Harris was thirty-six, six foot two and built like a basketball player. He had fought in every battle since he was fourteen but followed his heart to serve the Lord. He had a Glock 9mm in a shoulder holster and a bible in his left hand. His favorite motto was "The Lord takes care of those who take care of themselves." After the last person had entered the church, the pastor came in and waited until the choir stopped singing and welcomed the congregation and visitors.

As they entered, Josh noticed that there were numerous reporters and six cameras covering this event. They were ushered into a pew at the front of the church. He was seated next to John with Jenn on his other side. She filled him in on who was who in the ISA world. He quickly noticed that he was the only reporter that was actually even close to the leaders of the country. He could see the glares and almost feel the jealousy from the other reporters. One gave him a middle finger salute. It was just dawning on him how much he should feel honored.

Little Gus gave a hell fire and brimstone sermon that lasted for twenty minutes then yielded the podium to George Washington, the Vice President of the ISA. George thanked everyone for their service to the ISA and went on to cover the brief history of their country.

He spoke with passion of the sacrifices made by all, and the heroes that gave their lives to help give birth to this Republic. He mentioned big Gus's first wife Robin, Bill, James, Fred, Allen, Kristie, Fox and a host of others who gave their lives during the fight to establish this fledgling new country.

Little Gus then highlighted the diversity of this country born in fire and blood, and come out steel. He said that his father and mother, John and Beth, had found him scrounging for food for himself and his brother and sister. His first action was to shoot the future President of the ISA, yet they still took him and made him a part of their family.

He then mentioned his Godfather, Gus, and Godmother, Ginny, who had been wounded during the battle for Mobile. With that said, he introduced John to the congregation.

"How do you introduce someone that everyone already knows? Radio personality, war hero, founder of this country, and President of this country are some of the highest achievements a person can attain. However, I think his highest achievements are great father and friend. John Harris."

"Thanks, son," said John. He then went on to tell the people that he was honored to be a part of this great country and still alive to be able to celebrate its 25th anniversary. He briefly covered some of the early battles, trials, and tribulations and then spoke about the greatness of the people making up the country.

He then said, "All of you have heard every word that I've said and have been saying for the past twenty-five years. I never want our story to die away. We can never let the world forget the treason and the traitors. With that in mind, I want to introduce Josh Logan of CNG. Josh, stand up."

Josh stood up while John continued.

John added, "This young man is here to report the real story about the birth of, and the ongoing struggles of the ISA. He has promised to tell the story as it is told to him. Scott is opening up the archives and sharing all document related to the attacks on our country and the traitors that conspired with our enemies to kill over three billion people worldwide. If he does a good job with that, he will be commissioned to write my biography."

The crowd cheered, and Josh just about fainted. He sat down and thought that he was living a "once in a lifetime" event for a newsperson. This placed a lot of pressure on him to make sure that he reported the facts as he found them. John's offer to open up the ISA's archives was a tremendous help to him in assuring that he had backup info to support his findings.

*

Chapter 8

The Cavalry Finally Arrives

The Bunker

June 15, 2020

Ann knocked on the door and opened it yelling, "John, the Navy wants to talk to you."

John and Beth had only been asleep for a couple of hours when they were awakened by the knock on the door.

She walked up to their bed and said, "Get your hands off her ass John and get your ass outside to talk to these Navy guys."

John shook the sleep from his head and said, "What?"

Ann said, "The Navy is in our front yard with a big-ass helicopter, and they want to speak with you."

John quickly dressed and put his shoulder holster on with his Colt 1911 and headed out the door. Beth gave the finger to Ann and jumped out of bed.

Ann said, "Put some clothes on, hussy. John never slept naked with me."

Beth replied, "That's because I give him a good reason every night."

John walked out the door into a squad of Marines in full battle gear. They took his .45 and marched him over to the helicopter. Marine Colonel Hiram Stokes and his staff were inside. They welcomed John and immediately began by thanking him for leading the resistance against the DHS.

John said, "Look, friends, we are just trying to survive, and those bastards were trying to make slaves out of these good people."

The Major Bob Jones filled John in on the current situation across the United States. As John feared, the DHS was trying to control the entire country, and the Military was sure that the President and a large contingent of liberal progressives had been planning this for years. They weren't sure, but they may even have been behind the nuclear attacks around the world.

He also learned that Israel had used neutron bombs on most of the radical Islamic strongholds in the Middle East. Israel had been attacked by several countries. ISIS and Al-Qaida. The Jews nuked those bastards and took control of a strip of land extending one hundred miles around Israel. They moved all people out and mined the strip to stop all future attacks.

Back in the U.S., the President had declared martial law, suspended the Constitution and put his socialist friends into all key positions, but most of the military had refused to obey his commands, citing suspension of the Constitution. They were actually threatening to remove him from power, but the President still controlled a handful of nukes so the military, for now, left them alone.

He then told John that most of the country was without power and in the same shape as Lower Alabama.

The exceptions were several cities that appeared to have been prepared for the EMP blasts. Chicago, Charleston, Sacramento and several other liberal bastions still had power.

John said, "Charleston is not a liberal city."

The colonel replied, "The government moved a large contingent of the Navy, Army, and DHS to Charleston and intended to make it the new capital of the United States. The Navy and the preponderance of the Army did not go along with that and derailed the plan.

The Military stood up to the President and actually drove the DHS from Charleston and all other military bases."

After catching up on current events, Colonel Stokes got down to business. He wanted to know if John and his people were in the fight to take back their country.

John looked puzzled and said, "I may not be the sharpest pencil in the box, but since ya'll are the military, why don't you just kick their asses and take the country back?"

The colonel replied, "John, normally you would be right about that, but we have not gotten you up to speed on the state of the military. The good news is that we have almost 80% of the Navy, and 80% of the Air Force, both men, and equipment. The bad news is we only have about 40% of the Army and Marines following the attacks by our enemies. Also, two-thirds of the surviving troops are overseas trying to extricate themselves from local fighting. Therefore, the bottom line is we need every fighting man and woman that we can field to take back the country. Also, I failed to mention about ten percent of the armed service still supports the President. We have them bottled up and shaking in their boots in fear that we will nuke them."

John had to stop and think for a minute.

Finally, he said, "It goes without saying that everyone here will fight to save our country, but the only decent arms that we have are ones that we had to take from DHS dead bodies."

The colonel replied, "Did I fail to mention that we control nearly all military supply warehouses? We can supply you with every class of supply. We also will provide combat training personnel. Of course, we can't turn everyone into Delta Force, but you will have tactical training. Training will be coordinated by a cadre of Army Drill Instructors.

The actual trainers will be transferred to your location upon acceptance of your willingness to join us in the fight."

John replied, "I will have to meet with the team, but I'm sure they will be on board."

Colonel Stokes introduced John to the two Officers handling command and control, Army Captain Bob Jones and 1Lt Roger Teller. John was returned to The Bunker by helicopter, which made only a low rumbling noise as it left.

The pilot said, "One of our Special Ops helos."

The Bunker

John waited until breakfast was over and called everyone, but the children together to discuss the meeting. When everyone had settled down, John introduced the two officers and gave them a brief update on the state of the country and the armed forces.

He then told them that they were needed to help establish law and order. John waited to see their reaction, and when it was overwhelmingly positive, he told them about the conversation with the Colonel Stokes.

John then told them, "This means that we go to war against every scumbag and DHS agent in the South. This will be a long, bloody and costly war."

Ann spoke up, "I really don't want to go to war with anyone; however, we are under attack and unless we bow down to the DHS and go to that damned camp, we have to fight. Count me in."

All, but a few, raised their hands to volunteer to fight in this endeavor.

John asked several of the group members to volunteer to serve on an attack strategy team, a home defense team and a supply organization team. John asked Gus to lead the defense team, and George to lead the supplies team. John would be leading the attacking team. He asked Ann to manage the day-to-day operations at The Bunker. They quickly split up and held their kickoff meetings.

George went to John and said, "If it's okay with you, I would like to have my sons mixed in with the other teams. I'll keep Sonny with me and send Marvin and Sammy to Gus and you."

John replied, "Do either have any Recon experience? I'll need one."

George said, "Marvin has experience in recon, infiltration, and explosives."

"Good, good, welcome aboard, Marvin."

Sammy reported to Gus along with Mary and Ginny.

John's team quickly set up a command and control office in the basement of the house for operations security and privacy. Along with Captain Bob Jones, and 1Lt Teller they jumped right into planning surveillance of the DHS compound and harassing attacks on the DHS scout teams. John's thoughts on priority were not the same as Bob's. John caught Bob off to the side and confronted him with his concerns.

John said, "Bob, while we both want what's right for our country and its' people, I'm beginning to feel a difference in what I think is good for my group versus what I hear from you."

Bob replied, "We have the same goals, but maybe the difference is how we get there."

John stopped him and said, "That's right, you are gearing up for an all-out attack on the DHS compound. They have over two thousand men while we have just over a hundred men and women."

Bob replied, "John, you are right, we are going to attack the DHS, kill every one of those SOBs and take their compound for your base of operations. John, you have been thinking too small, we need you to buy into the big picture quickly."

Bob gave John the rest of the story that the colonel had hidden from him. The Joint Chiefs had been preparing for this type of scenario since Obama purged many combat experienced senior officers during his last term. The military had planes, ships, artillery and everything else an army could possibly need, but was very short-handed. The rogue United States Government actually had more loyal soldiers and DHS men than the military. If you will recall, former President Obama said that the Executive Branch needed its own combat force equal to the Military Forces. Well, he did it, and no one even raised a finger to stop him.

Look, we can blow the hell out of any enemy or even nuke them, but we don't have enough boots on the ground to take and hold large plots of ground. The Joint Chiefs did not want the US Government or our enemies to know just how few actual war fighters had survived the attacks.

Our plan is to have a hundred teams like yours defeat the DHS and take back our country. The Joint Chiefs do not want an open fight against the forces loyal to the rogue U.S. Government because they have more fighting men. We could bomb the U.S. forces back to the Stone Age, but fear there would be horrible civilian casualties, which would result in more support for the traitors in Washington.

John asked, "How do ya'll tell one side from the other? You both are the United States Army and wear the same uniforms."

Bob replied, "We are calling ourselves the Independent States of America and have the flag of the original thirteen states on our chests. Over the next few weeks, we will be going back to an earlier designed Battle Dress Uniform. That will give us another degree of separation."

John had seen the flag with the thirteen stars in a circular pattern instead of the fifty on the modern flag. "I like it."

Bob added, "Same for our ships, planes, and tanks. It's a start."

Captain Bob, as John now thought of him, and John kept the main objective, to capture the DHS compound, to their team, but left the rest out in the open. Bob gave the team a list of priorities, and then they started mapping out an action plan for each objective. They worked in the basement room for several days ironing out their plans and making lists of supplies and skills they had to have to be successful. The plan evolved to send scout teams to Mobile to recon the defenses around the compound and make up-to-date maps of that area as their first action. The rest of the group would concentrate on finding able-bodied men and women to arm and join their forces.

***

DHS HQ, MOBILE

Deke spent at least two hours per day sorting through the women in the relocation camp. He thought, Hell, ya take pleasure where ya find it.

He was the only one who knew the President's plan and certainly the only one who knew his addition to that plan. The President had ordered each Field Marshall to weed out the stronger willed men and women from the rest, put them in slave camps to be kept under guard, and worked to death.

The weaker ones would not resist and would become the citizens of the new United States of America. They would be glad to be fed and taken care of by the government.

Deke added his rule to the President's set of rules. Deke's rule was that he was going to have sex with every one of the keepers and impregnate everyone that he could. He wanted to be the father of the new state of Alabama.

Deke had no military training and actually thought that they were beneath him. Once the country was subjugated, he would knock them down a peg or two. This wrongheaded thinking filtered down throughout his team. There were many experienced ex-military men in his army, but most were in lower level positions, and the less experienced leaders did not listen to them when they pointed out glaring issues with their defenses and tactics.

The only exceptions were the complaints from the major who was in charge of the patrols along the Tennessee border and just north of Mobile. Major Davis was reporting resistance and lost patrols. Major Johnson who was a charge of defending the compound was pleading with his superiors to move the troops into

240

the underground bunkers instead of the barracks buildings just inside of the perimeter fences.

Deke was not about to hide his army below ground like some scared rabbits. Besides the ISA, military and the United States, loyalist forces have agreed not to attack each other, and no one else has any real firepower.

The captain reminded them of the Marines killed in Lebanon in the eighties when Regan sent them in to keep the peace.

Deke didn't have time for this nonsense about security since he knew that the country was a shambles and the people only had a few ARs and hunting rifles. His men were heavily armed and had heavy machine guns, LAWs, and mortars that would decimate any resistance.

He was very pleased with their progress in getting the people of Alabama into the relocation and labor camps. There were only about five hundred thousand people left alive in Alabama due to disease, starvation, and attacks by gangs and the DHS.

The President had requested that the Field Marshal comes to the new capital to meet with him in person. The government would send a plane for him and his wife so the trip would be safe and give them a chance to rub elbows with the leaders of the new country.

***

Captain Jones warned Gus to be careful not to make any changes that would be visible from the air. He also told John and Gus that part of the overall plan could have them moving from the bunker to a more secure location in a few months.

Gus gathered his team. They brainstormed ideas about improving the perimeter defense. Beth and Sammy volunteered to put a guard schedule together that would be effective and fair. Meg and Steve checked out the top of the barn and the house for potential observation platforms.

George gathered the trucks with the horse trailers and got the team ready to go on a supplies search along Highway 65 North.

He took the time to train the team to know when to hide and how to keep as low a profile as possible. Robin wanted to bring a Humvee along to protect them. Gus explained that a Humvee would stand out like a sore thumb and draw attention. He knew that their success depended on not being noticed while scavenging.

John caught George that evening and said, "George, keep an eye out for good men with combat experience and other skills that will be helpful when we go to war with the DHS. We're going to need a much larger force."

He then added, "Bring back all of the Ammonium Nitrate fertilizer that you can find and perhaps we can level the playing field."

Gus led his team north the next morning before dawn.

*

Chapter 9

Bad Things Happen to Good People

South Alabama

June 22, 2020

DHS HQ, MOBILE

George was hiding under the tandem wheels of a semi along with Sonny and Jill. They were watching a group of people trying to open the back of a trailer that had Kroger decals on the side.

Sonny told his father, "The dumb asses don't know what a reefer trailer looks like, do they?"

George replied, "They probably aren't the smartest bunch, but let's watch them for a while."

As they watched, a larger group of people walked up to the ones trying to break into the trailer. A tall woman pointed at the reefer unit and broke out laughing at the guy with the crowbar. The entire group broke out laughing and started towards the trailer hiding George's team.

George stood up while being careful to maintain cover. He waved at the group and asked, "Can we put the guns down and talk?"

The woman shouldered her rifle and walked towards George while the others stayed vigilant. She said, "I'd rather talk than shoot anytime."

George told his team to keep an eye on these strangers.

George extended his hand towards the lady, and they shook. George gave her the condensed version of their story and as usual held back some detail.

Sally Green was the leader of the group that was composed of three families that had left Montgomery to escape the ongoing turf wars between rival gangs.

The gangs were fighting for control of what drugs, supplies, and water that remained.

They were taking women as sex slaves and trying to raid the surrounding towns for arms, drugs and anything they could trade for drugs.

Meth making and prescription drug availability had exploded due to the gangs robbing the pharmacies and prescription drug warehouses. They had experienced several harrowing narrow escapes but were now concentrating on finding supplies and drinking water.

Sally pointed to George's M4 and asked, "How did you get the military style weapons?"

George replied, "We found them lying on the ground after someone ambushed a bunch of those DHS men."

She laughed and said, "Pardon me if I think that sounds a bit suspicious since I was a homicide detective for fifteen years. We actually thought that you might be in league with the DHS."

George replied, "I'm afraid that the DHS is enemy number one for most American people."

Sally agreed and added, "We feel the same way. We've seen several instances where the DHS has shot innocent people who would not go to the camp in Mobile. We could not help those people because we were outnumbered and as you see we only have a few pistols and some hunting rifles. We need some assault weapons like you have."

George turned and called the others in his group to come to the meeting. Everyone but Sonny walked out in the open to the group. He stayed behind just in case things went south.

George asked Sally to sit and talk with him for a while to see what common interests they held.

Sally said, "We don't have much time since we need to keep scrounging for food."

George waved, and Sonny walked into the group packing a SAW and smiling at everyone.

Sally said, "So, you don't trust us."

George said, "I didn't, and until you tell your guys over behind that truck to come on over, I still don't."

Sally waved to her men, and they joined the main group.

George said, "Forget looking for food today, we have more than enough and can quickly show you how to improve your search methods."

George had his team bring their vehicles and made camp. They feasted on Spam, rice, and beans, then, discussed forming a mutual alliance.

There were 23 men and 39 women in Sally's group. All, but five, had some experience with guns and could be quickly trained to fight.

George gave them 20 M4s, 16 9mm Glock pistols and one hundred rounds for each.

He had Sonny give them a pair of bolt cutters to speed up breaking into the trailers. George told them that Sonny would stay with them a couple of days to give them some rudimentary military training and to help them find a base of operations.

George told them that their base was only about thirty miles away and that they were looking for people to join the resistance to the DHS. Sally's group was amazed that George had so many running vehicles and asked if he could help them get a couple running. George told Sonny to help them find a couple of old trucks and show how to get them running.

Sonny took one of the men and headed out to the nearest town in one of the trucks. They came back in two hours with a 1973 F250 towing a trailer.

Sonny explained that he just got lucky. He explained to the group that there were hundreds of antique project vehicles all over the country. He gave them a short course on old technology concerning carburetors, points in distributors and setting gaps on spark plugs. He cautioned to not get shot acquiring them.

George gave Sally a walkie-talkie and spare batteries. He then told her how to check in without staying on long enough to be traced. He told her how to give short code words to say all is well or there is trouble. George demonstrated, "G1/30N/AG."

A voice came back over the radio, "J1/AG."

George said, "I told him where I am and all is good. He told me who he is and all is good. You are now officially part of John Harris' army, and your call sign is S2."

Sally asked, "Who is John Harris and how did he get to be our leader?"

"How many former Special Forces type badasses do you have on your team?

Actually, John leads about a hundred men, women, and children. We both knew this crap would happen and have been preparing for it for years."

Gus waved for everyone to come over to him. When they settled down, he said, "Do any of you listen to the radio program, "How to Survive," hosted by John Harris?"

Several said they did and the information from the show has been helping them survive.

Gus turned to Sally and said, "That radio host is our fearless leader."

George told Sally that they needed her team to find more people to join the cause and to contact him if any wanted to join. He would see to their vetting before allowing them to come to the compound.

He cautioned her to watch for DHS spies and gang members trying to enslave them.

Sally told him that several of her group would like to go back with him. They were two young couples with very young kids and a newborn baby.

***

Outside The Bunker complex

Shaniqua saw the two people first and waved for the others to drop and hide.

"Look they have assault rifles. We have to take the rifles and find out if there are more. Let's ambush them. Try not to kill them so we can see if they know where we can get more AKs."

She turned and looked at her ragtag team and knew that most had never been in a fight much less than a gunfight in their whole lives. When TSHTF, she killed her pimp, took his guns and joined this small biker gang. She killed the leader in his sleep and took over the gang.

"Marcus and Dashawn, y'all go down the fence line and wait until you hear me shoot before opening up on them. Shoot to wound."

Shaniqua saw her troops slipping down the fence line when one tripped, fell and dropped his rifle. The gun fired, and she saw one of the two intruders drop to the ground. She and the others began shooting at the remaining man.

***

Sammy and Robin were walking the perimeter fence on the west side of the bunker compound when they came under intense fire originating from nearby woods.

They dropped to the ground, and Sammy scanned the woods to determine where the shots were coming from. He noticed that Robin was lying face down in the grass and not moving. Shaking her got no response. He rolled her over and saw a bullet hole in her head. Robin was dead. His partner was lying there dead, with a bullet hole in her head. He became enraged. Sammy knew that nothing would bring his partner back, but he would make these bastards pay.

Sammy jumped the fence, crawled on his belly until he got to concealment below some bushes. He stood up and started shooting at the attackers, killing four in less than a minute. He dropped and crawled to a log and peered over it just in time to see some guys escaping on motorcycles. He took careful aim and shot one of the bastards off his bike. Firing several more times he dropped two more. He then opened up on full auto and sprayed the rest with .223s. He was mad because he did not get them all, but he was sure he hit some of the escapees.

With extreme caution, Sammy moved towards the downed bikers and finally stood over the closest two bodies. The first was obviously dead, and the other had a wound in his back. Sammy shot him in his head to finish him off. He bent over to roll the third body over to search for a sign of life when the biker suddenly kicked him in the shin and tried to escape.

He grabbed the jacket just as the biker got up to run and pulled him back with all of his strength. He then started beating the hell out of the biker who only put up token resistance. Sammy had noticed that the biker was a small man, but expected more fight from the bastard.

Sammy kicked the guy in the side and told him, "Roll over or be shot in the back."

To his surprise, a rather attractive young woman rolled over and gave him the finger. Sammy made her stand up, tied her hands behind her and then frisked her for weapons.

"Get your hands off my tits, you fucking pervert. I'll kill your sorry ass when I get lose. I'll kill your whole family."

He searched her bike then checked the tire tracks to determine how many bikers had participated in the ambush. He counted seven for sure and maybe another. He picked up their brass and found 30.06, 30.30 and some .357 shell casings which told him that they were armed with a couple of hunting rifles and pistols. Not much firepower considering the guns that were available in gun shops.

Sammy got her to her feet and then herded her back to the bunker.

Beth and Gus came running to the sound of gunfire and met Sammy at the perimeter fence. He asked Beth to guard the prisoner while he talked with Gus.

Sammy told Gus that Robin had been shot by a motorcycle gang and was dead. Gus immediately grabbed the prisoner and started beating her senseless. Beth and Sammy pulled him off, and Beth told him that he could kill her later, but they needed to interrogate her first.

Gus calmed down, and then kicked her in the mouth as he turned to go to Robin. Gus carried Robin back to the bunker, placed her on the porch and sat with her for several hours.

Sammy took the prisoner to the barn, tied her to a chair and left her with a guard to watch her. Beth rounded up the group and filled them in on the attack and Robin's death. She then asked if anyone had interrogated a prisoner before. Gus walked up and told them that he was an expert at getting people to talk.

John replied, "Gus, we need her to talk, then die, not die before she talks.

Gus said, "I will kill the bitch after I get what we need from her, but not a second before she talks."

Gus then sent everyone out of the barn except for John, Beth, and Sammy. Gus gave a list of items to Beth and Sammy to fetch and began to prepare for the interrogation. They came back with all of the items that Gus had requested.

Gus then took out a knife, cut her clothes off and piled them on the floor. He leaned her chair back until her head was slightly lower than her body and placed a towel over her face. He then picked up a bucket and slowly poured water on the towel, which made her start coughing and spitting. After about two minutes, he raised her up and took the towel off her face. She spat a stream of water in his face and laughed at him.

She said, "Everyone knows that you can't drown from being waterboarded, you dumb prick."

Gus lowered her back down and poured water on her for two more minutes with the same results.

Gus took Beth and Sammy outside and said, "Look, I hate the bitch and can easily shoot her, but I never tortured a woman before, I don't think I can cut her fingers off or burn the soles of her feet."

Beth said, "Give me a few minutes, and I will come back with something that will work."

John took Bob and Gus off to the side and said, "We have been so busy surviving that we have not thought about how to handle a prisoner or conducting trials for criminals. I would have easily shot her dead during a battle. Now that we captured her, can we execute her? I don't think we can release her to keep killing."

Bob replied, "We must avoid taking prisoners unless we need info from them, then execute them." Gus, John, and Bob agreed.

Beth went to the house and gathered Ann, Shirley and Alice to help her figure out what to do.

Beth said, "We need to get this degenerate bitch to talk, and Gus can't torture her like he would a man. What would scare the shit out of you and make you spill the beans?"

Several came up with ideas that were just too soft to make her talk, and then Shirley walked over to her and whispered in her ear.

Shirley ended with, "That was the nightmare I had as a child growing up in the ghetto in Atlanta."

Beth replied, "That is horrible and might just work."

Beth headed back to the barn, but stopped and asked several of the boys to go find a live rat.

Beth told Ann and Shirley to force the prisoner to lie naked on the floor of the barn and staked her down with her legs and arms spread out. Beth tied a string around the rat's neck, placed it on the woman's chest and let it walk across her body. The prisoner was visibly upset but acted as if nothing was happening.

Beth continued to walk the rat around on top of the woman's body. She started yelling about her rights and that this was inhumane, then broke down and cried between fits of yelling. Beth led the rat down between the prisoner's legs, and that broke her.

She yelled, "I'll talk. What do you want?"

Beth helped get a sheet over the prisoner while Shirley went to get Gus. Gus asked her several questions and made copious notes.

After about an hour, he looked up at the others and said, "Chain her to a post in a horse stall and keep a guard on her until her trial."

John gathered every adult that was not on guard duty and asked for six volunteers who could serve as jurors for the biker woman's trial.

One young lady, Cindy, asked, "Who will be her lawyer?"

John said, "You."

He got six jurors and told them he would be the judge. They brought the woman into the kitchen and asked her to tell her side of the story. She told them that she was with the bikers who killed Robin, but that she did not shoot at Robin and Sammy.

Sammy told the jurors that he captured her at the scene, that there were eight bikers, and all were armed including the defendant. He also recounted her threat to kill his whole family when she was loose. John watched the woman's face and body language throughout the brief trial.

John sent the jury to the living room to decide her fate when the Q&A was completed. They came back in fifteen minutes with a guilty decision.

John told them to chain the prisoner back to the horse stall and asked a volunteer to go with him. John stopped by the shed and got two shovels, led the prisoner to a spot behind the barn and forced her to start digging a grave. It took two hours, and the grave was about four feet deep, just big enough for the defendant.

"Cindy," the lawyer asked, "what are y'all doing?"

John said, "We are about to execute this murderer."

The two ladies started arguing and demanded that the woman should not be killed. John told them that she had been found guilty and would be shot immediately. He added that they do not have a jail and he would not set her free to kill again.

John asked, "Gus, do you want to shoot the bitch?"

Gus replied, "No."

Sammy pulled his Glock, put it against her head and pulled the trigger.

He said, "The bitch shot my partner on my watch. May God have no mercy upon her soul?"

Shirley and Ginny were watching the men gathering to discuss the day's events. Shirley said that she needed to pick one of these men and get a father for her children.

Ginny said, "It wouldn't hurt to have a man in my bed again. I really like Steve, but Janet has her claws into him. Mom, there are very few black men, and I really don't like any of them. I do like several white guys. Would that be a problem?"

Shirley punched her arm and said, "I just want you to have a man who loves you and the kids. A girl does get lonely, and I'm sorry, but your last husband was a worthless piece of crap. Try a white one."

Just then Gus walked by, and Ginny ran out to him and walked with him to the house. She followed Gus around like a puppy for the next year.

Shirley caught Ginny a while later and told her to be careful with Gus since he just lost his wife.

Ginny said, "I know that you're right, but since the attack, our lives are in danger every day. I think we need to pursue whatever or whoever makes us happy and feel safe. Gus makes me feel safe, and I know that he would be good for my kids."

Steve watched Ginny following Gus around the compound each day and was happy that a good woman was taking an interest in Gus even if he was oblivious to the attention. Steve even started sending Ginny when he needed Gus.

Gus was working on one of the pickups when Ginny came over and started talking to him.

"Gus, could you teach me how to fix things, and I would really like you to teach me how to protect myself," said Ginny.

Gus replied, "I'm sure your dad would be glad to help you with those."

She batted her eyes at Gus and said, "But dad doesn't have the time and always gets so upset with me. You're so calm, and I like the fact that you are a religious man."

Gus told her that he would be glad to help her and that he would call her when he had to fix something. He also scheduled her for hand-to-hand training with Jim, and he promised to teach her how to fight.

Gus caught John and told him that George's oldest girl, Ginny, was flirting with him and he needed it to stop.

John said, "Gus, you're a big boy. Why don't you tell her that you aren't interested in her?"

Gus said, "I am interested, but Robin just passed, and Ginny is so young. I need time to heal and find a woman my own age."

John replied, "Gus, times are tough and bad things are going to keep happening to us for many more years. Grab happiness when you can. Just in case you haven't noticed, there are very few women our age in our camp."

Gus said, "But damn it, she's younger than my daughter. That brings up another topic; I have to go find my kids if they don't show up soon."

Gus, I promise that we will go find them if they don't show up soon."

***

A guard saw George's group coming home and alerted the whole compound, who promptly came out to welcome them home. George's team rolled back into the bunker compound two days late and had filled every trailer-to-capacity. They had found four more trucks that they could get running and brought them back so they could take them to Sally's group.

He introduced the latest additions to their big family. In addition to the two families from Sally's team, they had found another twelve adults and seven kids. There were only two men in the whole bunch since six men had been killed saving the rest from a gang trying to steal the women. The good news was that three of the women had served in the National Guard and were handy with a rifle.

George reported into John and Bob to inform them about their trip. They had found Sally's group and several others like them.

They had given out all of the guns they had and needed about fifty more to pass out. He added that all of the groups wanted to strike out at the DHS for trying to run roughshod over them and trying to force them into the camps.

Bob said that he would have plenty of arms delivered that night. George told them that there were several bad groups of bikers and gangs from the larger cities raiding the countryside between Pensacola and Montgomery. They were too lazy to grow crops and just took anything they needed.

Bob said, "If you can get me coordinates on the biker gangs, I can get an Apache to wipe them out. I'll need someone to help point them out.

George replied, "I know just the group that will do that. I have to take guns to them, though."

252

Bob added, "John, what do you think about the Navy supplying some EDs to you so you can do some real damage to these gangs and the DHS patrols? I'll add them to the supply coming tonight."

John thought that was a great idea.

George also told them that several groups told him that most of the population had died off from starvation, disease or murder in the past ninety days.

Bob replied, "That matches what we're hearing from around the country. Very few were prepared for something like this, and if they were, others tried to take their supplies from them."

George said, "That reminds me, we brought in a whole trailer load of guns and ammo from a gun shop in Monroeville. We only found hunting rifles, shotguns, and pistols. Someone had taken all the ARs. We have half a trailer load of ammo of all types."

Bob replied, "You won't need to scavenge for arms. I have already made up my mind to add M4s, M60s, SAW squad MGs, mortars and more ammo than I hope you'll ever use.

I'll supply all of the MREs that you can stand, but I'd keep searching for food if I were you. You also need to bring back about ten pickups and grain type trucks that can be used by my men when the time comes."

John replied, "So you finally trust us?"

Bob said, "Yes, and we have to pick up the pace, so I don't want you to waste too much time searching for supplies to survive with. We need to start taking the battle to the enemy and hit them hard."

***

Steve assigned the new people rooms in the underground bunker and gave them chores. Gus talked with them and planned to schedule them for military training.

Shirley told George about Ginny's plans for Gus and told him to behave and not get in their way.

George said, "I feel sorry for Gus. When a woman sets her cap for a man, he's toast..."

*

Chapter 10

Mobile, Alabama

Watching the Enemy

Aug 1, 2020

Bob deployed three teams of scouts to scope out the DHS compound in Mobile. 1Lt Roger Teller was the leader, and he selected Scott, Jim, Marvin, Karen, and Meg. They traveled to Mobile at night, and Gus dropped them off a mile from the city.

It would take several days for Roger and Meg to get south of the DHS compound without being detected. They had the most difficult and dangerous assignment. Scott and Jim were to check out the docks and then check out the relocation camp.

Marvin and Karen were to make their way through Mobile's suburbs to see if they could find any other resistance groups that could help fight the DHS.

***

The streets of Mobile were deserted, except for an occasional DHS patrol. The patrols consisted of a Humvee containing a driver, passenger and a man who operated the machine gun on top. They appeared about every two hours and drove very slowly up and down all major streets.

Marvin and Karen traveled only at night, from midnight to an hour before daybreak to make sure no civilians spotted them. It took them two days to get to the middle of Mobile. They began to notice that there were almost no dogs or cats roaming the streets; however, they did find quite a few carcasses lying around. Many had been shot, but most were so decomposed that you couldn't tell what killed them.

There were no lights in most of the windows, but Marvin noticed that the only houses with lights were only large houses in very rich neighborhoods.

They traveled through numerous neighborhoods and did not see a single person other than the patrols. Marvin and Karen finally saw a group of people sitting on a patio with a fire in a fire pit having a barbecue.

They decided to get close enough to listen in and see what they could learn. Karen saw that these people had a lot of money before the attack. There was a five-car garage behind the house to the left of the patio. It contained a new Jaguar, Cadillac and three antique vehicles. There was a '65 Cobra, '49 FI pickup, and an old Jeep. Marvin whispered to Karen, "I'll bet that they don't know the old cars will run."

There were five women and three men in the group, and they were having a lively discussion about the state of the country.

They heard an older man say, "The DHS and FEMA are doing the best they can to help those people, and they have taken care of us with leadership positions."

A young lady replied, "They shot that black family for trying to sneak out of town to avoid being sent to the prison."

"Now young lady, you know that is a relocation camp to help feed them until a suitable place for them can be found."

A young man replied, "Many of the people that were forced to move into that prison had farms with plenty of food and water. Why were they forced to move when people like us are allowed to stay in our homes and live like this never happened?"

255

They listened for about thirty minutes and learned that the three younger people were fed up with the DHS and with the two older people's holier-than-thou attitude. The older man was a doctor and a Mobile Councilman. The younger man and two women worked at the hospital where the doctor worked.

They waited in the shadows for another hour until the three left the house and followed them back to their house. Marvin let them go into the house but pushed the door open before the man could close it. Karen and Marvin held them at gunpoint and forced the man to light some candles.

Marvin told them, "We are not here to hurt you, and just want to ask you some questions before we leave. We listened in on your conversation with that couple at the house and feel that you are not big supporters of the DHS and what they are doing to people around here."

One of the women said, "Why are you pointing those guns at us if you aren't going to hurt us?"

Karen replied, "Just being careful honey."

They frisked the three and then lowered the guns.

The man asked, "Are y'all resistance fighters?"

Marvin said, "And if we are?"

The reply from all three was, "We'd like to join you. The DHS and FEMA are killing innocent people and torturing women at their compound."

The man and his girlfriend were general practice doctors, and the other woman was a doctor of pediatrics. They were working at the hospital when the lights went out. As medical professionals, they were treated very well, but they quickly saw the DHS at its worst. They saw men and women coming to the hospital for treatment being placed on trucks and shipped to the relocation centers without the needed medical treatment.

While walking one Sunday morning at the edge of town, they saw a whole family shot down like dogs. They hid because they were afraid the DHS would shoot witnesses to these atrocities. They decided that day that they had to get away from Mobile and the DHS.

They had begun hoarding food. They scavenged at night for food, weapons, and ammo. They found several shotguns, a couple of hunting rifles and a dozen pistols from the abandoned homes. They stole medical supplies from the hospital and were only a couple of weeks from being ready to load up and walk out of town. They had a wheelbarrow to help carry the supplies.

Marvin asked, "Why didn't you steal one of the doctor's cars and drive it to get away?"

Ray said, "They told us nothing would run and all three of our cars are dead. Why would the doctor's car run?"

Marvin said, "They lied to you, pre-electronic cars will run just fine. The EMP blasts only fried the electronic components of new cars. If I were you, I would figure out how to steal that old Ford truck and join us. We will come back here in a few days and commandeer the Jeep at the same time."

Ray's girlfriend, Betty, asked, "Can we ask some more friends to join us?"

Marvin replied, "We just ask that we get a chance to vet them before they are allowed to come to our camp."

***

Afloat on the Chickasaw River
North of Mobile docks

Scott and Jim decided to borrow a small john boat in Chickasaw and float down to the Mobile docks after dark. They took turns rowing, and the trip was uneventful until they got to the Highway 90 Bridge when they saw lights approaching from downriver.

They hid behind a barge tied up on the Mobile side of the river. A patrol boat finally sped by them shining its search light back and forth. The boat was a good thirty feet long and had FEMA painted on its side. There was .50 cal. machine guns mounted on the fore and aft decks, but no one was manning them.

They let the boat get out of site and then continued down river. Scott and Jim paddled for another two hours when the FEMA boat came back down river. They hid again while it passed them before heading out again. In a few minutes, they saw the State Docks up ahead and saw five similar FEMA boats docked at the wharf. Even at two o'clock in the morning, there was a lot of activity around the boats. Scott and Jim took notes and eased on past the docks.

When they finally got to downtown Mobile, they saw several large warships docked at the Coast Guard base. One looked like a missile frigate, and the other was a destroyer or cutter.

Scott and Jim rowed to the town side of the river, disembarked and hid the boat.

They skulked around the docks long enough to know that there were also several cargo ships tied up, but none appeared to have much activity. None of the ships was getting ready to sail. They headed out beside Highway 10 to State Road 163, so they could head south to the relocation camp in Theodore.

***

Roger and Meg had to travel cross-country through Mobile's western suburbs to get to the DHS headquarters on outer Airport Blvd. This took a couple of days since travel was safer at night.

Roger had night vision goggles but really didn't need them since there was no one out on the streets except for the patrol vehicles. They arrived at the northwest side of the compound at 4:00 a.m., found a place to hide and went to sleep.

They took turns sleeping and watching the compound until 2:00 p.m. They ate and took whore's baths in a nearby stream. They took turns watching the west side of the compound until dark. They noted many things that pointed to very poor security and defense for the compound. Several of the guards were drinking and most paid no attention to what was going on outside of the fence.

That night, they again took turns sleeping and watching the compound for about five hours then moved to the south side of the compound and continued observation of the compound until daylight.

The main entrance was on the south side of the compound and had a guard shack just a few feet off Airport Blvd. They found much more movement on this side, and the guards seemed much more observant. They noticed that several black SUVs left and returned at 10:00 a.m. and at dinner time every evening.

Roger said, "Meg, the food must not be so good in the compound."

They continued to move to the east and north sides of the compound and made copious notes. The most helpful fact they discovered was that the large contingent of DHS men was living in barracks on the north side of the compound. There were only a fence and a few guard stations between the barracks and the outside world.

***

The relocation camp was approximately five hundred yards long by three hundred yards deep. The land was very flat without much cover. Five warehouses of various sizes inside the fence housed the prisoners. The DHS had bulldozed any structures not incorporated into the camp but did not keep the weeds and bushes trimmed.

Scott and Jim had to crawl most of the time, so going was slow. They spent four days watching the compound, a day for each side. They took turns watching the camp day and night so that they could observe the guards' routines and determine strengths or weaknesses.

There were two rows of fence around fifty feet apart with razor ribbon on top and guard towers every two hundred feet. The towers had two men at all times and had a .50 cal. Machine gun and small arms.

On the second day, they were hiding in a ditch just as the sun was going down when a German Shepherd started walking towards them sniffing the ground. Scott had been sleeping while Jim was timing the patrol driving just outside the fence.

Jim saw the dog, and at first thought that it was a guard dog. He was afraid the dog would point them out to the DHS. The dog got to within a hundred feet when he was mowed down by the machine gun in the nearest guard tower.

The noise woke Scott. He jumped and nearly gave their position away. The bullets ripped the dog to shreds, but the machine gun kept firing until the guards got tired of shooting.

Jim told Scott what had just occurred and they both agreed that they would have had some K9 patrols to prevent intruders such as them.

Scott said, "Hey Jim, it just dawned on me this is the first animal besides birds that we have seen since we got to Mobile."

Jim agreed but had no clue where they had gone. They completed their surveillance of the camp and started working their way back to the pickup point north of Mobile.

***

The Bunker

All of the teams reported back as scheduled, except for Marvin's, ten to twelve days after initial deployment. His team had to walk back to the meeting point in Saraland to be picked up.

Each team brought back a wealth of information about the DHS, their schedules, strengths, and weaknesses. They also witnessed several atrocities committed by the DHS men when citizens resisted their orders.

One team had seen a group try to escape by stealing a garbage truck and crashing the fence. The .50 Cal. machine guns located in the two closest towers shot them to pieces. Several men and women tried to surrender but were gunned down while throwing up their hands trying to surrender.

***

Marvin and Karen came back to camp two days later but drove up in an old jeep. They had several pickups, including the '49 FI following them with the three doctors, and friends that wanted to join the fight. There were more doctors, policemen, engineers, a lawyer and their families in the group.

Steve asked Ann to get rooms prepared for them in The Bunker. After the initial briefing, the new recruits were put on the duty roster. The doctors jumped right in and demanded a couple of rooms to set up a hospital.

John and Bob took a couple of days in-briefing them. Again, they were a wealth of information. The Med Team had even been in the relocation camp, and DHS compound to treat sick detainees.

Their stories filled in a few blank spots and confirmed that most of the DHS troops weren't professionals and there were quite a few seen drinking on the job.

They were also sexually abusing many of the female detainees under their care. This made Bob and John irate and filled them the desire to put an end to the DHS relocation camp. That included putting every DHS animal to a most unpleasant and painful death.

*

Chapter 11

Who Can You Trust?

North of Mobile, Alabama

Aug 23, 2020

North of Mobile

George's team had been very successful over the past month in finding supplies and new recruits. They had also brought more than fifteen extra trucks back to The Bunker for Bob's men to use.

The team shared food with those less fortunate if they appeared to be decent people.

They found many groups who wanted to join the fight, but as many that just wanted to be left alone. They helped supply the groups that would join in the fight with improved firepower and food.

The team politely thanked the groups not interested in fighting and left them alone. The Bunker Militia did not waste resources on anyone who would not fight.

The group at The Bunker had swelled to over two hundred and fifty people with at least one hundred that were being trained for the attack force. There were another seventy people capable of handling rifles, standing guard duty and foraging for supplies.

After they had finished unloading the supplies for the Pastor's group, Pastor Falls asked if that couple still wanted to get married.

George said, "They do, would you take a few hours and come to our camp to marry them?"

The Pastor agreed, and George told him that he would call and give him a date and time.

The Pastor told George, "We have attacked two DHS patrols since we last saw you. One was in Florida, and another was in Mississippi. We killed thirteen and captured four vehicles and a lot of light weapons and ammo. They acted as if they were out on a Sunday drive and drove right into the ambush.

We left a couple of dead motorcycle gang members at each ambush site to throw them off our trail. We also made sure to use only hunting rifles and pistols, so the shell casings fit a rag-tag bunch of motorcycle bums."

George patted him on the back and congratulated him for learning so quickly.

The Pastor asked George, "Can you tell me more about the attack on the DHS compound?

George replied, "I don't remember saying anything about attacking their compound."

"Oh, uh, sorry, I just assumed that would be the plan since that's where most of them are located.

George left it at that and did not reply.

Sonny trained the Pastor's group on how to handle the ED's safely, how to hide them so they could not be easily seen and then how to set them off remotely.

The Pastor told them a large supply convoy that had come down Highway 65 the past two Wednesdays just after noon. The vehicles were all military issue but were mainly tractor-trailers with a few heavily armed Humvees. He thought that the ED's would be used to take out a couple of the Humvees and then ambush the convoy to take the supplies.

George said, "As I mentioned, we are getting close to a major assault on the DHS, so let's clear this attack with John first."

The Pastor said, "Just let me know as soon as possible, so we don't miss a chance for some fat truckloads of food and supplies. I'm tired of the Sears catalog in the outhouse if you know what I mean."

George replied, "Oh, crap, no pun intended, I never thought about that. John and I stocked enough supplies for a year, and I really don't want to use an outhouse or a pile of leaves. Down the road, we've got to get a toilet paper factory up and running."

The Pastor asked, "Tell me about the attack. How soon, and how will a small group of us attack such a larger force?"

Gus replied, "Patience, old son, you just have to trust me for now."

The Pastor was not pleased by the answer but kept the disappointment off his face.

They laughed, shook hands and George's team left.

Near The Bunker

George and Bill were in the lead truck heading back to The Bunker discussing John and Beth's upcoming wedding when they came to the top of a hill. Bill saw the stalled vehicles blocking the road first and hit the brakes, bringing the truck to a dead stop. Just as the truck stopped, bullets peppered the front of the truck, and one crashed through the front window just missing Bill.

George said, "Crap, we should have had recon up front. We knew this was a good place for an ambush."

They quickly backed the convoy over the hill to safety. There were only eleven people on George's team, and he did not want to go charging down the hill to lose even one of them.

He sent Sonny and Jill to flank the bad guys on the left. Bill and Janet went to the right. He told them to take sniper rifles and pick the men off from long range and not to take unnecessary chances.

George guessed that they were about three hundred yards away from the roadblock and eighty feet above the ambushers. This made for much easier shooting, down onto the ambushers.

The ambushers were shooting steadily at George's position, but most of the bullets were falling well short or going very high due to the elevation difference.

There were a couple of long bursts from an automatic weapon, which resulted in bullets widely spread out over a range of about a hundred feet. He directed his team to also use their sniper rifles, wait until the flanking team started shooting and then rain hell down on these bastards.

George patiently waited for approximately twenty minutes until he heard the first shot from the left flank. George quickly found his preselected target and squeezed the trigger. The shooter fell behind a car.

George saw that several men hit. The rest scrambled for better cover when a stray bullet hit one of his team. She rose up for a better view and took a bullet through the right eye.

There were about ten men still able to return fire. They had taken better cover and no longer easy targets. Sadly, for George's team, the best cover to them was over a hundred yards from the roadblock.

George would not risk rushing them and possibly losing more people when patience would eventually win out. He radioed the flankers and told them to continue to pick off any of the men that showed themselves but to keep behind cover. He told them about Helen's death.

Bill said, "OK, option one, we can just forget them and go back to The Bunker before someone else gets killed. I'd hate to lose somebody fighting a bad bunch that we could just go around."

Sonny replied, "I don't think option one is good. We need an option 2. We can't leave them here to kill more innocent people who just want to drive by this place."

Bill reluctantly agreed, "Yeah, you're right. This world will be better if we turn 'em into fertilizer."

**

The Bunker

John and Bob were preparing the attack team for their first assault on a DHS supply convoy. The plan was to drive up Highway 65 and get off at Atmore. Then swing down to the northern part of Pensacola, seek out a DHS convoy, wipe it out and liberate the supplies.

The idea was to alternate between lower Mississippi and northern Florida to hurt the DHS, but to not get the Alabama DHS after them.

Bob and John wanted to sharpen their team's skills while weakening the government troops. Sun Tzu would have been proud. This would help them prepare for the attack on the DHS compound and relocation camp.

They would also scout for more people to join their militia to build a credible army large enough to defeat their enemy.

***

Ambush site

The team waited patiently until midnight when George felt they could sneak up on the ambushers without much chance of being seen by the enemy.

It was a cloudy night with very little moonlight, and George had found a dry wash that was about two feet deep and ran up to within twenty yards of the roadblock. George had recalled Sonny and Bill leaving the other two to watch for men trying to sneak up on them.

George told the team, "Sonny, Bill, and you two come with me to crawl down the wash to ambush those bastards before they escape.

I want all of you going with me to put on gloves, and wrap some extra cloth around your knees. We'll be crawling over rocks to get to these jerks." They all scrambled to protect their knees and were soon booted and suited.

George asked, "Is everyone ready?"

They were.

Sonny led the way. He crawled on his hands and knees for about a hundred yards before stopping to rest. The others, including George, were thankful for the break. They took a few minutes to observe the roadblock and did not observe any unusual activity.

They could see the glow of a couple of cigarettes and a head bob every now and then, but nothing else. Sonny began crawling again, and they quickly closed the gap to less than a hundred yards before checking the target again.

Sonny reminded them to make sure that their trigger fingers were able to fit into the trigger guard with the gloves on or cut off the trigger finger.

George radioed Janet when they got close to the roadblock and told her to start throwing some rocks to get the thugs attention.

He could see the men stir and shift towards Janet when the rocks clattered. The distraction was working. The five of them scrambled to the first car without being seen, took up positions and began shooting. It was a very intense firefight, but only lasted a few minutes and ended with all of the ambushers on the ground.

Sonny and Bill turned on flashlights, and they all began making sure that these bastards were dead except for one to interrogate. All but two were dead, and those two were wounded too severely to talk, so they were put out of their suffering.

George put out guards out and called the rest of the team to down to the roadblock for the rest of the night.

George did not want to travel in the dark and risk another ambush. He thanked everyone for their great job in taking out these scumbags and then told them to take turns at guard duty and get a little rest.

The next morning, they searched the area for weapons and any clues where the murderer's home base was located.

They found the usual biker gang looking men and women, some ARs and handguns, but saw some fully automatic Mac-10s and Uzis. These men were far better armed than any the team had faced in the past, but still biker trash. There were two workable pickups and three motorcycles.

Janet was checking the trunks of the cars for supplies when she found a woman and two children tied up in one of the car's trunks. They untied them and got them out of the trunk. They were dehydrated, hungry and very filthy.

The woman said that her name was Maria Sanchez and that she and her kids had been traveling from Washington, DC to her mom's home in Shreveport when the lights went out. The kids were two girls about fourteen and five and could have been Maria at those ages.

Soon after, they were captured by a gang outside of Tuscaloosa and eventually traded to this gang for some Mac-10s.

Janet gave them food and water while Jill rounded up some clothes to replace the rags they wore. Maria finished eating and told her kids to go play while she filled the team in on their story.

She said, "We were careful to avoid other people while walking towards Shreveport; however, we ran out of food and went into a small town to get food."

She went on to tell them how they were captured. There were only a handful of people left in the town. At first, they were nice and gave us food and water. Later that night one of the men told Maria that she had to pay for the food. She tried to give him money, but he laughed at her, grabbed the older girl and started to leave the room.

Maria caught his arm and said, "What's wrong? Aren't you man enough for a real woman?" She ripped her blouse off, exposed her breasts to him and said, "Leave the little girl alone and come and get some of this."

He shoved the girl back in the room and took Maria to a bedroom. He turned his back on Maria, and she stabbed him in the back, knocking him to the floor.

She put the knife to his throat and said, "You won't molest another little girl, you sick bastard."

She slit his throat.

The wife came running when she heard the noise and had three men with her. She pulled the .38 and shot two of the bastards, but the third knocked her down and out with one punch. When she woke up, she and the children were tied up and on the floor. The next day they were traded to the biker gang.

Janet asked, "Where did you get the knife and why didn't you escape?" Maria responded, "I had a knife in my boot and a .38 strapped to my leg. If I had only used them on that SOB's wife, we would have escaped."

Janet said, "Have you ever been in Idaho? You look familiar."

Maria replied, "Yes, why do you ask?"

Janet stuck her 9mm into Maria's chest and said, "You are a DHS agent, aren't you?"

Maria replied, "Yes, I was a DHS agent, but I quit right after the disaster in Idaho. John Harris talked me into getting the hell out of DC. He told me to take my kids to a safe place. Did he make it back to Mobile?"

George heard the conversation and was startled when Janet drew down on Maria. He drew his pistol to back Janet up and came on over to the two women. Janet filled George in on the "Trip" and the Chupacabras.

George could only say, "Holy shit."

They tied her hands behind her back and got ready to head back to The Bunker. George radioed for John, and they had to chase him down.

John said, "What's so urgent George? We are deep into the plans for our little picnic."

George said, "John, do you know a DHS agent by the name of Maria Sanchez?"

John replied, "Holy shit, yeah! Is she with you?"

George said, "That's exactly what I said when I heard that she was a DHS agent."

John said, "Bring her on in, but treat her like a prisoner until we get to know her better."

They left her tied up, finished loading up the trucks and drove back to The Bunker.

The Bunker

John gathered his key people to fill them in on what he knew about Maria Sanchez. When he said the words DHS agent, all of his team became alarmed. They did not want her to know where The Bunker was located.

John and the team put a plan together that would lessen the risk to the compound, but give them the chance to find out if Maria could be trusted. She would live if they trusted her, or die if she could not be trusted. All of their lives were at stake, and they would always err on the side of the Team.

Ambush site

Maria did not like for her daughter and niece to see her hands bound up like a common criminal. She had been with the FBI for ten years before joining the DHS and had put many criminals behind bars. This was very degrading and embarrassing for her. She kept thinking that John Harris, Gus, and Scott appeared to be decent people caught up in a bad situation back in Idaho. She hoped that they would treat her fairly.

She was in the back seat of a four-door pickup with George while Bill and Alice were in the front. Bill was driving with Alice riding shotgun.

Bill asked, "What happened when you reported into your bosses back in Idaho? Did they find the rest of the Chupacabras?"

"They filed the usual reports and told me to take a long vacation. It was as if they not care less. What happened to you guys? Did the authorities ever find out about your involvement?"

Bill thought for a moment and knew that he should shut up.

He replied, "I'll let John answer your questions."

The two girls were in a pickup with Janet and Jill. They were very worried about Maria.

The older one, Gladys, asked, "Why are you treating my aunt like a criminal? She is a respected federal policeman and works for the Department of Homeland Security. Bad guys attacked us, and she saved us from them only to be traded to those assholes. Please turn us loose, and we'll leave you alone."

Janet said, "Look, you two are very smart young girls so I will shoot straight with you. The DHS has become a very bad group in this area. They have murdered, raped and enslaved thousands of people. We need to make sure Maria is one of the good guys. We are fighting the bad guys and can't take the chance that Maria is one of them."

The younger girl, Angela, asked, "Are you going to hurt my mommy?"

Janet answered, "If she is as good a person as you say, we will welcome her with open arms and all of you can join our family. Now, answer some questions about your aunt."

Janet and Jill questioned the two girls during the trip to The Bunker. They felt they had learned what John would need to help make his decision.

The Bunker

The drive was short, and they arrived to see a large contingent of armed guards and several onlookers. They got out of the pickup and two guards ushered Maria into the barn and chained her to the back wall of a horse stall. A guard stationed himself in front of the stall and stood with his M4 at ready arms.

Shirley came into the stall and asked, "Is there anything that I can do to make your stay comfortable."

Maria replied, "Yes, you can take these chains off of me and set me free. I'm an official of the US Government, and you are breaking the law."

Shirley said, "The government and our President are the ones who bombed the country and killed over one hundred million people on the first day. Another hundred million have died since. The DHS and President are enemies of the US Our military, FBI, and CIA are preparing to arrest them as we speak."

Shirley left and closed the stall door.

The stall was dark. Maria could see well enough, and despite her chains was able to explore her cell. She walked around the stall and explored every. She then tried to pry boards loose from the outside and stall walls to no avail. She heard a slight knock on the boards to her left. She went to them and, in answer, knocked on the wall. A piece of paper and a pencil fell out of a crack onto the floor and startled her. She unfolded the note and read, "Talk to me through the crack, but keep your voice low."

Maria knocked on the wall, put her lips up to the crack and asked, "Who are you?"

"I'm a prisoner just like you. I'm an FBI agent. We need to get information on this group back to the home office in Mobile.

I heard that you are a DHS agent. We must work together to arrest these people before they do any more harm. I have friends in this camp, and they'll help us escape, but we have to overcome the guards. Are you in?"

Maria replied, "Why should I trust you?"

The reply was, "They will kill us as soon as their interrogator finishes with us sometime tomorrow."

Maria replied, "I still don't know who you are, but I do trust John Harris. Perhaps he can get us out of here. Do you know him?"

The voice was from a man who she thought was in his mid-forties and white. He replied, "Don't trust him. He is the leader of this group, and we need to get him and the other leaders behind bars."

The conversation went on for about twenty minutes when two guards opened the barn door and entered her stall. One unlocked her chains. Both led her to another room at the far end of the barn.

They sat her in a chair and tied her arms and legs to the chair. She was left alone for about an hour. Her hands and legs were beginning to lose feeling. She strained at her bindings a couple of times to no avail.

Suddenly two men walked in and sat down next to her; one was an older black man, and the other was a younger white man. They started asking her questions about her trip down to Alabama and her service in the DHS. She answered questions for over two hours and felt like she answered every question at least five times with the same answer. When they started to leave, she demanded to talk with John Harris. They ignored her and left.

John entered the room an hour later and sat down next to her.

He asked, "Have you been treated okay? I hope my Team hasn't been too tough on you. How are you doing?"

She replied, "I get it that you have to be careful, but please don't take any DHS issues out on my daughter and niece; they are innocent bystanders.

John, I am proud to be a DHS agent. I joined a little over two years ago but spent most of my career with the FBI. I don't know of any wrong doings by the DHS or the President."

John answered, "Your girls will be taken care of even if you end up on our bad side. Don't worry about them. Start worrying about yourself. Why should we trust you?"

She said, "I don't think that I can say anything that will make you feel safe with me in your camp. I mean you no harm and perhaps I can help you. There is a guy in the next stall claiming to be an FBI agent who has friends in your camp and is plotting to escape."

She went on to tell John the entire conversation. John reached over to Maria and untied her hands and feet, then told her to walk around to get her circulation going.

She walked around the cell for a few minutes and asked, "Well, where do we stand?"

John yelled, "Steve, come on in!"

An attractive black man about forty-five walked in and introduced himself as Steve. He and John talked for a minute when Maria interrupted.

"John, this is the voice from the stall. Oh, shit. You were testing me."

"Yes, and you should thank God you passed."

Maria asked, "Why, would you have killed me?"

"Yes."

***

While all of the secret squirrel stuff was going on, George went to the girls and filled them in on his talks with the pastor. Shirley, Ann, Janet and Alice chose a date and time for the wedding, then told George that they had everything under control. George radioed back to the Pastor and filled him in.

Shirley, Ann, and Joan were busy planning a wedding. They had to be careful communicating with the rest of the group since John and Beth were all over the compound. They finally decided that at least one of the two needed to be in on the plans since it would be terrible if they backed out in front of the group.

Beth was all in and told them that John had already proposed. They spent the next several days sneaking around planning the wedding.

***

John told Maria that they had been testing her, but what really made them change their opinions in her favor was what the girls told them.

John said, "First, their stories matched yours exactly. Second, your niece overheard you talking with someone in the FBI about some odd occurrences going on in the DHS. She said that she heard you saying some senior directors and agents were forced to

271

retire. Some new higher-level political appointees were taking all the key positions and had no qualifications for the job. She indicated that you had several conversations about your suspicions."

Captain Bob Jones came into the room, introduced himself and shook her hand.

He said, "I'll get a JAG lawyer to interview you as soon as possible. I'll have one flown in on the next supply run. Maria, eventually we will be back to normal, and we will be putting those treasonous bastards on trial. We want to make sure that we can execute them. Your testimony will fill in some of the holes." The Captain thanked her and left the room.

John said, "Let's go see your girls and get you settled in. You are now part of the family."

***

The Bunker

Captain Bob Jones and 1Lt Teller asked John, Gus, George, Steve and Scott to join them in a planning session. Bob told them that no one outside of this Team should hear what was said in this meeting. The meeting began with George giving reports on his salvage expeditions.

George reported, "We have emptied every truck and trailer for thirty miles around and most of the stores. We couldn't take everything because there are people out there that also need it."

Steve added, "George's team has almost been too successful. I don't have room to store anything else without piling it outside."

Scott said, "That's great news, but I'm not happy people out there think they can sit back and stay out of the fight. We need to stop worrying about them and perhaps encourage them to leave the area."

George replied, "I agree with Scott. How do we know that they won't turn on us when their food runs out? About half of them aren't even trying to farm and are just living off what they can find in stores and trucks."

They discussed these topics for a few more minutes and then switched to their recruiting efforts. George again gave them an update on his team's efforts.

He told them, "The strongest groups are the ones led by Sally and the Pastor. Sally's team has over a hundred fighters and another seventy or so who are kids, or people who can't fight.

The Pastor has over two hundred fighters divided into the Alabama and Mississippi Teams.

Basic training is progressing very well.

Next, we have nine other groups that are smaller, but very solid and dependable. They range from one hundred twenty to thirty-five fighters. These groups range from Biloxi to Hattiesburg on the west to Montgomery and Panama City on the east."

Gus said, "Sounds like we have about seven hundred able-bodied fighters and another thousand kids, and those too old or unable to fight."

Bob said, "We have reached critical mass and can move to the next phase of the operation as soon as the training is wrapped up. We should plan our attack out about thirty days before the DHS wakes up and realizes we are a force to be dealt with. That will also graduate our first Basic Training class."

John replied, "I have always heard that you need three attackers for every defender to overrun a well-defended enemy."

Bob replied, "That is normally correct; however, we will take out ninety percent of their force in the first minute of the fight. Our reconnaissance tells us that there are only a handful of guards actually on duty with most of their force in the barracks getting drunk. The Regular Army personnel were only used for convoy duty.

We have other things in our favor as well. First, we have the element of surprise, which in itself can be a great equalizer of armies. Second, they don't even know we exist. Third, we have land and air support from our military.

They will blast any enemy aircraft out of the air during the first fifteen minutes. We have fifty Special Force soldiers and Seals to assist in the attack."

Bob added, "We may have an issue with security. Our intelligence group thinks that we have a mole in one of the new groups."

That announcement rattled the group. Everyone started talking at once. Calm was restored when John raised his hand.

George said, "I'll bet it's the Pastor. I have to apologize for not sharing my suspicion."

John replied, "George, hold that thought for a minute. It is very important, but I want to make a point."

Scott said, "I guess we should have known that this was a possibility and prepared for it."

John replied, "We did plan for it and have been trying to find out who was talking to the DHS for some time now. I planted false info with each of you. Only one false bit of info got back to the DHS. Now before I tell who I gave the info to, I have to make sure y'all know that person isn't the mole, but he passed the info on to the mole."

Everyone looked at the other guy and started talking until John asked them to quiet down.

John said, "George, I gave you a tidbit about a planned attack on the DHS frigate in Mobile harbor planned for last Wednesday. The DHS moved in thirty men armed with Stinger missiles the night before."

George replied, "John, I didn't give the info to the DHS."

John replied, "Remember, I told each of you to share some info with only the leader of certain groups. George, you only did what you were asked to do. All of the rest of you were asked to do the same, and there were no changes in the DHS behavior."

John said, "No George, we believe you gave the info to the Pastor, and he gave it to the DHS. What y'all don't know is that the military still has access to all pre-EMP records from Government and civilian sources. They performed background checks on everyone with any access to confidential information and as many others as possible.

They also have their moles in all of the large groups. We narrowed our concerns down to the Pastor and just wanted to confirm the culprit."

George was still trying to apologize to John when John said, "George, you did exactly what we told you to do; so did everyone in the room, including me."

George said, "Now, what do we do to the bastard, he could have gotten us all killed."

Scott said, "Let me kill that dirtbag now. I'll sneak into his camp and make it look like an accident."

Bob replied, "No, we'll deal with him at the right time. We need the rat telling them everything that he knows, and we will keep feeding him false info."

*

Chapter 12

Weddings and Warfare

The Bunker

September 12, 2020

The Bunker

There were two major preparations going on in the camp; the preparation for the attack on the DHS and John's wedding. Since this was to be a surprise for John, there was almost as much secrecy about the wedding as there was for the major battle looming over them.

John and Bob kept everyone focused on the attack on the DHS attack and conducted numerous planning sessions with the key people.

Gus helped the women stay focused on their part of the attack while Shirley took the ladies' free time and prepared for the wedding. They kept most of the plans from Beth and everything from John by giving false information about a party before the attack. Gus couldn't help thinking that the wedding's information security was better than the DHS attack.

The wedding was planned for September 20. The ladies had been able to put some decorations together, and Shirley baked a cake.

The idea was to get John out of the compound by taking advantage of a short trip that Bob and John had already planned. They would set up the decorations and food and drink for the reception afterward while John was out with Bob.

The Pastor was already scheduled to come to The Bunker after lunch with the service planned for two o'clock. Shirley had warned Bob that he had better have John back in the compound by one o'clock.

Ann went to Beth's room and said, "Beth, I know that you did not get to bring any formal clothes down from Tennessee, so I want to offer you some of mine. I know you normally wouldn't want to use the groom's ex-wife's clothes, but the girls and I have scoured The Bunker and the surrounding area and have not found much that would be nice enough for a wedding."

Beth replied, "Ann, I am glad that you offered and will gladly take you up on the offer."

They hugged and went to Ann's room to look at her clothes. Ann showed Beth all of her dresses, and Beth even tried some on, but nothing struck her fancy. Ann went back to the closet and brought out a very nice off white satin jumpsuit. Beth tried it on, and Ann placed a string of pearls around her neck. She was beautiful.

Ann said, "You look fabulous. John will have an orgasm when he sees you. Hell, all of the guys will. Just stay away from Bob. I have plans for him, and we have been sneaking around. He is afraid that John might object."

Beth turned red and said, "Ann, I'm so glad that I was able to keep my jealousy in control. I need a friend, and I would like to be a friend to you. John really likes Bob, and I am sure he will be happy for both of you. I'll mention it to him if it's okay with you."

***

Mexico City

President of the Unidos Estados de Mexico Pablo Cortez was very pleased with the results of his partnership with the US President, Iran, and Columbia.

Europe was on its knees. The Middle East was a sea of glass. Russia and China were in major land battles, which neutralized them. Only the remaining US Military could possibly derail his plans.

The President had promised over eighty percent of the US Military would stay loyal to him and support the cause, but it appeared to be exactly the opposite.

The President was a fool, and Pablo thought that he had been a fool to count on him that much. The only good luck was that most of the Army and Marines had been killed or were busy fighting overseas. The rogue military would not nuke his forces on US soil.

Cortez had planned all along to double cross the US part of the coalition. The President had promised to give him the southwest part of the United States, from San Diego to Houston. This was in compensation for the US annexation the land taken from Mexico in 1849. The fact that the United States had purchased the annexed land from El Presedente Santa Ana in 1850 was not a consideration.

Cortez wanted the whole bottom half of the USA. He wanted the manufacturing and farming base to supply his South American operations. He planned to use the Americans as slaves to work the farms and manufacture goods. He had anticipated the EMP attacks. Technicians and electrical parts were on hand to get the grid back up to power his newly conquered land.

Iran had supplied Cortez's forces with all of the latest military hardware and training. They had ground-to-air missiles, shoulder-fired anti-aircraft missiles and light armored vehicles. His aces in the hole were two aging Soviet-era nuclear submarines that came into his possession through Iran, were stationed off the coast of Texas.

They were old, and hardly state of the art, but with an incredible amount of luck could take out the two USN aircraft carriers and their attending ships before being destroyed. They each had two nuclear mines aboard, which were intended to be set off in the middle of the USN Fleet.

***

DHS Compound, Mobile

Major Johnson had to demand a meeting with Deke Jones to inform him of the recent increase in chatter on the short wave and handheld radios. Johnson knew that this usually meant that something bad was about to happen and he wanted the compound prepared.

He had already told Deke about the Pastor's info gained from Harris' group, but Deke did not appear to take the information as a real threat. Major Johnson had been in the waiting room for over an hour and was beginning to wonder if he should take his men and get the hell out of Mobile.

A couple of his closest officers were urging him to head out west with the men who were loyal to them. They could find a nice area and start their own country.

Deke was busy sampling the newly interned crop of ladies and didn't want to deal with military crap. He truly felt that the old USA was invincible and no one could mount a credible attack on his army.

There were only a few ragtag biker gangs and rednecks out there to deal with, and they were poorly armed. Major Davis had told him that they had lost two patrols in the past two months and that did not worry him in the least. His fellow field marshals were losing five times that many to the west and east of him.

Deke allowed Major Johnson to enter his office and greeted him rather coolly.

Deke said, "What are you complaining about now? Have you heard about some grand plan to overthrow our government?

Major Johnson replied, "Mr. Jones, I assure you that I am not here about trivial rumors. We're hearing a major increase in chatter on the radio, and that suggests a concerted effort instead of random attacks."

Deke replied, "That's Field Marshal to you and don't you forget it. Come back when you know something and stop the guesswork. You are dismissed."

Johnson neglected to inform him of the latest information about an impending attack. He went straight to his officers and began developing their exit strategy.

***

John asked all of the leaders of the groups that had joined them in the fight against the DHS to a final planning session before the attack. They gathered in the barn, which had the only room large enough to hold all of the planning members. He proceeded to lay out the attack plan to the group of over twenty men and women. The plan was simple, should achieve total surprise and totally decimate the DHS before they have a clue what happened.

Bob said, "We will have three main groups plus the group that will stay behind and guard The Bunker. John will lead the first Team, and the goal is to free the detainees at the relocation camp.

Gus will lead the second Team, and that goal is to kill all of the DHS personnel and take the compound.

Our planned attack date is September 30. We will update you if our plans change before then. We have identified several large warehouses where we can pre-position our forces starting one day before the actual attack.

This will allow us to move smaller groups and not draw as much attention. We also will stage some small attacks on patrols in south Mississippi and Florida just across the Alabama border to keep the DHS attention away from our staging areas. The map at the front of the room has the location of the warehouses and the diversionary attacks."

There were several astounded team members in the group and some chatter about "How the hell can three hundred defeat several thousand?"

Bob said, "Hold your horses and have a little faith. I will explain in due time. Now back to the plan. George will have a smaller Team with a goal to set up a shit load of distractions around the Mobile area just before the main attack. Finally, Steve will stay back at The Bunker, lead the Team guarding The Bunker and keep the hospital ready for the wounded. We will also fly as many wounded as possible out to a Hospital Ship in the Gulf for medical assistance."

George said, "I have contacted all of our friends around Mobile, and they are ready to join the battle. Sally and the Pastor's groups are the largest, so Sally's Team will join Gus, and the Pastor's Team will join John's Team. All but fifty of the other teams will stand as a reserve force."

He went on for a few minutes on the division of the team members. He had already pre-positioned arms and ammo with them.

More questions followed George's briefing on the friendly groups that he and his team had brought into the family. Sally and the Pastor were a huge help in calming the fears of the leaders of the smaller groups.

George said, "My Team will have about fifty fighters and will divide up into ten squads that will attack as many DHS targets as possible. This attack will occur four hours before the main offensive.

We won't stick around for a major fight, but we'll make them think that a much larger force is invading their turf. This will draw some of the DHS from the compound, and set them up for an attack from the air by our Apaches. We should be able to take all of their reaction force out and distract the DHS leadership."

There were several targets designated for them to attack and George made copious notes.

John took his turn in front of the group to give a brief overview of the attack on the DHS Compound. He said, "As we have mentioned, we have the element of surprise on our side, and along with several hundred pairs of night vision glasses, we will attack the DHS Compound at midnight immediately following the successful attack on the Relocation Camp."

The Pastor asked, "What about the two thousand troops in the barracks? They worry me. How are we going to deal with them? They could be out of those barracks in a minute and slaughter our men."

John said, "Our intelligence says that most of the DHS soldiers are actually in the underground bunkers and we plan to set satchel charges at the three known entrances and bury them alive. The regular military force is encamped in the warehouse just inside the fence. I hope that most of them will be on the road for convoy security. I wish we knew how to best handle that wild card."

The Pastor replied, "I like that, and the plan makes me feel a little better about my men. Bob, can't the military give us any air cover? You have supplied a lot of arms, but no air power or tanks."

Bob glanced at John and said, "Pastor, I'm sorry, but we only have a couple of helicopters and a handful of fighters stationed at Charleston. We will have fifty men interspersed among you, but that is all we have. I know that is not what you want to hear, but it can't be helped as our main forces are fighting in several foreign countries, or dead."

The Pastor said, "Sorry for being such a pain, but my men are my family, and I just have to make sure that we have a successful plan."

John finally went on to say snipers would take out the guards while several squad sized teams infiltrate the compound and blow up the entrances to The Bunker. Other teams would attack the main office to get control of the communications room. The rest of the group would take out any other DHS threat that came out to fight.

The Pastor stopped asking questions, and the meeting proceeded at a much faster pace.

Gus said, "My Team will conduct the attack on the Relocation Camp. Our objective is to neutralize the guards No POW's are to be taken.

We will not release the captives right away. We will use the military resources to check out their health before we allow them to mix with our people. We have heard rumors that there may be several illnesses among the captives."

Gus took everyone to a representation of the compound to go into the details of the attack. Again, the Pastor asked several questions that had nothing to do with his responsibilities.

***

On the road to northern Florida

John and Bob left at dawn after a light breakfast. They were traveling towards Pensacola to scout out a warehouse that was supposed to contain several armored cars that had been used by banks. They took six men with them for security.

"John, this Pastor is my best guess to be their spy. He just asks too many good tactical questions for a pastor who has no military training."

"Until we arrest him, we have to move on with our plans. I don't like misdirecting the team with bad info, but it won't hurt our plans and might help us catch the DHS off guard."

The Bunker

Beth had pretended to sleep in but quickly got up after John left and started doing her nails and getting pretty. She took a long hot bath and then worked on her hair.

Shirley, Janet, and Ann directed the ladies and several men to decorate the barn and set up the tables and chairs. Many of the other women were busy in the kitchen preparing the food for the reception after the wedding. George had found several cases of wine in a wine cellar that was very good and would be a treat for the guests.

***

The Pastor's Compound

The Pastor convinced his team that he would travel to the wedding by himself. This worried his leaders and his bodyguards; however the Pastor frequently went off by himself to walk and talk with the Lord one on one. They were not happy because several of

281

them were attending the wedding and it made sense to all travel together, but they gave into their leader. What they didn't know was that the Pastor had been meeting with the DHS all along. He was feeding them information since the last major attack on their town.

The DHS had kidnapped his family. They would torture and kill them if he didn't spy for them. The DHS Agents took his youngest daughter and held her until he provided information on the local gangs. When he reported John's activities and the involvement of the military, they started paying him and let him see his daughter. They were very interested in Captain Jones and Lieutenant Teller and coached the Pastor how to get intelligence without raising suspicion.

The Pastor left his house and drove to the designated meeting place about a mile off Highway 43 north of Axis. He pulled off on a dirt road and into a barn where the DHS agent was waiting on him.

He passed on the information about the attack on Mobile, got his reward and quickly got back on the road. What he didn't notice was that two of his trusted men had followed him.

***

DHS Compound Mobile

Major Johnson and his men had come up with a very simple plan to send a force out to eliminate a fictitious gang that had reportedly attacked several patrols since the meeting with Deke. Of course, those patrols had not been attacked, as they did not exist, but in fact were part of Johnson's team.

Deke had been pissed when told that five ten man patrols had been attacked with total losses. He demanded that Major Johnson eliminate the ones responsible. He told Johnson to kill them and hang every one of them on trees on the road back to Mobile as a warning to the other gangs.

Under the guise of getting a force together to attack the rogue gang, Johnson's trusted cadre had staged over five hundred and fifty additional men to join them in their new adventure.

This force now had a convoy of trucks, armored cars, and Humvees loaded to the ceiling with weapons, ammo, food and gear needed to survive until they were established in the new land. They planned to leave immediately.

***

The Bunker

It was just after noon and Gus saw all of the plans coming together. Without any fanfare, all of the friendly groups except the Pastor's had moved to the real staging areas. None of them knew that the attack was actually planned for that night to keep the mole from alerting the DHS.

The Marines had an officer and five sergeants assigned to each group. They spent the afternoon going over the battle plans while their leaders attended the wedding... *and* dealt with the mole.

Bob and John returned from the short trip and parked behind the barn. They walked into the meeting room just in time for the last strategy session. Bob filled them in on the Military's plans at the last minute for operational security.

He said, "It's not that we don't trust you, but its need to know and you didn't have the need to know. We must achieve total surprise to make this go off without a hitch. I know we will accomplish our objectives, but I don't want to sacrifice any of our men."

Several of the leaders noticed that the Pastor wasn't in the meeting. John heard the buzz and said, "The Pastor has been delayed, and Bob will fill him in when he gets here."

Bob told them that the plan had been refined and that George would start the attacks on the DHS patrols at dusk today. The room started to buzz.

"Yes, today. This has been the plan all along. I'll explain why soon, and you will know why, but not now."

He told them, "First the Gerald R. Ford will supply F-18s to take out all enemy aircraft and communications and the ships in Mobile Bay...

Second, six Apaches will take out the guard towers at both the Compound and Relocation Camp. When that is completed, they will give cover for the trucks filled with C4 to get next to the troop barracks. After those are destroyed, they will assist in mopping up any stragglers.

Third, the attacks on the Compound and the Relocation Camp will be conducted at the same time, immediately following the F-18 Hornets departure."

Bob went on to tell the team about the multiple objectives that the various military teams would secure."

Scott said, "Not much left for us to do, but to mop up and try to capture the officers who are in charge of this hell hole."

Captain Jones added, "I'm glad you said that. We would like to capture some of the leaders and put them on trial for treason.

283

Most of the Command and Control personnel will be taken out by the F-18s during the first strikes; however, we still hope to catch a few. They will be wearing army style uniforms with army rank insignia. The highest civilian leader is Deke Jones who is the Field Marshall for Alabama. He is from the Mobile area and played football at Vigor High School."

Steve asked, "The football player from the late nineties? Is he the same one who traveled the world denouncing our military and having dinner at Hugo Chavez's palace?"

"Yes, the same jerk who hated his country became a friend of the President and helped him get elected."

Gus said, "I don't remember him having any military or government service. He'd better hope he picked some strong advisors to help run and protect Alabama."

Bob replied, "He is a mess. Even though he has credible military men at his command, he won't listen to their advice. That's good for us since we will be attacking his stronghold. Let's forget about Deke for a minute; we have presents for everyone."

Several soldiers brought bulletproof vests, grenade launchers, LAW rockets and assorted grenades into the meeting.

John said, "Come on up and take a look. Uncle Sam has brought some gear that should protect us and give us greater firepower. Make sure everyone has a bulletproof vest, helmet and a basic load of grenades."

Steve replied, "I didn't think they would trust a bunch of rednecks like us with the good stuff."

Everyone in the room broke out laughing. They laughed more than one would have thought at the joke. John knew that the laughter was a way to repress the stress levels. He feared that many of these men and women might not come back alive.

There was a commotion at the back of the room, and the Pastor was shoved into the barn. His two right hand men had his hands tied behind his back and pushed him to the front of the room.

One of them said, "John, we caught this bastard meeting with the DHS, and we think that he has been meeting with them for quite a while."

John thanked them and replied, "We have been suspicious of him for several weeks. We set a trap, and he took the bait. We planned to arrest him today after this meeting. Well, Pastor, what do you have to say for yourself?"

The Pastor wouldn't make eye contact and just hung his head down.

Bob said, "We will deal with him later; I need to bring you two up to speed."

Bob asked them to go back to their compound and await further orders. He strongly suggested that they attempt to find any other spies, and deal with them before the upcoming attack.

John said, "Good move. We can't fully trust them for a while. I would love to have their firepower, but would hate to get shot in the back."

Gus said, "You never know who to trust, do you buddy? Speaking of which, when you head to the house a whole bunch of women talked Beth into marrying you today. I wasn't supposed to tell you, but I figured that you might want to wash your face and put these clothes on. Oops, here is the ring for Beth. I got it in a jewelry store, but she doesn't need to know that you didn't pick it out."

John gave Gus a bear hug and pulled some clothes from a nearby stall. He reached in the pants pocket and pulled out a bigger diamond.

"Gus, do you really think a bunch of women can outsmart Big John?"

"No John, but you'd better damn well let them think they did."

While John got dressed, Gus scrambled to find another preacher. He was sneaking around to the visiting group's leaders when he found one who had been a Baptist preacher before the collapse. He was very happy to perform the ceremony.

The last of the wedding decorations were put in place during the briefing. The ladies had worked hard with very little to work with to make this a beautiful wedding.

Shirley and the other cooks had prepared a great meal and Steve had chilled the champagne.

Poor Gus had to explain to Beth that the attack had been moved up to that very night. Beth took the news rather well in front of Gus, then went to her room and cried for a few minutes.

Ann heard her sobbing and asked, "Are you okay? What could be the matter on this great day?"

Beth told her about the change in plans and then cried for another minute.

"Beth, you have found your true love, share every minute with him like it is your last minute on earth and your love will always stay alive and strong. John may not be my cup of tea, but you know he is worth the effort and will be true to you for the rest of your lives."

Beth said, "But tonight could be the rest of our lives."

Ann replied, "Now stop blubbering and get dressed. Your man is about to be dragged out to the Preacher any minute."

***

Bob brought John to the back of the house still discussing the day's events when they turned the corner and saw the crowd around the deck. He saw Beth standing with Janet and Gus on the deck with another man that he didn't recognize. Gus waved for John to join them on the deck.

John said, "It looks like someone is getting married, Beth. I wonder who it could be."

Beth gave him a hug and a kiss. "We are you big lug. Now stop acting like you don't know anything about this wedding."

"Now darling, this is a complete surprise, but a very good surprise."

"Liar!"

The wedding was conducted on the back deck, which was just large enough to hold the wedding party. The friends and family were seated in chairs on the deck. Gus gave the bride away, and the preacher started the wedding. Several people asked why the Pastor wasn't performing the wedding. They were told that his truck had broken down.

When John put the large diamond ring on Beth's hand, she gasped and said, "So the world had to come to an end for me to get a huge diamond. I'll hope you were able to get a big discount."

They kissed, and the preacher introduced them, "This is Mr. and Mrs. John Harris."

***

The reception and dinner lasted for two hours. The bride and groom ate a light meal and danced. The entire camp and visitors were excited about the first wedding since that day.

Gus and several of the guys told Beth to name their first child after them. Beth was already pregnant for several weeks but didn't know. John and Beth finally got away from the crowd and went to their room. Beth ripped his clothes off and made passionate love with John. She knew that this could be their last night together and wanted it to be the best of his life. They fell asleep until Ann knocked rudely on their door.

286

"Wake up sleepy heads, it's time to kill the bad guys and tear their shit up. Y'all were making enough noise in there to wake the dead. Beth, did Little John live up to your expectations?"

A shoe hit the door, and Ann laughed all the way down the hall.

*

Chapter 13

The Survivors Fight Back!

The area around Mobile, Alabama

September 15, 2020

Outside Mobile

George started the attacks on the DHS patrols, and roadblocks at seven o'clock at ten different locations spread out from lower Mississippi through southern Alabama over to Pensacola.

The actions were meant to harass the DHS and kill as many of them as possible, in rapid hit and run operations. These were attacks were not to wipe them out, but to inflict damage, distract, cause fear and then disengage without taking casualties.

George wanted each DHS unit to scream as loud as possible for reinforcements. They would hit, run and hit them again to draw as many of the DHS out of the Compound as possible so the Apaches could rip them to pieces.

George stayed in touch with each group by radio and had to remind the team several times to hit and run, not to engage in a pitched battle.

He radioed Bob and said, "But Bob, these DHS men are disorganized and not putting up much resistance. My team is kicking their asses with little resistance."

Bob replied, "Don't get cocky; remember, pride goeth before a fall. Hit hard, shoot straight, then run like hell!"

***

Outside DHS Compound, Mobile

At nine o'clock Scott reported that there were major movements going on at the west end of the compound. His team moved as close as possible to get a better view. They saw over a hundred vehicles lining up in a convoy. Hundreds of men were loading their gear into trucks and up-armored Humvees. This looked more like a relocation of forces.

Scott called Bob and said, "Something's fishy at this end of the compound. I expected fifty to a hundred men to mobilize and head out to help the patrols, but this looks like a major movement of manpower. I wonder if they are heading to the Relocation Camp to reinforce them. I'll keep you posted and get the Apaches warmed up. If they head out to repel the attack on the prisoner camp, the Apaches will catch them out in the open."

Bob responded, "I agree, it's too late to deal with this group unless they enter the fray. If they head southeast, we will attack, if not we wait and see."

***

Inside DHS Compound, Mobile

Major Johnson looked at his watch and said to his XO, "Captain, it is 2230. Let's get a move on. I want to keep to the scheduled time of 2245 to cross the Line of Departure. Take us to the bivouac site at Slidell. We'll rest for the night then go through Baton Rouge at first light."

"Sir, the convoy is ready, the men are ready, and we can move out of the Compound at your command."

Major Johnson replied, "Captain, mount 'em up and give the order to cross the LOD at 2245 hours."

He then got in his Humvee and prepared to leave. The convoy cleared the LOD at exactly 2245 hours and barreled away from the compound heading west on Airport Boulevard towards Mississippi.

His plan was to head west to Highway 63 in Mississippi, convoy south to I-10 and continue to Texas.

Intelligence covering the southwest pointed out several communities that were in relatively good shape and had not been taken over by the DHS.

Port Arthur, Austin, and Prescott, Arizona were cities that had fared the best after the attacks. Major Johnson preferred Port Arthur because it was on the gulf coast and was on a river that had a deep-water port.

No one in the convoy noticed the helicopters following them from a few miles behind.

***

DGI Relocation Compound

The Relocation Camp had several buildings inside of the double fence line. The location had been a major warehousing complex. The prisoners were kept in the six largest warehouses with minimum security. The compound's walls were eight inches thick, and the guard towers had machine guns. No unarmed people were going to get out of that camp. Each warehouse had hundreds of bunk beds, five-gallon slop buckets and little else. These were holding pens until the people could be relocated to the planned labor camps.

The EMPs had knocked out the electricity at the labor camps so there was no need to bring in workers until the engineers could repair the power plants.

The good news was that the warehouse walls should protect the prisoners during the attack to free them. Bob was afraid that the guards would try to massacre the prisoners when they realized they were being overrun.

The plan was to attack one side of the Relocation Camp with only half the attacking force to get the DHS to send reinforcements from the Compound. Apache helicopters would follow the convoy and eliminate it before reinforcements could get to the Camp. John's men would then attack, and overrun the camp to free the prisoners.

Bob expected to lose twenty percent of the prisoners if there was a major firefight inside the warehouses, but the planning team could see no other way to take the camp and free them.

The attack began with Meg's snipers taking out the guards before the main attack. This did give the prisoners some time to find cover.

Meg and Alice had eight other snipers on their team. They had the Camp surrounded and were using night vision telescopes to eliminate guard after guard. It took less than two minutes to decimate the guards stationed in the watchtowers.

The first missile fired by an Apache took out the Communications tower.

Meg looked up at Alice and saw a big grin on her face each time she brought down a guard.

"You really enjoy killing these scumbags, don't you?"

"Yes, I do. I think back to being captured by those drug running bastards, and pretend that I am killing them."

"Bad luck for these worthless shits. Most are small-time outlaws paid by the DHS to rob and rape the same people they were supposed to be protecting before The Collapse (TC)."

John's team then attacked the East end of the Relocation Camp by ramming several trucks through the fence. This made an opening for John's force to flood through to attack the center of the Camp.

John told Marvin, "Take your men to the mess hall and clear it, and the Admin Building. I'll take the barracks and the Command and Control Center."

Marvin said, "No prisoners accept high ranking officers, and no quarter given. We will make you proud, John."

John called Bob, "These men are lightly armed, and there doesn't appear to be an active reserve. Deke will have to send reinforcements if he wants to try to keep control of the Camp."

Bob replied, "His ego won't allow for him to lose the Relocation Camp without a fight."

As expected, it only took fifteen minutes for Deke to send armed Humvees and several trucks full of men to reinforce the Camp. Deke also sent five helicopter gunships to cover the reinforcements as they counterattacked.

The convoy got about two miles from the Compound when the Army Apaches began strafing them. The DHS helicopters flew towards the convoy to protect them when the hell arrived from above, in the form Navy F-18s. The Hellcats blew the DHS choppers out of the sky from two miles away. Fire and wreckage rained down from the sky. One of the gunships fell in the middle of the convoy and destroyed four trucks carrying fifty DHS soldiers. The fuel from the chopper burst into flame as it rained down on the men in the trucks, incinerating any crash survivors.

Marvin had fifty men and women in his group to secure the section given to him. Half were regular army, and half were Bunker Militia whose squads were led by army sergeants. Marvin ordered the army force to tackle the Admin Building, while he took the rest to secure the mess hall.

"Karen, take five men with you and guard the back door to prevent anyone from escaping while we enter and kill all of these bastards. Shoot anyone who comes out of that door."

Marvin tossed two flash-bang grenades through a window and led the charge past the door with his M4 blazing away. He had killed five men before his team got inside.

There was an intense firefight, but the enemy was disorganized. They didn't take effective cover and fired wildly with very few hits.

Marvin was hit in his chest vest and knocked down. He recovered quickly and painfully rejoined the fight. He thought, Thank God for the flak jackets, and kept firing.

His team quickly cleared the main dining room and started on the kitchen and supply rooms when they heard shots from the back door.

The DHS men came running out the door and ran right into the trap. There was a brief shootout, but the agents were mowed down to a man. The last three raised their hands a little too late and died begging for life.

Karen yelled, "Cease fire. They are trying to surrender."

Mary replied, "Too late, they are dead and good riddance. Karen, we are here to kill them, not to save them."

Karen turned and looked at Marvin saying, "We won," then she fell to her knees and passed out.

Marvin saw the blood on her shoulder and leg. He yelled, "Get a medic. Man down."

Pat checked the wounds and held pressure on the leg wound, which had been bleeding profusely. He could not stop the bleeding and continued to yell for a medic. Karen bled out before the medic arrived.

Command Center, DHS Compound, Mobile

The command center only had a few men left to man the radio. They were burning documents when John and his team broke

292

through the doors. The flash-bangs immobilized the defenders. This allowed John to capture nearly all of them.

"John, behind you!"

John dropped, turned and fired his .45 at the man who was trying to kill him. The shooter missed. John rolled and fired again.

A bullet slammed John's chest, and he fell. He fired on the way down. Firing again, he hit the shooter in the middle of his forehead.

"Damn, John, you cut that close. Do you always give the bad guy the first two shots?"

"Hell no, I try not to give them any shot. I do think I'll have to check my underwear when the opportunity arises. That scared the shit out of me.

This crap is for the young. Thank God, and the Army, for these flak jackets, still, though, it hurts like hell. I'm going to have one hell of a nasty bruise to explain to Beth."

The Gulf of Mexico, at sea

At midnight, the Navy began its attacks on the DHS airfield. F-18s took out all of the aircraft that the DHS had around Mobile. It was a lopsided battle with no losses for the Navy and complete destruction for the DHS Air Corps.

A Seal Team seized the Frigate without any losses, while the helicopter gunships took the Gunboats.

DHS compound Mobile

Bob ordered the snipers and trucks into action, and Scott took two men with satchel charges to bury the doors at the south end of the massive underground bunker. The training of these Sappers proved to be excellent. Their satchel charge attacks went off without a hitch.

Jim took his men to the north end, where he and his men accomplished the task with élan. They set the charges and established themselves behind a berm seventy-five feet from the doors. Scott's team had just placed the first charge when twenty DHS men charged out of the remaining door, a hundred feet from their position.

His team began firing at the DHS and surprised them. Bullets were hitting all around Scott. One hit his back, and another bore into his butt. He grabbed a grenade and pitched it at the DHS attackers. Seconds later the explosion pitched one man through the air. The firing abruptly stopped, and Scott's men came over to him.

"You set the last charge. You, help me get behind that truck so we can watch both doors. I'm not bleeding a lot, so take care of business."

Both Teams watched from safety as the bombs blew the compound entrances closed. The rubble was at least ten feet deep. No troops would be able to get out for days, if ever.

Scott's ass felt like a huge yellow jacket had stung him. The hit in the back was stopped by his flack vest. He felt good about the successful entombment of the men below ground. Little did he know that all but a handful of the men either had left with Major Johnson or had been in the barracks?

The Apaches thundered in at ground level firing missiles into each of the guard towers. They made three passes to get them all. On the third pass, a defender fired a Stinger ground-to-air missile at the last chopper.

Scott saw bright white flares pop out of the back of the chopper. The missile detonated when it was drawn into the heat of one of the flares. The explosion, however, was too close to the chopper and a fragment hit the tail rotator. The Apache started spinning and hit the ground very hard. There was no explosion, but Scott feared the crew must be injured.

Scott yelled, "Guys, let's go help the crew before those DHS creeps get to them."

"But Scott, you're injured."

"I'll live a long life, but those men look like they need some help and protection, now!" Several more stingers were fired which caused the Apaches to back off.

A squad of DHS Agents raced toward the downed chopper. Jim's team began firing to pin them down so Scott's team could go to the aid of the crew. Scott's men got to the chopper while Scott helped pin the enemy down. The chopper crew was dazed and shaken up, but otherwise okay.

Bill drove the lead truck, filled with explosives, in the ten-truck convoy. He enjoyed the irony of using terrorist tactics against the DHS.

Bill directed his five trucks to his designated targets while Imelda handled the remaining bomb laden vehicles. They were receiving only sporadic small arms fire. The trucks had DHS markings, so they were thought to be fresh troops coming to reinforce against the attack. The trucks were parked beside their targets. The drivers and ran to the safety of a retention pond wall in the center of the Compound. They timed their escape with the explosions that would seal the underground bunker.

Their escape to safety went unnoticed as they ran the hundred yards. Coming around the last building, they saw the downed chopper and ran over to assist.

Bill was in the lead with Ginny and Mary on his tail when he saw the enemy behind a couple of cars. They were firing at the downed chopper. Bill realized that they had no cover and the enemy was just seconds from spotting his team. With no cover Bill yelled, "Charge!" and ran into the fray, firing.

Bill yelled, "Die, you sumbitches!"

The DHS Goons were caught by surprise, and before they could return fire, the rest of Bill's crew ended their lives. It was a fierce firefight, which became hand to hand in two cases. Bill killed five of the enemy, but they shot him several times before falling.

Imelda was a few steps behind Bill and took rounds in the left leg and forearm. She continued firing until the enemy shooter fell. Ginny dropped several, but one shot her in the shoulder. Mary caught lead in the leg.

Scott bent down to check on Bill who plaintively whispered, "The truck bombs?"

Bill died just as Scott remembered the explosives in the trucks.

"Take cover. The....."

At that instant, the trucks exploded one after another. The explosions flattened the barracks and blew huge amounts of debris around ground zero. The five story buildings fell on the troops inside, and a thousand men were entombed within seconds.

Bricks, glass and burning boards fell over everyone. Scott looked up and saw the debris falling. For an instant, he felt a terrible sadness and nausea. Many body parts were mixed in with the building debris. Several warfighters of The Bunker Militia were injured, but none was killed.

As the dust and debris settled, a lull descended upon the battlefield. Everyone stopped and peered from their cover, into a vision of Dante's Inferno. Some militiamen later said they felt as though the whole area looked like a scene from a cheap zombie movie with dead and dying everywhere. Thank God, it was mostly the enemy doing the dying.

***

Command Bunker DHS Compound

Deke yelled, "What the fuck is happening? There are explosions all around Mobile."

Deke's aide called for Major Johnson's second in command.

He had a brief discussion and quickly slammed the phone down.

"Sir, I am afraid that we have lost this battle. The enemy has destroyed all of our aircraft and is systematically bombing all of the buildings. What fighters are still alive are trying to surrender.

Deke cursed for several minutes and said, "Gather my staff and tell them to meet in my bunker."

It took several minutes to round up what was left of Deke's staff. These men were loyal to Deke to a fault. They were loyal because without him, they had no power. He knew that he could count on them until all was lost and they tried to escape like rats from a sinking ship. Explosions and gunfire continued to rake the compound.

Deke looked at his men and ordered, "Give me an assessment of our situation. What are our chances of winning this fight? Can we hold out until reinforcements arrive from Pensacola?"

The men looked at each other. None wanted to tell the Field Marshal that there was no chance of winning. They all knew that he would blow up, and heads would roll their heads.

Captain Davies stepped up and said, "Sir, the ISA Navy, Army, and Marines are conducting a major offensive against us. Our communications tower was the first target. It's gone.

We don't stand a chance against such a superior force. They have FA-18 Hornet attack fighters and Apache helicopters attacking from the air and large numbers of seasoned troops hitting us on all fronts. We need to evacuate...if we can."

Deke's aide stood up and said, "We'll have to sneak out in the darkness because any vehicle will be shot to pieces. I have a plan."

The inner circle of Deke's force discussed their plan and then scurried around gathering everything they needed to make their escape.

***

DHS Compound, Mobile

Gus' team came charging in on the west side of the Compound. Roger's team attacked from the east side. The DHS was caught in the middle.

As planned, the Apaches came in ripping up the DHS positions. There was a fifteen minute period of chaos, with bullets flying in all directions before the firing subsided. Resistance crumbled, and the enemy threw down their weapons and tried to surrender. The Bunker Militia asked no quarter and gave none. The DHS Compound was now in control of The Bunker militia.

Gus called Cpt. Bob Jones, "Dang, Bob, we caught them before they could drop their cocks and grab their socks. Those damn trucks obliterated the building and the troops. The attack was a complete success."

"Great job Gus, pass on my compliments to your team. How many losses are on our side?

"I don't have a count yet, but only a couple of dead and a handful wounded, so far. I'm still nervous that this has been too easy."

Gus ordered the men to search each building and warned them to watch for any live officers. He wanted to interrogate the officers and try to get Intel on the DHS in the rest of Alabama and the surrounding states.

Gus walked around the corner of the building and saw Scott tending to Ginny with Jim hovering over Imelda. He ran over and began caring for Ginny. The bullet just creased the top of her left shoulder. The medic only had to apply antibiotics and a bandage. He made her take a couple of naproxen and released her.

Gus looked at her and said, "Hey Ginny, did you forget to duck? I'm calling for a car to take you back to The Bunker so your mom can look after you."

"Gus, I want to stay here with you. I feel safer with you."

Ginny, I know you do, but your mom will raise hell with me if I don't get you home."

He kissed her on the forehead, and she grabbed him and planted a deep kiss on his lips. He then helped her into the ambulance returning the wounded to The Bunker and waved goodbye.

Sally had Beth, and twelve other women set up around the compound ready to pick off any DHS men who may still be trying to get past the now occupying force. They decided that there would be no attempt to allow the DHS to surrender while deserting their comrades.

They steadily picked off stray DHS men trying to escape in the aftermath of the battle. Alice had killed over twenty, while the others had five to ten.

Alice and Beth covered the West entrance to the compound and dropped more DHS trying to get away from their lost cause.

Alice pointed towards the compound and said, "See those people? They are walking too slowly. It looks like all of the men, but two, are carrying a very heavy bag. We'll take out all but the two without bags to interrogate. Don't shoot the women unless they are hostile. Alice assigned targets to each of her shooters.

They waited for the group to get about twenty yards away before opening fire at near point blank range. The group was caught by surprise. Only two were not hit. They ran over to the men, tied the survivor's hands behind their back and then tied their feet.

The women fell to the ground and begged for mercy.

Beth looked in one of the bags and exclaimed, "Damn, the bag is full of gold coins and jewels."

She poked one of the men in the stomach with her M4 and said, "Where did you get the treasure? You bastards robbed the people of Mobile, didn't you? I should kill both of you right now. You are just thieving scum."

She pointed her rifle at a large black man who immediately began begging for his life.

"Don't shoot me, please. I'm an innocent civilian. I didn't hurt anyone."

"He's a lying bastard! He's Deke Jones, the Field Marshal. He was in charge of all of Alabama, and he tortured us."

Beth questioned the other women and their stories matched. She called for Bob and filled him in on the captives. Beth then asked the women what they meant by torture.

"That son of a bitch raped every woman that he got his hands on. He had us beaten and then passed us around to the guards to be gang raped."

Beth told the women, "There he is. Don't kill him, but you may make him wish he was dead."

The women took turns kicking Deke in the balls or slapping his face. He passed out a couple of times before Beth ordered them to stop.

Beth said, "He will be questioned and hung. I promise you that!"

A squad of Marines appeared in short order and took all of the captives. The squad leader thanked the women before slipping into the darkness.

Bob's men used the same tactics John had successfully used. They knocked down the fences with the five-ton trucks as the snipers and helicopters took out the guards.

Meg's team switched from taking out the guards to picking off any DHS men who raised their heads. Alice continued to lead the pack in kills, but the others were quickly catching up to her body count.

Bob had fifty marines and fifty local recruits charging into the Camp expecting a major firefight and heavy losses.

They ran into the compound finding little resistance. They used normal urban tactics utilizing as much cover as possible, but only encountered a dozen men and quickly eliminated them.

Bob waved at John and said, "Let's check on the civilians. I'll bet they have no idea what is going on out here. Let's meet with them and explain that they are no longer in any danger. They'll be free to return home soon."

The plan was to interview every single detainee and weed out the problem people first. Crooks, gang bangers and thugs would stay in prisons. Police, firefighters, doctors, and nurses would be released first. Then essential workers would be released to get the city running again. Those remaining captives would receive an evaluation of work history. They could then go home.

As soon as the area was secured, the Navy planned to bring in the George W. Bush Aircraft Carrier Group. The Carrier has the capability to supply nuclear powered electricity to a city of 50,000 people. It also houses a full surgical hospital onboard.

This capability would provide the essential power source for Mobile until both naval and civilian engineers could get the power plants back in operation. Mobile, Alabama had less than twenty thousand people still alive. Pensacola had less than fifteen thousand people. The Navy had the same plan for that city, in its turn.

*

Chapter 14

Founding Fathers and a Few Soreheads

Theodore, Alabama

September 16, 2020

Former DHS Compound, Mobile
Now ISA Militia Headquarters, Mobile

Colonel Stokes' group arrived at 1:00 p.m. in five helicopters accompanied by a large security force. One helicopter took Deke and several of his top men back to HQ for interrogation.

He thanked the team for their successful elimination of the DHS and for the capture of the Compounds.

Colonel Stokes then asked for a meeting with John and Captain Bob Jones. He quickly got to the point.

"John, we'd like you to take charge of an area which will encompass Alabama and Louisiana. You are being tasked to create a stable government. It is hoped that elections can be held within the next 2 years.

John, we want you to start today to begin the long road to remaking America. Build a nation we can all be proud of, but you will not be allowed to create another DHS style dictatorship. I mean this, John. If you do, we will be back to replace you, just as our combined forces replaced the DHS here tonight. Am I clear on this?

"Whoa, Colonel, while I am pleased that you have so much faith in me, I really don't have the experience to govern anything, much less Alabama and Louisiana."

"John, you are wrong about that. Times are tough and what we need is a tough, fair minded benevolent dictator. One that must rule by hand selected committees, until a stable constitutionally centered government can be democratically elected. Though I would prefer we keep the word dictator to ourselves. Let's make your title, Governor.

Your interim government must get the citizen's of this region back on their feet and must prepare them to govern themselves.

We must begin to rally America. The current anarchy cannot continue. We intend to begin rebuilding this nation based upon the ideals of our founding fathers. The Constitution must be the law of the land."

John replied, "Well, I really don't think I'm qualified for this undertaking but okay. I'm overwhelmed, but with your help, we'll give it our best shot.

I guess the Marines say it best, John: 'It only takes all you got.'

I must admit I really like the plan, and I do want to be a part of this nation's rebirth. I'll do the best that I can.

Now we really need to figure out the support that I am going to receive from you."

The Colonel smiled, and said, "Well I'm glad that we, at least have a starting point. Tomorrow morning at 0800 hrs a chopper will arrive here to pick you up for transportation to the G.H.W. Bush Aircraft Carrier. You'll meet with the Admiral representing the Joint Chief of Staff for Naval Operations.

You'll be able to make your needs known to him."

Bob and John arrived in front of the largest warehouse with a hundred armed men. They drove a flatbed truck to the front of the building and asked the men to round up all of the detainees. Colonel

301

Stokes, John, and Captain Bob Jones climbed up on the bed of the truck where Bob introduced Colonel Stokes.

"Hello, I am Captain Robert Jones, and this is Colonel Hiram Stokes. Colonel Stokes is in charge of the Alabama and Louisiana relief effort, under the direction of Governor John Harris."

Colonel Stokes said, "As you probably know by now, we have either killed or driven all of the DHS troops out of Mobile.

After the bombs had fallen, Socialist elements of our government used the DHS to take over major parts of our country. Some of our senior elected officials were involved in the destruction of our country. Fortunately, most of your military did not betray their oath to the Constitution of the United States of America. We now plan, and intend, to take back our country."

The crowd cheered.

He went on by presenting their plan to bring Mobile back to a functioning city and seaport. "The initial part of this plan is to evaluate your ability to assist in this grand effort. After a medical evaluation, you will be released to return to your homes."

The former detainees were not happy that they would have to stay in the warehouse for even another day. Using 5-gallon buckets for human waste removal was unthinkable to them. Colonel Stokes promised to provide porta-potties to help ease the stress of the repatriation process.

Captain Jones was told to form a team to scour the city for portable toilets, and have 300 of them on site no later than 0800 hours of this morning.

The Captain saluted, turned and said, "Sergeant Mullens, gather 100 men and 50 trucks. I want them ready to move 5 minutes ago. Oh, and don't forget the trucks to suck 'em clean. Any questions?"

"Sir, no questions, on the way!" The Sgt. immediately began to gather his NCO's and left to accomplish the mission. He was soon able to find the addresses of three portable toilet outlets in Mobile via the yellow pages. Sgt. Mullens appropriated the toilets and paper. They were up and running by 0600 hours.

This helped, and most understood the reason for staying in the compound for just a little while longer.

Colonel Stokes then went on with requests for help.

"First, we need to know if any of the DHS men are hiding in your ranks. Turn them into us, and they will receive a fair trial.

Second, please go to the eastern corner of this building if you have prior military or police experience. We need to secure this area and establish order before we start moving people out of here.

302

Third, I'd like to introduce you to the new Governor of Alabama, Mississippi, and Louisiana. This is Governor John Harris. Many of you know him through his local business or his radio show.

Governor Harris has proven to be instrumental in eliminating the DHS and returning Mobile to you. Please give him the help, and latitude he needs to do his job.

What you may not know is that he has the leadership and military experience to lead you through the tough times ahead. Just as important, he does not want the job and will willingly turn the reigns over to personally selected committees, and later to the properly elected officials when that time comes."

This started discussions throughout the crowd. Most appeared to be pleased, and others were very angry.

One angry man said, "We have elected officials; why can't they take over their old jobs?"

"That is a very good question, and I will answer very bluntly. Many of your senior officials turned against you and worked with the DHS. Most of them were killed in the battle to free this Camp and the DHS Compound. I might also ask, other than those who fought with us tonight, how did those other elected officials work out for you?

Next, the military will assist you in building a strong city with a strong and well-trained militia to protect it.

Lastly, we want to ensure that this region has every opportunity to get back on its feet. Once that happens, elections will be held, and you will decide on the next governing body."

Most of the crowd applauded; however, a few were still angry.

John addressed the crowd, "Ladies and gentlemen, please listen to what I have to say about how we are going to govern this area.

Currently, there are zero jobs. We have no long-term source of food. We have to have a crash program to get water, farming, and fishing back up and running quickly, or we will all die.

The DHS has left us with approximately a two months food supply. The military can only supply another 2 months of MREs. For those of you who do not know, MRE stands for Meals Ready to Eat. The standing joke is that it really stands for Meals Rejected by Ethiopia." Many in the crowd visibly chuckled easing tensions a notch.

"There will be no welfare, no food stamps, and no handouts. The truly physically handicapped beyond the capability to do any work will be cared for. You will have to work, or you will leave. To set the bar, being crippled or in a wheelchair does not make you unable to work. There will be a plethora of sedentary jobs to be done.

At 0800 this morning, all farmers, commercial fishermen, mechanics and truck drivers, are to form a line in front of warehouse 1. Mr. George Washington will begin the process of directing you to those who will be assigning appropriate quarters, and equipment needed to begin operations concerning food supply. Time for this effort is critical. Speed is of the essence.

Former police and military will report to warehouse 2. At 0800, Captain Jones will begin registration and initial organization.

All other vocations will report to Mrs. Beth Harris at warehouse 3 for further processing."

A great enthusiasm began to blow through the crowd. It seemed to ease the sadness and depression that had, only moments before, permeated these former prisoners. The past had to be dealt with individually, through friends and family. The future begins now.

This meeting brought a round of laughter and applause from the crowd.

"All right, you all know what must be done. Now, let's get to it."

John added, "Friends, we are burning daylight. Before we can even think about recovery, we need to bury the dead. The DHS personnel will be buried in a mass grave.

Our own fallen heroes will be buried in a place of honor, separate from any other cemetery. We will not ever forget what happened here today. One day a marker will be placed on the site honoring this Day of Emergence from Chaos.

Captain Jones, please organize your people into squad leaders and take charge of burying the dead.

People, let this grisly task be the first step in rebuilding Mobile, and this great nation!" The crowd cheered madly and began lining up to complete this first task. **"Today, America is reborn!"**

John was pleased to see that the crowd was made up of about the same population mix as the general population before the collapse.

At 1500 hours, Governor John Harris installed the committee heads. Criminal behavior, racism or laziness would not be tolerated in this new beginning. Violators would be banished from Governor Harris' area of responsibility. "We haven't even begun to wrap my head around all the skill sets needed to rebuild

Mobile, much less the entire country, but having said that, we are off to a good start. Now let's Git 'er dun!"

Militia Compound, Mobile, Day 2

Shirley walked up to John, accompanied by two well-dressed older men who appeared to be nagging at her every step of the way.

Just as they got to John, Shirley yelled, "Shut up and zip your freakin' lips. John, pardon my French, but these two are getting on my last nerve. I would shoot them, but God might not hate Socialists as much as I do, though I would bet that He does."

She waved her M4 in the air and scared another ten years off the old fart's lives.

"Shirley, what the hell did these two men do to get on your bad side? Oh, by the way, gentlemen, before now, I have never seen this side of her, and I don't want to see it again. Now, what is the problem?"

"My dear sir, the problem is that this ruffian told us that our courses are canceled, and that we must find honest work. She obviously has no education and should not be the Secretary of Education."

"What courses do you normally teach the children?"

"We don't teach children. We are University professors, I teach the Fundamentals of Socialism versus Capitalism. I cover why capitalism has failed modern society. My associate teaches Modern Art."

"Well, I think I see the problem. Shirley, what did you recommend that these two esteemed professors do for a living?"

Shirley replied, "I think that they should try farming, but they are definitely too old, and far too out of shape for any physical labor. They have no useful skills that I have been able to discern."

"Did you ask if they could teach reading, writing or arithmetic?"

"I did, and they laughed at me."

"Well, kind sirs, it's cleaning up rubble and trash, or banishment. Come on, what's it to be?"

Both protested and started blubbering. "Why this is insane! We shall do no such thing. We know our rights, and you sir, shall hear from our legal department."

John said, "Remember those people at the first meeting who didn't like what they heard? I think that what is best for all is for you to join them. I don't care where you go, but you will not remain here. Doctors, mechanics, and nurses will be paid with potatoes and chickens until we can establish a workable monetary system. Who would pay you to teach that bullshit? This discussion is ended. Happy trails."

Beth, have these two arrested and placed on the truck with the rest of those too good to earn their way in this brave new world.

Shirley poked one with the M4 and said, "Let's go boys."

They boarded the trucks. Those worthless bastards were never seen again.

*

Chapter 15

Don't Mess with Texas or Rednecks

Port Arthur, Texas

September 17, 2020

The G.H.W. Bush Aircraft Carrier
Admiral's conference room
 Admiral Jones, holding out his hand to John said, "Governor, I want to thank you for coming this morning.

 I have been briefed on your history, and based on that and your present successes; I think you are ideally suited for this opportunity to excel. You have, without question, my complete backing.

 As we have a considerable amount to discuss, I would like to bring in the staff officers heading the classes of supply, which may fit your need. Now, let's see how we can be of assistance to you.

 Lt. Miller, please send in the briefing staff."

 "Aye, Aye Admiral."

 The selected staff entered the conference room, saluted the Admiral, and stood at attention until he said, "Gentlemen, please be seated."

Introductions were made, and the briefing began.

"Class 1, please begin this brief."

"Aye Aye, sir. Governor Harris, our classes of supply staffs, have all prepared a short list of how we may be of assistance.

Class 1 supply encompasses rations. At this time, we can, if needed, supply MRE ration packs for approximately 2 months. That is, of course, based upon your current level of population. This population will grow exponentially should your nation building experiment be a success.

The man droned on for hours, and John's head spun. All e got out of the meeting was that he had to assign someone who paid attention to detail to handle supplies.

***

Hwy 10, North of New Orleans

It was a little before midnight, and the sky was clear. Jets were seen flying in from the ocean towards Mobile. Major Johnson thought that these must be supported from the government to help Deke stave off the attack.

Johnson's group was camped along Highway 10, just north of New Orleans. He watched as one of the Sergeants posted the guards and sent scouts out to ensure perimeter security.

Johnson just wanted to move his team to a town. His Battalion would provide safety and security for the local inhabitants. He planned to live out his life as a Feudal Lord without all this bullshit hassle.

He had served in two Gulf Wars, the Canadian-Russian conflict and the Second War in Cuba.

Johnson was too tired to sleep. He sat down by the fire and reflected on his past accomplishments and failures. He had risen to the rank of Colonel in the Army, but one little issue in Cuba had ruined his career. The young girl was a piece of human trash, and she died accidentally during rough sex in his quarters. It was a pure accident, but her dad was a high-ranking officer in the Cuban resistance. That bitch had cost him his stars.

The moon was full, and he could see the jet contrails crossing the sky. He fell asleep and dreamed of being the leader of his own principality, similar to Luxembourg. Being able to have his way with all of the young women without anyone being able to stop him pleased him.

He did not hear the helicopters bearing down upon his bivouac.

A few minutes before the Apaches were to make their strafing run on the convoy, they received urgent orders to return to Mobile. The lead pilot fired two missiles and headed back home. The missiles struck their targets. One armored personnel carrier, model M-113 and a Humvee disappeared in a blinding flash that killed over thirty men.

Johnson woke up and went into action. He rallied the men and had them get Stinger missiles ready for the next run on them. They stood ready for several hours, but nothing happened. Johnson had no clue what had happened.

***

Port Arthur

Jack Mays, the Mayor of Port Arthur, banged his gavel and started the meeting on time.

"Come to order. That means stop yakking. We're here to govern, not swap stories. Pete, I do want to hear about the widow over in Grove City after the meeting, but now is not the time. Let's get our asses in gear and do some serious business."

His city had spent the last few months improving their defenses, preparing all able-bodied adult volunteers to defend their city. The council also focused on increasing the amount of land being farmed.

Every adult was now required to be armed at all times, kids fourteen and above were trained along with the adults in gun safety, marksmanship, and self-defense.

"Y'all begin as usual and give us an update on your areas. I'd like to hear from Charlie first, as usual."

Police Chief Charlie Adams started, "We have over twenty thousand trained militia and weapons for all. Only about half could be considered a real fighting force. The rest can definitely shoot and kill any enemy in their sight, but would not last long in an extended campaign, or against a well trained determined attacker.

We have armed checkpoints at all roads into our city. We have placed sensors and cameras covering all possible ways into our city about five miles out that will give us warning if anyone tries to approach. This makes it very difficult for anyone to enter in force around the roads without our knowing.

There are observation posts around the clock, so there shouldn't be any surprise attacks.

309

Blackout rules are in place from dusk to dawn, and my patrols are authorized to vigorously remind anyone not complying to douse those lights.

There are rumors about some pretty bad boys over towards Stowell. It's rumored they's building a regular army of gangbangers and bikers. They are kidnapping children."

"Great work, Charlie. Thanks for staying on top of security. Charlie, we trust you to handle the Stowell situation. The only advice I'll give you is to go in with stealth and overwhelming force. If the rumor of gangs is true, then wipe them out. No negotiations. Kill them and tear their shit up."

This brought out a mixture of cheering and a few blank stares. Everyone wanted a strong defense; however, a small group was very much against expanding their influence.

The Mayor spoke up and said, "If we let them alone, they grow stronger. When that happens, they will attack us. We need to kill them now before they kill us. And, no, I don't want to hear one whiny word about thou shall not do no killing. We kill them. End of discussion."

The crowd died down, and the meeting went on.

"All essential services are working with no issues. The water plant is up and running, thanks to Tim's hard work last week."

"Thanks, I will pass the praise on to the guys who work their asses off to keep the city ticking."

The Mayor pointed at Mike, who was in charge of agriculture for the town and said, "Mike, how are things going on the farms?"

"Sorry, but not all is well. We still need more tractors and fertilizer. Charlie took a large amount of our stores to manufacture those damned Improvised Explosive Devices of his."

"Now damn it, Mike, we've had that discussion and those bombs will serve us well when not if, we are attacked. Remember, it's not if, it's when someone tries to take what we got."

"Okay, okay, I get it. We are farming enough land to supply our current needs, but we need more so we can build up a reserve of corn, wheat, and other semi-perishable foods. We are only one drought away from starvation."

"Mike, I'll send out my deputies to the surrounding counties to search for tractors and other farming equipment. Just give us a list. We'll also search every farm supply, hardware store, and Wal-Mart in a 50-mile radius for fertilizer. We won't steal from any new owners, but it appears most of these items will be found to have been abandoned. If not, then we'll try to trade."

The group applauded Tim and his team's efforts for repairing a long list of electrical issues caused by the EMP blast.

The Mayor and Chief of Police were very pleased with the progress in such a short time. They were becoming self-sufficient and living almost as well now as before the attack. They had electricity, city water, and sewage, which eighty percent of the United States of America did not have. They had several old fashioned round ups and had over twenty thousand cattle, fifteen thousand hogs and ten thousand sheep on their surrounding farms. No one tried to count the chickens, ducks, and geese.

Jack and Charlie left the meeting and went to Jack's house to have their weekly private discussion. "Charlie, I need details on your plan to expand our territory and give me numbers of men, supplies and potential losses. Will Sowell be your first target?"

"I have a written plan and have the data that you need. Yes, to taking Sowell first. Those men rape young girls and if left alone, will get too big to handle without major losses. My plan will always be to strike first without mercy to overwhelm the opponent."

"Do you have any fresh intel on other groups like us in Texas or Louisiana that we could join up with for a common defense against the DHS and gangs?"

"Not much change from last month. There is the group outside of Dallas that is slowly clearing Dallas and the one west of Houston.

The Houston group is having a tough time with biker gangs and disease. They are barely holding their own. They have plenty of citizens willing to fight but are poorly armed.
There has been a lot of chatter the past couple of days about a group in Mobile that is standing up to the DHS. A few ham operators said that this group may actually be attacking the concentration camp."

"Thanks, Charlie, is there anything that we can do to help the people in Houston? If we don't, we'll end up fighting those animals alone."

"Mayor, I think we can spare enough arms to help make a big difference, and we can conduct some hit and run attacks that will weaken their enemies."

"Can we secure the Stowell area and help Houston?"

"I am one hundred percent sure that we can be successful in both operations. In fact, the Sowell operation is the springboard to take all of Houston into our new country. You might want to think up a name for it that suits our conservative roots, Mr. President."

The Mayor thought for a minute and said, "I'm a small town mayor and know it. We will need a strong man to lead our new country, but we'll cross that bridge when we get to it."

"Or woman," said Charlie.

"Charlie, do you know a woman with balls big enough to run this country?"

"Well, Clinton certainly had balls, but socialism and welfare are not my cup of tea. I hope those last nukes fried her sorry ass. You know, that could be the best thing that happened during this disaster."

***

Outside Sulphur, LA

Major Johnson saw the sign that said Sulphur, LA. He directed his battalion to get off Highway 10 on 27 South.

"We'll camp at the Sabine Pass Battleground Park for the night. Captain Bensen, send one scout team ahead to check out Port Arthur from the north, and three teams from the south. Do not make contact with the locals."

"Sir, what if we're spotted? Should we take out the locals?"

"No, first do not get spotted; but if that happens, be nice and ask for directions. We want to win their hearts and minds, not kill them. Always remember we need workers to grow food and manufacture goods. We are not just a roving band of killers, raping and pillaging."

"Yes, sir," said the captain.

The captain turned and said, "Lieutenant Kreel, take your squad out along Highway 10 and make camp north of Port Arthur. Report back every hour and do not engage the locals."

He passed on the orders but noticed the Lieutenant was not paying close attention.

"Yes sir, we will scout out North Port Arthur and won't rape any women."

"Lieutenant, if this were the regular Army, you'd be in the stockade for that smart assed remark. Now get you're your ass out of here before I have you arrested."

The Lieutenant gathered his men and passed on the orders.

"What good is it to have the only army within a hundred miles if you can't take all the beautiful women and steal anything you want?"

"Don't worry about that, once we take over one of these towns, Major Johnson will have an unfortunate accident."

The Lieutenant sent one scout team on down Highway 10 to approach Port Arthur from the north, and he sent a three-man unit to keep an eye on Major Johnson.

Major Johnson was one step ahead of his two wayward officers. He had a team following them.

"Sergeant, those SOBs are doubling back and spying on us. Keep an eye on them and kill them if they make any hostile moves. Keep in communications with that captain, but don't give up anything about our attack plans."

***

Outside of Port Arthur

The sun was peaking just above the pine trees chasing the shadows away. The roosters were crowing, and the birds were chirping as if to tell the world that this was going to be another beautiful day on the Gulf Coast.

The VW Bus was rocking a bit, and there were moans and groans coming out of the window. Joe got out of the bed, looked out the window and saw the sun coming up.

"Darling, this morning is almost as beautiful as you are. There is a light wisp of a fog as the sun burns the night away. When are we going to tell your dad, so we don't have to keep sneaking around? I love you and shouldn't be forced to hide all of the time."

"I'll do it when I get the courage to tell daddy. He thinks I'm still his little girl and haven't even had sex yet. He might come unglued if he caught us."

Joe kissed Jenny and said, "I'd better leave first today. See you at work."

"Joe, let's go to the beach this weekend. I miss the water."

"Okay, darlin'. I'll make sure we have the weekend off. We can camp on the beach and make love all night."

She laughed and said, "All night or fifteen minutes?"

He blew her a kiss and left before she got the best of him again. Jenny cleaned up, had breakfast and went into work.

Port Arthur, Command & Control Center

The surveillance office was manned around the clock, and all sensors and cameras were vigilantly watched. They saw mostly deer and only an occasional group of people drifting through the area. There was a beeping sound for the sensor for sector three, which covered the Northeast.

"Joe, please pan camera thirty-five left and right. That's it. See those men in the bushes; they are spying on our northern border. Jenny, call the Chief. Joe, call the water tower and tell the men to man the defensive positions until further notice. Warn everyone and tell them to stay vigilant until we know who these men are."

Charlie ran all the way from the town hall when he got the alert about the soldiers at the north end of the town. He walked into the room, went over to Jenny and gave her a kiss on the cheek.

"How's my favorite daughter doing this great morning? Please, hon, get your boss a cup of coffee while Joe fills me in on what's going on this morning."

Joe played back the camera feed and then showed him the live feed from several cameras covering the area in question. Charlie watched the live camera for several minutes and gathered the team around him.

"These guys are soldiers, but they're sloppy. They are military, but not currently trained to regular army standards. They appear to be grunts surveying the area for a larger force. I'll bet that there are several more like them coming at us from all directions. Keep a close eye on the sensors and cameras. My men would have found the sensors and cameras and disabled them or avoided them by now."

Charlie had Joe call the council and tell them to go to the town hall ASAP.

A couple of hours passed before all of the council members could get to the town hall. Several had been south of town, fighting a small house fire and were still in their firefighting equipment. Charlie was pleased to see that every one of them had their M4 and pistol with them as they arrived.

"Our initial surveillance has found three small recon teams watching our city. These soldiers are armed to the teeth and have the latest military equipment. This is not some bunch of crooks setting up a raid to steal drugs.

It probably is the DHS or a rogue army unit trying to find a base of operations. We would be a prized plum for any group to conquer. I'm sending several small scouting teams out to find their camp."

"What should we do to protect our town? We can't ignore them, and we need to find out if they are friend or foe."

Chief Charlie spoke up, "First, they cannot be allowed into our city. Second, we meet with them to find out their intentions.

314

Third, we wipe them off the face of the earth if we even suspect they plan to attack."

The mayor banged his gavel and said, "Charlie, put the plan into effect."

***

They kept watching the men who were observing the town for three more days without any movement on either side. Then at ten o'clock of the fourth morning, a Humvee drove towards town from the south with a white flag waving on its antennae. The men guarding the checkpoint were heavily armed and had bulletproof vests. One noticed that a soldier in the Humvee had a camera and was recording every move they made.

A soldier wearing captain's bars got out of the vehicle and said, "We are peaceful and want to meet with your city leaders. Can you take us to them?"

"No, we won't take you to them. Who are you? Why are you here and what do you want?"

"We are the US Army. We are here to help protect you and establish law and order in this area. We want your help in accomplishing our goals."

"Be prepared to prove you are with the Army. I will inform our leader of the conversation and get back to you. What channels do you monitor?"

The captain told them the channel to use, then got back in the Humvee and drove away.

Charlie had been listening in on the conversations through a microphone placed on one of the men at each checkpoint. Everything he heard pointed to these men being regular Army soldiers, but his gut told him that the Army would not have sent recon teams out for several days to watch his town.

Charlie had his radio operator change to the frequency supplied by the soldier.

"US Army, this is Port Arthur. Do you hear me?"

"This is Sergeant Brown; we hear you loud and clear. Here is Major Johnson."

"This is Major Johnson, with whom am I speaking?"

"This is Charlie; we don't need your help or protection. Our town is self-sufficient and does not need the government interfering in our affairs. Move on and find some other town that needs your assistance. You are not welcome here."

"Charlie, our orders are to set up a base of operations and re-establish law and order on the Gulf Coast of Texas. We would like to use your town as our base of operation. We can protect your town and begin turning the lights back on."

"Major Johnson, you only have about five-hundred men, five up-armored Humvees and six Humvees armed with M60's. With that compliment, you cannot even protect yourselves.

We have over twenty thousand heavily armed citizens, mortars, LAWS, and several 90mm cannons."

Charlie heard Johnson gasp when he found that the town's people knew more about his army than he knew about them.

"Look, Charlie, you're messing with the US Army, not a bunch of ragtag civilians playing soldier. You have until noon tomorrow to lay down your weapons and join us, or be destroyed."

"Major, you're just another thug trying to set up your own little kingdom.

The real Army would have tried to win us over not try to run us over. You are the pretenders, and your ego will get you and your men killed."

Johnson cut off the call.

"Well, Charlie, what do you make of that conversation? The major didn't scare off as we'd hoped, did he?"

"Joe, tell everyone to go on highest alert and be ready for an attack before daybreak. Mayor, the major just about shit his britches when he found out that we knew more about him then he knew about us. His ego kicked in and he is going to pull a sneaky surprise attack to overrun us before we can react. He thinks he is dealing with a bunch of rednecks."

"Charlie, are you sure about this? We are a bunch of Rednecks. What if they are the real US Army?"

"Jack, you really need to trust me. You know I was in the Army for over twenty years, and these guys have served, but they are the dregs of the army."

"I'm sorry, you know I trust you; tell us what to do."

"Joe, tell the team to arm all of the IEDs and tell the company commanders to position all forces in their defense positions after the sun sets.

We do not want them to see us strengthening our positions. Jack, if they were legitimate, they would be trying to assist us and win our hearts and minds, not threaten to wipe us out. I pushed the bastard to find out how he would react. I hoped for the best, but got the worst."

Charlie was in the command center watching the video feed from the numerous cameras around Port Arthur and saw the enemy slowly moving into position. He watched them set up their mortars and gave their coordinates to his own mortar teams, which greatly outnumbered the enemies.

He had seen men like the major's before, all cocky and full of themselves. The major was over confident and had committed all of his troops, in the hope of one successful, overwhelming attack, which would be his downfall.

Charlie continued to watch the troops move in towards the city and kept making counter moves. The Port Arthur fighters were perfectly positioned to repel the attacking soldiers

Charlie decided it was time to resolve his issues with Joe before the fight started.

"Joe, come outside with me so we can work out some personal issues."

They walked outside, and Charlie led him out to the parking lot and stopped beside Joe's VW bus.

"Joe, you know my daughter, don't you? Do you know how much I love my daughter and how protective I am of her?"

"Yes, sir. What are you trying to say?"

"How long have you been defiling my daughter and what are your intentions?"

Joe was stammering and trying to collect his wit to give a coherent answer, when he said, "I love Jenny and plan to marry her if she'll have me. I'm sorry if I've upset you sir, but I love her and will fight for her if I need to. You can't keep us apart."

"Damn, son, we have enough fighting about to happen tonight without fighting each other. I know you love my daughter; hell, everyone knows that. What I want to tell you is to stop screwing her in my parking lot, which everyone also knows. Son, you need a lesson in discretion. Ask her to marry you and get a home and give us some grandkids."

He slapped Joe on the back and said, "Now get your ass back to work."

Charlie looked up and saw Jenny, with eyes glistening, standing in the doorway watching them.

"Darling, marry the boy and get the hell out of that damn bus."

She gave her dad a kiss and went back to work.

Johnson's men started moving in at four o'clock sharp with two major groups. The captain was attacking from the north just above Bridge City, and Major Johnson led the group attacking from the south

"Captain, you are free to move down from your position. You are free to eliminate any resistance, but, if possible, keep civilian losses to a minimum."

"Yes, sir. We will sweep through and meet you for lunch at the town hall."

"Don't get too cocky and watch for traps. These people are not soldiers, but many of them are experienced hunters. Do not advance past Groves without orders from me.

I plan to be a mile south of Port Arthur about the time you get to Groves. Pacify that city and be prepared to advance on Port Arthur tomorrow morning as planned."

Both forces only met token resistance and sniper fire, which slowed them down and made them keep taking cover. Resistance increased as the captain's men got north of Bridge City.

The captain found his men under heavy attack from the front and rear of his column. Just as he noticed that his vehicles were bunching up due to the withering fire from the south, the trap had sprung. There were explosions from both sides of the road, and the men and vehicles were peppered with shrapnel. A fourth of his men were cut down in the first couple of minutes.

"Sergeant, recover to the woods. We'll regroup at that barn. They're killing us."

"Leave the wounded and get your asses over to the barn. We'll get them later."

Before the soldiers could move the Humvees and armored vehicles, there were thunderous explosions that flipped two of the Humvees and destroyed two personnel carriers.

"Retreat, head back to Highway 10. Fuck this place and fuck the major."

They fled as fast as they could while still taking heavy fire and mortar fire from the left and right. There were only six vehicles and seventy-five combat capable men left by the time they got back up Highway 10.

Charlie gave orders to the mortar teams to begin firing on the enemies' mortar emplacements first and then the advancing men. He also told the leaders to blow the IEDs when the enemy got close enough for maximum killing power. Many of the IEDs were bombs wrapped with nuts, bolts, and washers, secured to trees at chest height. The Port Arthur forces outnumbered the enemy forty to one.

318

"Don't use the cannons unless I give the order. We only have about a hundred rounds, and I want to save them for a real threat."

Major Johnson's team was taking small arms fire when he heard his captain yelling at his men to take cover. He heard several thumping sounds in the distance.

"INCOMING!"

The men scrambled for cover under or behind trees, logs or their vehicles. The mortar shells rained down on them for several minutes killing twenty-four and wounding as many.

Johnson yelled, "Start returning mortar fire at will! Blast them off the face of the earth."

Before the mortars could be fired, numerous IEDs exploded around them, and they were attacked from all sides. His men were dying all around him, and there was nothing he could do. He grabbed a white T-shirt and waved it out the window of the Humvee.

"Men, stop firing. We are surrendering. Please stop shooting, we surrender."

"Throw your guns down, come out with your hands up and walk to the crossroads. We will shoot anyone who runs or makes a sudden move."

"Men, do what you're told. We surrender."

Only fifty men were able to move on their own, another twenty-three were wounded, and the rest were dead. Charlie's team rounded up the enemy and forced them to walk to a holding area outside of town.

The wounded were placed in the backs of dump trucks and driven to the holding area. They waited in the dump trucks until their comrades finished walking to the holding area.

Major Johnson saw his men were still in the back of the dump trucks and started yelling, "Why aren't my men receiving medical treatment? This is a violation of the Geneva Convention."

"Shut up, or I'll knock your damned teeth out, you worthless piece of shit. Joe, take the Major, and his officers and have Fred interrogate them. Your men were going to kill, then rape and take over our town; screw the Geneva Convention."

"You must treat my men, and I, as prisoners and..." Charlie hit Johnson on the side of his head with the butt of his rifle just enough to shut him up without knocking him out.

***

The Bunker Compound, Mobile, AL

"Captain Jones, we've just established radio contact with the Police Chief of Port Arthur. He says that a group of five-hundred men claiming to be US Army attacked their town a few days ago."

"I'll have to check with Stokes before I can send help to them. See how long they can hold out."

"Sir, they don't need help. They want to know if we know a Major Johnson and what we want them to do with a couple hundred prisoners."

"That Johnson is the traitor that was guarding the Compound in Mobile. Put the Chief on the radio."

The radio operator called for Port Arthur and had the Chief on in just a few minutes.

"This is Chief Charlie Adams; I am the Police Chief and head of our local defense force. We have one hundred fifty-six prisoners, and about eighty of them are wounded. Do you want them? We believe them to be traitors to our country. They intended to take over our city and use it as a base of operations for their own gain."

"Charlie, this is Captain Jones. We know of Major Johnson, and you are right, he and his men are the bad guys in this disaster. Yes, we would like to take charge of them. Can we approach your town and take them to Mobile? I'd like to send a helicopter over too quickly pick up Johnson and his officers."

"Certainly, but you need to know that about a hundred escaped and went on towards Houston."

"Thanks for the heads up, I'll send some Apaches to find and destroy them."

"Sir, could you take a look at Sowell and Houston while your birds are over that way? We were going to see if we can help those folks out and need some Intel on the bad guys."

"I will have them recon those areas for you. By the way, are y'all interested in joining our team? We won't force you or send soldiers to protect you, but we can send arms and supplies to help you take back the area around you. We'd really like you to help us take back our country."

"I'll talk it over with the Mayor and town council, but I'm sure we will want to join in with you."

"Charlie, tell me, how did a bunch of civilians defeat a battle tested company of soldiers?"

"Captain, they assumed that we were a bunch of redneck civilians without any training or fighting experience. It was a deadly mistake. It's true, we are a bunch of rednecks, but we have Major Charles F. Adams, 101st Airborne."

"Charlie, we have found another guy from Mobile that sounds a lot like you. Have you heard of John Harris?"

"Yes, and tell that old fart that I still owe him an ass kicking for that bar fight in Bangkok."

"Then I guess you also know Gus McCoy; he appears to hang out with Harris."

"Damn, it's old home week on the Gulf. How'd those two amateurs survive The Collapse? Have you checked your back pocket? Those two need to be watched closely."

+

Charlie stopped laughing and added, "Captain, come on over and let's see what we can work out. I think we have the same goals. Bring John and Gus. I'll feed all y'all well."

***

Captain Jones said, "I talked with an old friend of yours. Do you remember Charlie Adams?"

Gus spoke up, "Hell yes, we know Charlie. We go back to our wet-work days. What did that old sumbitch tell you?"

Bob filled them in on Port Arthur and the recent events including Major Johnson's failed siege of the city.

"I almost feel sorry for Johnson; only five hundred men against Charlie Adams. That wouldn't be a fair fight even if Charlie were all by himself," John added.

"We'd like to visit with old Charlie. Can you make that happen?"

"Yes, and remember, you asked to visit with him."

*

Chapter 16

Mopping Up and Rebuilding

Mobile, Alabama

September 25, 2020

Mobile

John chose Mobile to be the capital of the New Territory of Alabama, Mississippi, and Louisiana. Not a lot of thought had to go into this decision since the Navy was supplying a reactor to power the city until the Mobile's power plant could be restarted.

John picked the Compound to house the new government, mainly because it was relatively safe from attack and had an enormous amount of food and other supplies prepositioned that would be needed.

He also wanted a complete separation of Mobile's city government and later the state of Alabama's government. He thought of the compound as one would think of DC, the home of the ISA Government.

Tom and Sam took up the task of cleaning up the compound and getting it ready to house the new government, while Sam healed up enough to get back to work with his dad.

The Compound had thousands of bullet holes and hundreds of broken windows but was in good shape otherwise.

Of course, the DHS barracks had become a pile of rubbish. This was being remedied by those with skills, and those who needed training. Part of the day was remaking the ISA Capital, and the rest for training. Aptitude testing was the buzzword of the day. People who had been on the government teat since birth were discovering abilities they could never have dreamed of in the lost world. Perhaps even more importantly, they were learning the satisfaction of being a part of something, and actually working toward a new and better world.

John banged the gavel and then threw it in the garbage. The ten people around the table laughed and gave high fives to each other.

"Gavels are for people with weak voices. Now, let's get this meeting going and figure out how the hell we are going to govern this land, how much land we are governing and who is going to do what."

"John, you need to pick your cabinet and brush up on Robert's Rules of Order. We don't need any fist fights in the middle of one of these meetings."

"Alice, you are correct. Bone up on the rules and guide us on the rules until we can choose a parliamentarian. Thanks for volunteering."

"I don't plan to rule by decree. I want your input, but I will make the final decisions until we get elections established.

Now, I open the floor for nominations for the territory made up of Alabama, Mississippi, and Louisiana. The first job is temporary Governor of Alabama. I nominate George Washington. I see all yeas and no nays. George, you are temporary governor. Choose the people that you want to help you run your state and the city of Mobile."

George replied, "I can pick anybody that I want?"

"Yes, I don't have the time to help you, and I trust your judgment.

George quickly said, "Sally, I want you to be the leader of the area north of Mobile. Take a team and survey the area up to Jackson, on Highway 43 and Evergreen off 65 North.

Find some leaders that can handle some of these small towns, and make 'em Mayors. Watch for thugs and kill them every chance you get. My best advice is to call for air support if you find any large groups of gangs. Tom, I want you to be the Mayor of Mobile."

This continued until the break for lunch. Gus was appointed Secretary of Defense, Anne Secretary of Treasury, and so on until all key positions were filled. John backed off his ban on lawyers. He now knew that differences needed to be settled through a legal process.

He did, however, ensure that those with a history of liberal, nose wiping, hand wringing attorneys were escorted out of the new ISA. There would be no ACLU in the ISA.

He chose the most conservative lawyers from Mobile to make up the three-person Supreme Court and had all of the doctors and nurses select a Surgeon General.

"Gus, please beef up our defenses quickly, and then send teams to take charge of all of Alabama. Make friends and arm them. Eradicate all the bad guys with extreme prejudice. We need to get our backyard cleaned up before we can clean up Mississippi and Louisiana. Remember this; the old government is gone. We are solely responsible for this restart.

Oh, wait, that reminds me, Gus, please get with Colonel Stokes and ask if he can help you get any remaining National Guard and Reserves to sign on. I'd like to be kept closely in the loop.

Send Steve and Jim over to Pensacola to make friends and see how they are doing. Tell them to go with enough force to fight their way back in case the situation goes south.

Gus, see if we can get a couple of warships to make an appearance, but only if needed. I'm talking showcase here, not combat."

"How much help can we really expect from the Military?"

Bob replied, "Same as before, unlimited arms and supplies, but only the trainers and advisors currently on board."

"I almost forgot to bring up an opportunity that Bob told me about just before the meeting. He told me about a group just like us that has made Port Arthur a model city for what we want to achieve. Port Arthur borders our area, and I think we should go over and invite them to join us."

Gus replied, "What if a group doesn't want to join our new country? We have assumed that everyone would, but I think we need a plan if they don't."

"Damn Gus, I never thought that any of the good guys would not want to be a part of our new country. The answer is simple, join or leave. We will not have a divided country from the start. We might as well cull out the undesirables in the early days of our republic."

"John, that's a slippery slope. I think a lot of people don't deserve to live in our country, but should I be the one to make these decisions?"

John replied, "I have discussed this very topic with everyone of you in this room and our military leaders. I received the same answer from every one of you. It is the same as our Founding Father's plan for our country. It will be a Judeo/Christian country based on Christian values and laws. Non-Judeo/Christians are welcome but must assimilate into our society and obey our laws. The only exception to this rule is that all followers of Islam must leave. We will help them to do so, peacefully. I want no gunplay here unless it is truly forced upon us.

Each state will have its own set of laws per the constitution. Kids will pray, and say the Pledge of Allegiance to the Independent States of America, in schools again. So, I guess the answer is that anyone who wants to stay in our new country has to have our same values or we will fail again.

I know how this sounds, but I hope you each understand that we are at war with Islam. We will not round them up for internment, but we will bus them to Washington DC."

"Thanks for the clarification; out with the bad guys, in with the good, even when we aren't sure if the individual is a bad guy."

John looked at Gus with tired, sad eyes and said, "Yes Gus, we live in a new, different and dangerous world. I know of no other way to make our position any clearer, or our lives a tiny bit safer."

***

The drone of propeller blades quickly put John to sleep on the flight to Port Arthur. He awoke just before the landing at the Southeast Texas Regional Airport. The sun was behind them, and only wispy white clouds were in their path. The Gulf Coast was beautiful and had no activity, which made the scene almost scary to behold. There were no boats, ships or people to be found. Just as

325

they were landing, Gus saw several groups of people camping on the beach and found that comforting.

"John, wake up. Look at the city. There are people everywhere, farming, driving and just living a normal life."

John snapped to attention and looked out the window and said, "Damn, look at all the people. Gus, we need to know how they are doing this."

They landed at a small, but modern airport that appeared to be functioning, as it normally would have been before The Collapse.

"These guys are way ahead of most of the country," Bob said "and we have found that there are dozens of small cities like them that were much better prepared than the rest of the US. We need to find them and get them into the fold before the President, and DHS send them to concentration camps."

The plane taxied up to the terminal. The pilot cut the engines, and they left the plane. There were about twenty people at the terminal waiting to greet them. There was a banner above the entrance to the lobby that read, "Welcome to Port Arthur – John and Gus."

"John and Gus, you are the two ugliest old bastards I have ever seen. How the hell did you two survive?"

"Well Charlie, you are still dumb as a box of rocks and where are the old folks home that you hid in when the world came crashing down around our ears? Who's been packin' your sorry ass?"

The rest of the Port Arthur crowd did not know what to make of the name-calling and taunting and then saw John give Charlie a big bear hug.

Gus shook Charlie's hand and said, "I don't hug men, and I really don't hug men as ugly as you."

Charlie slapped Gus on the back and gave him a hug while Gus was protesting. Charlie then introduced the visitors to the Mayor and other town dignitaries, and John introduced his team to the town folks.

Charlie guided the visitors to a small school bus and had his men load their gear into a pickup. They went to city hall while the pickup took their gear to the hotel.

"First, I want to thank you for inviting us over to visit your city. Second, we want to assure you that we mean you no harm and finally we want you to join us in rebuilding our country into what the founding fathers meant it to be."

John and Bob took turns explaining the military's role and abilities to the Port Arthur town council.

Mayor Jack asked, "So how do you plan to govern this new country, Bob? The US Military is the best in the world, but I don't like them being in charge of civilians."

"Mayor, the military will lead, support and protect you until you can elect a President, Congress and Supreme Court. Then and only then, will we go back to the traditional role of the armed forces. We can only promise that we will back out of a leadership position; however, we also promise that we will never let a bunch of progressive socialists take charge of our country again.

We have wiped all federal laws off the books except for those outlined in the Constitution. The states, through their congressmen, will govern the country. The Supreme Court's charter will be changed to only enforce the constitution and not change or enact laws."

He then told them about the three districts being set up and John's leadership role in Alabama-Louisiana.

"John, so you swear that we will be part of your district, but we are free to run our own town and surrounding area."

"Jack, I'm not over your area, but I swear that we will live up to the promises made tonight. Also, we want you, Mayor, to govern this end of Texas, including Houston.

Bob interrupted and said, "Mayor, if it makes you feel better, we can add Texas to John's responsibility."

John shook his head in agreement.

"That would make us feel much better since Charlie already trusts John and Gus."

Bob continued, "We plan to see what's going on in DFW, Austin, San Antonio and Corpus Christi as quickly as possible, but don't be surprised if we ask you to help get those areas ready to govern themselves.

Port Arthur has the largest army in this part of the country. The army will embed advisors to train and help with tactics. The Navy and Air Force will also provide air support, transportation, fuel and all the ammo and guns you could use in the next hundred years. We also have warehouses full of spare parts for most vehicles and machines that you will find useful.

What we will ask in return? Mayor, the only form of repayment is already printed out in a document called, The Constitution of The United States of America. The only change will be in the name, The Independent States of America.

"Damn Bob, I like what I'm hearing. Council, raise your hands if Port Arthur should join this motley crew."

Every councilman voted yes.

Charlie loaded them into three jeeps, gave them a tour of the city and surrounding area. John's team was astounded at the level of preparation that the town had accomplished before TC.

Bob saw thousands of cows and asked, "Is there any chance of us getting some of those cows from you?"

"Of course, how many do you need? We can have them ready for you to pick up in a couple of days."

"Jack, I don't know how many, but I'll call our Mess Officer and find out. We haven't had fresh meat since a week after the bombs fell."

***

The most pressing task John's team faced was to get the militia organized and strong enough to defend the new territory without the help of the military. John had been warned several times that the military would help as much as possible but was stretched thin guarding the whole country and fighting on three fronts across the world keeping their enemies at bay while the country regained her strength.

Sally and her team quickly cleared the bad guys out of the area north of Mobile and expanded their territory on up to Montgomery and Columbus. Their several calls for air support quickly eliminated the criminals and gangs. She reported that most of the larger groups had headed towards the east coast where they thought the pickings would be easier.

She reported that her biggest problem was not enough people to farm the land. So many people had been killed off, that there were only a couple of people for every one hundred square miles. The people that were left mostly congregated in and around the cities.

Scott's team spent most of October mopping up around Mobile all biker gangs and criminals. They always used excellent intelligence, overwhelming force and took no prisoners.

They freed over eight hundred people, mostly women, and children from these animals. The captives who had farming experience were relocated to the various farms around provide support to get their farms in production. Scott made sure that he repopulated one area at a time with a good mixture of men and women who could fight and those that were not able to fight but could farm or perform other valuable services.

Gus' team worked along with the Navy technicians to install everything from air defenses to maintenance garages for the vehicles.

John was very happy to see the radar installed around Mobile and was surprised by the hundreds of pallets of Stinger missiles given to his team. They now had more weapons than most small countries. The Navy was also arming Port Arthur in the same manner.

"John, I just learned that we are getting five Apaches to help protect us as we build your empire."

"Whoa! Gus, you can stop that empire shit right now. Someone might hear you and take you seriously."

"John, I am serious

"Gus, what do you think about offering some of the land in Alabama to people from Port Arthur? They have Port Arthur, Grove City and a bunch of stragglers from the Beaumont area that know how to farm, but don't have land. We have land and no people."

"John, I think that is a great idea. Let's fly some of their leaders over on the next supply run."

Steve and Janet decided to make their home at The Bunker. Many of the original group from Mobile also decided to stay there to farm and get away from the city.

*

Chapter 17

The Birth of a Nation

Headquarters of the Resistance

USN Gerald R. Ford

Dec 20, 2020

Admiral Walter Jones moved his Flag from the Aircraft Carrier George H. W. Bush to the Carrier Gerald R. Ford after he was given command of the Gulf Coast states, all of the Gulf of Mexico and the Atlantic Ocean through Virginia.

Two other Navy admirals had the west coast and northeast parts of the country. The Army and Marines had been decimated during the early days of the attack.

The Air Force and Navy had only lost approximately twenty percent of their planes and personnel. Nukes had taken out most of our large foreign bases and desertion had taken another large chunk of men. Many took their weapons and went home to protect their families.

The Joint Chiefs were counting on getting these soldiers back into the fold as they stabilized the country one region at a time. There was to be no recriminations or charges. An understanding of family needs seemed an excellent way to restart the military.

The major fly in the ointment was that the President of the old United States had secretly placed several of his loyal men in some key positions and had about ten percent of the remaining Army and Navy loyal to his cause.

Colonel Hiram Stokes and Captain Bob Jones were summoned to meet with the admiral to give a personal update on the successful battle to liberate Mobile.

Their commanding officers were not alarmed since the Admiral was well known for conducting ship level meetings to find out what was really going on with the sailors.

The colonel and captain saluted the admiral as they entered his office. He welcomed them, asked them to sit around his conference table and offered them a drink.

"Well, let's cut through the formal shit and get to the point. If this thing is going as well as your bosses have told me, you two must walk on water."

Stokes replied, "Sir, it is going much better than we could have expected. While Captain Jones deserves a medal for his accomplishments, we both agree that we got lucky with the caliber of the team that John Harris had already assembled. He was already planning an assault on the DHS to wipe them out and to free the detainees. Bob and I believe that they would have succeeded, but would have suffered much higher casualties without our assistance."

The admiral thought for a minute then asked, "Bob, what makes this group so special? As you know, we have had mixed results in Florida and Texas but have gotten nowhere in Mississippi."

The captain answered, "John Harris is their leader. He is former Special Forces and Black Ops CIA. His second in charge is a former Marine who also worked for the CIA. They met on an assignment and have been best friends ever since.

They have surrounded themselves with men and women who have former military and police experience. We assisted them by putting a top notch boot camp together to train the civilians. Several of their women are Grade A snipers, and every adult and kid over ten can shoot several weapons."

The admiral soaked all of this information in and then asked about the two about their families and their safety. Both mentioned that the few hours' notice before the bombs fell had saved their families and most of their men's families.

The admiral asked, "Did either of you know how we got that advance notice that saved over five hundred thousand uniformed personnel?"

They both replied that they had wondered, but had been too busy to think about from who, or how the warning had come.

Admiral Jones said, "A former Army Special Forces guy stopped two nukes from destroying Dallas and Memphis. He also called a friend in high places to warn the military. That guy was John Harris."

Their jaws dropped, and they were speechless.

Admiral Jones asked, "Is John Harris strong enough to lead a major section of the country in a battle against gangs, thugs, the DHS and even the rest of the military loyal to the President?"

Both replied at the same time, "Yes, sir."

The captain added, "If he were running for political office, he would find it difficult to win because he speaks his mind and is too honest. I would feel comfortable with him in charge of my town or state."

The admiral replied, "I want you to invite them out here to celebrate their victory and discuss future plans. Tell them to bring their wives and key members of their team. We need to get to know these people.

Son, go to my cabin and see your mom. She's been worried to death."

***

The trip to the Ford was uneventful but fun for a group who had seen nothing but hardship for the past several months. None of the women, including Beth, had ever flown in a helicopter so that part was especially exciting to them. Everyone focused on how large the Gerald R. Ford was even from several miles out. It continued to fascinate them until they finally landed on the flight deck. They were ushered to their cabins and given time to clean up before the celebration.

Bob met them on the flight deck and said, "I'll be your escort while aboard the Ford. Please let me know if there is anything that I can do to make your stay more comfortable.

The Admiral and his team welcomed them made sure that he introduced everyone before he spoke.

He gave them a brief history of the events that caused the mass destruction in their country. Then he brought them up to speed on the military's efforts to take back control of the country from gangs, the DHS and a morally bankrupt federal government.

He gave them thanks for their results and heaped praise on them for eliminating the DHS threat in this region. He then challenged them to assist in cleaning up the rest of the country.

John thought about what the admiral had said and thought that maybe there was a chance to get the country back to normal.

John said, "Before we get started, I noticed that Captain Jones looks a lot like you, Admiral."

"John, you have a good eye, Bob is my son, and he has two brothers and a sister. All of them serve in the military. We have not heard from our oldest son since the lights went out.

"Sir, I'm sorry for you and your wife, but I'm sure that you raised them right so don't give up on him, he might show up anytime."

"Thanks, John. I hope that you are right, but he was stuck in DC when it got nuked."

John thought for a minute and added, "Gus and I will be glad when we finish our task so we can get started with our new lives. We need to stabilize Alabama and get teams started in Mississippi and Louisiana so we can retire back to private life."

Gus looked at Admiral Jones and said, "John, you have done a damn fine job so far, and you know that we can't just turn the reins over to any Tom, Dick or Harry. Why don't you lead us for a few more years until we get stronger and are better able to stand on our own? There are still lots of bad people hiding among the good folks, and they are just waiting to take over and mess this new country up all to hell."

The admiral spoke up, "Most of the country is under Martial Law until we can establish a new government.

The Southern Territory of the ISA is made up of the lower southeastern states including Arizona and is under my command. I am not going to turn control over to just any tin pot dictator who gets himself elected by a bunch of idiots that he promises handouts for votes.

John, I want you to be the first President of the Southern Territory of the ISA. This is a temporary position for about two years until we can hold proper elections. This will be the nucleus for the new stronger Independent States of America."

John asked, "What form of government will you try to establish?"

"John, I'm glad you asked. Here is a copy of the US Constitution. The laws contained in that document will be the only laws for the new Federal Government.

Each state will have its own laws per the Tenth Amendment. As you know the Federal Government's main duty is to protect the states. I highly recommend that you stick to the constitution or not take the job. The military will not allow a President who runs roughshod over the states ever again."

"Admiral, I couldn't agree more with what you've just said. It's a shame that you didn't get a chance to hear me rant and rave about our recent string of socialist Presidents who trampled the constitution."

"John, I have listened to most of your broadcasts. We had recordings of them, thanks to the NSA who thought that you might be subversive. I liked what I heard, and the founding fathers would feel safe with the country in your hands."

The admiral went on to say, "I will also have three governors watching over the states to the west and east of you. I have a couple of people in mind, but John you are the only leader with the whole package. Our new nation must have men like you leading the new USA."

Gus said, "Sorry, Admiral, won't that be confusing, sort of like the uniforms?"

The admiral laughed and replied, "Okay, I know that you have used the Independent States of America. Personally, I think that is a grand name. If you agree to make it official, then ISA it is."

John said, "Admiral, throw in military support and get the power back up and I'll be your man until you find someone better."

"John, you will get all the support my team has to offer. I wish that I could give you a more definitive answer to both requests. Mr. President, you have the full support and loyalty of the military. Electric power, however, may not be as easily remedied as we had hoped. Our engineers and technicians are hard at work to turn the lights back on the grid. The downside is that grid no longer functional on a nationwide scale. Each area will have to be rebuilt using new technologies. I am confident they'll figure it out.

Bob will be your liaison to the military and report directly to me.

Now, let's celebrate. I've got some fifty-year-old Kentucky bourbon to toast to our new country and its first President."

They all congratulated John with a few drinks.

*

Chapter 18

Chupacabras

Brownsville, Texas

December 24, 2020

Mexico City

Twenty miles to the south of the old border between the US and Mexico life remained normal. Power was still on, TVs worked, and cars still ran. The effects of the EMPs, which struck the USA, did not reach far into Mexico. In El Unidos Estados Mexico, the Generals were very excited.

Headquarters Cortez Drug Cartel
Brownsville, TX

The citizens of Matamoros didn't notice much change in their lives after the attack on the US. While they had no power, the new Cortez Drug Cartel began providing food, clean water, and jobs by reopening some of the closed factories. The Cartel brought in massive generators on semis and got the city power plant back in operation within a few weeks.

They began manufacturing ammunition, canned food and the old air-cooled VW Beetle along with a host of other manufactured goods that were being shipped south.

The factories spread all along the border, which was closed when the power was lost and all of the workers in Mexico City went home.

The Cartel took over the factories and retooled them to make products that were more useful. There was not much use for cell phones, tablets and TV's, but there was a huge need for simple farm tools, basic transportation, and food items.

Drugs had now become only a small part of the Cartel's enterprises since there were no longer Americanos crying for drugs.

There was a steady flow of Mexicans and South Americans crossing the border to return home. The loss of electricity and the chaos resulted in a lack of jobs for these low-wage workers. Millions returned to their home countries. Others died of starvation or gangs murdered them on the way home.

The Black, White, Latino and Skin Head biker gangs killed the men and raped the women. The lucky women and children were turned into slave farm workers and sold on the open market in Mexico and the lower southwest United States.

***

Lucio watched another convoy of soldiers heading north in the dark to cross the bridge to Brownsville and said to his wife, "That makes over ten convoys this month heading into Texas. Every one of them crosses the bridge after midnight with their lights off, and the drivers all have night vision goggles. The gringos must have no army or police left to allow these drug hombres to run wild in Texas."

"Keep your nose out of it, and we will live longer. I know you are proud of your work with the American DEA, but these men will kill our family and us if they find that you helped their enemy."

Lucio knew that even though their lives were getting better now, bad times were just around the corner. A well-fed slave was still a slave. He knew he had to do something to get help for his town and family. He also knew that the Chupacabras were behind this cartel and they were well known in South America for removing heads off with machetes and killing the entire families of anyone who stood in their way.

He kissed his wife and left to go back to work making his rounds in the northern section of Matamoros. He was a patrolman for the city police and could travel at will as long as he didn't leave his home territory.

His partner liked to sleep a lot since he worked the day shift at the VW plant. Lucio would leave the district command post and drop him off at his girlfriend's home most nights so he could get some tail and rest. That made it easy for him to report troop movements back to his contact in the US.

Lucio had also found a local cantina that the Cartel's newly uniformed Army frequented. A few beers and tequila always loosened their tongues.

The rumors floating around the cantina were that Corpus Christi had been taken and a major push to take San Antonio had begun.

***

"Gentlemen, a toast is to honor General Sanchez's victory in Corpus Christi. General, congratulations to you and your men for taking the town of Corpus Christi, the land around it and acquiring several thousand workers and citizens for our Nuevo Mexico."

The room broke out in cheers and clapping. When the celebration died down, the wives left the room and the men lit cigars and got down to business.

"Senor Wolf, what is the latest intelligence coming out of Mobile and this new country, the ISA? They may be the largest threat to our new country."

"Sir, the group in Mobile does not worry me. They are a bunch of ex-military rednecks that are playing soldier and kicking the ass of a bunch of biker gangs.

The US Military presence, however, is much stronger than we were led to believe. We need a plan to get rid of them for good.

As you know, the US President was not able to keep most of them on his side. Even though they have a nuclear stalemate, they are supplying training, weapons and air cover for operations, to these rednecks."

"I will discuss this with the Iranian Commander and see what we can do to take care of this, potential boil on our ass."

337

***

"Senor Cortez, our latest surveillance tells us that the US Navy has two aircraft carriers, three cruisers, ten missile frigates, at least two submarines and twenty-five support ships in the Gulf. They keep them spread out to cover more territory and to keep one nuclear strike from taking them all out. It will be very difficult to destroy them, but we can cut them down by half without much effort."

"What are your plans?"

"A large part of their fleet is within one hundred miles of Mobile. We can never sneak up on the US Navy. Their radar and surveillance equipment is just too good for that.

We will plant two nuclear mines as close as possible to them and then draw them out to fight. We plan to set off the nukes in the middle of their fleet."

"Can't they detect the mines?"

"The mines have had thicker lead shielding installed which makes them difficult to detect until they are very close. By the time, they know what they are; it will be too late to run.

The main thing you should be worried about is that we can hurt them, but we cannot eliminate them. You poke the bear, and the bear gets pissed. If they know where you are located, they can nuke you out of existence."

"How will they know who destroyed their fleet? Even if they do find out, we have very few concentrated assets in North America that would be worth an Intermediate Range Nuclear missile strike. I will worry about their counter attack after I see how many ships we can sink."

"They will know, because, they always know. If not immediately, then a while later, but they will know."

"How do we draw them out of Mobile to the mines? Their airplanes can cover the whole Gulf from Mobile."

"Ah, but their Apaches can't. You just took Corpus Christi, and they know it. So, we just need to get their attention so that they have to come to its rescue.

Perhaps kill a few hundred women and children. That will piss them off and get them moving. I think your Chupacabras can think of something so insulting that these foolish Americans will rush to their deaths trying to save a few infidel women."

Pablo was a Catholic and hated these Muslim bastards, but knew he had to keep using them until he could do without them.

The US and Israeli Military had destroyed Iran, which made it easy to use these remaining Iranians against the US. He would turn his Wolf loose on these godless heathens when the time came.

*

Chapter 19

Day after Independence Day

Smyrna, TN

Dec 21, 2048

Scott had been at the podium for ten minutes thanking all of the warriors and hardworking people who had fought to build the nation and keep it free.

He ended the speech with the Lord's Prayer and a warning about complacency. "There are still enemies trying to destroy our country."

He walked towards his parents and gave them a big hug, then hugged the rest of his brothers and sisters. He walked up to Josh and looked him in the eyes.

"I hear that you are the one who will tell our story accurately and not be afraid to stand up to the media pressure to put out the bull shit lies from the US?"

"Mr. President, I have promised your sister and father that I will do exactly that, and I make the same promise to you; however, I also promise to tell the truth, and follow the evidence to wherever it takes me."

"Son, that's all I ask anyone to do. Always tell the truth and do your best to treat people right."

"I will."

"Now we need to load up and get back to my parent's house and get some of mom's great cooking. Momma Anne and Momma Beth both cooked this meal. It will be some of the best grub that you have ever eaten."

The security group ushered the Presidents and their families out to their cars before the congregation was released. Again, John waved to Josh and directed him to his limo along with Beth and Jenn.

There were three limos with three Humvees leading the convoy and three following. Josh also saw Humvees on side streets and several Apaches hovering over the neighborhood.

Jenn sat next to Josh and was flirting with him while Beth and John discussed Anne's new boyfriend.

"Josh, when are you going to ask my daughter out on a date? It's obvious you like her, and you never take your eyes off of her."

Josh started to reply when the limo came to an abrupt halt. A garbage truck had rammed the lead Humvee and several other large trucks were smashing into other vehicles in the convoy. Shots were being fired, and several bullets hit the windshield leaving stars in the glass. Josh saw everyone pull guns out from under the seat and from several hidden compartments.

Jenn yelled, "Uzi or M4?" to Josh.

He replied, "M4," and grabbed the assault rifle checking the magazine then jacked a round into the chamber.

Suddenly, a large truck backed into their limo right over the driver's door. The collision knocked the driver out and crushed his door. Josh saw the door on the back of the truck start rolling up and saw a small cannon mounted on the back.

"Get out of the car!"

Josh jumped over to the open door and started shooting into the back of the truck killing most of the crew manning the cannon.

Josh kept firing into the back of the truck while the others escaped the limo. Josh turned and crawled out of the limo when he saw Jenn return and begin firing at some men who were charging them from an alley on the driver's side. She dropped three and had to reload. Josh killed another two but saw there were too many to deal with.

He grabbed Jenn and yelled, "Let's go."

The cannon fired, and the engine compartment of the limo exploded in a fireball.

John and Beth covered their escape with steady and accurate fire, which kept their attackers pinned down.

They heard several explosions and saw two of the Apaches blown out of the sky. John motioned for them to slip away while enemy eyes were drawn to the choppers.

They ran into an open garage door, through a house and out the back doors before running into a barn at the back of the property.

"Check your ammo."

Beth, John, and Jenn each had a bag held by a strap around their necks. Jenn looked up and saw that Josh didn't have an ammo bag.

"Damn, I forgot to tell you about the ammo bag under your seat. We keep five hundred rounds in each bag. I've got about two hundred left."

Josh had one additional full thirty round mag and ten rounds in the M4. John and Beth had five hundred between them.

Josh said, "Y'all believe in being prepared, don't you? That's a lot of weight to carry."

Jenn replied, "It's very hard to protect yourself with an empty gun."

Beth said, "John, let's rest a minute, then head towards Stones River and hide out until the army can clean this up."

"Beth, I want to head back in and help protect Scott. We can't let the bastards kill our President."

"John, the attack was designed to kill you, not Scott. His car took off with most of the security. Our vehicle was the target. They want to capture or kill you."

"Dad, Mom's right, the focus of the attack was on our car. We have to get you to safety. Scott is in good hands and is probably twenty miles from here."

"Okay, I've caught my wind. Let's head out, find a car and get the hell out of here."

***

Scott said, "Gus, we escaped. Is there any word on the rest of our team? We are heading towards the base and do not have any bogies chasing us."

"Scott, I don't have any good news. The bastards caught us with our pants down. We just did not have enough resources in place to repel a full assault on our President."

"Gus, the attack was on dad, not me. They are trying to get even with the old man."

"Damn, that explains everything. It's not the US attacking, it's the damn Chupacabras."

***

"What is happening? Have you killed Harris?"

"Senor Wolf, we have him pinned down and surrounded. It is a matter of minutes until we kill him, his wife, daughter, and that damned reporter."

"Fool, don't underestimate the man and his family. They have kicked our asses all over the world for the past twenty years. I want the old bastard's head brought to me now. I will kill you and your whole family if you don't deliver."

***

Jenn went to the door and looked out towards the back of the house. She saw several men crawling along the side of the house and several more coming towards the barn from the east.

"Josh, take a peek out the back of the barn, but be careful, I think we are surrounded."

Josh peered around the edge of the door, and a bullet smashed into the door just above his head. It was followed by a barrage hitting the front of the barn. Jenn knew that they had to get her dad to safety even if they had to die to do it. Losing John Harris would be a devastating blow to the country.

John yelled, "Pile up these hay bales for cover. We've got a fight on our hands."

The End of Hell in the Homeland

If you like my novel, please post a review on Amazon.

Thanks,   A J Newman

To contact the Author, please leave comments @:

www.facebook.com/newmananthonyj   Face Book page.

To view other books by A J Newman go to Amazon to my Author's page:

http://www.amazon.com/-/e/B00HT84V6U

❋ ❋ ❋ ❋ ❋ ❋

*

Books by A J Newman

Alien Apocalypse:
The Virus   Surviving (Oct 2017)

A Family's Apocalypse Series:
Cities on Fire – Family Survival

After the Solar Flare - a Post-Apocalyptic series:
Alone in the Apocalypse   Adventures in the Apocalypse*

After the EMP series:
The Day America Died New Beginnings The Day America Died
Old Enemies The Day America Died Frozen Apocalypse

"The Adventures of John Harris" - a Post-Apocalyptic America series:
Surviving   Hell in the Homeland   Tyranny in the Homeland
Revenge in the Homeland...Apocalypse in the Homeland   John
Returns

"A Samantha Jones Murder Mystery Thriller series:
Where the Girls Are Buried   Who Killed the Girls?

Books by A J Newman and Cliff Deane
Terror in the USA: Virus: Strain of Islam

These books are available at Amazon:

http://www.amazon.com/-/e/B00HT84V6U

To contact the Author, please leave comments @:
www.facebook.com/newmananthonyj   Facebook page.

About the Author

A J Newman is the author of 17 novels that have been published on Amazon. He was born and raised in a small town in the western part of Kentucky. His Dad taught him how to handle guns very early in life, and he and his best friend Mike spent summers shooting .22 rifles and fishing.

He read every book he could get his hands on and fell in love with science fiction. He graduated from USI with a degree in Chemistry and made a career working in manufacturing and logistics, but always fancied himself as an author.

He served six years in the Army National Guard in an armored unit and spent six years performing every function on M48 and M60 army tanks. This gave him a great respect for our veterans who lay their lives on the line to protect our country and freedoms.

He currently resides in Owensboro, Kentucky with his wife Patsy and their four tiny mop dogs, Benny, Sammy, Cotton, and Callie.

Made in the USA
Lexington, KY
08 July 2018